Blame It on Eve

Blame It on Eve

Philana Marie Boles

One World
Ballantine Books • New York

A One World Book
Published by The Ballantine Publishing Group

Copyright © 2002 by Philana Marie Boles

www.ballantinebooks.com/one/

Library of Congress Cataloging-in-Publication Data

Boles, Philana Marie.
Blame it on Eve : a novel / by Philana Marie Boles
p.   cm.
ISBN 0-345-44712-3
I. Title.

PS3602.O654 B57 2002
813'.6—dc21   2002067571

Text design by Holly Johnson

Manufactured in the United States of America

First Edition: October 2002

10   9   8   7   6   5   4   3   2   1

Once there was a little girl who imagined.
And her parents taught her to *believe*.
And so, of course, she dedicated her first novel to them.
Philip and Patricia Boles, my wings, I love you.

And for Butterscotch.
(Any girl who has ever had a dog knows why.)

ACKNOWLEDGMENTS

I am eternally grateful, Mom and Dad, for your unselfish love, never-ending support, and constant guidance. The most valuable gift you've given me is the knowledge that any and all recognition belongs to God. I thank you for that—and *for everything.*

Ginger, my sister, thanks for always having my back, for your proud enthusiasm over the years, and for supporting my addiction to the written word ever since you gave me my very first magazine subscription when I was ten.

To my loving Grannie—who saw it then, and whose hugs I can still feel, here is your pudding. Thank you for being so proud. I know you're smiling in heaven. I miss you.

Mel Berger, thank you for giving *Blame It On Eve* a home. I sincerely value your guidance and support. Anita Diggs, my editor, I truly appreciate your patience and helpful insight.

Melanie Okadigwe, thank you *Melanie "O."* for your kindness and assistance.

Dr. Fred Zackel, I am so grateful for the generous way you have shared your knowledge over the years, the lessons you've taught me, and the way you've been there when I needed you.

Acknowledgments

So many teachers, from elementary school to St. Ursula Academy and on through Bowling Green State University have inspired me and been instrumental in my journey. Mr. John Rowley, my very first mentor, you believed in me, we were a great team, and I thank you for the opportunities to hone my skills. Dr. Richard Messer, *thank you* for lessons that continue to guide my writing today. To all of my workshop peers, fellow thespians, numerous incredible instructors—both high school and college—and all of the casts and crews of my plays, *thank you.*

For the people who have consistently been in my corner—family or true friends, please know that your love and support continues to inspire me. You know who you are!

To all of "the great ones, the few"—keep your heads up, and don't forget to kiss the wind as you continue to press on in life, and in your chosen fields. I believe in you.

My appreciation is also extended to the ACT-SO program, 40 Acres & a Mule Filmworks (especially Ross and Andre), *Glamour* magazine—and Martin Blair, Carol Green—who taught me about the baby chick and other things, and to the Gerity-Schultz Corporation (for the clovers).

To my buddies in office services at Conde Nast who kept asking, *"How's the book coming?"* It's finished! Thanks for the encouragement.

Thank you *always*, Ms. Donna M. Bagdassarian, for your early guidance and faith!

To Paul Morris and Ike—*thanks* a million times again for the computer rescues!

And to Miss Jada Marie Boles, my precious niece, *this* is what Auntie was doing on her " 'puter." One day, when you're all grown up, you'll understand. Thank you for making me giggle when I was tired. Be good to yourself!

CONTENTS

Blame It on Eve

ONE

School Is in Session

"*Y*our mother called," Ernie informs me. He's standing behind the swivel chair that I'm sitting in as he ties the satin cape around my neck.

I study the cream-and-gold cape as if I haven't seen it every week for the last three years. Same script, same words. *House of Elegance*, and then an outline of a pair of golden shears, followed by the slogan, *Leaving No Head Uncut.*

He parts my hair down the middle, separating two oceans of earth brown waves. "Did you hear me?" he asks.

I roll my eyes. "Yes. What'd she want?"

"She said for me not to tell you that she called." He laughs and then begins massaging my scalp.

I sigh. "Well, if she calls back—"

"If she calls back, nothin'," he cuts in. "*You* need to call *her*. This has gone on entirely too long. She's all sayin' how she just wanted to know if you had a hair appointment today, and tellin' me how I should sneak a call to her to let her know if you showed up. I tell her, yeah right, that the only way you would miss your weekly conditioning—and then I stopped myself right there and told her

1

that there was no way you'd miss your weekly appointment." He laughs.

"If she calls again, tell her I moved back to Milan."

"You're tripping."

"I'm serious," I say, making an earnest attempt to sound as if I am.

He pops my shoulder with a thick black comb and stands there with his hand on his hip.

I shrug. "What?"

"It's been a week since you've talked to her, Shawni. Your *mother*. Call her. You want highlights today?"

When Ernie ends a discussion, it's over.

I accept the subject change, and hold up the sample book of little swatches of hair—dyed, looped, and stapled into the book for consideration. You have to imagine your hair one shade lighter or one shade darker, and debate whether you'll be satisfied with either. The color is never exact. Why don't hairstylists ever tell you that? I tap the one I've been eyeing for the last twenty minutes.

He frowns. "You like that color?"

"Yes."

"You don't think it's too bright?" His facial expression suggests that he does.

I close the book without glancing again. "No. I want it."

Only a month ago I had everything. I was a fashion model. No. I was a fashion model with international acclaim, an overzealous contract offer from the incomparable king of fashion—Ricci Malone—who was willing to pay me to smile, flaunt, and provide the illusion of being perfect or ideal. I had even been showered with promises of infinite modeling possibilities for the future. I had all that I'd ever closed my eyes and wished for since I wore pigtails and braces.

As Billy Dee Williams once said: Success is nothing without someone you love to share it with. Bo, my fiancé, is my someone, and I have a three-carat platinum Cartier engagement ring to signify his love. My dreams had become my reality, yet I wanted to snap out of it. And so I did. Modeling, that is. Bo's still here.

I didn't sign the contract. I won't be signing the contract. I can't recall the exact words I had used to break my mother's heart.

Shawni! She held her breath, paused—probably considering whether or not to bite her tongue. She exhaled and said it anyhow. *You're breaking my heart.*

I knew that was coming.

I was living the life she had sought. I grew up listening to her stories of unattainable dreams, and I wanted to be like her, to achieve those dreams for both of us. Although her name was never as recognizable as someone like Beverly Johnson or Iman, my mother was a well-accomplished model in Italy. This was before the days of Alek, Naomi, and Tyra. Long before Shawni was even thought of. I don't care what any fashion magazine says, my *mother* is my epitome of beauty.

My fascination with makeup was born when I was a child, watching Mommie apply hers with gentle strokes. Already beautiful before the makeup, she was a movie star with it on. I started sneaking her Chanel lipstick and eye shadow, and eventually progressed to loose powders and thick mascara by the time I was nine. When I was a little girl, I used to chase butterflies, fascinated that they had evolved from being caterpillars, enthralled by their delicate beauty. Mommie was a butterfly. I was a caterpillar—eager to become like her, anxious to see what I would look like as a woman. So, I used makeup to paint the picture of my future. Mommie eventually caught me with the brush in my hand. She wasn't upset. She just smiled gently.

"The lipstick goes on like ice cream," she told me.

I thought then that there couldn't possibly be anything more spectacular than that velvety feeling across your lips.

"Chanel," she said, "is the only lipstick suitable for a lady's lips." She held up my chin, and applied a delicate coat of Russet Moon to my lips. "Close your eyes," she said. "The eye shadow and powder are going to feel like sensational bursts of fairy dust." Her wrist was a wand as she handled the brushes.

A shiver swirled up my spine, and then I giggled—regretfully. I had felt so mature as I sat there, and that nervous laugh had ruined it all. Then, she laughed, too, and that made laughing okay. It was great. Before that day it had never felt like that—tingling.

She was so tall, so sophisticated, a giant Barbie Doll, only with skin like melted Godiva, ebony hair, and eyes like an ocean of caramel.

She winked. "Never use your index finger to apply or blend— it's too strong. The pinky and ring fingers are weaker, gentler." So much patience in her voice, so much pride from sharing her beauty secrets. She tapped my nose playfully.

"Makeup, darling, must never be forced. It should have the impression of just happening to be there, unnoticed at first. Always keep it elegantly simple."

Things weren't "elegantly simple" with our family. Far from it. Everything was so complicated. I wish Mommie had applied the same rule to us.

It's been eight days since I told her I didn't sign the contract. She was calm at first, putting her rage on simmer until she could get the full explanation. Then she exploded. "Shawni! What devilish possession has come over you to make you even *dream* of not signing a contract with Ricci Malone?"

"Mommie," I pleaded, "I'm changing."

"I see," she said suspiciously. "Well, I hope you don't think that just because you're getting married you have to give up your dreams."

"Mommie," I sighed, "I'm sorry."

I was sorry—not for the decision that I'd made, but because I knew I was not fully expressing myself, providing a sufficient explanation for my sudden change in desires. It was agonizing. I was also truly sorry that I was the cause of the disappointment in her voice.

She was crying. "And it's not even about me," she insisted. "Darling you deserve that contract. You don't understand how it's breaking my heart to see the entire world within your grasp and you not grabbing it, taking it for all it's worth. Most girls don't even get a glimpse of the world you have access to."

I'd heard it all before.

She hadn't been there a month ago, the last show. And I couldn't explain the emptiness. The room full of applause, of people, of energy. Yet, eerily, not one clap sounded without a lonely echo. Years of growing up wanting this. Runway. Print. Paris—after the show. The biggest show of the year. Smiling, pouting, sashaying, defining style. But it never turned out like that. Suddenly I realized that it wasn't about the fashion anymore. I was standing there for approval—not of the snakeskin dress I was wearing, but of *me*.

"Mommie, I'm nothing but a paper doll," I finally said. "And I'm sick of it."

"That's really unfair." She was stern. "Suppose modeling isn't what you want to do with your life now, okay! But don't reduce the entire concept of personifying beauty and illustrating fashion to being a mere paper doll, Shawni. It's much more than that."

Fashion, modeling, and beauty are the things that made sense to Mommie. It's what she had helped me to acquire an appreciation for, a passion for. How could I tell her that at this point in my life I thought I'd missed a moment in my youth where I could have discovered other dreams?

I heard the clinking of her glass after a few moments of silence, and then the pouring of something soon after. More than likely it was her usual—vodka mixed with iced tea. Mommie's Brew. She sniffed, "I'll call you back in a few."

"Okay," I agreed. I had already done the damage, why make it worse by saying more?

Ernie, who had been sitting there beside me while I broke the news to her, smacked his lips and turned to me after I hung up the phone. He cleared his throat. "A paper doll?"

It's what I had always dreamed of becoming. I nodded.

"See." He huffed. "Hell naw. Ain't *no-ooo-body* gonna pay me to be nobody's damn paper doll, havin' me all propped up somewhere just to sit there and be cute, livin' a life where all people do is look at you? Oh, hell naw. I can't go for that. I've got too much to say."

I stared at the phone, accepting that Mommie probably wouldn't be calling back any time soon. Then I looked at him and forced a smile. Despite the usual attitude and neck rolling, Ernie understood.

A giant contraption that resembles the rings of the planet Saturn is humming quietly as it orbits my head while I sit still, having been instructed by Ernie not to move. This satin cape is making me sweat. Does it really take this long for this stupid machine to fix the bronze highlights into my hair, or am I just feeling anxious? And if I'm feeling anxious, why?

It's not as if I have anywhere to be after I leave the salon. Time isn't important today. In fact, this is the beginning of my four-day, fiancé-free weekend, and I'm thrilled about all of the possibilities. I plan to embrace every moment of my temporary freedom while Bo is away on business. I may just decide to spend my entire weekend doing nothing.

I'm going to buy a box of Snackwells, rent *Pretty Woman* for the sake of Richard Gere, *Mahogany* because of Billy Dee, and as many Pierce Brosnan flicks as are available. I have even entertained the idea of skipping my morning jogs tomorrow and Saturday.

Even this morning, on my way to Helena's for a manicure, I was feeling so good that the Manhattan traffic didn't bother me at all. The November air was unseasonably warm, as it's been lately, and I refused to allow anything to upset me. I ignored all the gypsy cabdrivers as they maneuvered and even outright bullied their Lincolns in front of my baby blue Lexus SC400, affectionately named "Baby Blue."

I deliberately chose not to focus on the traffic in which I had been cemented for nearly an hour. Instead, I allowed Tina Turner's "Private Dancer," still as beautiful as it was in the eighties, to tune out all the honking—as if sitting on the horn will miraculously solve the traffic that hasn't moved since forever.

Now, as I sit here at the salon, I wonder, Where's Ernie? And why is it so silent in the salon today? Usually Kenny G or Sade is playing softly. I close my eyes and concentrate until I can hear the water pumping in the fish aquarium in the front of the mauve-furnished lobby. Then I hear the faint sound of the telephone ringing. A pause. Ernie's tasseled black leather shoes clicking closer and closer on the marble floor. He's standing in front of me, the cordless in his hand, his smile sly, his eyes narrowed. He purses his lips.

He sighs heavily, and then holds the phone out to me. "It's your *huuussssband.*"

I dangle my fingers. "I don't see a band around this solitaire yet, Ernie."

"Y'all might as well be married." He pouts and laughs.

I snatch the phone. "Hello?"

It's Bo. "Baby, I got your message that you'd be at the salon. You should turn your cell phone on, I tried to call it." He pauses. "What's that about a solitaire?"

Whoops. Didn't think he could hear me. I pull out my cellular and turn it on. "Oh, nothing. You know us, always kidding around." Before I continue, I give Ernie a deadly "you are getting on my last nerve" glance and he scurries away. "You didn't have yours on either. I called earlier, while I was stranded in hellish traffic."

"Naw," he responds. "I was in the shower when you called, couldn't get it. Baby?"

"Yes?"

"Can I ask you why you insist on going to that salon? You can't find a sista salon or one of those Dominican shops?"

"Bo?"

"S'up, baby?"

I take a breath. "We've had this discussion before, so I will refrain from responding, okay?"

He laughs, and I have to laugh, too. I mean, how many times have we had that discussion. Really.

And then he says, "I'm runnin' late for this meeting. So . . . "

"Who are you meeting?" I look down and admire my French manicure.

"Aw, baby. You forgot? Remember, I told you? Sherm and Mark Hoyt hooked it up—the groups."

"Oh, okay." Always meeting with some new group, to convince them that they need powerful representation from an entertainment attorney before they actually need an attorney. Convince them that he is the one they should work with when that time is at hand. Do all of this before the group blows up and every entertainment attorney comes knocking and calling. That's always the plan, he told me once, to be a step ahead of the game.

"Yeah," he says, his voice so incredibly sexy. "I'll hit you up later, at the crib. Cool?"

Of course he thinks I should be at home on a Thursday night, waiting for his call, just because he's out of town and I supposedly have nothing else to do? With a fresh facial, a barely dry manicure, new stiletto boots needing to be broken in, and a to-die-for set? Right. "I'll have my cellular if I'm not home," I say.

"What?" He laughs. "So, a brotha goes out of town for a second and his fly girl wants to get really really fly, huh? Okay. I see how it is. You just make sure you keep it on, all right?"

Damn, I miss him. I sigh. "I'll be good. Don't be too late for your meeting."

"Yeah."

"Love you."

"Love you, too, baby."

So now I'm sitting under the dryer thinking about how it never takes this long for my hair to dry. I'm thinking about how three days is actually a pretty long time to go without Bo, and how incredibly stupid it was of me not to get on that plane with him when there is plenty of shopping I could have done in Chicago. And what am I really going to do without my man? Then I hear a faint ringing coming from my Louis Vuitton purse (compliments of my man), and I hesitate before I answer. Probably Mommie.

"Hello?" I skip the pleasant tone of voice and try to sound busy as I manage to position the phone under the hood of the dryer.

"Shawni?" It sounds like my brother.

"You have to speak up. I'm under the dryer," I shout. "Duran?"

"Yeah," he shouts back, a grin in his voice.

I try to lift the hood of the dryer over my Martian-style rollers, only Ernie walks up as I do and immediately pulls it back down over my head. I roll my eyes and twist my body around to turn the temperature of the dryer down to low, which also lowers the volume of the noise it makes. The change in temperature instantly causes Ernie to pout.

He frowns at me. "Don't hold me responsible if those curls don't last, Shawni," he says, and then struts away.

"Duran?" I say again, relieved that I don't have to shout now.

"Duran the man." He recites his favorite rhyme.

"What's up?"

"Hey, baby girl. You still want a gig?"

"What's going on?" I ask.

"Got a gig for you, as promised. Last minute though." He sounds excited.

"Who? How last minute are we talking? Explain," I say. Of course I want to do this. A career woman—with something to say, an opinion that matters, not just a paper doll who doesn't talk. Use what you know. I know fashion. My brother knows that I know fashion. Who better for him to call upon when he needs a stylist? This isn't about nepotism. I had my very own subscription to *Vogue* by the time I was seven, and I became a runway fashion model by the time I was seventeen. I *know* fashion. I'm qualified. "Details, Duran."

"Okay. Hold up." He laughs. I smile at the thought of how cute my younger brother is, probably driving his black Navigator down Peachtree Street in Atlanta. Surely he's dressed in some casually fly Calvin Klein and demanding all female eyes to take note of the walnut complexioned fly guy driving. "Check it. One of my groups— The Gentlemen—is doing a charitable gig for the NAACP. Raising money for the ACT-SO program."

"The what program?" I ask.

"ACT-SO, right. Some youth program, I don't know. Yo, so The Gentlemen is covering for another group that had to cancel. Last minute. Need gear for the show, and tuxes for the dinner. And you know, whatever else."

I didn't like the "whatever else" part. "What kind of gear? And what do you mean 'whatever else'?" I pull my electronic notebook out of my purse and wait.

"You know, some fly Armani. Nothing stiff. The publicist'll fax you a press kit to get their vibe. Four fellas in the group."

"And what else?"

"Really, the gear is top priority. You know, you can talk to them and see. Pays twenty-five hundred and two tics to the event."

"You never did tell me the date."

"Remember, I said last minute." He takes a deep breath. "They're leaving Atlanta in an hour, and they'll be at the Grand Hyatt in Manhattan tonight."

"Tonight?" I close my notebook. No use typing anything else— no way am I going to meet, get to know, and style four men on such short notice. I may be new to being a professional stylist, but I'm no novice to the particulars of quality styling. Adequate time is essential.

"Your brother needs this favor," he says. "Do this for me, all right? Don't I always look out for my sis? Always have. Daddy said be the man, look out for my sister and—"

"We're not kids anymore, Duran," I interrupt.

"I'm just sayin', you know? I said I'd get you a gig, look out for you. Yo, if I don't do nothin' else in life I'm takin' care of you and Mommie, right? You wanted a gig, I got you a gig."

"I know, Duran. And I appreciate the thought, but it's too last minute. Forget it."

"Come on. Today is only Thursday. Show isn't until Saturday— *night*. What's up? Plenty of time. You down or what?"

"Next time, Duran. Providing you give me more notice. I promise."

"What else do you have going on this weekend? Nothing. Like I said, the show isn't until Saturday night. You can meet them tonight, and have all day tomorrow *and* all day Saturday to do whatever you need to do. I could call a dozen other stylists right now. You want me to? It's part of the game, you gotta be ready to roll when opportunity hits you on the cell, sis. Come on, now. You owe me."

"*Excuse me? Owe?*"

"Yeah, yeah. Let's not forget I hooked you up a couple of years ago. 'Oh, Duran, you have to introduce me to your sexy bald friend. Oh, Duran I have to meet him.' Need I remind you who you're marrying?" He laughs, his voice cracking. Duran is so adorable when he isn't doing things like blackmailing me.

"I did not say all that. Furthermore, if Bo weren't my man I would have found another. Men are a dime a dozen and I have five dollars."

Duran laughs again. "Right. You love him, though. Love that slick-ass bald man that's got you all locked down with a condo and a Lexus coupe. Yo, don't front."

Okay, I admit, Bo is all that. It's funny, because the first time I saw him I thought he was really handsome—fine in fact—but definitely didn't seem like someone I'd be interested in. Too smooth, too cool, too suave. I figured he was pompous, slick-talking, an ex-football player turned car salesman or something. And he did turn out to be charming, just not in the sleazy way I initially thought.

It was at a party that Millennium Rush Inc. was throwing for Duran and one of his groups that'd sold like a gazillion records or something. The first time I saw him, he immediately consumed my attention—dark, bald-headed, and attractive. And, being the super observant woman that I am, I saw that he was courteous to the women who approached him. He'd talk with them for brief moments, smiling politely, but then he kept moving through the crowd.

I asked Duran who his friend was. Duran wanted to know if I

was checking Bo out. I told him no, that although he was sexy I just wanted to know his story. You know, who he was or whatever. Duran didn't buy it, and as soon as Bo neared where we were standing, Duran introduced us.

He was even more handsome up close. "Bo Delaney— entertainment attorney." His voice was a tad raspy. He kissed my hand.

I smiled. "So, what brings you here?" I asked, glancing around at the room full of people celebrating.

"Entertainment attorney," he repeated as if he was giving me a clue. "Means I represent entertainers. My clients just went platinum. It's a beautiful day." He laughed.

I nodded. "Gotcha."

"So," he asked, "is music your thing?"

"No," I replied, "fashion is."

"Ah," he nodded. "Designer?"

I shook my head. "No. Model."

"Thank God." He looked me up and down, shook his head with a *whew* noise escaping out of the corner of his mouth.

"What?" I asked defensively.

"I meet models all the time," he said. "But, believe it or not, *gorgeous* models are hard to come by." He smiled with a wink.

I liked that. I thanked him with a modest nod, and tried to continue the conversation, wanting to be captivated some more.

"So," he said, "it was a pleasure meeting you."

What? Was he brushing me off? Annoyed, I sensed that he was ready to move on, to keep working the room. I copped an attitude, let him know with my eyes that he could carry on for all I cared, that there were other conversations I could find, seeing as how the party was jam-packed. Please. He seemed nice, but I am not the persistent, going to sweat you, type of girl. I decided to channel my curiosity about him into something else. I started looking around the room to see who else I could mingle with.

Then I felt something in my hand, looked down, and swallowed my annoyance. Staring up at me was his very simple business card, which just happened to be baby blue, my favorite color.

Cute, I thought, and smiled.

"If you know any gorgeous models who wouldn't mind giving a brotha a call, okay?" he asked.

I was flattered. He hadn't done *that*, given his card, to the other girls, I would have noticed if he had.

"Perhaps." I gave my shoulders a shrug and him a sexy smile.

I didn't call. I never call a guy first—something Mommie always told me on no account to ever do. Since he hadn't asked for my phone number I silently hoped our paths would cross again some day, and tried to forget about him in the meantime.

A few weeks later I came home—at the time I was still living with Mommie—and there was a note on the refrigerator.

Shawni,

You had two phone calls. A young man named Bo Delaney called. He says he's a friend of Duran's—wants to know if you're free this weekend! He sounds nice. I told him I thought you *might* be free (wink), but that he should call you back tonight around nine o'clock. Duran called also. He said to tell you that he gave your phone number to his friend—the bald one. I take it Mr. Delaney is bald? (smile)

Mommie

At nine o'clock he called. Two days later we had our first date. The opera. I was delighted. It was a fantasy come true. When I was a little girl I used to lie on my stomach across Mommie's bedspread as she sat at her dressing table getting ready to go to the opera with Daddy. Her hair pinned with an occasional curl falling, her perfume womanly, she'd rise from her seat and walk effortlessly in high heels. Of course, there were many other nights, many other men who took her to the opera or to some social event, but they were only substitutes, and those nights were never as exciting to watch her get dressed for. Daddy was the only one who inspired such wonderful anticipation.

So, of course, I was elated when Bo told me where we were going. But a quarter of the way into the show I realized that I would have preferred a Pierce Brosnan flick. I was bored.

"Duran," I say now as I realize that my defense has weakened. I feel cozy inside as I think about the memories, and I feel twinges of delight as I think about my man, who hasn't stopped trying to please me since that night at the opera, two years ago. I sigh. "I'm just saying that it's not as if I couldn't have found another man. I am *choosing* to settle down with Bo, not like I'm some desperate woman who's just dying to have a man, just *dyyy*-ing to walk down the aisle. I've had my pick, and I chose him."

"Yeah," he clears his throat. "I hear you. If you say so. But I already know that the man you chose, or whatever, is down in Chi-Town with Sherm and them, so what else do you have to do this weekend? Nothing. So, what's up? You down?"

"Fine, Duran." I whip out my notebook again. That's one of the problems with Bo and my brother being friends, Duran always knows too much.

"They're staying at the Grand Hyatt under the name Jack Daniels," he informs me.

"How clever." I roll my eyes.

"They'll be checkin' for you around ten o'clock."

"So, in other words you already told them I'd do it?"

"No, but I knew you wouldn't let big brother down."

" 'Bye Duran."

"Peace."

I barely hear him end the conversation because Ernie turned the dryer back on high and is standing guard so that I don't turn it back down.

At least I'll look good for this meeting.

"You like?" Ernie swings my chair around after nearly a half hour of toying with my freshly released curls. My new bronze highlights add a subtle glow to my dusty brown hair, and further define the natural-looking curls that are now cascading down my shoulders. It feels good to look in the mirror and see a refreshed me.

I give Ernie a quick kiss on the cheek and a fresh fifty-dollar bill from my white-laced bra. Question answered.

"So, where to?" he asks. "Looking for trouble while Mr. Clean is away for a few?" he teases.

"Trouble?" I overdramatize. "Now, why would I, Shawni Baldwin, being of sound mind and body, go out and look for trouble just because the man who spoils me silly is out of town for a few days?"

He fakes a yawn, and then laughs.

"Anyhow, I was planning on enjoying myself—my temporary freedom—and just doing whatever."

"So, why don't you?"

"Duran called. He needs me to fill in as a stylist for some group called The Gentlemen."

"Shut-*uuup*." His eyes widen. "Girl, you mean to tell me you get to deal with them boys that sing about winin' and dinin' and all that jazz? *Girrrl . . .*"

"I've never even heard of them."

"You're askin' for trouble, Shawni," he warns. "You might as well stand out in the middle of Broadway and Forty-second and yell 'Trouble, here I am!' "

"Whatever."

"Tell me you won't go this entire weekend, without Bo, mind you, and not find yourself in trouble with one of those Gentlemen?"

"It's a gig, Ernie. A job."

"Yeah, but considering the source . . ."

"What's that supposed to mean?"

"Considering that we're talking about you. And, well, you know, seeing as how you're a little weak when it comes to the opposite sex."

"What!" I mock scream. "Excuse me. I am a lot of things, but weak is not one of them."

He puts his hand on his hip. "Let me break it to you like this, girlfriend. You flirt, hopelessly, when Bo is and isn't around, and with any and every man you can. Despite you running around like you're such a so-called independent woman, you need a man."

"Shut up."

"What? I bet if you had to go this entire weekend without a man, on Monday morning you'd be in a straitjacket somewhere. Chile, sometimes I think I know you better than you know you. Ya know damn well you can't be without a man. Man-crazy bitch." He cracks up laughing.

I get up from the chair and grab my purse. "I paid for my hair. I did not ask for and I'm not paying for your sarcastic and totally stupid remarks about my personality. I don't believe in gambling, but I could go more than a weekend—months or even years. However, I am not going to sit here and continue this conversation, okay? I have a job to get ready for—for my *brother*. Thank you."

He pouts. "Get agitated if you want, Miss All That, but my observations are free of charge!" For dramatic effect he wipes nonexistent sweat from his prematurely receding hairline.

"'Bye Ernie."

"The truth hurts, Shawni—like a Tyson to the chest. I still love you though."

"Like I said, good-bye, Ernie."

He smirks. "I know you love me, too, bitch."

"Jack Daniels, please." I smile at the young man at the information desk and catch a reflection of myself in the clock behind him. I could have dressed up, illustrated a much more professional look tonight, but . . . no, this is a last-minute gig and I'm going to treat it as such. I look perfectly fine in my black-and-yellow Donna Karan warm-up suit and matching sneakers.

"Sure," the front deskman says, "What's your name?"

"Shawni."

"Baldwin?" A voice from behind me asks—a male voice.

As I turn to say yes I plan to offer a pleasant smile, but it's just some guy with cornrows wearing a leather jacket with all sorts of race-car logos on it and a pair of oversized Polo jeans—about four sizes too big in fact. And Kenneth Cole boots. *Those* are nice.

He extends his right hand. A gold ring with a diamond horseshoe screams hello at me.

"Zin." He smiles and waits for me to shake the diamond ring— the hand with the ring I mean. "From The Gentlemen." He nods at front-desk boy.

"Oh." I finally put my hand in his. A quick exchange of warm energy. "I'm Shawni. Duran's sister. Nice ring."

He looks down at his diamond horseshoe. "Thanks. Not that I believe in luck, but a good friend of mine gave it to me."

"Don't believe in luck? Never heard that one before. Don't go to Vegas."

He laughs. "Nope, what I *do* believe in is karma. You get what's coming to you."

"Interesting," I say.

"You know, I figured it was you when you walked in. You and 'Ran could be twins."

Is that Joop cologne? He smells good. "So, *Zin*? Is that your real name or some catchy stage name?"

He's got a slow grin going on, kind of a crooked smile. His eyes are a piercing shade of gray—two worlds of hazy feathers.

"Yo," he laughs. "You're not hip to The Gentlemen? To the fellas?"

"Your publicist is supposed to fax me a press kit. I'm sure that'll help."

"So in other words, you're not hip."

"Excuse me?"

"I'm sayin', don't sweat it. It's cool." He looks at me in a way that feels like he's taking me all in from head to toe just by looking into my eyes. It's so annoying.

He leads me toward the elevator. "Anyway, Zin is my stage name. And all I'm saying is that you just need to gain some knowledge on what The Gentlemen is all about to understand. It's all good though. I'll introduce you to the fellas, and we'll just have to school you on The Gentlemen tonight. Ya dig?"

I'm a blink from being appalled. No, I don't *dig*. Why doesn't he just tell me whatever it is that I need to know? I came here to do a favor for my brother! That's all. I did not come here to get schooled on anything. If I had wanted schooling I would have put my modeling career on hold and gone to college!

He does his little laugh again. "Relax," he says, and pushes the button for the elevator.

Up to Gentlemen 101 we go.

TWO

The F Words

Zin and I are uncomfortably silent during the elevator ride, and I am peeved because of it. He, on the other hand, is still smiling. Or is that a smirk? I roll my eyes and ask him, "Excuse me. Is there something funny, Zin from The Gentlemen?"

He laughs and says sarcastically, "Zin from The Gentlemen"—he clears his throat—"is just checkin' you out. Don't sweat it."

"Who said anything about sweating?" I say, and then decide to look up and watch the numbers above me light our ascent: 3, 4, 5 . . .

"You all right?" he asks.

I cut him a look, give a quick smile, pretending not to notice how fine he is (because Ernie's theory will not be proven true tonight), and nod. "Super."

He reaches into the inside pocket of his coat and says, "Okay. Well, here's a copy of our CD." He hands it to me as the elevator doors open.

I look at the cover—four guys in fur coats, bare chests, and too much jewelry, and I decide not to roll my eyes again, reminding myself that this is a paying gig and that I must make an attempt at being cordial. "*Take a Sip,* huh?" I read the title of the CD.

He swipes his entry card, and leads me into the suite. Incense. Too much of it. Three pairs of eyes are staring back at me. A tall Gentleman wearing wire-rimmed eyeglasses and tiny twists in his hair stops flipping channels on the remote to the large-screen television. The short one with the seemingly wet curly hair is sitting on the couch and pauses from filing his fingernails.

The muscular one with waves in his hair stops doing his push-ups and breaks the silence. "Damn. Thought that was Robin Givens for a second. Got my heart racin'."

If only my cheekbones were as well-defined, and if I had her trademark dimples, then maybe I could see a slight resemblance. It's quite a stretch, otherwise I'd be flattered.

Zin gestures toward me, "Gentlemen, I'd like you to meet Shawni—as in Shawni Baldwin, our manager's sister, our stylist for this weekend."

Mr. Push-up seems to be the only one in the group with vocal cords. He widens his eyes. "For real? Damn. I forgot 'Ran said you're a model."

The others just stare.

"Actually," I say, "I'm no longer modeling. I'm an independent beauty and fashion consultant—stylist, if you will." My voice comes out sounding too high-pitched, too close to my flirting voice (and I will not be using that voice tonight), and so I make a mental note to deepen my register the next time I speak, to sound professional. Why am I so nervous? I should be more relaxed than this.

Mr. Push-up Gentleman gets up, revealing his sweaty and chiseled abdominal muscles, and walks over to me. "You ought to be a model, for real." He tenderly takes my left hand and kisses it. What is it with these rough men being so charismatic? He nods. "Mo. Nice to meet you."

"Indeed." I snatch my hand from his. "Now, is Mo your real

name or is it your catchy stage name?" Yes. Now I have power behind my voice. Much better. Be strong, Shawni. Ernie doesn't know what he's talking about.

Zin clears his throat and pulls up one of the suite's cream-colored chairs. "Have a seat Shawni. Gentlemen, I have assured Shawni that we will school her on what The Gentlemen is all about. So, Shawni, you just sit back, and chill, all right?"

The short one finally remembers that he can talk, "Hold up, baby doll isn't even hip to The Gentlemen?"

"Shawni," I remind him, "Not—*'baby doll.'* And this gig is a favor for my brother. No, I do not know anything about you or your group, and as a matter of fact . . ." Oh, forget the voice, I'm ready to leave. This is not the audience I had wanted for my new highlights. I can head over to the Sugar Bar while it's still fairly early. Duran will just have to get over it, because I am not in the mood for this!

"H-h-hold up." Zin offers a soft grin, and looks so far into my eyes that I don't know whether to be irritated or afraid, and he motions for me to be quiet. I just met him, I know, but something about him makes that seem irrelevant.

I shake my head. "Look, I'm sorry. Maybe you should just get someone else."

He whispers, "Shhhhh . . ."

I do. My mother didn't even have that kind of control over my tongue.

He continues cautiously, "I believe that what Cris is saying is that in order for you to understand what you've gotten yourself into, you have to be schooled on what The Gentlemen is all about, dig? Remember what I told you on the elevator?"

The room is too silent, and I refuse to be mesmerized by the soft gray color of his eyes and his soothing voice!

I detest you, Ernie.

He continues, taking his time. "I told you, it's cool. What you don't know, you will."

I almost retreat back to my usual "I don't give a piece of lint about you or your group, so whatever" attitude, but it suddenly feels wrong, unnecessary. I take a breath and nod an okay. Zin bites his lip, brushes my shoulder, and gathers the four of them in front of the window. The curtains are still open, and the starlit sky offers a soft glow in the room. I take another deep breath and examine each of the men standing in front me, suddenly realizing that I have seen these men before. *Jet* magazine, a few weeks ago. The cover. I particularly remember the one in the Armani wire-rimmed glasses—*because* of the glasses. Duran has so many groups these days; I hadn't even realized they were one of his! Without intending to, I smile at the sudden recollection.

"See," Zin says, "you're smiling already and we haven't even begun. Much better. Gentlemen?"

Suddenly Mr. Push-up, Mo, clears his throat, hums a note, and in a soft and patient alto begins, *"Taaake . . . uhhhh . . . siiiiiip."*

The group joins in with a subtle, gradual harmony, each one managing to look into my eyes no matter how hard I try to turn away, *"Pour some wine, pour some wii-iiine . . . pour a tall glass oooof it. Pour some wine, pour some wiiiine . . . pour some champagne baaaabaaay."*

Mr. Push-up slices the harmony into a solo, *"Pour some Mo . . ."*

Their voices and gestures are leisurely as they support his solo with a harmonized afterthought, *"Moet baby dollll."*

The one in the Armani glasses bears down to seize his tenor note, *"Pour some Al . . ."*

They are really into this now as they harmonize, *"Alizé . . . baaaabaaay . . ."*

The curly-haired, fingernail filing, short one with the attitude comes in now. Attitude is gone, energy maximized, a near soprano high voice, *"Pour some Cris . . ."*

As if they are one, they instinctively look up, their eyes following Cris's pitch to the sky as they sing, *"Cristal daaarliiiin."*

Zin is the most delicate, barely audible. *"Pour a little . . ."* he licks his lips, takes his time, as if all the time in the world is his. The whole universe, or at least the whole room, is quiet. *"Pour a little . . . Ziiiinnnn . . ."*

The group's harmony complements his tone as they simultaneously sing, *"Ziiiin . . . fiiiiin . . . daaale . . ."*

There is a moment where I have to consciously remember to breathe, where I realize that I am more relaxed than I was a few moments ago, where I actually feel my head tilt to the side a little, batting my eyes.

I want to run from this room!

Think about Bo, Shawni.

They continue softly and sincerely, the tempo picking up, *"Pour some wine, pour some wiiiiine, pour a tall glass oooof it. Pour some wine, pour some wiii-iiine, pour some champagne baaabaay. Pour what 'cha wanna pour darliiiin . . . to get in the mooooood. When you're reaaady . . . foooor it . . ."*

Mo concludes earnestly, *"Taaaake uhhhhh . . ."*

They nod before the final harmony, *"Siiiiip."*

And then a silence that is neither awkward nor easy, just sort of, well, silent. I am anxiously waiting for them, and they for me. I don't know whether I think there should be more, or whether I just want more, but Zin speaks before I have time to figure it out.

"So, Shawni Baldwin," he says, releasing the group from their concluding stances. "There you have the introduction to our CD. Moet, Alizé, Cristal, and me—Zin, Zinfandel."

What am I supposed to say? How am I going to say whatever it is that I am supposed to say if I don't know what to say? This type of music shouldn't fascinate me! I like real music, good lyrics. Whatever happened to songs like "My Girl" and lyrics like the Temptations' "Just My Imagination"? Whatever happened to Motown? And where is Berry Gordy, anyhow? This group is singing about drinks!

But I have to admit that they are good. My breath is coming back to me. Be cool, Shawni.

"Nice." I blurt out. Nice? Quit being such a hard-ass, Shawni. Tell them their voices made you feel mellow and in the mood, and you needed this. Tell them you want to hear more. Apologize for having not been "hip" to The Gentlemen before tonight, because you will listen to their CD, and you will listen to their music. You will be hip. Tell them. Yes, now I am officially hip to The Gentlemen. I have been schooled. Thank you. Thank you for schooling me! Tell Zin his sexy eyes are making you nervous because they're so sincere and it seems like they've seen you before, but you know that you've never met.

Then, like a shot of cold water in the hot tea that was warming my insides, Cris, the small one, gets his attitude back. "Yeah, she liked it. Stuck up honey probably doesn't know how to handle The Gentlemen's effect. That right, fly girl?"

Mr. Armani Glasses, Al, speaks with a laugh, "Cris, chill out man. This is Duran's baby sister."

"Shawni!" I remind him. I can't believe Mr. Shorty called me stuck up!

"My bad. Damn." Al pushes his glasses back, *"Shaaawni,"* he whines playfully, "why you so tense? I mean what's the deal? We botherin' you by hirin' you or somethin'? You been actin' kinda stank since you got here."

"For real." Cris adds, which is a lot of nerve, as if his attitude is comparable to Barney's theme song.

Mo goes down to start his push-ups again, pausing long enough to say, "I'm like, she can act how she wants to act, fine as she is, long as she gets the gear together." Then he resumes his push-ups.

Al and Cris both sit down on the cream-colored sofa. Cris picks up one of the peach pillows, punches it, stuffs it behind him, leans back, and then situates his head into a comfortable position. "So, what's a fly girl like you gonna do with four sexy men like us?"

I don't believe him! It's past time to go.

Then I glance back to the window, where Zin is standing. He's still smiling at me. He lowers his chin. He waits. He finally speaks. "So?" he says, "can we talk business?" He gestures for me to follow him, and I do.

He opens the door to a small office adjacent to one of the suite's bedrooms, where there is now relief from the incense and the insulting comments, and he nods at a chair in front of the cherry wood desk. "Have a seat."

I turn around, watch him close the door. Just the two of us now. I feel a strange uneasiness inside, a mouse faced with cheese, knowing the consequences, but it's so tempting.

"The others?" I ask.

He stands behind me and pulls my black cropped leather jacket off my shoulders a little and then pauses, "Unless you're cold?"

"No." I smile. Did I just smile? Again? "No. Thank you."

He proceeds to take my jacket. "The fellas are cool right where they are. I'll handle this." He puts my jacket on the coatrack and then removes his jacket to reveal a black short-sleeved muscle shirt.

Muscles.

Bo! Bo has muscles. *Bo!* Think, *Bo!* Shawni, think *Bo!*

Zin sits on the edge of the desk, his jeans so baggy, way too big for his . . . looks like thirty-four-inch waist. He looks at my ring fin-ger. "So, you're married?" he asks.

"Oh," I laugh nervously. Why am I laughing nervously? Check yourself girl! "No, I'm engaged." I smile.

He nods, takes a toothpick out of his pocket, puts it in his mouth, and then nods again. "Okay, so . . ."

"So?"

"Soooo," he chews his toothpick. "So what about the gear?"

"Right." Jeez girl. Get a grip! I sit down on the chair, and glance down at my outfit. Was it really this tight before I left home? Maybe I should have worn something looser? I hope they don't think I'm a hoochie. I wonder if I look like a hoochie. Who cares? Forget it. "So, I understand you guys just need some clothes for the dinner?" I take out my electronic notebook.

"Dinner?" he asks, confused.

Oh, please don't tell me that Duran didn't tell him about the dinner!

"Yes," I reply. The dinner that you and your fellow alcoholic beverages are attending on Saturday, I want to say. He looks at me blankly, so instead I add, "The ACT-SO program?"

He shakes his head no. He's serious. He has no idea what I'm talking about.

I immediately snatch my cellular out of my purse. I'm going to tell Duran about himself and his little last-minute gigs. I dial a one, but Zin takes the phone out of my hand.

He's laughing.

"What?" I roll my eyes.

"Chill. Chill." He leans back on the desk. "I was just joking. You're all tense. I'm just trying to lighten your mood, that's all. Chill, Shawni."

Shawni. I'm Shawni, right? Did I slip myself a Mickey in my vodka or is this guy getting into my head? Okay, laugh. I laugh. Ha! Ha! Funny joke. "Okay, so you do know what I'm talking about?"

He nods. "Girl, you are so tense." Then suddenly he jumps up and down a few times, laughing. "You gotta loosen up, right? You having a bad day or do you and your brother just have opposite personalities?"

"Actually," I say, "I just have a lot on my mind, if you really wanna know."

"Word?" He sits back down on top of the desk. "What's up?"

"Nothing." I laugh to myself, just some silly comment my best friend said to me earlier. "I just had a conversation with my best friend, and I guess my mind is still there, or something. I'm sorry. It's no big deal. Anyhow, how do you want to look for the dinner?"

He gets up and pulls one of my curls, lets it go, and watches it spring back as he smiles that crooked smile.

"What?" I flutter my eyes. "Why'd you do that?"

"Bounce up off it. Life's too short, ya dig? Whatever it is that she said to you, bounce up off it."

"He." I correct him and nod in agreement. "I know. You're right." He's right. Forget about it, Shawni.

"Whatever you think." He stands up and stretches.

"Think about what?" I lean back in my chair.

"About the gear." He walks over to the window, pulls the curtain back and stares out. "I'm answering your question."

"Oh, right. Well, yes, but if you have some idea."

"We'll trust your judgment to find us a few choices, you know, do your thing." He stares out the window for a moment, lets go of the curtain, and then turns to me. "Cool? You can handle it, right?"

"Handle, uh, what?"

He laughs. "You are always like two pages behind, girl, I swear. Can you *handle* picking out the gear for us? You know, why you're here?"

"I see." I type one word into their file in all caps. WHATEVER. Then I close it, put it in my purse, and stand up. "That's it, then? I'll send a car for you tomorrow once I have some things for you to check out, okay?"

"Cool." He looks out the window again. "Let's go have a drink."

"What?" Did he just ask me out on a date? Didn't he hear me tell him that I'm engaged? Didn't he see the platinum and ice on my ring finger?

"I'm sayin', you've had a bad day, and you need to unwind. It's still early. I'm trying to revisit New York. What? Your man won't trip if you have a drink with a client will he? Let's roll."

I watch him glide toward the coatrack. He doesn't know Bo. Yes, Bo *will* trip if I have a drink with a client. I allow him to help me on with my jacket. I wait as he puts his jacket back on. I swallow. "He's out of town for the weekend," I say.

"Should I call a car?" He hands me back my cellular phone and waits. "Or do you wanna drive?"

"Uh, sure. I can drive."

What am I doing?

"One thing." He sniffs and steps in closer and speaks casually, but with a hint of authority. "Let's just chill for the rest of the night. The attitude, the prissy eye batting, leave all that right here in this room, cool?"

What did he just say? Prissy? Eye batting? I hardly do it on purpose; it's the mascara I'm adjusting my eyes to. Really.

He nods with a laugh, and then, "Let's roll."

I follow him back out into the living room area of the suite.

Al is on the phone in the corner. Cris and Mo are both leaning back on the couch engrossed in the television. I check to see what has their undivided attention, and see a naked redhead standing on a pool table licking an eight ball. Perverts.

Zin pauses on the way to the door. "I'll be back, gentlemen," he says.

"Hold up." Cris doesn't take his eyes off the screen as he talks. "What's the deal on the gear?"

"It's being handled. I'll be back." Zin opens the door and gestures for me to go out.

It's just a drink with a client, right? Stylists do this all the time. No big deal.

He steps out of the room and lets the door close gently behind us and goes over to push the elevator button. As we wait he softly hums the song they sung and I recall the words.

It is Joop cologne he's wearing!

Bo, Shawni. Think Bo.

I can't believe I'm sitting in a dark corner of the Sugar Bar with a cornrow-wearing singer, that I have just finished a second Long Island iced tea, ordered a third, and that he and I have been talking nonstop for almost two hours! I am completely comfortable with this, and I shouldn't be. Something about this seems inappropriate for an engaged woman. Perhaps it's the palpitations of my heart each time this incredibly sexy man licks those bubbly lips of his. I peak around, feeling as if Ernie is somewhere laughing. He isn't.

"Your Long Island." Our weave-wearing waitress places my drink in front of me. I really shouldn't be having another one. I haven't had this much to drink in awhile—my tolerance may not be high enough. I take a sip before continuing. She gives Zin his second Molson Ice.

"Don't laugh?" I say shyly.

"Laugh?" He pours a serious expression over his genuinely interested face. "There isn't anything funny about a person's feelings. Feelings are always valid, *never* funny. I won't laugh as long as you keep it real and help Zin understand where you're coming from. Why didn't you sign?"

I nod, sure that I'm not going to sound stupid even if it's the craziest thing he's ever heard. I'm intrigued by his sincerity, amazed by my own willingness to be so open with him. "To be completely honest, I turned it down because it just didn't feel the same all of a sudden. I was at the point where I was questioning what I was doing in a place where all I did was chase approval. I didn't want to just be a paper doll anymore."

"A paper doll?" He smiles. "I'm sayin', I'm not laughing, but help me out here."

"I know it's hard to understand." I prepare to ramble through my reasoning. "Being a model was incredible, my dream. I mean, I got to see the entire world, you know? I was being offered a huge, insane amount of money to put on fly clothes and strike a pose. So much money, right there. Only it was never about the money. I used to get a rush whenever I worked that runway. Then it all just got old for me—the money, the runway, the people. It's like no one cares about anything else about you. I love fashion, I love fashion designers. But when you're a paper doll, all people do is look at you."

His jaw drops. He understands. "Word? That's deep. I'm sayin' . . ." He looks pensive for a few moments and then, "It's like that with me . . . with singin'. I'm trying to do interviews and talk philosophically, and all folks want to hear about is the money and who I'm layin' with. I'm sayin', there's more to Zin than that, a whole lot more, right? Women in every city, waiting, willing—just *willing*, ya dig? And I don't mind chillin'—gettin' to know new folks—but it's never enough for the ladies. They always want more of the image but never the real. It's crazy. I dig what you're sayin', believe that." He sighs, and for a while just looks mellow, sort of distant.

Neither of us speak. The silence is comfortable, though, appropriate.

And just as much as Zin seems to understand what I'm saying, there seems to be a connection between this glass and me, because I can't get enough of it.

He finally asks, "So, how'd your man feel about it?"

"Oh." I nod. "You know, well, he's always wanted to just take care of me anyhow, so he's cool with it. He'd be happy just spoiling me, letting me live as carefree as I want. He's said that, you know. He's that type of man, can give me, and is willing to give me, anything I want. I was born into the good life, the finest things, and he's willing to keep giving it to me."

"Dig that." He nods. "So, you're *his* paper doll now? Like a trophy for him?" he asks.

"What? What do you mean"—I shake my head—"trophy?"

He smiles, eyeing my now half-empty glass. "I'm sayin', some fellas are cool with havin' a lady just to have for the mantel and say she's theirs. Doesn't he want you to have your own thing goin' on?"

"No, see, the thing is, *I* made the decision to stop modeling. He's just cool with it."

"So, when's the wedding?"

I gaze down at my ring. Wedding. You're going to be someone's wife. "He really cares about me, you know? He's so good to me. It's a good situation, too. My mother adores him. He's good friends with my brother. And Daddy, well, Daddy still lives in Milan and he hasn't exactly met him in person yet, but he did give me his blessing."

He crosses his arms and looks even more intrigued. "Word? So Pops lives in Italy?"

"Yeah, well, that's where Duran and I were born, you know? We only moved to New York when I was nine. Duran was seven."

I was nine, right? Or was I the one who was seven?

Yup, last drink for me.

"Naw, Duran never mentioned it. So, Moms is still in New York?"

I nod. "Fifth Ave. She's happy there."

"And Pops is still overseas?"

I nod again. "He's happy there."

"So, are they still—"

"A couple? Yes. They're still in love, too, after all these years with Mommie being in the States." Is that a tear welling in my eye? Where did that come from? I take a swallow of my drink to shut myself up.

"So, what about you?" he asks.

"I live here." I say as I put my glass down. Duh.

"No," he leans into the table. "I'm asking what about you. You said Moms is digging fiancé man. Obviously your brother does." He pauses. "Zin didn't hear one word about how Shawni feels. So, what about you?"

"I love him." I say without hesitation. "I adore him." I giggle. "He's the best man I've ever had in my life. He's attentive. He's romantic. He spoils me. We're compatible. He's superfine."

He's nodding repeatedly, encouraging me to continue.

"I wouldn't be marrying him," I remind him and myself, "if I didn't love him. He buys me whatever I want, and I deserve that. Every woman does. Money is of no consideration when it comes to the things he buys me."

He shrugs. "Okay. Check it. I have a Benz. A Vet. A Hummer. A pad in Atlanta, a pad in L.A., and I'm looking at a spot in Vegas. I'm well invested, stocks and all that, money working for me, dig? I go to Aruba three times a year, been to Africa—when I'm not out promoting or touring or doing some charitable shit. Any man can buy you things, me included. What's unique with fiancé man?"

No, he didn't. *Whoa.*

I strain to twist my neck that is suddenly tight, and this weird laugh comes out that suggests I'm getting pissed off. "Excuse me? What are you implying?"

He sits still—stone still. "Nothing. I asked a question."

"Kind of rude, don't you think?"

He drinks a little bit of his beer, puts it down, slides it to the middle of the table, and shrugs. Then he takes a knot of money out of his pocket and drops a fifty on the table. He finishes off the remaining sip in his beer and stands up. "Let's go ride. I wanna check out the city streets. Cool?"

"I need to finish my . . ." I really don't. I take one last sip of my Long Island, grab my jacket, and follow him out the door. I feel a rush to my head but manage to deal with it as I keep walking. I unlock Baby Blue's doors, and he and I both get in.

He reclines the passenger seat and tells me to just drive—and I do. We're silent until we get further uptown and he points out various places that he remembers from living in New York, and I assume that he's from here.

"I lived here for about three years before I moved to Atlanta. Shorty and me—uh, that's Cris in the group—moved to Atlanta together. That's where we met your brother. 'Ran introduced us to Al and Mo."

"Oh, so you guys didn't grow up singing together, with a pact to stay together forever?"

"No." He laughs quietly at the thought. "I'm from Ohio. Toledo. Cris grew up in Brooklyn. Al and Mo grew up in Georgia."

"Farmland?" I ask, surprised. "Isn't Ohio in the heart of the Midwest?"

He closes his eyes, and it changes the way he looks—less intense, relaxed. He laughs. "You're trippin' for real." He opens his eyes, looks at me, and stares in disbelief, before laughing. "Girl, no. Hell no. Ohio is cool—different from New York, true enough. Yo, I did not grow up on a farm!"

I hope I haven't offended him. Maybe I've had too much to drink. Maybe I couldn't possibly care any less, anyhow! I shrug. "I've never been there."

"Toledo's cool. Not a whole lot to do in terms of the industry, but it's cool. My cats are all there still. I'm the only one that busted out to do this thing for real. My main cat owns a record store. That's the closest any of 'em got to the business, you know. They're all doin' all right though, maintaining. You know, it's no New York, but it's home for us farmers." He laughs.

My head feels funny. My stomach is starting to get a little queasy. "Interesting," I say to be polite, realizing that I may be getting ill. "Do you go back often?" I ask.

"Yeah, my Moms and Pops, you know? Four brothers, my little sister."

"I'm sorry if I offended you, about the farm."

"Naw, you're straight. It's not New York, but you should check it out."

"I live here," I reply, distracted by my stomach.

"Awww . . ." Zin laughs. "Toledo, girl. You should check out Toledo. I forgot you're always a couple pages behind."

I just drive in uneasy silence, hoping my stomach will settle.

We have been riding around for nearly an hour, and I definitely feel the effects of those drinks. We drove uptown, through Harlem, and he showed me where he and Cris used to live above a barbershop near Washington Heights, and then we drove back down Broadway to Times Square. Something is in his memories that you can't get in Atlanta, or from being on the cover of *Jet*, something he enjoys thinking about tonight, enjoys sharing. He seems warmed and inspired by the recollections. I'd like that, to enjoy remembering.

Stories about the times he and Cris sang outside the barbershop to get money for hair cuts, struggling, and too proud to call home for help, they did what they had to do. Maybe I'd admit that it's all very inspiring and commendable—the way they persevered—but it's also almost two o'clock in the morning, and all I can do is focus on the fact that I drank too much, I feel really tipsy, I need to concentrate on what I'm doing, *and* I hope I'm not going to be up sick all night.

"You mind?" He gestures to the window, feeling good, enjoying being back in New York.

"Go, ahead," I say. "Maybe the fresh air will help. I'm not feeling so well."

"Straight? You need to pull over?" He sits the reclined passenger seat back up.

I answer him by doing exactly that. I turn down traffic-congested Forty-second Street and manage to pull over. I barely make it out of the car before letting my stomach out alongside a building. Awful, just awful, sour and intense—the smell, the feeling. My head is spinning. I know better than to drink so much. Ugh. I hear a car door. Footsteps. Then, from behind, I feel his arms around my waist, pulling.

"You gotta let it out." It's Zin. He pulls my stomach in. "That's how you'll feel better."

He pulls harder, forcing whatever is left in my stomach to flee to the ground. Doesn't he see that I *was* letting it out? Now there is absolutely nothing left to let out. I hear a phone in the distance. Is that my cellular? Who cares? I'm sick. Zin eases the hold on my waist and I try to decide if I'm going to throw up again. Oh, Heaven, please make it go away!

I will never never never drink again.

Why is everyone honking so loud?

He completely lets go now. "Hold up. I think your phone is . . ." He walks away, goes back to the car.

"I don't care," I moan. "I'm sick."

"Hello?" Zin answers the phone. My phone. Oh no! What if it's—"You looking for Shawni?" Zin walks back over to me with an aww-shit expression on his face. It must be.

"Hello?" I moan into the receiver.

"Shawni?" Yup, it's him.

"Bo," I say. "Honey, I don't feel so well."

"Shawni?" Bo's breathing is heavier than usual.

"Bo, you've been jogging? You're breathing so hard." I swallow and hold my stomach. As Zin holds me up, my knees and my legs weaken.

"Shawni!" Bo shouts. "What the hell is going on? Why do you sound drunk? And who is Zin? And why the *fuck* is he answering your phone?"

Silence.

Oh, no. I suddenly realize what's happening. My fiancé thinks I'm creeping. "Ooooh . . . noooo . . . Booooo . . ." I giggle. Hey, that rhymes. "He's just a client." I close my eyes.

Silence.

"Bo," I whine. "Please don't yell. It hurts when you yell."

"A client?" He replies, ignoring my request. "Since when does a client answer the damn cellular phone that I pay the fucking bill for, Shawni? And client, for *what*?"

"Please stop cursing at me, Bo. You don't understand." I manage to get this much out as Zin leads me to Baby Blue's passenger side. "I'm getting back in Baby Blue now, honey," I say to Bo.

"Oh, really?" Bo laughs. It's a fake laugh, not a "ha ha, that was really funny" laugh. "You ridin' this dude in the Lex?"

"Noooo . . . I mean, I don't know." Whatever. "You're tripping."

"H-h-h-hold." Now Bo is laughing a "ha ha funny" laugh, and then there is a rather enjoyable silence, and I try to stop my head from aching. Then he shouts, "You're telling me you don't know? You riding some fool in my Lexus, and you're drunk? And you're trying to lie about it? What's going on?"

So much for the silence.

"Bo. Shhh. Not so loud," I plead.

Zin takes the phone from me as I climb into the passenger seat. "Look, man, Shawni had a little too much to drink. She's cool, though. I'm a client of hers. I'll see to her getting—" He closes the passenger door and a while later I hear him open the driver's side door and get in. I don't hear him saying anything else, so I look up only to realize that he's not on the phone anymore.

"What'd he say?" I ask, but Zin doesn't answer me, just pulls Baby Blue out into traffic and starts driving.

"Why'd you drink so much if you couldn't handle it? I didn't know you were all tripped out like that, man. You should've said somethin', girl. Why'd you drink so much like that?" I hear him talking but I don't answer. Partly because my head is splitting, and partly because I really don't know why. I was nervous. I don't know. I didn't know I was going to get sick. As if I would consciously drink so much that I would throw up in full view of the immediate world.

It's Zin's fault. He's the one who kept looking at me. He's the one who kept asking me questions like he could read my mind. He's the one who . . . urgh! I slap the power button on the stereo, make Montel Jordan shut up. "Get It on Tonight" is not the most appropriate theme song for this occasion.

The silence is inviting. If I take a quick nap all the drumming will end.

"Damn!" he shouts, reminding me that my headache isn't going anywhere anytime soon. "Why didn't you tell me you had a pony up in here?" Zin backs out of the doorway leading into my condo, and pulls the door closed. My Doberman, Sanford, sits in the hallway with his head tilted, good-naturedly waiting for our guest to enter.

"Oh, please." I pull the door open. "Come on in. He's fully trained. He won't try to get you unless I tell him to." I walk past Sanford and head toward the kitchen. I need four Tylenol, water, and some Alka-Seltzer—*fast*. I turn on the light switch. Did I really choose all white for my kitchen? This is just too bright for my eyes tonight.

I finally hear the door close and Zin whispering, "It's oooookay dude. Dooon't bite."

"Just go on and have a seat," I say. "He'll only get nervous if you seem nervous."

I grab a liter of seltzer, a bottle of water, and a few Tylenol before I join Zin in my plush baby blue and white living room. He's standing there studying a framed picture of my mother, which is hanging above my white sofa. I'm standing behind him, gazing as well.

She was just beginning her modeling career, wearing a red sundress, a white flower in her loosely pinned up hair. A fake waterfall was the backdrop, as she nonchalantly leaned against a wooden railing, staring off into a place only she could see.

I swallow a Tylenol. "That's Mommie."

"Word?" He looks down, noticing Sanford sniffing at his Timberland boots. Zin whispers, "Niiice doggy doggy doggy."

I must be feeling better. I actually chuckle a little. "Sanford, listen to me." I say. He looks up at me, unsure of whether or not he should trust our guest. "This is Zin, from The Gentlemen."

Zin raises his eyebrows at me with a questionable look, looks down at Sanford, "Nice to meet you, Sanford? That's what I'm supposed to say?"

I laugh. Sanford takes a final sniff and retreats to his bedroom.

"See," I sit on the edge of the couch, "he's off to his bedroom."

Zin gives me a strange look. "Dude has his own bedroom?"

"Well," I pop another Tylenol, "I don't have any children."

He laughs, looks at me quietly, a thought, and then he looks back at Mommie's picture. "You look like her." He pauses. "She's stunning. Beautiful."

"Thank you." I swallow my third pill, deciding not to take the fourth, and put the glass on the coffee table.

"So, is it true, every picture has a story, a thousand, plus some, words?" he asks.

I nod up at the picture. It was before she had even met Daddy. Before she'd realized that her success as a fashion model, who just happened to be a woman of color, would be limited. Before she'd given birth to Duran and me. Before she would move her two children far away from their father, to another country. Before her last hope for a successful modeling career was to lie in the palm of her daughter's hand, who would then just toss the opportunity away. A perfect title for the picture could simply be *Before*. "Definitely a thousand plus." I tell him.

"Are the two of you close?"

"Mommie and I are best friends."

"Dig that," he replies, impressed. "Like me and my pops. That's my main cat right there."

"How old are you, Zin?" I turn to him and ask.

"Been rollin' for twenty-eight years."

I nod. "And in your twenty-eight years, how many times have you and your father argued?"

He looks perplexed for a moment, as if he's thinking about my question, and then he bites his bottom lip. "Probably just once. I was seventeen. I had found out on a Thursday that my girlfriend was pregnant. That Friday I was like whatever, I still went down to Cincinnati with my cats to kick it. It was mad crazy, I was down there just kickin' it, doin' whatever, tryin' to forget about it, right? I didn't call her once while I was out of town. I dogged any thoughts about it, like she didn't even exist. I was raw about it, just cold. Came home Monday morning, wasn't even out the car good, my pops was standing outside, threw me up against the side of the house, held me up by my collar, told me how my girl had been calling there all weekend cryin' and all that. Pops said he'd put me out of his house before he'd allow me to live there and run from my responsibility. I'd never seen him look so pissed."

"Wow," I reply.

"Yeah, it was crazy, 'cause my cats were still in the car. Man, I was so embarrassed. I'm tellin' you"—he shakes his head—"but I needed that. Then again, it wasn't really an argument, just when Pops went off on me. I was too scared to say a word. Naw, we never really had a real *true* argument. He's a military cat, so you just take it as he says, you know? Mad respect. It's just the way it is with him. He's a cool cat, though."

"Was he strict?" I ask.

"Nope. Just stubborn as hell. His way or I-75."

"And the baby?"

"He'll be eleven. Stevie."

"Oh." I nod.

"What about you?" He looks at Mommie's picture again. "Do you argue a lot?"

I sigh. "We never used to. Now we do, all the time."

"Why now?" he asks.

"What do you mean?"

"I'm sayin', all of a sudden you're arguing all the time. Why now?"

"Okay," I reevaluate my exaggeration. "Maybe not *all* the time, but a lot recently."

"Right, right . . . But I'm saying, what's going on in your lives that's causing animosity that was never evident before?"

I laugh. "What are you? A singer *and* a therapist?"

"You started the conversation"—he shrugs—"I'm just probing."

"Let's just drop it."

"It's your call." He nods and looks up at the high ceilings and skylights. He smiles before getting up and walking around my spacious living and dining room area, eyeing everything with approval. "Nice pad here, Shawni Baldwin."

"Thank you." I say and then suddenly remember how awful I

must look. I've been so busy throwing up, falling asleep in the car, and dragging myself into my condo, that I haven't looked in the mirror once. My breath must be really funky. "Excuse me," I get up, grab the master remote control to the entertainment center, and toss it to him.

He catches it, "What's up?"

"Feel free to check out the stereo or the television. DVD"—I open the glass doors to the entertainment center—"I'll be right back."

"Cool."

In the bathroom, I am amazed that my curls are still decent. Had I not received such a thorough facial, I would probably look hideous, but I don't. A quick Clinique 3-Step, some Colgate and Scope, a change of clothes, and I should feel okay. I'll take a dip in the whirlpool after my company leaves.

It's not like I'm having company. He's a client who helped me get home safely after I got sick, right? I convince myself of this as I scrub my face. I apply some Mac coffee eyeliner and then a little cherry Chapstick on my dry lips before heading to my bedroom. I turn on the light to my baby blue and white bedroom and sigh at my king-size waterbed. I should be diving in and going to sleep. I glance at the clock. It's late, almost three in the morning. I catch the reflection of a blinking red light on my nightstand.

"You have three messages," the answering machine woman says.

I anticipate my mother's voice. She should be giving in by now.

It's Bo. "Shawni, I'm trying to be calm here. Call me as soon as you get in from your little drinking engagement 'with your client.' I don't care what time it is."

Click.

Beep.

"Yo, sis." The next message is from Duran. "Where are you? Talked to the fellas. Seems, uh, you left with Zin hours ago. Hell's going on? Tried your cell, turned off or somethin'. Hit me up." Still playing big brother, even though he's my little brother. I don't remember turning my cellular off.

Beep.

"Shawni." Bo's voice again. "I don't know what's going on, but I just tried your cellular again, and it said the shit is either turned off or out of the service area. Now, did you turn the shit off or are you out of the fucking service area with your *client*?"

Click.

I don't feel like dealing with this, but I better call him.

"Hilton front desk. How may I direct your call?" A woman answers.

I peel off my sneakers and plop down on my waterbed. "Bo Delaney's room, please?"

"Just a moment." She puts me on hold. I stand up and pull off my spandex warm-up pants, decide to wait on changing my shirt. I'll change into sweats and a T-shirt in a sec.

He answers, his teeth apparently still clenched. "Shawni."

"Bo, baby." I close my bedroom door and fall out onto the waterbed.

"Don't give me that Bo baby stuff. What's going on?"

"Bo, nothing! Nothing. Nothing. Nothing. You are overreacting to Zin answering my cellular, and you're not giving me a chance to explain. Now, I don't feel good, and I don't feel like arguing."

"I call my fiancée in the middle of the night, she's not home. I call her cellular, another man answers. You're talking all drunk, gigglin' and shit, and I'm supposed to be understanding? This better be good, woman. This better be some damn Shakespeare. Drinkin' and carrying on, you ought not feel good. This is some bullshit right here."

I wait a moment. I'm really not in the mood for this but, "First of all, you know how I'm trying to start my new career as a stylist. Well, Duran needed me for a last-minute gig for this group—"

"Get to the Zin part, Shawni!"

"I will if you let me finish."

"Finish."

"Okay!" I sigh heavily. "Zin is one of the members of the group, and I met the group at the Shark Bar to discuss the gear for the show I'm dressing them for, and since there wasn't enough room in the cab for me, I had to drive. Really nice guys, Bo."

"Keep talking."

"Okay. Okay. So, I had a little too much to drink, you know, just caught up in casual conversation. The group caught a cab back to the hotel, but Zin, one of the members of the group, offered to drive me home since I wasn't feeling well."

"Hold. You let this fool drive the Lex?"

"Oh, no. Of course not, honey. He offered, but I told him I'd be okay, and would he mind just riding with me in case I got sick. And then I *did* get sick, and I asked him to answer the phone. He rode home with me, I called him a cab, and he's gone back to his hotel now. It's all cool. See?"

Silence.

Silence.

"Look." He finally speaks. "Damn! All right, maybe I over-reacted, *maybe*. But there's nothing cool about you drinkin' with a bunch of men when it's supposed to be a business meeting. What the hell was I supposed to think? I call you, you're not home. Call your cell phone, and some fool answers? That's not exactly what I call a professional meeting, baby. And how the hell was I supposed to know you were handlin' business for 'Ran?"

Perfect transition—business. Whew. "So, how did your meeting go, honey?"

He takes a moment, and I know he's deciding if he should let the argument go or not. He finally does, but unenthusiastically. "Stale. The groups were all right, but that's it—just all right. There's another show tomorrow night. Hopefully it'll be worth my time."

"I love you," I say on impulse. I do love my man. Whenever I feel like saying it, I say it.

"I love you, too, baby."

" 'Kay. Call me tomorrow. Let me know how it goes?"

"Yeah."

"Good night." I kiss into the phone.

"Yeah, all right Shawni." He kisses back before we hang up.

Whew.

Now, back to my company. I run out into the living room and find that Zin has removed his jacket and is standing in front of the stereo, comfortable, as if he hangs out in my living room all the time. Just as I walk in, Otis Redding's voice fills the room. *Otis. So many nights—Bo and me and Otis.*

"Having fun, yet?" I say over the music as I stand in the doorway to the living room.

He turns around with an angelic and inspired smile on his face. "This is my dude." He closes his eyes and hums along to a tune. Suddenly, however, one of his eyes pops open. "Shawni," he eyes me with one eye still closed, looks down, and his eye immediately looks back up.

I look down to see what he's looking at.

Oh, no!

He opens both eyes, turns away slowly, "You forget something?" He laughs.

I ease back into the bedroom, thinking How the heck did I forget to put my pants back on? It's a good thing my legs aren't ashy, but that's irrelevant. The fact is that I was standing there, in front of him, with no pants on. What was I thinking? Why was I in such a rush to return to the living room? How embarrassing. This can't be happening.

Just act as if it didn't happen. Don't miss a beat. Pretend. Act your way through it. This has nothing to do with anything except the fact that I've been a little tipsy tonight and that's it. I hurry into my bedroom and throw on a pair of black cotton sweatpants and a Calvin Klein T-shirt. There is no reason to entertain further thought about this. Just walk right back out into the living room. Accidents happen.

I dismiss the voice in the room that sounds exactly like Ernie, laughing, and saying "yeah right." I march back out into the living room, determined to have as professional a conversation with my client as possible.

He looks up at me, smiles at my sweatpants, and gestures with a CD. "So, I see you're a big Motown fan," he says, as if nothing happened, as if the only thing on his mind is my music collection.

I sit down on the couch. "Motown was the best. You like?"

"Marvin Gaye. Whaaaaat? Smokey! Man, I'm diggin' all those cats."

"That's surprising." I smile.

He looks at me with a concerned expression now. "You feel better?"

"Yes. Thank you." I do feel better.

"You need to freeze up when you drink, for real. Just have like a mellow Amaretto sour or something. You were drinking alcohol like water, girl."

"I know."

"Yeah." He nods. "So, is your dude all right?"

I clasp my hands over my knees. "He's calm, now that he thinks you're back at the hotel."

"How come you didn't just tell him you were hanging out with a client?" he asks, confused.

I look at him closely, and I do not see anything abnormal about him. "You don't know Bo." I tell him.

"Word?" He looks sincerely interested, but continues instead, not giving me a chance to answer. "Way I see it, I mean, realistically, sometimes we all have to lie, but yo, you didn't have anything to lie about. All right, you had a couple of drinks with a client. Now, I'm just here chillin'. Not like anything else is goin' on, right?"

"So much easier said to me than to him," I say.

He sits back a little. "Yeah, I'm just sayin', we are just chillin' out, right? I was just tryin' to hang out, get to know you. That's my thing. I wasn't tryin' to step to you like that. For real."

"Right." I nod. "Chilling. That's all."

He smiles. "Chill-*in*', Shawni," he says, as if he's correcting me.

"That's what I said."

He laughs. "All right. Yeah." He leans forward, toward me, looking at me. "I'm like, it's just whacked to step to another man's woman, knowing that she's another man's woman, and that they're engaged. I don't push like that."

Right. I'm supposed to believe this big bag of bullshit from the brother who outright said that he was checkin' me out? Oh, he was just trying to get to know me better. Right. Did I just imagine that he called me stunning, or didn't he?

"Look, Shawni," he says, folding his hands into a prayerlike position. "Why are you rollin' your eyes at me? Yo, on the real, just because a dude sees a beautiful woman and has a few drinks with her doesn't mean he's trying to step to her. Look, the type of man I am,

I'm always trying to meet new people. That's it. I mean, you're a beautiful woman, don't get me wrong. If you were fair game, I'd be trying to get to know you with an agenda. I won't deny that. But don't think that I'm here trying to step to you ill. Bad karma, you dig?"

Do I dig? If I told him right now that I am not the faithful type, that I'm willing to introduce him to my waterbed, he'd be on me like a leather glove. So, whatever.

Instead, I reply, "I totally understand what you're saying, but Bo wouldn't understand it if I explained it to him that way."

Zin smiles but still seems frustrated. "Check it. That's because he's used to reading between the lines. If you two focused on saying the absolute truth, he would believe every word you say to him, no question. His mind is so programmed, like most, to hear the subtext, that he can't roll with just truth. I function on the literal. I don't bullshit. Relationships should be all-out honesty and trusting, and honesty is essential for trust. I shouldn't even have to tell you that, if you're marrying this man." He pauses. "I'm stepping to you as a fella trying to meet a friend. That's all."

Either I'm still drunk or he just thinks I am. This is complete bullshit, the other *f* word that I've always hated for men to use. Friends. We sit in silence for moments. Well, it isn't actually silence, because Otis Redding is singing, so it's like we just let the music replace conversation for a while.

It's too quiet for too long, so as corny as it sounds, I say, "Friends are nice."

"True dat. I'm always looking to get to know people."

"Right." I smile. "True that."

He laughs. "*Dat,* Shawni. True *dat.*"

"That's what I said." I shift positions, get really comfortable before I say, "Yes, but, at the same time, the only reason I was even at the hotel was to talk about gear for the show, as a favor for Duran. I wasn't looking for any friends, okay?"

"No?"

"No."

"No?" he asks again.

I clear my throat, roll my eyes, and speak as clearly as possible this time. "No! I mean, what makes you think I was looking for something?"

"I just asked." He shrugs. "Just a question, that's all. You're funny, you know that?" He laughs. "The way you dismiss things with a flutter of your eyes, the way you have a 'been there, done that' approach to everything, the way you. . . . All that, Shawni. I don't buy it. None of it."

"You don't even know me," I say.

"True dat. I don't. But, yo, that's why I'm here." He yawns. "I dig getting to know people, right? I'm serious about that. That's just me, how I am."

"Well, what a friendly camper you are." I do a whoop-ti-do twirl of my finger in the air.

"Friendly camper, huh?" He laughs. "Is it just my imagination or were you being friendly to me, too? I mean, I'm up here, chillin' in your pad, right? That's a friendly camper sort of thing to invite someone to do, isn't it?"

"I was just being polite. I could go the entire weekend if I wanted. It's ridiculous."

He looks confused. "Entire weekend?"

"I'm sorry. It's nothing. It's so stupid. Would you like something to drink?" I ask.

"What you got?" He yawns again. "Then, I'm gonna have to head to the hotel."

I go into the kitchen and use the light from the refrigerator to light up the room. "Raspberry seltzer, grapefruit juice, carrot . . ." I close the door and go back into the living room. "Unless you want a real drink."

He's sitting there, stretched out, leaning back on the couch. "Naw, I'm sayin' I think we both had enough tonight. Seltzer is cool."

I don't answer him. I go back into the kitchen, pour the seltzer, and consider the consequences of repeating what Ernie said. Then I remember what Zin said earlier about not laughing if I tell him something. But it could be funny, and maybe that would be okay if he laughs if I tell him, because it is funny, ridiculously hilarious.

I hand him the glass. "My best friend doesn't think I can go the weekend, while Bo is away, without being in the presence of a man."

He raises an eyebrow, pauses from drinking his seltzer. "Word?"

"Whatever. He's always saying things."

"Oh, so that's what had you buggin' earlier! Yo, well, it's botherin' you like that, that he said that to you, maybe there's something to it. Can you?"

"Are you kidding? Of course I can!"

"How long has it been?"

I shriek. "I am not going to entertain Ernie's suggestion. I only told you for the sake of a good laugh."

"Oh, yeah? Well, all right," he says, and sits there quietly.

The phone rings. Uh-oh.

"Hello," I try to sound asleep in case it's Bo.

"You get my message?"

"Oh, Duran. Hey." I relax and sit on the edge of the leather recliner and play with a few of the leaves on my hanging plant. "Yes, I did. Actually I was just getting ready to call you."

"What's goin' on? Fellas say you left with Zin forever ago! What's the deal?"

"Oh. Yeah, we just hung out a little. Went by the Sugar Bar and talked about the gear for the dinner."

"He still there?" Duran asks.

"Here?" I clear my throat. "Oh, no. He should be back at the—"

"Shawni, look," Duran interrupts, "I did not set you up with this gig to go gettin' in trouble. Now, I don't know what the deal is, but call him a cab right now, and be cool, all right? I'll hit you up tomorrow."

"Duran—"

"Call him a car right now. You're a bad liar, Shawni. I'll see you when I get to town. I'll be there early Saturday morning. Holler at you then. 'Bye." And my brother hangs up on me.

I listen to the dial tone for a moment before hanging up. I look at Zin. "My brother thinks he's my father or something, like I'm not an adult."

"I can dig it. I have a little sister, too. And I drive her crazy, too. Call me a cab?"

"Yes, but only because I know you're tired, and I am, too, and not because my brother suggested it." I dial the number to a car service.

"Five minutes." I inform Zin after I finish.

He stands up, stretches, and pulls his jacket on. "Yeah, I need to grab some shut-eye. I'll talk to you tomorrow. How's that?" He smiles, extends his hand to shake.

I don't want him to leave. I shake his hand.

He doesn't let go of my hand for a few lingering moments, and I'm glad for that. He leans in, kisses me on my cheek, and then lets go.

He starts to say something, pauses, smiles, and then nods. "You seem like a very special young lady. Just take it easy, all right?"

I smile. "Always."

He nods again, and then leaves. And that's for the best.

I tossed and turned all night. Too many incomplete thoughts. I couldn't relax. I watched the night through the cracks in the blinds for hours as I waited for sleep to come. I tried, but was unable to rest. I'm thrilled, now, to see hints of dawn, and I decide to get out of bed.

Sanford's chin slides off my stomach where his head has been resting. I sit up and immediately recognize this feeling—groggy from drinking last night, borderline sick, irritably achy, blah. Hangover. Why did I ever think Sanford would allow me to skip morning exercise? It's routine. His eyes scream in delight as I head toward the hallway.

I should be able to run this feeling off me. I pull my hair into a ponytail and throw on my running gear. I just need to clear my mind, get mentally prepared for the day. I also need to study The Gentlemen's press kit, and start shopping.

Sanford stops at every tree, every pole, and every bush. It takes awhile to get my momentum going, but the brisk morning air is pleasing to my face. I run until I feel my sports bra's soaking wet, until the sweat drips from my forehead, until I can feel the sweat, like raindrops, falling down my back. Even my hair is wet. I don't care. I run away from thoughts of last night's drinking, of Duran's chains of authority, of Mommie's stubbornness, of Bo's tantrums, of Zin's eyes. I run away from echoes of Ernie's accusations. Then, as if he can read my mind, Sanford looks back at me with pleading eyes and a droopy tongue, begging for mercy. So instead we lightly jog back toward home, but it feels just as good.

I fill Sanford's dish with fresh spring water and again go over the press kit. Based on pictures from various magazines and newspapers, their style seems to be "conservatwist," a term I use to describe someone who likes the safeness of conservative dress and the appeal of a little funk or, for women, a little cleavage and a dab of color—a term for those who don't like to necessarily turn heads but who want people to take note if they happen to look.

I sip from a glass of carrot juice as I flip through the kit. The thing that's really distinctive about The Gentlemen is that they each have their own individual look. I mean, never mind how diverse their personalities are, their looks are different. Their hair for instance. Zin is wearing cornrows, Mo waves, Al twists, and that little arrogant Cris's hair is curly. A collective variety of men—supposed gentlemen—and each of them is unique.

Now, if they each have their own vibe, each one a different style of singing even, why are they always matching, wearing the same clothes? They're like four different definitions of gentleman. Yes, that will be my inspiration.

The buzzer rings.

"Ms. Baldwin?" It's Otto, the doorman, a retired radio disc jockey who used to always brag, on air, about the fact that his name was a palindrome.

"Yes?" I reply.

In a voice reminiscent of his radio days, he booms, "A delivery for you. Just for you, for you. Shall I send it up?"

I didn't order anything, but then again, maybe I did. Oh, well. "Yes. Thank you," I say.

I stand at the door and crack it open as I continue to flip through the pictures. In each picture they are dressed exactly alike. They shouldn't be. They're all so different, even the drinks their names represent.

"Shawni Baldwin?" A heavyset man appears from the elevator. "Delivery." Oh, my. I gasp. A huge white vase at the bottom of a covered package. I hope it's roses.

"Yes, uh, thank you." I take the heavy vase from him and slip him a tip. He nods a thank you and I close the door. I rush into the dining room, put the vase on the table, rip off the tissue paper, and . . . The most beautiful dozen of pink roses, nearly in full bloom, emerge from beneath the wrapping. I tear open the white envelope, and stare at the card.

> *Baby, I am so sorry that I overreacted.*
> *I love you always,* forever.
> *Bo.*

Now, that's an *f* word that I adore.
I love you forever too, Bo. I truly do.

———

THREE

Physics 101

"So, what did you do last night?" Ernie asks from the other end of my phone.

I wish I hadn't answered. "Nothing." And for the fourth time I reposition my new pink roses on the center of the glass coffee table.

He laughs. "Chile, well you know me. I didn't do much either. Hell, if I'm not out somewhere with you, I'm at my House of Elegance, leaving no head uncut, or at home. I stayed in, ordered some Cambodian, had a few glasses of wine, watched the tube. That's it. Did you call Miss Mommie?"

"No."

"You're tripping."

"Ernie"—I sit down on the couch, satisfied with the positioning of the vase for now, and take a deep breath—"I need to talk to you."

"What happened last night?"

"I had a nice time. Nothing happened."

"Tell me first. Which one? Not that it really matters. I mean, they're all fine. I just wanna know which one you were kickin' it with last night."

" 'Bye, Ernie. Just forget it."

"Call your mother. She called me again last night."

"Are you serious?" She keeps calling Ernie, why doesn't she just call me?

"Call her. She's worried about you."

"Whatever."

"Pick me up at six. Let's do dinner—the Sugar Bar," he suggests.

"Fine." Just forget that I said I needed to talk to you about something.

I hang up, dial Mommie's number. It rings but there's no answer. I'll just stop by there later after I finish picking out clothes for the aphrodisiacs.

I'll spend the next few hours looking for outfits for The Gentlemen, get that over with, and then I'll stop by Mommie's, let her tell me again what a terrible decision I've made, come back home, change for dinner, pick up Ernie, and enjoy the evening. Sounds good.

Oh, no! Am I imagining things, or do I hear keys jingling? A doorknob turning? Sanford isn't barking! No barking could only mean one person.

A voice. "Hey, boy." It's *him*, talking to Sanford!

I glance around. Is there any evidence to destroy? No. Of course not! Evidence of what?

What's he doing back in New York? He's not supposed to be back until Sunday night! Why is he here?

"Bo?" I shout toward the hallway. "Is that you?"

He's standing in the doorway to the living room, so fine in his business suit, so virile. It isn't that I forgot what Bo looks like, or anything like that, but as he walks in I get this "oh my goodness can I just stare at you for a little bit" flutter in my stomach. Bo is the finest, smoothest-complexioned, sexiest bald-headed, pencil-thin-mustache-wearing—and he knows just how to walk—man I have ever known. And then I suddenly think, is this man really mine? Have mercy.

"Is that me?" he asks, totally calm, but an uneasy smile. "I'm the only one with a key, right?"

"Bo." I get up. "What are you doing here?"

"What difference does it make?" he asks, looking around, casually, but suspiciously. "Party over yet?"

I walk over to him, want to hug him, but I'm apprehensive. He seems too rigid, like if I reach out to hug him he may not hug me back. "Are you okay?" I ask, not sure if I want the answer.

"Oh, I'm fine." He walks past me. No hug. No kiss. He unbuttons his suit jacket, sits down on the couch, and waits a moment before asking, "How are you, Shawni?"

"Great." I smile, chin up. I'm not in the least bit intimidated by the prospect of a face-to-face confrontation, but now is not the time. "Just on my way out to go shopping for the group, the gig I told you about. Thanks for the flowers."

"Shopping, huh?"

"Yeah." I walk over to him, stand there, and wait a moment. "You look really good, baby. I missed you."

He eyes me, my Gucci stilettos, the slit up the front of my black slim-cut skirt, the hug of my baby blue off-the-shoulder sweater, my hair—pulled back into a sexy bun. He smiles, nods. "I could say the same about you. Damn good. Damn good for just shopping. Shit."

"Um, honey?" I begin.

He nods up, a "what's up" nod.

I sit down next to him. "You weren't supposed to be back until Sunday. Why didn't you tell me you were coming home early?"

He glances at the roses. "I'm glad you like your flowers."

I look at them. "They're beautiful."

"The caliber of talent wasn't there last night, and I'm not wasting my time when it's probably going to be the same thing tonight and tomorrow. Kind of a low-budget showcase. Sherm didn't know what he was talking about."

"Oh," I get up, sit on his lap this time, and lean in to him, testing him. Will he respond if I hug him, kiss him? "I'm sorry to hear that." I put my hand on his leg. I lean in. Then I kiss him on his neck, the soft, quick kisses he's crazy about.

His mood softens, and he smiles. He leans in, and then he gives me a long, slow, melted butter kiss on the lips.

I reply with another creamy kiss, and then a gentle blow down his neck.

"I swear you drive me crazy, woman." He looks at me with determined eyes. His jaw muscles are clenching. He takes a deep breath. "I was trippin' last night. Let me make it up to you?"

Like magic, his words blow my eyes closed. My head is pulled back by a magnetic energy, allowing ample room for my neck to accept each and every one of his tenderly placed kisses. As he pulls me in closer to him by my waist, I think to myself that this is how I want to spend the rest of my life, in this man's arms, on the receiving end of this man's patient kisses and tight hugs.

He whispers between soft kisses, "You smell so good."

He whispers between soft kisses, "I love you so much."

He whispers. Soft kisses. He whispers.

I swallow the flaming passion growing inside, try to contain myself. "Bo, baby?"

He pulls back, looks at me with that vein throbbing on his right temple.

I give him a fast kiss. "I'll be back in a little bit, okay? I have to go take care of this stuff for Duran."

His eyes widen, a heavy blink. "Say what?"

"I'm sorry," I say as I stand up, straighten my skirt, and reach down to grab my purse. "I need to get going. I have an appointment with Caroline in a half hour—she has some things she thinks are perfect for the group—and you know, I want to get this over with so we can spend time together."

He sucks his teeth. I hate when he does that.

"Look," I say. "By the time you go to Brooklyn, unpack, check on your place, do whatever, I'll be finished. You can go with me over to Mommie's to visit."

"Oh," he looks surprised, pleased. "You finally talked to her?"

"No, but I'm going to—today."

"After you finish shopping?"

"Yes."

He stands up. "All right then, I don't need to go to Brooklyn—already went, dropped my stuff off before I came here. So, I'll just roll with you."

"What?" I laugh. "Roll with me where?"

"Caroline's. Shopping, right?"

I smack my lips. "Bo, please. You hate shopping."

"So, who said anything about wanting to shop. I wanna spend some time with my lady. Is that all right?"

"Bo, do I tag along with you when you're working?"

"W-w-w-wait. Hold up." He scrunches his eyebrows, looks at me like I'm a goofy clown. "Tag along? What the hell is that supposed to mean? You're going shopping, I go with you, that means I'm tagging along? Any other time it's 'come help me pick out this, see if you like me in this.' What's up?"

"Bo—"

"No." He holds up his wait-a-minute finger. "And I did ask you, woman. I asked you to come to Chicago with me. What'd you say? 'No, I think I'll pass, just wanna chill out this weekend.' Woman you know, if you ever wanna go anywhere with me, business or no business, you're coming. First class. You know this. See, this is some shady shit right here."

I almost laugh but manage to hold it in, and sigh instead. "Bo, if you want to come, fine."

He walks over to me, gives me a hard, forceful kiss on the mouth, and starts walking toward the hallway. "Just keep your cell phone on," he says.

"Bo!" I shout after him. "I said you could go!"

The front door slams shut.

"No, *you* chill. Honey's talking all crazy, and I'm the only one with enough balls to say somethin'?" Of course that's Cris, responding to Al's plea for him to chill it out. I don't know if Cris is the catalyst to another headache or if I'm still hung over from last night, but I am personally about two seconds away from walking out of this store in pursuit of some relief. In fact, I would have, *twice,* if it weren't for Zin grabbing my arm both times, and again now as I get that urge-to-flee look in my eye.

"Hold on, Shawni," Zin insists. "Try and understand where Cris is coming from, you know what I'm sayin'? Your idea is just different from what we're used to."

"In other words," Cris adds, "we're a music *group.* Means we dress *alike.* We coordinate, understand?"

Ugh! It's almost as if he has not listened to a single word I've said. I spent hours in Sky Limit, Caroline's upscale trendy boutique that I simply adore, looking for ideas for them. *My* time, spent looking for clothes for *them.* I dedicated my entire day to this, and this is what I get?

Caroline and I had set aside two dozen "looks" that complemented my concept for The Gentlemen's dinner performance on

Saturday, and after sending a car for them to come check it out, what is the thanks I get? Strange looks and a bucket of attitude from the midget. I will explain myself one last time, speak my peace, and then say "whatever" to this entire ordeal. If they don't like the concept, I'll just call up Brekke at Armani and have her arrange for a simple tuxedo wardrobe, and tell Duran what he can do with his gigs in the future. That's what I should have done in the first place.

"Well, Cris"—I clear my throat—"the concept simply mirrors what each of you represent—different styles stemming from a similar base. I'm not suggesting that you wear—"

"Yo," he interrupts and talks through his teeth, "I'm not rockin' plaid while Al is in Fubu and the other fellas in tuxedos, feel me?"

"As I was saying," I growl. "Look, would you at least just—"

"Ms. Baldwin?" Caroline approaches me with an understanding smile. She slides her reading glasses on and says, "Why don't we show them what we have set aside? How's that? I can have the girls pull the things from the back. Maybe it'd be easier to explain the concept by showing them."

Then she looks around at the group and smiles at Cris before continuing, "I happen to think Ms. Baldwin has gathered some remarkable attire. Shall we take a look-see?"

Mo replies, "It's worth at least seeing, Cris."

"Very well," she winks at me, "I'll have Allison and Natalia bring the garments to the showroom."

I smile back at Caroline before she goes to find the girls. I would really like to get this over with. The tension is doing nothing for my lingering hangover headache. I need a Kirk Whalum CD. A steam treatment. Something.

Cris frowns and murmurs to Al, "Now we're supposed to wait on Martha Stewart and her little helpers, right?"

Then again, they say when you have a hangover, you're supposed to bite the dog that bit you. Perhaps another Long Island is in order.

The first five pieces are too "corny" for even Mo and Zin, who are the most open-minded of the group. Cris is just sitting there biting his bottom lip, and Al is still on his cellular.

"Could you ask him to take his phone conversation outside at least?" I whisper to Mo. "That's rude."

Al overhears, and snaps at me. "Yo! I heard that. I'm sayin' that none of these are workin' for me. Show me something I like, I'll get off."

"Perhaps," Caroline whispers, "we should show them the Lance Colvert collection?"

I nod. She whispers to the girls, and a moment later they return with a rack of leather clothes.

"Oh no, she didn't!" Cris yelps. "I'm not doing the Eddie Murphy *Raw* leather pants wearin' thing. Hell naw. Zin, man . . ."

Caroline looks at Zin, ignoring Cris. "Lance Colvert specializes in leather, but it's leather like you've never seen," Caroline begins her spiel that hooked me earlier. "Natalia?"

Natalia holds up the one-piece baggy black leather coveralls.

"We've all seen," Caroline continues with contained excitement, "the sharp-cut leather, but not the extreme baggy look in leather."

Caroline goes on to explain the four different cuts that we selected for their consideration. I notice that Cris is silently awestruck by the baggy leather pants with the delicately thin zebra print suspenders, just like I suspected he might be. Mo's eyes light up at the sight of the leather muscle T-shirt, with the square-neck, which is sure to show off his cherished abdominals. Al can't take his eyes off the coveralls that Natalia is still holding up as he hangs up his cellular. I already knew they would fall nicely on his tall frame. Caroline winks at me before having Allison reveal the final selection.

It's the black leather vest set with the tiny, barely visible, tropical blue-black feathers hanging like cowboy fringes across the chest, along with a pair of hip-hugging blue-black baggy pants. It screams Zin! Zin! Zin!

I watch him out of the corner of my eye. That slow smile is on its way as he closes his eyes, and then he simply nods before clearing his throat and finally, looking at Cris in particular, he asks, "Fellas?"

Cris doesn't answer as the others voice their approvals, but that's okay. He doesn't need to. He slightly rolls his eyes at me, but it's forced.

"What's this fool's name?" Cris asks Caroline, trying to maintain his attitude.

"The designer's name is Lance Colvert." Caroline ignores the "fool" part and continues, "He's West African. Self-taught. Unique concepts. Innovative. And he's truly a nice man."

Cris nods reluctantly, but he definitely nods. That's all I need.

After showing them the shoes we had also selected and making a purchase so expensive that Caroline asks to have an autographed copy of The Gentleman's CD, to which they oblige, we exit the boutique with the guys toting the dress bags and shoe boxes. I'm wondering if they all shamelessly carry copies of *Take a Sip* in their pockets.

"I suppose you might be needing facials and cuts tomorrow?" I rub my temples and ask no one in particular, but look directly at Cris.

"What? Why you lookin' . . . why is everybody always lookin' at me?" Cris cuts his eyes at Zin. "Ask your boy. He's the one you seem to want to get to know, right?"

"Actually, Cris," I reply. "I was speaking to everyone in the group. No one in particular."

Al's deep voice interjects. "Facials sound kinda fly. But I don't know about all that."

"I'm cool," Mo surprisingly heads toward the car. "No sissy facials, and yo, my barber is back in the A.T.L. Feel me? I don't know nothin' about these barbers in the Big Apple," he says.

I thought I liked Mo. I don't.

Al and Cris follow Mo to the limousine and they put their things in the trunk before piling in. Zin looks at me, takes his time, as if he doesn't realize that his posse is already in the car, as if he doesn't really care if they realize that he is the only one still standing over here with me.

Zin gestures, tipping an imaginary hat on his head. "You did a nice job, Shawni."

"Thank you," I say, and I do appreciate it. He's the only one to comment as such. "I know it was my job, but it feels good to hear a sincere thank you."

"You know, I'm not making excuses for Cris, but he's just tense. He's been in this business for a long, long time, and you know, it's like he's just on edge now that things are panning out, ya dig?"

Whatever. Then we stand in silence for a moment, and I wish he would say what it is he wants to say, because my headache is elevating, and I'm ready to go.

"And, uh—" Thank goodness he finally says something. "It was mad cool coolin' out last night, you know?"

"Sure." I decide to hurry this along. "I had a good time also. We should do it again sometime." I turn and walk up the block toward Baby Blue.

"Tonight," he says.

I ought to keep walking, pretend that I didn't hear him. Instead, I turn around and whisper back, "Tonight?" I make myself utterly sick sometimes.

Zin sniffs, throws his garment bag over his shoulder, that diamond horseshoe ring screaming as he walks toward me. He stares into my eyes again.

"Right now." He waits.

"Excuse me?" A squeaky voice coming from my body seems to imitate me.

"Right now." He smiles. "Let's go get some sherbet."

"It's November." I look up at the winter sky.

"Hot chocolate then."

"Carbohydrates."

He laughs, out loud, *very* loud, and then says, "Let's go get some water, and add a twist of lemon for some flavor. How's that?"

"Yo!" Cris gets out of the limousine and throws his hands up in the air as he shouts to Zin, "What up dude? You comin'? We're ready to roll, man."

Zin nods at Cris, and then turns back to me.

"So?" He lowers his chin and raises his eyebrows, "You want me to go get in the car with them, or am I rollin' with you?"

"Listen," I say, "Bo's back in town. I really have to go. I'm sorry."

"Oh, for real?" He smiles. "Well, you know, handle your business." He looks like he's going to walk away, but then he doesn't. "The fellas want to hit Club New York tonight, then we'll probably do the Blue Note. If you and fiancé man aren't doing anything . . ."

I nod. "Sure. And let me know if any of you decide to get a facial or a cut. Just call my cellular."

"Word." He turns, and walks away.

The Blue Note? That's surprising. I thought they'd prefer a hip-hop-inspired joint, like the Tunnel or something. A jazz spot like the Blue Note?

I don't mean to watch him walk away, in fact I consciously try not to, but I do. Even his walk is relaxed. My eyes snap to a pair of eyes staring back at me. Cris! He's staring at me with a mean smirk. He's an evil gremlin. I glare back at him. Zin is oblivious to the eye war going on between Cris and me as he puts his things in the trunk and then goes to the other side of the limousine to get in. I'm not sure if Zin looks at me before he gets in or not because I refuse to lose this stare down with Cris.

" 'Bye Shaaaawniiii," Cris calls out sarcastically. He slides down into the car and pulls his door closed.

I pivot around. This gig is pretty much over with, and I won't have to see Mr. Munchkinland or Mr. Let's-go-have-some-water-so-you-can-be-hypnotized-by-my-eyes ever again. I climb into Baby Blue. My man is back in town, and we have a wedding to plan.

"Honey," I say to his voice mail as I walk into Mommie's Fifth Avenue apartment building, wave at the doorman, and head down the hallway to her apartment. "This is the third time I've called. I wanted you to come with me over to Mommie's. Meet me over here, okay? Love you."

Mommie opens the door to her antiques-furnished apartment, wearing a white-laced camisole and navy slacks. At fifty-six she is as gorgeous and as sophisticated as ever, her long hair now tinted with thin streaks of silver.

I smile nervously.

"Hello darling," she says warmly.

"Can I come in?"

"Of course." She opens the door all the way. "Hazel's here," she says as I enter. We hug, and I immediately get a whiff of her vodka/iced tea brew and the peppermint she's sucking on. The smell combined with her floral-inspired perfume reminds my head that I'm still hanging over, so I quickly pull away.

Hazel is a petite blonde in her mid-forties who wears far too much eye makeup and perfume. Mommie says that she has been a consultant for some of the most successfully fabulous weddings in the fashion industry. I'd be happy to plan my own wedding, just Mommie and I.

Hazel greets me with a dramatic embrace. I pull away and sit down on a chair on the opposite side of the room.

"Well, Shawni," Hazel picks up her wineglass, "what do you say to a toast?"

"I have a headache."

Hazel and Mommie clink glasses. "To wedding plans," Hazel says. Mommie laughs before drinking. "Indeed." She then sits down on the sofa next to Hazel and they stare across the room at me as if I am being interviewed.

Several wedding planning books are lying open on the coffee table.

"We were thinking eggshell for the invitations," Mommie says.

"Yes," Hazel adds, "and of course the traditional calligraphy script."

"Oh." I nod. "Actually, I was thinking blue."

She brushes me off with a flutter of her eyes. "We're just looking at books. Nothing has been decided."

Well, thank goodness I got here when I did. I may have missed the wedding itself!

Hazel reaches over and picks up a stack of invitations from the couch. "I brought some samples. You'll see that Lauren Chrystaldon selected eggshell as well. Oh, it's the absolute rage!"

I halfheartedly flip through the stack. "Well, maybe you'll be able to find something in baby blue?"

"Blue?"

"Yes, blue. You know, the color of the sky?"

"I hate when she does that," Mommie says to Hazel. "Shawni

has had a fascination with baby blue since she was a teenager. Don't be surprised if she wants a baby blue wedding dress!" She laughs a really fake laugh.

There isn't a single thing funny. Now that she mentions it, I hadn't thought of my wedding dress in terms of any other color except white. But a blue wedding dress . . . Hmmm . . .

"Okay," Hazel sips her wine. "I'll see what I can come up with in baby blue. How's that?"

"You know darling," Mommie adds, "Z. Z. Peters had eggshell also. Did you notice that?" She looks at Hazel. "Z.Z. was one of Shawni's mentors when she first started modeling. Shawni wanted to do *everything* Z.Z. did. Z.Z. is leaving for Paris next month."

"Oh," Hazel responds, impressed. "Will you be joining her, Shawni?"

I look at Mommie and say through clenched teeth, "No, Hazel. I'm not doing much modeling these days. Or didn't Mommie tell you?"

I should just tell Mommie and Blondie over here that I don't care what any fashion people did for their weddings. And I don't care that Z.Z. is doing Paris. I've done Paris. I could still be doing Paris if I chose. And I want what *I* want, not what anyone else had.

Hazel winks at me. "Well, let's move on and talk about the guest list. Have you decided on a number?"

I'd be happy with immediate family, Ernie, and Sanford. But, let's see what the powers that be think. "Well, Mommie?" I sigh.

"Darling," she replies, "I specifically told you to give me an exact head count. Please tell me that you have a list prepared?"

I shake my head no.

She sighs and takes a long sip of her brew before saying, "Darling, I have a list, but I thought you'd have a few names to add."

Hazel smiles at me. "Perhaps Shawni needs a little more time?"

Mommie raises her voice. "It's already the twenty-first of November. Time is not a luxury at this point in the game. Shawni, at least tell me you have a final list from Bo's family?"

I cringe.

"If you recall, we also agreed to settle on a caterer by Thanksgiving. Do you remember that conversation, Shawni? Do you realize that Thanksgiving is next week?"

Hazel pulls out a white folder from her attaché. "Well, that brings up a good point, we should schedule tastings with the caterers."

"Excuse me," I reply as I grab my Chanel purse and stand up. "I need to use the rest room. I'll be right back."

I hear Mommie say something about me being just like my father as I make my way into the bathroom. I hurriedly lock the door behind me and sit on the edge of the bathtub. I snatch open my purse. No Tylenol. No aspirin. No nothing. I'm fighting the tears, but it's hard, so hard. Just sitting in there like nothing is wrong, unable to stand up to her, tell her that I don't want all this fuss for my wedding. I splash cold water on my face, avoid my reflection. I don't want to see the strain. I flush the toilet to make it sound as if I actually went.

The important thing is that Mommie and I are communicating again, and that's what I wanted, right?

I give myself another final splash of water before going back to the living room.

Mommie's voice greets me before I've even fully entered the room again. "I like the idea of Caribbean food. Don't you? Your father's favorite."

"You know what, Mommie?" I quickly retort. "You decide, okay? I don't care. I don't care about the food. The food is unimportant to me. I'd be happy with lemon cake. Just cake. What difference does my opinion make, though, I'm only the bride." I'm on a roll and can't stop myself even though both of them are staring up at me as if I'm speaking in Japanese. "And you know, I really don't like eggshell. I like blue—baby blue! I don't care about the stupid guest list because I only have one friend, and *he's* my maid of honor!"

Mommie stands up and her smile fades. "I suggest you lower your voice! I don't know, nor do I care, what happened when you went in that bathroom, but you march yourself right back in there and pick your manners up off the sink where you left them."

Hazel stands up and puts her glass down on the table, "Maria, perhaps we should schedule a meeting next week when—"

"Hazel, no!" Mommie stares at me. "It doesn't make a second of sense to put off what could be taken care of right now. Shawni, get on the phone and call the Delaneys and get the list together. But before you do that, apologize to Hazel, and then to me. And before you do any of that, you need to put it out of your mind that your little confused friend is going to attend this affair as anything more than a groomsman, usher, or attendee. Do you understand?"

I look at Hazel, and fight off tears before saying, "Hazel, I'm sorry." Then I stare back at Mommie and say, "I'm sorry. And I love the way you can call Ernie to ask about me, but now you can stand here and disrespect him to my face."

Hazel has gathered her things. She whispers to Mommie, "Call me. Bye, Shawni." And she leaves.

The room is silent for excruciating moments.

Mommie shoots me a warning look.

I'm still fighting tears, unable to move.

Mommie snatches her glass off the table, spills a little, takes a sip, and asks. "What is it? Why do you resent me so? Let's just get it out, okay? What is it that we're really arguing about?"

I clear my throat. "Mommie, I didn't come over here to discuss wedding plans."

She sits down on one of her thronelike, antique chairs, takes another drink, crosses one long leg over the other, and says calmly, "What, then, Shawni, should we be talking about?"

I take a deep breath and sit down on the chair opposite her. "I came over here because I haven't talked to you since I called you last week. You said you'd call."

"And I had every intention of doing so. I've been so busy, getting ready for the trip to Aspen."

"Mommie, please." I roll my eyes. "You've called Ernie. You could have called me."

"Well," she shrugs. "Quite frankly, darling, I really haven't been in the mood to speak with you."

"Oh, right!" I reply. "You don't want to talk to me, but you feel like planning my wedding?"

"Hazel has been scheduled for weeks to come over here today. There was no point in canceling. Now she's gone. Happy? I thought I'd at least keep the plans for the wedding going—at least hold on to the hope that you'll be going through with your wedding. I know you wouldn't dream of not going through with that, would you?"

"Would you stop speaking to me if those plans changed, too?"

She gets up, goes over to the bar, pours a little more vodka, and says, "If you don't want to get married, Shawni, so be it."

"As if you don't care! Why else would you be here planning?"

"Shawni Kaye!" She raises her voice. "I don't know why you're not hearing me! It's not about me, darling. I never had a wedding, but it doesn't bother me, if that's what you're thinking—that I'm trying to live my life again, vicariously, through you. I'm not. I have no regrets about my choices. I just don't want to see my only daughter make stupid mistakes. Is that so terrible?"

She nods toward her bedroom. "Go get Mommie's ciggys, will you?"

I frown at the open suitcase on her bed. Lingerie. Lots of it. I snatch a pack of Misty's from her nightstand, march back into the living room, and shove them at her. "So, when are you leaving?"

"Tomorrow." She shakes a cigarette out of the pack. "My lighter?"

I snatch my purse off the table. "I don't know where your lighter is Mommie. You said you were quitting. Why don't you?"

She sighs.

"I've gotta go," I say.

"Darling," she gets up, walks over to the dining area, and gets a lighter from under the candelabra. "Bo Delaney is good for you. He's a fine human being. I don't need to tell you that. But if you decide you don't want to get married, there's no law that says you have to. You don't have to have a wedding if you don't want to. The marriage isn't the thing, the love is." She lights her cigarette.

"Yeah, Mommie." I bite my tongue to fight the tears.

I don't wait for her reaction, don't look at her face. I just leave.

Where's Bo? It's way after six, and he hasn't returned a single one of my pages, or responded to any of the messages that I left at his house, or the ones I left on his cellular! I've been driving around for almost an hour and a half. Nowhere to go, needing to talk to him, and he's nowhere to be found.

Finally my cellular rings. "Hello?"

"Chile, I'm hungry!" Ernie sings. "And I'm ready to go."

Ernie. The Sugar Bar for dinner. I completely forgot. "Hey, Ernie. I'm sorry, I forgot. I'm really not hungry."

"What's wrong?"

"Bo's back in town. I went by Mommie's. We had a fight. I'm not in the mood to eat. Bo won't return my calls."

"He's back? Whaaaat? When did he get back?"

"This morning."

"Come by and get me. I'm dressed. And did you hear me? I'm hungry."

"I need to find Bo, Ernie. I'll call you back." I sigh. "Okay?"

"Fine." He hangs up.

"It's almost nine o'clock!" I shout as he finally enters, closing the door behind him, making his way into the living room, and he looks at me as if the time is unimportant. I bite my bottom lip, try to hold my anger in. I can't. I do, however, manage not to shout again. "I've been calling you all day!" I whisper loudly.

"How'd your shopping go?" He responds composedly, looking so good in his black pants, red turtleneck, and black leather jacket.

I decide that I, too, can try to compose myself. "You look awfully nice."

"Did you find what you were looking for?" He sucks his teeth and sits down on the La-Z-Boy—on the opposite side of the room.

I ask, "Why are you sitting way over there?"

He shrugs. "Where's the remote?"

I eye it, sitting on the coffee table, grab it, and put it on top of the entertainment center. Why is he acting like this—like it's no big deal that he hasn't returned my calls today? I slap the power button on the television off. "What's going on?"

"All I did was ask for the remote."

I walk over to him. "I wanted you to go with me over to Mommie's."

He reaches up and pulls my hand, easing me onto his lap. He takes a deep breath. "Let's just start this conversation again, okay? Pretend I just walked into the room." He rubs my shoulder for a while, calming me, soothing me, and then he says, "Hey, baby."

Melting. My heart is. "Hey," I reply. I give him a shoulder shove, lean in, and kiss him on the tip of his nose.

He squeezes my hand. "How was your day today?"

"It was okay. I got everything finished with the group, and then I went over to Mommie's."

"I'll tell you what. Why don't we go out to dinner and we can sit down and you can tell me all about what happened when you went over to your mother's, okay?"

"Like where?"

"I don't know," he replies. "Are you hungry?"

"A little."

"Cool. And I need to mellow out. You wanna go hear some jazz? The Blue Note is hittin' tonight."

The Blue Note?

"How about the Sugar Bar?"

"Sounds good to me. You ready?" He glances at me. "Hell yeah, you're ready. Lookin' all fine." He kisses me playfully.

So I grab my purse, kiss Sanford good-bye, and leave with my man.

Rolling up Broadway in the passenger side of his sleek black Denali with leather interior, I feel so safe, so good. Frankie Beverly and Maze coming from the speakers sets the mood with "Don't Wanna Lose Your Love," and I wonder if maybe Bo had it cued up on purpose.

I crack open the window, let the crisp air blow in, close my eyes, and enjoy the heavy comfort of his hand on my thigh. I take a breath, open my eyes, look over, and for some reason a tear sneaks out of the corner of my eye. I let it fall as I reach up and rub his head, so smooth, and so sexy. I love you so much, I try to say with my hand as I massage his head. He steals a glance at me, and winks.

"Honey," I say, "Mommie and I had another fight. I'm so tired of it."

"I know you are, baby."

"I don't want you and I to fight, okay? That's the last thing I need."

"You need to get along with her, too." He notices my tear stain. "Baby, don't cry."

I close my eyes. "Things have never been this bad."

"She'll come around, Shawni. It might take awhile, but things always work out in time." He takes my hand from his head, pulls it to his lips, kisses it softly for a few moments, and then holds my hand to his chest—so solid, so strong.

I allow my eyes to survey his entire body, "Tonight, after we eat, I don't want you to go home to Brooklyn. Stay with me, okay?"

"You got it."

"As a matter of fact," I hum. "I'm not hungry anymore."

He eyes me, makes sure he's reading my vibe correctly. "No?"

"No." I soften my eyes.

He glows knowingly.

It seems to take too long to get back to the condo, so once we're back inside we don't even bother to stop, to slip in Johnny Gill or LSG or Otis. It would take too much time. I love it when it's like this. Urgent.

We make our way down the hallway, clumsy. Bo mumbling, holding me, telling Sanford to go. I'm laughing, so happy, so thrilled. Bo's laughing, too, at us, at how we can't move fast enough, at how much fun this is, at how good it feels to hold me, to have me holding him back. I'm laughing at how good it feels to be laughing.

The waterbed is an ocean beneath us. Never-ending motion. Fingertips, pulling my face closer to his kiss, soon tiptoeing down my body and to the small of my back—his spot. Pulling my entire body closer.

My eyes flutter and gaze up in sheer satisfaction at first, like always.

"Baby . . ." he moans.

He keeps talking, his voice making it even sweeter. I'm his. He's mine.

He moans. "How'd I ever get so lucky, baby?

"Baby . . . ?" He moans.

"What?" I whisper, irritated by the thoughts that are suddenly muffling my passion.

Shake it away, Shawni. Mind over matter.

He pulls me closer. "Baby, what's wrong?" He moans. "Stop."

What'd I do? Why's he telling me to stop? Can he read my mind?

I try to turn over. If I move I can make my mind concentrate.

"No," he groans. His fingertips pull me, won't let me get away.

I can't move.

Lucky diamond rings are yelling at me, laughing at me. Diamond horseshoes, lucky, dancing on the ceiling.

Close your eyes, Shawni!

I can't close my eyes.

"What's wrong, baby?" he whispers.

"Can we . . ."

"Baby . . ." he pleads.

"Bo . . ."

"What?" he whispers louder.

I try to wiggle my body out from under him.

"What?" he speaks in standard volume.

I completely maneuver my way out from under him and sit up.

"What?" He's shouting now.

I've ruined it. He's upset. What's wrong with me? "I'm sorry, honey." I bite my lip to calm the quivering.

"Sorry?" He looks dumbfounded. "What's going on?"

"Let's stop."

He sits up. That soft vein that protrudes out of the left side of his head in the heat of passion is flaming intensely. He sucks his teeth, flaring his nose. "You want to tell me in a complete sentence exactly what's going on?"

"I just don't feel like it, okay?" I attempt to get up, but he snatches my wrist and holds my arm.

"What's up, Shawni? You didn't feel that way fifteen minutes ago."

"Would you let go of my hand?" I snap.

"Let go of your hand?" He waits a moment, sucks his teeth, and then drops my hand to a thud on the bed. "Dropped," he says.

I want to say something. I want to make the tension go away, but the words do not come to my head or my mouth.

The silence is too loud.

His heavy breathing eases into a forced exhale, trying to calm himself. "Would it be asking too much for you to get my robe for me?"

I get up, thankful for something to do because just sitting here is unbearable, and after slipping on my own robe, I hand him his. He takes it and doesn't bother to look at me as he slips it on and fumes out of the bedroom.

A moment later I hear the water running in the bathroom, and I fall back onto the waterbed, and I wish I could keep falling. I feel myself drifting away to the sound of faint trickles, and I can't help thinking that I'm starting to know too many moments like this, moments of uncertainty when I'm not sure why I'm feeling what I'm feeling, or even what I'm feeling. I only know that in the midst of sharing blissful intimacy with an incredible, my incredible, man, I froze. Images of a diamond horseshoe ring taunting me.

"You didn't hear me calling you?" Bo's voice jars into the room, interrupting my thoughts, or dreams, as he dries himself off. He glares at me. "I guess it's asking too much for you to bring me some lotion now, too?"

"Oh," I sigh, and toss him a bottle of Curel from the dresser before I get up and head out into the hallway. "I need a drink."

I'm fixing a Mommie Brew—vodka and iced tea—and my hand is shaking. Maybe I should eat something.

Bo's voice follows me into the living room. "Correct me if I'm wrong about this, but it seems to me that something strange is going on. And, uh, maybe I'm out of line by asking this, seeing as how I don't seem to fit in around here, but is your mind on something else?"

"No!" I reply, annoyed, wanting him to just be quiet so I can figure my feelings out.

"Or is it someone else? Some sort of infiltration that I need to know about?" he asks.

"Infiltration?"

"Damn straighter than a yard stick, infiltration." He enunciates precisely. "You want to tell me why the hell I had to go in there and take a shower, when you're standing here fully capable of handling that for me? I get off a plane two days earlier than I'm supposed to, get in a damn cab, rush home, then rush over here—like a damn fool—walk in the door, and all I can think about is making love to you, holding you, and instead you have to go shopping? Then, tonight, I have to take a shower by myself? Damn straight infiltration, woman. Who is it?"

"You don't know what you're talking about," I say calmly. "I told you that Mommie and I had a fight."

"And? That's never stopped you before."

"I have a lot on my mind, okay? Can you just accept that?"

"No. Something or someone is occupying the space that I should have in your mind right now, and I want to know what or who it is." He readjusts the towel around his hips, pulls it tight, and sits down on the couch and waits. Damn, his body is all that!

I look away from him. "Bo, look, I know what you're thinking."

"Oh, so you're gonna turn your back on me now?"

I need food, a cucumber or something. I head toward the kitchen.

"Shawni, don't walk away from me!" He raises his voice. "What do you know that I'm thinking, Shawni? Huh? What?"

Urgh! I do not feel like this drama. I've had more than enough today.

"Answer me, Shawni! What is it that you think I'm thinking?"

I grab a carrot from the refrigerator, slam the door shut, and march back into the living room. "I don't know. You're thinking something ridiculous, like I'm sleeping with someone else and that I don't want to make love to you because of it."

"Are you?" He stretches both of his arms out on the back of the couch and smirks a smile. "Is there somebody else, Shawni? Lay it on me. I'm a man. I can handle it. But what I can't handle is bullshit!"

I take a big bite of my carrot—smack on it loud. "Of course not, Bo. That's silly."

"Silly, huh?" he says. "So, why'd you say it?"

"Say what?"

"You said that that's what I was thinking, that you were thinking about making love to someone else while you were making love to me. Your words! Must have been your conscience talking."

I take another big bite of the carrot. Crunch it. Yummy. Really good carrot.

"You seem kinda nervous, baby. What's wrong?" He walks toward me.

"Nothing." I take another bite. Yummm . . .

He smirks. "Hand's shaking, could barely even fix yourself a drink. Do you want me to fix it for you baby?"

"No."

"Second time you told me no today, baby. Third times a charm, they say. Answer me yes or no, did you sleep alone last night?"

"Bo, would you stop it?"

"Third times a charm, baby. Yes or no?" He sucks his teeth.

"What are you talking about?"

"Simple question. Answer me." He gets closer, bringing his Zestfully clean scent with him, and stands right in front of me before saying, "Better yet, I have something else I want you to answer for me, okay?"

"What?"

"You know, I felt like such a fool last night when I got off the phone with you—like such a fool, Shawni. I sat there in that hotel room thinking to myself—'Damn Delaney you tripped out over nothing.' You know? I was thinking that I tripped out over *nothing*."

"Bo—"

"No! No, you let me finish." He shouts before he draws his index finger to a deliberate point on my forehead, forcing me to back away.

I try to regain my balance. "Why are you acting all insecure?"

"Insecure?" He looks dumbfounded. "Woman, have you forgotten who I am? I call you in the middle of the night and you're out with some fool drinking and carrying on. I sent you flowers. All I'm thinking about last night is seeing you. Caught an early flight because I wanted to see you so bad." He clears his throat, stretches his arms while clinching his fists. He grunts a few times, and clears his throat again before calming himself down enough to continue.

He glares at me. "I skip the business that I'm taking care of to come home to you, and all I can think about is making love to you! Then you push me away? What have I ever asked you for? All I've ever asked you to do is to *be there*. I've never asked you for anything else. Now I'm insecure?"

"You're still overreacting, Bo."

"Oh, yeah? Well, why don't you do me a favor and just come straight with me?"

"Why don't you just sit down, and we can talk about this?"

"I'm finished talking. I'm all ears now."

"Okay . . ."

I don't know where to begin. What's there to say?

He glares. "Is he the reason?"

"Who?" I ask.

He goes over to the dining room table, snatches a CD. I catch a glimpse of the cover—*Take a Sip*. "This fool." He smirks. "Zin." And then he hurls the CD across the room. It hits the wall an inch away from Mommie's portrait, leaving a small, dull, black scuff.

"Bo, that's ridiculous. And I thought you said you were going to let me talk?"

"So talk." He flings one of the dining room chairs around and sits on it. "I'm waiting. Did he sleep here last night?"

"Of course he didn't sleep here. Can we just end this, already? Please?"

He glares at me. "Please what?"

"You can't understand what I'm going through right now."

"Shawni"—his jaws are clinching—"you have no idea how I feel right now."

"Bo, *nothing happened*," I say, tired of repeating myself.

"Don't lie to me."

I suddenly remember what Zin was saying last night about not lying, and subtext, and the absolute truth, and I wish it were that easy.

He gives me a final look before turning around and heading toward the bedroom. Where's he going? I hear the closet door opening, slamming shut.

I'm pacing this room, thinking, wanting to cry, wanting to scream, wanting to be alone so I can do all of this, but wanting him to come back in here so that I'll know he's not mad at me.

Within minutes, Bo returns, fully dressed in his purple-and-blue fraternity sweatsuit. He even stopped to put on his gold herringbone necklace! And is that . . . ? Yes, I look closer; he has even oiled his head.

I stand up and tighten my robe. "Where are you going?"

"Home."

"Excuse me?"

"Home!"

"Why?"

"You don't need me."

"Are you serious?" I ask. "You're really leaving?"

"Yes," he says, looking around at the floor.

"No, you're not," I say adamantly.

"I need some damn air," he looks around and then yells, "where are my damn keys?"

"I don't know." No way am I going to help him leave by telling him that his keys are on the floor, at the end of the hallway, where he dropped them when we came in. His eyes follow mine. I can't move quick enough to grab them before he does.

I run over and push the door closed.

"Move out of my way!" he demands.

"No! You're not leaving."

"Move."

"No."

"Shawni, move, *now*! I'm not playing."

Suddenly I'm consumed by desperate passion, and nothing means more to me than having every inch of Bo Delaney's body back in that bedroom. No more lucky rings. Whatever I have to do.

"Bo," I plead, "come on, let's go make up, okay?"

"What?" He gives me a "you must be crazy" look.

I plead with my eyes. "Let's just go back in the bedroom and make up."

His eyes are unaffected, unimpressed. "I need some space."

"Space?"

"Let me bounce."

"Where are you going?"

"Shawni, for the last time, home. Now move!"

"But you *are* coming back, aren't—"

"Shawni, just move, okay?"

I immediately think of a hundred things to say, but then I think of the two hundred responses that Bo will give to each of them, so I don't say anything. Instead I try to conjure up my "I love you" eyes, but the glare of his "move out of my way" look won't allow them to work their magic.

We've had arguments before; I've seen Bo upset before—but not like this. I've never been stomachachingly afraid of letting him leave in the heat of an argument. Why can't I just snap into my whatever attitude and let him leave, go home and cool down, and trust that he'll come back over later?

He looks at me, his eyes distant, hurt, and confused. And he calmly says, "Shawni, there is a proven fact that I learned a long time ago, okay?"

I am afraid to hear it.

"Law of physics, baby. No two objects can occupy the same space at the same time." He pulls the door open, and takes a step out. "I won't compete for the place that I should already have in your mind."

And he leaves.

FOUR

The After-party

"Good morning," I say, and I'm so happy to see my baby brother. He pulls me in for a tight hug. "What up, baby girl?"

I look up into my brother's always bright eyes. He's so handsome, wearing the black leather jacket I bought him last Christmas, a brown ribbed shirt with blue jeans, his wavy hair is gelled back into its stubby ponytail, and a diamond-hoop earring glistening. This pretty boy even looks a little buff since the last time I saw him.

I nudge him teasingly. "Have you been working out?"

He laughs. "A little sumthin', sumthin'. What's wrong with you? You look beat."

I look beat because I've only slept for two hours. How was I supposed to sleep with two of the most important people in my life upset with me?

I try to sound cheerful as I smile at Duran. "I made omelets. How was your flight?"

"Too early. But, hey, the fellas say the gear is tight. I can't wait to see it. I knew you wouldn't let your big brother down. He here?" He looks around as he walks down the hallway.

"Duran," I yell after him, "I'm older."

"Yeah, yeah," he shouts back, and laughs.

I join him in the kitchen and he's already diving in. "Duran, at least take your coat off!"

"Where's m'man?" he says with his mouth full. "Got any o.j.?"

I open the refrigerator, grab the pitcher, and pour him a tall glass. "Bo's not here, and I don't know where he is."

He takes a gulp of his orange juice. "Don't front. Aren't you glad he came home early?"

"Not hardly. I'd planned on renting videos and just doing whatever—"

"Yeah, right," he interrupts. "You, at home, alone, with just videos to keep you company? Anyway. Have you talked to Mommie?"

I sit down on a chair directly across from him. "Yes . . ." I begin, and then decide to leave it at that. When he goes over there I'm sure he'll get the whole story about what a horrible daughter I am.

"She told me you stormed out on her last night. What's going on?"

I should have known. "She told you already? And you just got in town this morning?"

"She had to meet Daddy in Colorado this morning. She called me last night." He tosses a piece of omelet down to Sanford. "Go on, dude. Let me eat in peace." He laughs as Sanford plants himself in front of Duran's chair, hoping for as many scraps as possible.

"What was her version of what happened?" I ask.

"Somethin' ill, like you're trippin' 'cause you think she's trying to plan your wedding, and all she was trying to do was help. Some-thin' like that. I don't know."

"Duran, I went over there. She and Hazel had wedding books out—without *me*! She didn't even know I was coming over!"

"So, don't sweat it. She's just excited, all right? Something she never got to plan for herself."

"It's not fair," I say.

"Fair is irrelevant. You know that. We both know that we can't help the cards we're dealt. But you can turn any hand into a winning one. Believe that. You just have to play it right." He gets up and tosses another omelet on his plate. "You're just mad spoiled. Always have been."

"I'm not."

He widens his eyes, freezes in mid-motion, and then unfreezes. "Yes, you are!"

"That's not the point."

"So what's the point? Damn, can't we all just get along?" He flings a piece of egg across the kitchen floor for Sanford to catch. "Now, go on, dog. Damn, Shawni, don't you feed him?"

"Go, Sanford!" I command. Sanford looks at me, can't believe that I betrayed him, and goes out into the living room.

"Duran," I look at him, wanting him to match my mood. "Can we be serious for a minute?"

"Man, forget being a lawyer. Delaney should've been a chef. These omelets are good as hell."

"Duran, I cooked the omelets. I told you that."

He laughs. "My fault. Good job, baby girl." He catches my annoyed expression, and he nods. "All right, all right. What's up?"

"What do you think of me as a person?" I ask.

He drops his fork on his plate, wipes his mouth, and holds his hands up, committing to listening. "Okay, I'm all ears. What did Mommie say?"

"Nothing. It's not Mommie, okay?" I get up, tighten my robe, and start cleaning up the kitchen. It's so hard to talk to my brother sometimes.

"Shit, then. What is it?" he asks.

"Why'd you say that I wouldn't be able to stay here alone and watch videos?"

"Oh, it's possible," he says. "But think about it. Nobody in the entire spot except you? Yeah, right. No Bo. No Ernie. No me. Not even Mommie? That's my point, baby girl. You're not the type of female to just kick it on the solo. When's the last time you spent the night alone?"

"Last night. Bo didn't stay over last night."

He waits. "And?"

"And I'm fine."

"You sure about that?" he asks. "How'd you sleep?" He folds his arms across his chest.

"Peacefully." I flutter my eyes. "So there."

"I wish I could believe that, sis." He smiles, but then a curious expression comes over his face. "And why were you alone? He's back in town, right?"

"We had a fight. He thinks I'm seeing someone else."

"What? You creepin' on my boy?"

"Did you not hear what I just said? He *thinks* I have someone else in my life. Just because I'm getting married doesn't mean I can't have friends."

He waits, looks confused. "True, but why would he accuse you of something like that?"

I look down at my hand, my ring peeking through the soap suds as I wash the pan that I cooked the omelets in—the pan that Bo usually cooks omelets in. He never cared that I couldn't cook. He cooked for me. He taught me how to make omelets, and he does make the best. "How do I know for sure I'm ready for marriage, Duran?" I turn to him. "And it hurts that I can't ask Mommie that."

He looks away, dismissing the subject. Then he stands up, finishes off his omelet, and hands me the plate. "Don't be stupid, all right? I mean, I don't know shit about marriage, but I do know that he's good people. Yo, Delaney's down for you, and maybe it's just that simple, you know what I'm sayin'? Maybe it's just about findin' somebody who's down for you and rollin' with it. Don't mess that up. And you *can* ask Mommie, but she'd tell you the same thing."

"But isn't it normal for me to wonder about such things?"

"No." He kisses me on the forehead. "Yo, it's a done deal. And, come July, big brother is going to walk you down that aisle, and you're going to live happily ever after. Believe that."

And he goes out in the living room to play catch with Sanford.

Bo didn't call all morning. Fine. I pick up my cellular as I turn up Madison Avenue. I'll call Ernie, maybe he'll meet me at Saks. I call the salon.

"Go shopping with me?" I ask when he comes to the phone.

"Chile, please. I have a perm at noon, and a Broadway diva's weave at one-thirty. I have zero time for looking for clothes. Plus, I think I'm supposed to be mad at you about something."

"Yeah, well, Bo and I had a huge fight last night."

"Oooh. You're just turning into Holyfield these days, huh? What's up with you and all these little fights?"

"Please. I told him I had a lot on my mind, but all he can think about is himself. He's just being selfish and insecure, that's all. As if my entire life revolves around him."

He coughs—a fake cough. "That's a lot of nerve. Pot don't need to talk about the kettle, okay? Both, black as hell."

"What?"

"You got a lot of nerve. But, hey, I'm just Ernie, tryin' to survive."

"Ernie, I've had enough of your criticism."

"We'll have to talk about it later, okay? I have dos to do."

"I have to go anyhow," I reply.

I can shop by myself.

"Are you finding everything okay, ma'am?" A man's voice from behind me asks quietly as I flip through the rack of men's robes. Bo is very particular about logos. He doesn't like anything with anyone's name written across it, and nothing where the logo is too prominent. So far I haven't found anything that I think he'd like, and I must, soon. I need to make up with him by this evening. I can't go another night like last night. I'll die.

"Yes, I'm fine, thanks," I say without bothering to turn around.

"Just holler Jerving if there's anything I can help you with," he says.

I turn around to give a polite smile, at the same time wondering what ethnicity the name Jerving is, when I see the face of the man who has just told me to holler his name—and I feel like hollering it right now. He's so handsome. Perhaps Trinidad or Barbados. Oh, my.

I smile. "Jerving?"

"Yes, ma'am." He answers politely. His eyes innocent, his clean-shaven face chiseled, just like his body, adorned with Versace—for whom he ought to be modeling. Dark skin, hair soft and smooth, nails clean. He's borderline choirboy type—and he's gorgeous.

I tilt my head a little, twist my lips, and pose with a flustered expression. "Um, can you help me?" I ask.

He nods. "Well, hopefully. What'd you need?"

"I'm looking for a gift—for my brother—and he likes robes without a lot of fuss, you know? Something fashionably simple, without any fancy logos or names written across the back."

Jerving looks at the surrounding racks, giving me ample time to glance at his shoes. Bruno Magli. Nice.

"Preferably, something in a solid color," I add.

"Right." He turns around. "Follow me."

"Okay."

"We just got this in from Calvin," he says, holding up a charcoal gray robe.

I answer by slipping him the plastic. "You're good." I smile. "My brother will love it."

"What size is he?" Jerving asks as he holds the credit card in one hand, and begins looking through the sizes with the other.

"The biggest size you have."

After ringing up the purchase, he looks down at the card, and then gives me a curious look. "Bo's your first name?" he questions.

"No," I reply.

"That's your spouse?"

"No." I easily rotate my engagement rock to face the inside of my palm. "I'm not married."

He sighs. "I'm gonna have to ask for identification."

"For what?"

"Are you an authorized user of this account, ma'am?"

"Of course. What's the problem?"

"No problem. It's just that in order to protect the security of the account, I need to verify authorization. I can call Mr. Delaney, if you have a valid driver's license."

"I'm a respected customer here."

"I imagine you are, ma'am, but it's our policy."

"I've never had this problem before," I insist.

"Ma'am, trust me, it's no problem. Really simple. I just need identification from you and a phone number for Mr. Delaney and we can proceed."

"Here," I say as I slap my driver's license on the counter and ramble off the phone number.

He must be new to this job, and too zealous about having a

little hint of authority. I should snatch the card back and say forget it, but I want him to feel really foolish when Bo gives him the okay.

He hangs up the phone after a brief conversation. "Okay, ma'am," he says, giving me back my license. "I'm sorry. But according to Mr. Delaney you are no longer an authorized user on the account."

"Excuse me?"

"Do you have another method of payment?"

I nod at the robe. "Forget it. I don't want it."

He shrugs. "I'm very sorry, ma'am."

"Hope you don't work on commission." I snatch the card back, and walk away.

"The commission on one robe isn't astronomical, as you can imagine," he calls after me.

"Maybe I would have purchased more," I say back without turning around.

I don't wait to fully exit the store before I take out my cellular and dial. I try to be as composed as possible when Bo answers. "Are you trying to be funny?" I ask.

"Attorney, baby, not a comedian."

"Were you trying to embarrass me? Was that your goal?"

No response.

"Let's not play games, Bo."

"Who's playing games? They called here asking if you were authorized to use my Saks. Hell no."

"Very mature."

"Gotta go," he says before hanging up.

Dial tone.

Okay, the only reason I need to talk to him is to redeem myself for losing my cool earlier. I refuse to be that woman, the one who raises a fit about every little thing and lies here all evening wondering why he won't return my pages, and won't answer his phone. If he wants to be silly and revoke my access to his Saks card, so what? I don't need his card. But he could at least have the decency to call me back.

I sit up in bed, frown at the moonlight, and snatch the phone from my nightstand. If anyone knows where Bo is, it's definitely Duran. So I page him with a double 911 behind my number, pour another glass of Mommie's Brew, and then call Ernie while I wait.

"Ernie?" I say.

"Oh, boy." He laughs, and I hear the volume fading on his television. "What's going on now in the life and times of Lady Baldwin?"

"Bo won't return my phone calls."

There is a long silence because I stop talking and Ernie doesn't say a word.

Finally he speaks. "And let me guess: You're losing your mind now, right?"

"Just listen, okay?"

"Isn't that what I do best?" he replies. "I'll listen, but don't ask my opinion if you don't want it."

My other line beeps.

"Ernie, hold on," I say before clicking over.

Maybe it's Bo.

I answer. "Hello?"

"What's the emergency, Shawni?" It's Duran.

"Duran, have you seen Bo? I've been trying to call him all night and he won't return my pages."

"Uh, yeah, we just got back from Justin's. Yo, the fellas tore it up at the show. The gear was out of sight, sis! I thought you were gonna come?"

"Justin who?"

"Justin's—the restaurant."

"Who is we?"

"Me, Bo, and Yusef."

"I can't believe you went with him. So what happened?"

"What do you mean what happened? We slammed on some catfish."

"I've been paging him all evening and I haven't heard from him."

"Well, if I see him again, I'll tell him to ring you," he says.

I can't believe what I'm hearing. Bo was out to dinner the entire time that I was sitting here paging him, wanting to talk to him all day, and he didn't even bother to call back? What kind of practical joke is this?

"Okay, Duran. Thanks."

"Yo, Rush is throwing a party tonight at the Kit Kat. Comin' through?"

"Where is he now?"

"You're buggin'. I don't keep tabs on my boys. Just you and Mommie."

" 'Bye Duran." I click back over. "Ernie, you are *not* going to believe this."

"Try me."

"That was Duran. He said that Bo was out to dinner tonight."

A long silence.

Finally, Ernie gasps. "So what part is going to be hard to believe?"

"Ernie!"

"What? A man does need his nourishment."

"All he was doing was eating dinner and he didn't even bother to call me back!"

"Girl, why are you sweatin' him like that?"

"I'm not," I say, glancing up at the clock. "Ernie, let's go hang out tonight?"

I'm fuming. How dare he go out to eat and not even bother to call me and try to make up? I paged him somewhere between two and four hundred times, and he couldn't take a moment away from stuffing his face to call me back?

Maybe he didn't get my pages?

But I also left messages on his voice mail at home.

Well, maybe he hasn't been home since he left?

But he had to have changed his clothes to go to Justin's.

He must have gotten my pages, and my messages.

"Shawni!" Ernie yells. "Are you listening to me?"

"Yes, I heard you," I lie. I can pretty much fill in the blanks with Ernie.

"Good. So why don't you and Sanford come over here tonight? I made a cheesecake, and I can chill some Merlot. The Jackie Kennedy movie is playing on Lifetime tonight. We could watch that, get your mind off things. The last thing you need is to hit the scene and get yourself in more trouble."

Not tonight. I'm in the mood to go out. If Bo wants to hang out, so can I.

"Cheesecake sounds good," I say. "I'll think about it. I'll call you back, okay?"

"Don't do it girl! Don't you go out tonight!"

" 'Bye, Ernie."

"I mean it, Shawni," he shouts as I hang up.

So Bo wants to go out and have a good time with his friends and not return my pages, huh? Well, it takes two for almost every game except solitaire, and I'm in the mood for a little Ping-Pong.

I flip through my closet and zero in on three of my hot new dresses. Should I go with the pink leather Kristee Holm, the sleek black spaghetti-strapped Donna Karan, or the zebra-printed Dolce & Gabbana halter dress? After trying on all three three times each, I decide on the Dolce & Gabbana. I'll wear my new Bruno Frisoni stiletto boots, and my cropped leather jacket, and I'll be stunning.

I put on a Phil Collins CD and let "In the Air Tonight" be my theme music while I bathe myself in vanilla bubble bath and shout "no" out loud each time I find myself thinking of Bo. Obviously he isn't thinking about me, so why should I think about him?

I put on my signature Russet Moon lipstick—by Chanel of course—and do my eyes in smoke eye shadow before pulling my hair into two Pocahontas braids. Chanel's Coco is the fragrance of choice tonight, it never fails, and I switch my purse's contents into one of her small handbags before taking a final glance at myself in my full-length mirror. Mommie would be proud.

Mommie.

I sigh. No, Shawni, don't think about it. She's in Aspen, having a good time with Daddy, not thinking about it. Why should you?

I give Sanford two quick kisses on his nose and ignore his please-don't-leave-me whining. "I love you baby poo poo poo," I say. "But I'll be back."

My heels click to an upbeat rhythm as I make my way to parking space number 237.

Empty.

Where's Baby Blue?

I look around—empty; 238, 236—no Baby Blue anywhere.

My heart heavy, my skin throbbing, my eyes frantically searching everywhere, as I run, as I bang on the security officer's bullet-proof little room.

He looks up from an Archie comic book. He smiles, as if he doesn't notice that I am having a serious occurrence right now. "Ms. Baldwin, hello." His voice booms from the microphone.

"Excuse me," I glance around again, "my car—my Lexus—is missing. Where is it?"

"Oh," he smiles jovially, nods agreeably. "Your boyfriend took it a couple of hours ago."

I bat my eyes, replay in my mind what he just said. "My what?" I repeat. "Bald guy, you mean?"

"Yeah, yeah. The dude you're always with."

"You saw him leaving in my Baby Blue?"

He nods cautiously. "Everything okay?"

"Thanks." I walk away. I run through the parking lot, nearly breaking my heels, to the elevator and can't think in complete sentences during the ride up. I walk down the hallway to my door, hurry to get it open.

I hate you, Bo. I hate you. How can you do this to me?

I look around for the cordless, can't find it fast enough, but dash for it once I do. I can't dial. I'm too upset. So, I throw it across the room and watch it crack open, the battery slides under the table. I stand in disbelief.

Okay, think Shawni. Think. He's just assuming that without Baby Blue you can't go anywhere. Don't even give him the satisfaction. His little tirade of insecurity will not get the best of you.

Ernie would let me borrow his Jetta for sure, but I would have to explain where I'm going first and why I don't have Baby Blue to go in.

I could borrow Mommie's Benz, but she's in Aspen and only Duran has a spare set of keys. And I'm not going to call him—that accomplice!

I need a car, quick.

Oh, forget this! I run into the kitchen and snatch the phone off the hook, bang his phone number, and wait for the four rings that I've been listening to all day.

"You have reached the home of Mr. Bo Delaney, leave a message and I'll return your call as promptly as possible," his voice says.

"Bo," I say after the beep. "I am *really* tired of talking to this voice mail! I know you took Baby Blue. I don't care. Don't bother to call me back. Forget my messages from earlier, okay?" I slam the phone down, snatch my engagement ring off, and hurl it across the kitchen. I watch it slam against the refrigerator door and then come to rest in front of it.

Good.

Now, how am I going to get out of here? I could have a drink to help me stomach a funky yellow cab ride. No, I'll just call a really nice Lincoln car service.

I wait impatiently after making the request, and jump when the night doorman finally calls.

"Ms. Baldwin, a car has arrived for you," he informs me.

"I'll be right down."

I sashay out into the night air, determined to feel vibrant. I smile at the driver. "The Kit Kat," I say, forcefully cheerful.

"You got it," he responds as he opens the door for me.

I walk to the front of the line and glance inside the doorway to see if I can catch a glimpse of someone I know, because there is no way I'm going to wait in line. I get even more excited as I hear a Lucy Pearl song playing from inside. I hope the music is good all night.

The bouncer standing behind the velvet rope smiles and says over the music and noise from the crowd, "What's up, fly girl?"

"Hey," I reply.

He poses awkwardly. "You don't even remember me, do you?"

I don't remember him. Where would I know him from? "Vaguely. Help me out, here. I remember the face," I say.

"You're Duran's little sister, aren't you?" he asks.

"Shawni." I roll my eyes. "Duran is my brother, yes."

" 'Ran's not here yet." He unhooks the rope for me to pass through. "You know I gotta look out for 'Ran's sister, man. Go on in there, girl. Have yourself a real good time."

It's so annoying—Duran's little sister—everywhere I go.

He takes my hand and escorts me to the door. "They should be here any minute."

Normally, when I enter a club scene or a social event, I put on my Mona Lisa barely there smile and assess the room. Then, after walking around for a while, I usually stand near the bar, wait until an attractive man offers to buy me a drink, accept it, flirt a little, and then find a spot to situate myself until I'm high enough to hit the dance floor. That's ordinarily. Tonight I feel like hitting the floor right away, unwinding, with every thrust of my hips and snap of my fingers more intense than the one before.

But for some reason I feel a little nervous about going straight to the dance floor. So I make a detour and head toward the bar, debating whether or not I should order anything. A part of me wants to be thrilled while sober, but another part of me can't imagine going out there without something to coat the surfacing nervousness.

All of a sudden a female voice shrieks from behind me. "Shawni!"

I whip around and I'm face-to-face, because we are almost the same height, with a familiar face, and I'm immediately happy to see her trademark jet-black hair, her Asian-styled bangs, and her warm smile. I'm in awe seeing the green-eyed and soft-dimpled beautiful woman, old friend, that I have not seen in a very long time, and actually never imagined I'd see again, or at least not this soon.

I pull her into a brief hug, notice her cream-colored slip dress, and wonder where she got it. "Abigail! What are you doing here?" I scream.

She steps back and grins. "You look so awesome, Shawni! You always do."

"You, too." I nod at her dress. "Cute."

"How are things?" She looks at me sympathetically, probably remembering all the rumors she's heard about me not signing the contract for Ricci. "I hear you're engaged, anyhow. That's cool. Bo's awesome. We miss you, though. Everyone does."

I look around, wondering if he's here, hoping he isn't, and then hoping he is so he can see that I'm here without him. I nod. "Yeah, I miss you guys, too. You'll have to come to the wedding."

"No question." She offers a perky grin and taps my hand. "What are you drinking? Let my new boyfriend buy you a drink?" She pulls my hand over to the end of the bar.

He's quite handsome. Sitting at the bar, holding a martini in one hand and a burning cigarette in the other, he looks up as we approach him. Never mind the fact that I hate when men smoke, this man's seemingly sunburnt skin is glowing, his mostly unbuttoned black silk shirt—Armani—looks fabulous against his platinum jeweled chest.

Abigail nudges him. "Trip, this is Shawni." She leans into the divine creation in front of me, and smiles proudly. "Shawni, this is my boyfriend, Trip."

He looks at me with his chestnut brown eyes, and pearl white glistening teeth, puts his martini on the bar table, and delicately takes my hand and kisses it. "A joy to meet you, Shawni. Such a beautiful name."

Abigail smiles at me proudly. "Shawni and I used to model together."

I slide my hand out of Trip's. "Thank you."

He picks his glass back up and frowns. "Used to? Please tell me you're still modeling?"

"Actually, no. I'm a personal stylist now, not doing any modeling."

He makes a tsk-tsk noise. "Oh, what a shame, my dear." He looks me up and down approvingly. "Truly, a shame."

Abigail sits on Trip's lap. "She turned down Ricci Malone. Huh, Shawni?"

He kisses her neck, but continues to look at me. "You must be kidding me?"

"No," I say. "I was tired of the modeling thing."

Abigail chimes in. "Trip's a photographer."

"Really? My father was, too, at one time," I say.

"Interesting." He drinks some of his martini.

Abigail nudges me. "What are you drinking, Shawni? It's on Trip, right, babe?" She kisses him again.

He gestures with his glass. "Whatever she wishes to have, I'll pay for. The sour apple martinis are splendid."

Trip motions for the bartender, who promptly comes over.

I'll just have a quick drink and slip away.

"Trip!" Abigail says. "Shawni was born in Milan."

His eyes glisten in amazement. "You must be kidding me!"

"It's true," I assure him. "We moved here when I was a little girl."

He rubs his chin a little and his eyes continue to beam. "Milan! What a splendid place. You must have loved it. I'm from Florence, originally," he says.

I tilt my head. "Really? Lovely place as well."

"You guys are so lucky," Abigail interjects. "I wish I was from such an exotic place as Italy."

"Boston is nice," I suggest.

"Indeed," Trip agrees as he puts his cigarette out, and glides Abigail off his lap before standing up to retrieve his platinum money clip from his pocket. Abigail slips her hand in his. He looks at me curiously. "You're Italian mixed, I presume?"

"No, my mother is Creole and my father is half Trinidadian and African. The only connection with Italy is having been born there."

"I see," he says. "Now I understand where your beauty comes from. Trinidad, Africa—that's enough in themselves. Creole also? No wonder." He laughs.

I blush. "Trip, that's quite flattering."

"Oh," Abigail picks up the martini that the bartender has just delivered and seems to almost thrust it at me while Trip pays for it. "Here's your drink, Shawni." She raises her eyebrows. "Enjoy the party." She widens her eyes, completely refrains from blinking, and waits. Her vibrant smile has vanished.

What's wrong with her all of a sudden?

Trip takes my hand and kisses it. "Shawni, I'm so absolutely pleased to make your acquaintance."

"Likewise." I want to smile, but Abigail still hasn't blinked yet, and it's rather distracting. I lift my drink up and look back before walking away. "Abi, it was nice seeing you again."

She looks at me blankly, still not blinking. "Of course."

Maybe she's a Gemini. Those are the only people I know whose moods can change so easily from one extreme to another.

I find a spot near the dance floor, assume a sexy stance, and drink. Almost immediately, however, a hand rests on my waist and turns me around. I almost spill my martini, but manage to balance it before I do. I start to roll my eyes in annoyance, but I smile when I see who it is.

He smiles, too. It is Yusef, Duran's right-hand man. "I thought that was you," he says to me. "You're lookin' good."

He's such a sweetheart. Duran's primary assistant and just a well-rounded nice guy. His mustard-colored suit and matching fedora, tilted to the side, are a little gaudy, but it complements his otherwise average appearance—it looks good against his chestnut-brown complexion. Yusef is the guy in Duran's crew who always has to try a little harder to look good, but he always manages to pull it off.

"You do, too, Yusef."

He nods at my dress approvingly. "Yo, that dress is sayin' somethin'."

"Oh, and what's it saying?" I ask.

"Well, I'm not fluent in dress language, but yo . . . It sounds a little like don't get too close because I'm being worn by someone who is off limits and you might not be able to control yourself!"

I join him in laughing, and give him a quick hug. "It's so good to see you, Yusef."

"Always good to see you, too. You lookin' for Bo?"

"No," my smile melts. "Why?"

"Oh, dang." He raises his eyebrows. "Didn't mean to spoil your mood. I was just askin'."

"Is he here?" I glance around.

"You didn't know? Yeah, he's around here somewhere. Duran and them should be here any minute."

"Wanna dance?" I ask.

He eyes me, and whistles playfully. "Yeah."

"Here," I hand him my drink, "have a drink on Trip."

He takes it, doesn't bother to look down into the glass or ask who Trip is, and downs it. "Let's boogie, Shawni B.!"

I put my hand in his and lead him out to the dance floor.

Once I find a spot for us on the floor, I turn around and look at

Yusef, and I'm glad he's out here with me. This is going to be fun, and who better to have fun with but a guy who can appreciate it?

A nice sexy groove is playing. Good.

I very gently place my hands around his neck, give him a little rub right above his collar, pull my hips close to his for a quick tease, then pull back a little. I look into his eyes, wanting to hypnotize. This'll never work if he's not into it, too.

He looks at me, tripping out; he can't believe this. He's slowly getting into the feel of the music, to the slow motion of a fantasy come true, to my lead.

Our eyes are locked, and he's moving easily from side to side with me. I lick my lips, let my neck relax, let my head fall back, keep it there, hold on to him, wanting him to hold me tighter. He does. I snap my head up, look at him, and pull away completely. Just stand there, Yusef, I say with my eyes.

He's enjoying every second.

I can't believe I'm doing this! I'm having so much fun doing this!

I reach up, my hands slowly illustrating the music, my head one with my hips—back and forth. No, no, no, I say with my eyes every time he tries to move closer. Be still, now. Just watch, Yusef.

Someone from behind me snatches my arm, yanks me out of my world. I'm so jolted it takes a moment for me to focus in to see who the villain is. My brother.

Duran looks at me, breathing hard, eyes narrow, like he just caught me actually doing it or something. His ponytail shining and his clothes crisp, he looks fly and like a madman at the same time. He shouts over the music. "Shawni? What's wrong with you slow groaning all up on 'Sef? Man!" His eyes snap in Yusef's direction. I look over but Yusef has gone. Duran leads me off the dance floor, but when we get near the bar I snatch my arm away.

"Duran, I was just dancing!"

His eyes are glaring in disbelief. "I can't believe you're out there all up on 'Sef, man. That shit ain't even cool, Shawni."

I try to walk away.

He snatches me back, forcing me to look at him. "Shawni!" he yells.

"I was just dancing, Duran! Am I not allowed to have fun on the dance floor?"

His eyes are looking around for someone. "You need to go holler at Delaney."

"I don't want to see him," I say. And suddenly, as I glance across the bar, my eyes are locked with eyes that are magnetic, gray in color, and intense. He's at the bar, ordering, and he pauses to smile back at me. I can't help returning the smile.

Duran turns to see what has my attention, and laughs. "Thought you saw Bo, the way you were glowin' like a nightlight and shit. You're trippin' up in here tonight. Flirtin' with all my boys."

I pull him down by the neckline of his shirt, pull his ear as close to my mouth as I can get it, and say, "Duran, I'm leaving." And I shove him away from me. I'm sick and tired of him treating me like I'm still a child. I turn and walk away, intent on getting out of here as fast as I can.

I storm past the bar, but a hand grabs me, stopping me, pulling me in. "Leaving already, my dear?" he asks. It's Trip. And he nearly pulls me onto his lap, but I pull back just in time.

I look around for Abigail. No Abigail. I look around for Bo. No Bo. I look around for Duran. No Duran. Good, I have time for a quick smile, so I give him one. "It was nice meeting you, Trip. But I really have to go. Another party to hit."

He forces a sad face. "But this one is just beginning, and we haven't even danced yet."

I look down, realizing that he is still holding my hand.

"Please." He cups my hand with both of his, and then kisses it. "Tell me that you will at least allow me one dance before you leave?"

"I'd love to, but I really have to go." I pull my hand away. "Some other time?"

He playfully pounds his chest. "My heart is breaking."

" 'Bye." I wave before I walk away.

As I make my way toward the door, I see Al first. And then Mo. And then Cris. And then Duran. And then Zin. They're all at the end of the bar. I whisk past, just wanting to escape this room full of enticement. I do, however, pause for a quick second, after I pass them, because I'm stunned at how striking they look in their leather gear, and I think to myself, I did that, and I'm proud for a moment. But the joy is fleeting, and my determination to leave resurfaces.

Maybe I should have finished that drink.

No, Shawni, just get out of here.

I gain my composure, settle into my Mona Lisa smile again, and proceed to the exit.

My friend the bouncer smiles. "Leaving already?"

"I have another set to attend before the night is over," I say convincingly.

"Be safe," he says as I'm walking away.

I should be able to catch a cab in the next block or two.

Footsteps behind me.

I am not turning around.

I will ignore Duran. I can catch a cab by myself. I do not need him to hold my hand crossing the street. He's my brother, and I love him, but he has no right to dictate my life. He's so controlling.

Footsteps, getting closer.

I walk faster.

They walk faster.

I snatch my head around. The eyes stare back at me, smiling.

His voice is its characteristically gentle tone. "I thought you were gonna start sprinting."

I stop walking. He stops, too.

I sigh. "Hey. I thought you were my brother. The vest looks nice."

He laughs, his gray eyes glistening like sterling silver. "Come here." He nods toward a space in between the two brick buildings we're standing in front of.

I follow him into the alleyway, and ask, "So, how'd the show go?"

"It was cool." He pauses and tugs at one of my two braids. "I dig the look. Cute. Why didn't you come?"

"I was so busy today."

"Sorry to hear that," he says. "Listen, are you cool? You looked kind of upset in there."

I roll my eyes. "It's nothing."

"There you go again, rolling your eyes, acting like it's all good. Straight up, are you okay?"

I tilt my head and force a smile. "Zin . . . I'm okay."

"Still a lot on your mind, huh?"

"Always."

"Yeah," he nods with a concerned look. "Well, look, don't, you know, be too mad at your brother, all right? I peeped it all. He's just looking out for you. And, yo, I dig why."

"Whatever." I roll my eyes. "It wasn't that serious. You don't know how Duran is."

"True dat," he says. "But I know that he'd kill for his baby sister. As I would for mine."

"I'm older." I look away, down the alley, back at the street. Now, I'm really ready to go.

"My fault." He laughs. "He always calls you his baby sister."

"I know."

"Well, look here, Shawni. I just wanted to holler at you before we get up and outta here in the morning. Hopefully we'll do business again. We're in New York often. You know, it was fun coolin' out with you. And I wish you and fiancé man the best." He glances down at my ring finger, and looks back up at me with his left eyebrow raised. It's so funny, the way he does that, with just one eyebrow.

"I took it off," I say. "We had a little disagreement. I was upset, that's all."

"Oh." He nods. "Dig that."

"Yeah, it's okay. It's a good thing."

His eyebrows scrunch up, "Breakin' up is a good thing?"

"Maybe it's for the best. Things happen, you know?"

"For sure. Like the way I encountered one of the most intriguing women I've ever met in my life, could hardly contain my desire to get to know her, but respected the fact that she's engaged. Then I see her again and she's commitment free. Dig that. Things do happen."

I ask him, "Are you coming on to me?"

"Full-court press," he replies without hesitation. "Kill the defense."

He's serious.

"Wait," I say. "Bo and I just had a little disagreement. We'll be okay. It's just one of those things that couples have to go through. I never said I was commitment-free, Zin."

"All right." He thinks for a moment. "But yo, that's what we've been conditioned to think—that love has to be this big complicated arrangement where you have to constantly work. Yo, it's about finding someone you truly connect with, and then it's as simple as what the

Book says—patient, kind . . . A relationship with the right person can be a beautiful thing if you have enough faith to wait for that person— and if you're not afraid of feeling some real shit once you do."

"What are you saying?" I'm totally annoyed. "And why are you always coming at me with some theory? You don't even know me! You have no idea what my relationship with Bo is like. You think you can just plug your little theories into every situation and it'll make sense?"

He waits a moment. "Yes, I do."

"Look, you seem like a really nice guy, but trust me, some things *are* complicated."

He sticks his chest out sarcastically and says in a baritone super-hero voice, "Name me one!" He laughs.

I glare at him, "My family."

His smile fades. "Yo, all I'm saying is that everything can easily be understood, that all things can be simplified. Every situation has a reason why it is the way it is. I don't know jack about your family, but . . ." He waits with reservation.

"Let's just drop it, okay? Bo and I will be fine."

"I hope so." He nods. "You found someone you've connected with on such a tight level that you're committing to loving him for the rest of your life. That's the way to live. It would be a shame to lose all that." His eyes wonder at the possibility of something like that happening. "But, check it. No matter what, somebody better always comes along. Believe that."

And we're silent for an awkward moment or two.

Finally, because I've wanted to ask him ever since I met him, I ask, "Are those contacts?"

He laughs and shakes his head. "Hell naw. But I get that a lot. I could never rock contacts, though. That's ill."

"Why not?"

"You gotta keep it real. The eyes are the window to the soul. You can't shield that—it's not even cool. Wearing blue contacts, and your eyes are really brown? Man, that's denying your true self."

"Oh." I nod. "Window, huh?"

"Have you ever just stared into a person's eyes for a long time?"

"No."

"There's an infinite beauty," he says. "If you're quiet, and stare long enough, you can feel the rhythms of a person's soul. You can feel the flow of their thoughts."

I blink my way out of his trance and look away.

He frowns. "Yo, don't do that." He steps over to me and gently pulls my face, forcing me to look at him.

"What?"

"What is it that you don't want me to see, Shawni?" he whispers.

"Listen, I gotta go." I look away again, refusing to look at him.

He lets his hand linger under my chin for a moment and I think I could get high off the smell of his cologne if he keeps it there long enough. But then he brushes my cheek and lets go.

"Yo," he says, "I don't know why we met, but I personally try to learn something from every person I encounter, and I can't for the life of me figure out why I met you. What's goin' on up there underneath all that pretty hair of yours? Why do you keep closin' a brotha out?"

"Maybe I'm just tired, okay? Maybe I just don't feel like talking."

"You seem so distracted. I'm just trying to understand."

"Why do you care?" I abruptly ask. "I told you, I'm fine."

He gestures with his index finger for me to wait. "Yo, you don't have to say anything else. I'll cool out, okay?" And then he takes a step back. "I guess Duran will take care of the fee for your brilliant services. We got mad compliments on the gear."

"I'm glad to hear it."

"I don't want to hold you up from going where you need to go."

I nod. "I really do have to go."

"Who knows when I'll ever see you again, but in the meantime, you be cool, all right?" He leans in and gives me a quick kiss on my cheek. Then he leads me out of the alley. "And ease up on your brother. It's not such a bad thing that 'Ran's mad obsessed with your well-being, all right? He made it real clear to me today just how serious he is about that."

Whatever. I don't even feel like asking what Duran said to him. "See ya," I say.

He turns to the right, back toward the club.

I turn left. I have a cab to catch.

After walking two blocks and waiting and waiting and waiting and waiting, and realizing that practically every Lincoln that drives past has a passenger, I decide to take advantage of the first empty yellow cab I see. Yellow cabs are so stuffy, but at this point I don't care, I just want to get home.

Home. To no one.

Well, at least there's Sanford.

So, Shawni, what did you do Saturday night?

Spent the evening at home, alone. With my dog.

Bo's out dining, partying, and not returning your calls, and you are going home alone?

My mind is pleading for a cab to pull over before something humiliating happens, like Bo driving by and seeing me get into a yellow cab. I sigh as one finally pulls over.

Just as I am about to get in, I hear a car horn honk. It's a dazzling silver Porsche with a black convertible top. The driver rolls his window down.

He smiles from behind the wheel, his sunburnt skin shining, and his smile eager. "So, where's the after-party? Let me take you."

"Nevermind," I tell the cabdriver before slamming the door

shut, and I stroll over to the passenger side of the Porsche. I get in, and it smells like vanilla.

"Where to?" the divine Sicilian asks as I close the door.

"Where's Abigail?" I whisper.

"Who?" He shrugs as if he has never heard the name before.

"Soho." I nod in the direction of where I live. "Nice car."

An after-party with Trip has to be better than an evening spent alone, paging Bo, waiting in vain, on the phone, whining to Ernie. Besides, Ernie is probably asleep by now, and a Porsche beats a yellow cab no matter how you look at it.

"I have a dog," I warn him, just in case he's having criminal thoughts. Then again, Abi would never date a psycho.

"I like dogs." He smiles. As a matter of fact, he's been smiling ever since I got in the car.

"A big one," I add.

He glances at me questionably.

"But if you're nice to me, he'll be nice to you."

"Easy enough," he says.

Sanford immediately trots down the hallway toward us.

"Whoa. He is big." Trip pauses at the door.

"Doberman," I emphasize. "Come on, in. Don't be nervous— he's fully trained." I grab Trip's hand and pull him in, letting the door close behind us.

I pat Sanford on his head. "Sanford, say hello to Trip."

He barks.

"Shhhh." I laugh as Sanford barks again, unsure of whether Trip should be leery.

Trip laughs, too, tiny wrinkles forming at the corners of his eyes. "Hello, Sanford."

After giving Sanford a chewing bone, and instructing him to "go," he reluctantly obeys, but not before giving Trip's shoes a final sniff.

As Sanford retreats back to his bedroom, Trip nods. "Nice pooch you have there."

"Thank you." I take off my leather jacket and hold out my hand for Trip to hand me his. I hang them both up in the closet, and then join him on the couch.

He looks at me, shaking his head in amazement. "I'm so glad I caught you before you got into that cab." He slides over to me, and takes my hand in his.

"Where's Abigail?"

He rubs my hand in circular motions. "You must hear all of the time how beautiful you are?"

"What about Abigail?" I ask again.

He gives me a look bordering on annoyance at first, and then he slides back into a pleasant manner. "Abigail is pretty. You, Shawni, are a living portrait of classic, elegantly written poetry." He moves closer.

Cool Water cologne. It's nice, it's very nice, comparable to Joop, even. "You smell nice," I say.

"You do, too," he replies.

I pull back a little, feeling a little uncomfortable.

"What's the matter, beautiful?" He smiles, and I notice those peculiarly premature wrinkles around his eyes again. I wonder how old he is? I'm guessing forty-five.

"Can I fix you a drink?" I ask.

He answers by pulling me closer, and sighs, "Awww, I'd rather just hold you."

I pull away anyhow. "Stay here," I nod at the couch. "I'll be right back." I get up, flip on the power to the CD player, and hand Trip the remote control before heading back into my bedroom. I want to sneak a peek at the answering machine and see how many "I know you're there, so pick up the phone" messages there are from Bo.

"You have . . . no messages."

A Taurus is equally as stubborn as he is bullheaded. He'll call soon.

I turn on the light on my vanity table before having a seat and examining myself. He said I look like elegant poetry. No man has ever said that before. How lovely. Wait until he sees this, I think to myself as I begin undoing my two braids. The result is a soft wave effect as my hair falls down my shoulders, I tousle it around with my fingers, and give my head a few shakes, and smile at the wild effect that it produces.

See what you're missing out on, Bo? Party on without me, if that's what you want to do.

Just as I finish dabbing a little more CoCo behind my ears, the sound of Keith Washington's "Kissing You" comes from the living room. I'm getting up from the vanity when suddenly I feel someone staring at me. I do a double-take when I turn around and see that it is Trip peeking into the room from the doorway.

He grins. "How is it possible that you could be even more beautiful than a moment before? Your hair is like ripples of silk . . ."

I tune out the rest, because, no, he didn't just take it upon himself to walk down the hallway and come into my bedroom. "I'll be out in a second," I tell him.

He walks toward me.

I am not in the least bit aroused. I stand up and put my hands on my hips.

He smiles. "May I have my dance, now?"

"In the living room," I remind him. "And I'll be *out* in a second," I insist.

"Your hair . . ." He brushes it softly with his hand, which produces a surprisingly pleasant shiver from my body.

"Trip!"

"Yes?" He wraps his arms around my waist, pulling me into him by the small of my back. And then he kisses me. And then I pull out of his grasp.

"What's the matter?" He leans back in to kiss me again.

"Why did you just kiss me?"

"Pardon me? You didn't want me to?"

I put my hands on my hips. "No."

"This is a joke, right? A riddle with an answer?" He raises his eyebrows.

"No."

"No?"

"Okay, now you need to leave," I say.

He bursts out laughing and then covers his mouth with his hand.

"What's so funny?" I ask, irritated.

He drops his hand from his mouth, but continues to hum a laugh. "You're kidding, right?"

"No."

"So, you didn't want to kiss me?"

"Nor did I give you permission to come into my bedroom!"

For the first time since I met him, he isn't smiling. In fact he's frowning, with a wounded look in his eyes as he says sincerely, "I'm very sorry. I thought that you wanted me to kiss you. I'm very confused. I didn't mean to . . . But you invited me up? In the car, you said 'did I want to come up.' I thought we were going to have an after-party."

"Well, not in my bedroom, if that's what you were thinking."

He pivots around and walks out. I turn off the vanity light, and follow him down the hallway and back into the living room—where he retrieves his jacket from the closet. "It was nice having met you, Shawni," he says.

"Right."

He proceeds to put his jacket back on, adjusts the collar, and then turns to me. "I hope I didn't give you the wrong impression of me. I just thought since you asked me to come up, that you wanted to have fun."

"Did I say come on up so we can kiss, Trip? No. Ever hear of conversation?"

"Sure, over dinner, after a movie, walking through the park. Not in the middle of the night. I didn't know. Honestly." He looks puzzled. And at the same time he looks harmless. "What is there for us to talk about?" he asks.

"I don't know. I just didn't want to be alone tonight. And you seemed nice."

A smile in his eyes. "I am nice," he says. "Just an easygoing artist from Florence. I mean no harm. We can talk, if that's what you're looking for. You shouldn't have to be alone."

I sigh. "If you're willing to forget about what time it is, and as long as we just talk."

He shrugs. "I need a smoke. Do you mind?" he asks.

"If you must, but I hate cigarettes." I sit down on the couch.

He peels off his jacket and hangs it back up before lighting one up anyhow. "Then I suppose I shouldn't offer you one," he jokes before joining me on the couch.

"Precisely," I say.

He sits there for a moment, and then chuckles.

"What's funny?" I ask.

He exhales with one long, continuous, dreamlike flow of smoke. "Just thinking about what just occurred," he says. "And how I never thought I'd see the day when it would be intriguing to have a woman turn me down. An evening spent smoking and just talking is not something I experience too often. It's pleasantly different."

"There is nothing wrong with just talking."

He takes another puff of his cigarette.

"How long have you been a photographer?" I ask.

"Fourteen years old," he finally says, after another long exhale.

"And when did you move to the States?"

"Twenty-two years old."

"Oh."

And the room is quiet except for the occasional sounds he makes when he puts his cigarette to his mouth.

"Are we going to talk, or not?" I finally ask.

He grins. "We are talking. You asked me how long I've been living here. Be calm, my dear."

"Would you like a drink?" I offer.

"No, thanks," he replies. "And you've lived in the States since when?"

"I was a little girl."

"Do you ever go back?" he asks.

"Rarely."

"I can smoke something else, you know, since you don't like cigarettes."

"Cigars bother me, too."

He reaches into his pocket and pulls out his billfold.

"From your wallet?" I ask.

"Laced with a little of the white lady." He kisses the thin joint that he removed from his billfold. "You want?" His smile is smug.

"Oh," I say. I haven't had any since . . . In fact, the last time was with Abigail, after the show, my last show. But even then I hadn't done it in awhile, but it was my last show, and Abi always had the best. "I'll pass."

"Sure?" he asks. The flame from the match is as enticing as the immediately familiar stale smell of cannabis. Trip's lips tenderly caress the paper.

"Yes, I'm sure," I say.

"Sparks good conversation, you know. Conversation is what you want, isn't it?"

"I said I'll pass, thanks."

I have to look away. The aroma is filling the room, suffocating my repressed desire. I should get up and run.

He scoots over to me, crosses his leg, and puts the joint to my lips. "Good stuff," he whispers.

"I don't mess around anymore," I say, the joint touching my bottom lip. I could let it go. If I really wanted to, I could drop it.

He whispers, "You don't model. You don't kiss. Won't dance with me. You don't go back to Italy to visit. Come on. Live a little." He takes it from my mouth, licks the tip again, and glides it into my mouth with one hand, while easing his other hand onto my left thigh.

I feel myself push his hand away.

"You're so alluring," he whispers.

I close my eyes.

"Breathtaking," he replies, putting his hand back on my thigh. "You must realize how remarkable you are, no?"

I reply, "I'm not even sure what beauty is anymore."

He laughs. "You're kidding, right?"

I open my eyes. "No."

He puts the joint to my mouth, and speaks quietly. "Come on . . ."

I try to lean away, but the back of the couch won't let me. Trip is on my right, and there's no room on my left, only the end of the couch. I could just get up. I should. The paper, dry, is resting on my lip, and there's a taste, a familiar smell mixed with Trip's cologne, and it feels as if I'm hugging an old friend. The paper on my lips. His hand rubbing my thigh. Both waiting for me to surrender.

What am I fighting? What can it hurt?

A hand is coming toward my face. French manicured—square-shaped, thin, natural-looking fingernails that resemble mine are delicately touching the joint. I'm the only woman in the room. It must be me. I'm holding it. I'm inhaling . . .

A recognizable twinge in my chest, and then there is brief pleasure before I exhale, and a relieved feeling after I do.

Back and forth. His lips. Mine. His hands. Mine. The smell is thick and hungrily it consumes the room. Trip is nodding, or is that me? Am I nodding? He's smiling. Am I?

I remember this. A seemingly uninspired laugh comes from my mouth. It's the first sign.

His smile shines amid the smoke. "You like?"

I inhale again.

His hand is still on my thigh. I look down and watch it.

I touch his wrist, study his platinum-linked bracelet for what is probably ten minutes, or maybe even longer, or maybe I really don't know how long it's been. "Is that Gucci?" I ask.

"You like?" he asks. "I could buy you one if you do." He leans in as if he's having a conversation with the side of my neck.

I laugh. I'm laughing because I am laughing, and it wasn't even funny. "You would buy me one? Is it Gucci? I adore Gucci."

He nods. "It is. Gucci, Movado, Rolex. Tomorrow. I'll buy you something tomorrow. Whatever you want." He kisses my neck. He kisses me the way he kissed Abigail, down my neck.

Abi, we used to call her. She and I were so excited when we did a Jhon Manuel show here in New York once. He gave us Fendi makeup cases with our names engraved on the handles.

She isn't really a "friend," so this isn't so bad. We only did shows together.

I'm laughing.

He grins. "Funny?" He kisses my neck continually.

The Gucci bracelet is crawling up my thigh.

I cross my legs.

"Uncross them," he pleads.

I laugh again, and I shouldn't have laughed. I shouldn't have laughed because whatever muscles in my stomach that moved when I did must be good friends with the muscles that are now rippling in disturbance. And they're having a good time down there, rumbling, tumbling. I attempt to sit up, but his mouth on mine won't let me.

I kiss him back because I can taste the joint on his soft lips, and I suddenly feel greedy for that taste. I kiss him back again, and he makes a moaning noise.

My moan matches the pitch of his pleased one, only mine is a result of the increasing discomfort in my stomach. I push him away.

He looks stunned. "What, now?" His eyelids are heavy.

"I don't feel so good," I reply.

I use the coffee table to brace myself as I stand up. These boots are now too heavy for my feet to carry, and I manage to kick them off. I take a step, a really gigantic step, way up, high, unnecessarily high, and I laugh because I can't believe I stepped that high, and I laugh because I realize that I don't remember where I'm going anyhow, so why was I stepping so high?

"Let me kiss you again." He reaches up and pulls me back down to the couch.

"What don't you understand?" I snap. "I said I don't feel good." And I consider getting back up again, but I can't remember where I put my boots, and my thoughts concentrate on that.

He smiles.

I reach for his hand. "Help me up."

He leans back in to kiss me again. "Let me help you feel better."

"I said help me up."

"This is fucking bullshit," he raises his voice.

"You better leave." I grimace as my stomach feels as if it is a towel ringing itself dry.

"Leave?" he asks.

"Yes. Would you just leave?"

He doesn't move. He sits there, his eyelids growing heavier by the second, and then he says under his breath. "You're such a bitch tease."

"Whatever." I grab the side of the couch and try to pull myself up as another shot of pain runs from my stomach to my chest.

I really hope I don't have to use my pepper spray on him tonight.

He pushes me back, leans in on me, and puts his elbow in my chest.

"Get—" I start to say.

Swiftly, he covers my mouth with his hand, and with his other arm he digs his elbow deeper into my chest. And then even deeper.

I try to push him off of me. Dead weight, we both are. I can't move. Neither does he.

"You're a bitch tease." He glares at me, whispering into the side of my face—my ear, it feels like—and he presses his hand even harder against my mouth. His elbow continues to press deeper into my chest. He hisses, "One minute you don't want me to kiss you, the next minute you don't want me to leave? You think I came up here to talk? I didn't. You bitch."

The increasing spasms of panic throughout my body are more numbing with each passing moment. All that I can do is breathe.

I'm thinking of the little pink case in my purse, the pepper spray that I've never had to use, of the stern expression on my brother's face when I opened the box the day I left for Paris. I'm thinking of what he told me about his gift to me. *No one should know you have it, but don't you ever forget that you do.*

If only I could move. Anything to defend myself.

I'm thinking of Christmas two years ago, when Bo gave Sanford to me, and all of the training we put him through because he wanted my dog to be able to protect me if ever he wasn't around.

The pink case, in my purse, is across the room on the table, beyond my reach.

My faithful companion, so obedient, is in his room, as instructed, and is unable to hear me. And what good would it do if he could? I can't scream.

"You don't know what I could do to you." Trip breathes onto my ear, his breath spicy and his breathing hard. "I could do it and leave you lifeless if I wanted. If I had it in me."

And he shoves me fiercely before he gets up.

I clutch my chest, overwhelmed by the stabbing reverberation of pain caused by his elbow. A sound finally escapes from my mouth, but it is faint, barely audible. "Sanford?" I reach for him, and close my eyes, hoping that he comes.

"Trip, you stupid bitch!" he mumbles as he walks toward the closet.

"Sanford!" I shout with every ounce of my pain.

"Who the hell is Sanford?" he yells back at me. "My name is Trip!"

Sanford's breath on my wrist lets me know that he is next to me now.

"Sanford," I say, "Get him *out*!" I feel his warm wet nose snap away from my wrist.

Sanford immediately begins growling, as he urges Trip to get his "I'm from Florence, Italy, and you look like a poem" ass out of his domain.

I hear Trip stomp his foot. "All right!" he shouts at Sanford. "I'm going."

I watch him walking down the hallway toward the door with Sanford growling right behind him. Finally, the door slams shut. A few moments pass as I listen to Trip's footsteps going down the hallway. Not until I hear the elevator door closing does Sanford's growling stop, signifying the end of the "after-party."

FIVE

Monsoon Season

It's three-thirty in the morning, and I'm finally recovering from a stomach war comparable to Vietnam. Dare I call Duran and listen to his speech about how careless I was to even allow Trip in? Ernie will say the same. If only Mommie were in town. If only Bo would call me back. Balled up pillows, now wet from my tears, do not provide the illusion of security the way his chest does.

I ease out of bed again, and it's relieving that finally I don't need to rush to the bathroom to purge the residue from the cannabis and scrub away the memories of Trip's touch. I kiss Sanford again, and he whimpers in response. I slip on a white Guess babydoll T-shirt, pull on a pair of denim overalls, lace up my Reeboks, and pick up the phone on my nightstand.

Ernie answers after five rings. "Whoever is calling me this late, call me tomorrow," he says—with attitude, as usual.

"Hey, Ernie. Are you doing anything?"

"Chile, no you didn't," he says. "I know this isn't Miss U.S. of America calling me this late. What do you mean 'what am I doing?' Can we infer that maybe I was sleeping?"

"I'm sorry," I say. "Can you wake up, please?"

He moans. "I ate the cheesecake by myself, by the way. What is it, diva?"

"I got tied up earlier. I'm sorry I couldn't make it over. I need a ride."

"A ride?"

"Yes."

"Chile . . ."

"Come on, Ernie. I'll pay you."

"A ride to where?"

"Brooklyn."

"What's wrong with Baby Blue?"

"Long story. I'll tell you when you get here."

"Why are we taking a journey to Brooklyn at almost four o'clock in the morning?"

"What difference does it make?"

"You're the one who needs a ride, okay? You better talk."

"I need a ride over to Bo's."

"Chile, you better call that Hershey bar and tell him to come pick his lollipop up."

"I want to surprise him. Come on."

"So he doesn't know you're coming?"

"Exactly."

"I smell something fishy. I'm on my way."

Give Ernie a hint of drama, and it's like honey to a bee.

The night air is refreshing for my tired body and my troubled nerves, but jolting to my dwindling high as I wait on a bench at the end of the driveway. Sure enough, Ernie's white Jetta comes creeping up. He sees me sitting here, and as if it's the middle of the afternoon, he honks and waves.

I pull the door shut after I get in. "Why are you honking? Do you know what time it is?"

"I'm out in the middle of the night to star in Driving Miss Baldwin. Don't ask me no questions. What's the scoop?" He puts the car in park. He's wearing a brown bomber jacket and a brown cotton jogging suit. Maybe he *was* sleeping. His eyes are tinted red.

"Can you just drive? I'll tell you on the way to Brooklyn."

"This must be juicy."

"Let's just go, okay?"

"So," he says as he pulls out of the drive, "what happened? You called him and another woman answered the phone or somethin'?"

"It's not that serious. I just haven't heard from him, and he won't answer his phone."

"Umm hmm. You better give me something juicier than that. Got me out here in the middle of the night." He reaches for something on the floor, and retrieves a brown paper bag.

"What'd you do, pack a lunch?" I laugh.

"You know me and my munchies. Want a Twinkie?" He balances the wheel and pulls one out of the bag. "You smell like you could use one, too."

"Excuse me? How can someone smell like they need a Twinkie?"

"Chile, the smell of weed got in the car about five seconds before you did."

"Are you serious?" I shriek.

"Damn, don't go breaking the glass, I need my windows, chile." He rips the plastic off the Twinkie and bites half of it off as he continues to talk with his mouth full. "Got some Nutty Bars and some Kit Kats, too. Who'd you get high with?"

"I'm not high, Ernie."

"If you say so. So, what's the scoop?" He finishes off his Twinkie and licks his fingers.

"To make a long story short I just need to see him."

"Oh, no! That's for news briefs. Give me the evening edition."

"He found out I went out with Zin, and now he thinks I'm cheating. He still won't return my calls."

Ernie breaks off a stick of a Kit Kat and takes a bite.

I continue, "And, it was nothing. All we did was hang out."

"Liar!" He hits his hand on the steering wheel. "And who did you get high with tonight? It wasn't me. Since when do you have another friend?"

"Bo shouldn't be so insecure."

"Shawni, you're killing me! Insecure? Please." His excitement causes him to speed up a little bit. "Shoot, I bet you were checkin' out all those guys in the group, weren't you? Even that little one with the high voice."

"Slow down, please," I say. "Cris? He's an asshole. I was bored. Zin was just there."

He clears his throat. "Bored? How about a Freddie Jackson CD and a bottle of wine, chile? You weren't bored, you just couldn't stand to be alone."

"Just because I'm engaged doesn't mean I can't have fun."

"You're just resisting the leash, that's all."

"Whatever."

"That's what you're afraid of. And who was the guy you were kickin' it with after the club?"

"Filler companionship. I didn't feel like being alone tonight. That turned into a—"

"Boo-yow! Whoop! There it is." Ernie cuts in, "Thank you very much! You just proved my point."

I don't even bother to respond because I don't feel like it, but after a moment I can't help saying, "The only person I need is me, okay? I can choose to kick it with whomever I damn well please, if and when I choose."

"If you say so."

"Can we talk about something else?"

"Umm hmm."

But we don't talk about anything else. The only thing on my mind is what just happened with Trip, and I can't tell Ernie about that. And Ernie doesn't say anything else, which is unusual. He just sings along to the radio and munches on his treats.

When we are a block away from Elliot Street, I say, "Make a right up here."

Ernie slows down. "And I thought you said you don't get high anymore?"

"I don't. It was a spur of the moment thing. An old friend stopped by."

"Who was he?" he asks.

"What difference does it make? Just slow down. You have to make a right up here."

He turns the corner onto Bo's street. "Which one is his?" he asks.

"The only one on the entire block with the lights still on." The street is still and dark, except for Bo's brownstone.

"Shawni?" he whispers.

"What?" I say as I am looking up at the windows to Bo's living room. The lights are on but I don't see any shadows moving. He's probably on the couch sleeping. He always falls asleep with the lights on.

Ernie doesn't answer, but I follow his eyes to see what has his lips tightened. First, I notice the Denali, and then directly in front of it I see a familiar license plate.

I squint. "Is that Baby Blue? Pull up a little."

"Chile, you can get on top of it and bounce up and down, it does not take twenty-twenty vision to see that that's your car." He grudgingly drives up some. "Now, Miss Shawni, you know you need to march those Reeboks up that stoop and ask that Lou Gossett Jr. wanna-be why he took your baby blue whip from you like that." He pushes the power locks and unlocks the door.

I look up at the light-filled living room window again, and this time I see a shadow. "Ernie, look!" I nod up. Just as Ernie looks up, however, the lights go out.

"He's home. Now, go on up there," Ernie replies.

"Wait a second, do you have your cellular?" I ask. "Pull over and park."

Ernie eases the car down a little farther and parks in front of a Minivan. "Who're you calling?"

I hold out my hand. "Just give me the phone."

He does so reluctantly. "You gonna call him from out here, and all you have to do is walk up those stairs? Chile, you're better than me. I'd be up those stairs three at a time."

"Shhh." I dial Bo's number.

"Yeah," Bo answers, his annoyed tone startling to me. Although he sounds irritated, he is definitely wide-awake.

"Bo?"

No response.

"Bo? Hello?" I shout into the phone.

"What is it, Shawni?" He sounds even more annoyed.

"What do you mean, what is it? Did you get my pages? I've been calling you all day."

His response is dry. "Yeah, I got 'em."

I wait for him to say something else, but he doesn't, so I ask. "Well, so how come you didn't call me back?"

He clears his throat. "Let me call you back, Shawni."

My heart clenches. "What?"

"I said let me call you back. Damn! I'm dealing with something right now."

For a brief moment I can't speak, everything seems so vague, as if I'm dreaming, but then I remember where I am. "Bo, I'm outside. I need to see you. I'm on my way up."

Click.

Did he just hang up on me?

Ernie watches the shocked expression on my face, and asks, "Girl, did he just hang up on you?"

I go to push redial, but Ernie snatches the phone from me.

"Get your butt out of this car and take your self up those stairs. Use your key."

"I don't have a—"

"What?" Ernie shouts. "Mr. Clean has a key to your spot and you don't have one to his? Oh, that's some simple shit that Ernie don't have time or tolerance for."

I walk up the stairs only one by one, but just because I'm still in shock that he hung up on me. Maybe the plug came out.

I lift the knocker of the huge black door and knock several times, and then wait, and wait, and wait. No answer. "Bo?" I say as I knock again. "Bo, come on! I need to talk to you!" I shout.

No answer.

I rush back to the car, and snatch the door open. "Ernie, Bo is stubborn. He's not gonna let me in. He's pissed," I say as I get back in and slam the door shut.

"Pissed my ass." He rolls his head from left to right. "He ain't too pissed where he can't open the door and call you a bitch or something face-to-face. I'm not buying it. Chile, it's fishy. I'm telling you. Perch. Catfish. Tuna. Fishy."

"He's just being stubborn."

"Umm hmm. I'd be willing to bet my Denzel movie library that there's someone up there."

"You must be crazy."

"You think I'm wrong?" Ernie reaches into the backseat, onto the floor, and pulls up two black balls of wool.

"What are those?"

He unfolds one of the balls and stretches it out, taking three of his fingers and poking them through the holes. Then he pulls the entire thing over his face. "Come on." He hands me the other one.

"Ernie!" I shriek. "I don't believe you. You came over here with ski masks? We're not robbing a bank!"

"Put it on. I'll be Clyde. You'll be Bonnie." He smiles.

"Why? He already knows it's me, and do you have any idea what wool does to hair?"

"Shawni, shut the hell up. Here." He holds out the remaining ski mask.

"This is outrageous." I snatch the mask from him, pull it over my face, and position the holes over my eyes and mouth. It smells like mothballs, and I have to pull a few stray strands of wool off my tongue while Ernie turns the car off.

I follow his lead as we tiptoe over to Bo's brownstone, which is mostly dark except for the flickering of lights from the television in the living room.

Ernie pulls me by my hand over in front of the stoop next door to Bo's and whispers, "Okay, I'm gonna lift you up to the living room window."

"What?" I raise my voice.

"Chile, hush. You wanna be able to sleep tonight, you gotta get some answers. Just tap on the window. He's gonna freak out, like 'what the hell is that on the window,' right? When he opens the curtains to see if it's a bird or whatever, you peek in, okay?"

"Ernie . . ."

"Trust me. It works."

"You've done this before?" I whisper.

"Like I said, trust me. I mean, what can you lose? He's already mad. This'll just prove to him how much you care."

"You better not drop me," I say as I step into Ernie's cupped hands.

"I got you. I got you," he whispers, and steadies his hands as he prepares to boost me up. "You ready?"

"Yeah," I whisper back.

The next thing I know I'm being elevated, and although the flight is a little wobbly, it does smooth out. In a matter of seconds, I am directly in front of the living room window.

"Go on and knock," Ernie whispers from below.

I grab the windowsill with one hand, and tap on the glass with the other. There's something very liberating about being this high up, I think as I wait.

"Knock again," Ernie whispers louder.

Just as I am about to, the curtains snatch open. Bo leans into the window from the inside and jumps back when he sees me. I remember the ski mask that I am wearing, and realize that I must look like a burglar, so I shout, "It's me."

"Shawni?" The window muffles Bo's voice as he shouts back. He leans all the way against the window and looks down to see what is holding me up. "What are you doing?" he shouts louder.

"Is that him?" Ernie whispers up and steadies his arms after he sways a little.

"Bo," I shout as I hold on to the windowsill.

He unlocks the window and pulls it open. My heart melts at how good he looks without his shirt on—his gold herringbone necklace so sexy against his solid dark chest. I notice the top of his purple silk pajama pants. A smile crosses his face for a moment, and then it changes into a defiant stare.

"Woman, you must be losing your damn mind. What the hell is wrong with you?" he shouts out the window, and leans out to look down below me. "And who the hell is that?"

I am about to tell him to let me in, that I need to talk to him, but as he leans out the window I catch a glimpse of what is behind him on the black leather couch. A blurred silhouette at first, a strange surreal image. With each blink, however, my eyes focus in and realize what it is that I am seeing. She stands up and fixes her robe.

She stands up.

She fixes her robe.

She wipes her cheeks. Are those tears?

She looks directly at me and forces a smile.

She walks out of the room.

I slap Bo's chest. "Who is that?"

He nods down below me at Ernie. "No, who is *that*?"

Ernie whispers, "Reveal no names, Shawni."

"Bo!" I shout. "Who is that? I just saw someone get off the couch!"

Bo reaches up to close the window, and I hurry to try to pull myself up by the windowsill before he does, but he lifts my hands off.

Ernie whispers louder as he staggers to hold me up. "Be still."

I shout down to him. "I'm going in, Ernie."

Ernie whispers back, "I said no names!"

Bo continues to hold my hands, preventing me from grabbing the sill. "You're not comin' in here, Shawni."

"Bo, let go," I plead. "You're gonna make me fall."

He lets my hands go.

I immediately grab the sill for a second time and try to pull myself up.

He grabs my hands again. "Woman, didn't I tell you to get down?"

"Who was that?" I shout.

Ernie's voice sounds strained. "Shawni, come on down. You're moving too much, now."

A sudden rage takes over and the next thing I know I am obsessed with slapping Bo's chest, and as I do so I can feel Ernie's grip wobbling. Bo ignores each slap and desperately tries to close the window.

I try to grab the sill again—if I can just grab it—but Ernie loses his grip. As I fall on top of Ernie I hear the window above me slam shut. My hand skids across the concrete and I scream.

"Ernie! I'm bleeding."

He pushes me off of him. "And my legs are broke. Get the hell off me."

His legs aren't broke. I know this because he immediately stands up and wipes the dirt from the ground off his butt.

I hold my hand up so that Ernie can see the scrape marks. "Look at my hand."

"Girl, all that fish up in that brownstone to fry, and you're worried about a little scrape? Who was she? What'd she look like?"

"Ernie," I feel my lip quivering as I realize that my hip is also hurting. "There was another woman in there!"

"No shit, Sherlock. I told you," he says. "What'd she look like?"

I try to get up. "My side hurts."

"Chile, if you don't get up and shake that off—" He pulls me up by my nonbloody hand. "What'd she look like? Who was it? What was she doing?"

"I don't know!" I shake my head and try to feel reality. Is this really happening? Did I just fall? Did I really just see another woman sitting on my man's couch?

She stood up and fixed her robe.

Why was she there in a robe?

"Ernie, she wasn't dressed."

"What?" He jumps up and down and his shout snaps me out of my daze. "She was naked? Titties out and everything?"

I grab hold of the garbage can next to me. "No, I . . . I mean she had on a robe," I say as I pull my ski mask off.

"And what'd she look like?" He shakes me by my shoulders.

"I don't know. I don't know. Ernie, you think Bo would actually—"

"Shawni." His eyes widen. "I'm about to say something to you that might hurt your feelings, but I got to say it to you, okay?"

My eyes search for comprehension of where he's going with this. "What?"

"Sometimes," he says, "you's a real dumb bitch." Then he pulls my arm and marches back to the car—pulling me behind him. I'm glad he's forcing me to walk because I doubt I would have otherwise. He opens the door as I stand here shivering quietly, in shock. I don't know if I'm crying or frowning or numb or what. I don't know what I'm supposed to be feeling right now.

Ernie rips the paper off another Kit Kat bar and holds it out to me. "Here."

"I'm not hungry, Ernie. How can you think about a candy bar right now?"

"Chile, I'm not talking about eating it this time." He nods in the direction of the Denali.

"What?"

"Damn, you don't know?" He smacks his lips. "Go put this in that fool's tank so we can get the hell out of here."

"What? In the tank? What's the point of that?"

"You know—*sugar in the tank*." He waits for me to comprehend.

"What?"

"Chile, at least you'll know that he won't be taking her home in the Denali if you put this in his tank. That's for sure."

I take the candy bar. "Really? It'll mess his car up?"

He nudges me. "Handle your business, girlfriend."

I must be crazy. Then again, Bo must be crazy. How dare he have another woman over in the middle of the night? I make my way over to the Denali.

The next thing I know, I'm breaking each of the four sticks off the candy and stuffing them, one by one, into Bo's gas tank.

I hear Ernie whisper from the sidewalk behind me. "Go on, girl!"

I'm twisting the top back on, but as I do an odd emotion consumes me, and each twist inspires more of this emotion. All I can think about is that woman, standing up, fixing her robe, inside my man's house!

Bo closing the window—on me! And he locked it!

"Shawni, that's tight enough, girl," Ernie whispers. "Come on."

I can't stop. It'll never be tight enough.

My neck is stiffening. My heart is racing. My breathing is increasing. My thoughts are dashing all over my mind, and I can't complete any of them.

"Shawni, come on," Ernie whispers. "Let's get out of here before he brings his big football self out here."

I hear Ernie. I hear every word. But actually, I want Bo to come out here. Yeah, come on out here. Asshole.

I see a brick by the fire hydrant. I run over to it. I pick it up. It's heavier than I thought it would be. Good. I run out into the middle of the street, and stand there holding the brick, and I pivot myself into position.

"Shawni, what are you doing?" Ernie whispers louder.

Glass from the driver's side window cackles into a rainfall of shattered pieces—everywhere.

Ernie's eyes widen, and I watch him, wait for him to tell me what to do now, but suddenly there's more noise. A look of absolute fear covers Ernie's face now as he looks back toward the brownstone. He turns back to me, panic on his face. "Here he comes!" He tosses his balled up ski mask in the air, grabs my hand, and begins running back toward the Jetta—forcing me to run with him. We dash back to Ernie's car.

I reach for the door handle, but suddenly someone grabs my shoulders and abruptly pulls me up in the air.

Ernie yells from the other side of the car, "Put her down!"

Bo yells as he holds me up in the air and shakes me into feeling like a rag doll. "Woman, have you lost your mind?"

"Who is she?" I hear myself yelling as he carries me back across the street to the Denali. He dumps me down in front of it and makes me look at the damages.

He grabs my shoulders. "You see this? You see this?" He continues to shake me. "You see what you just did?"

"Come on, Shawni." Ernie is by my side now. "Put her down, Bo. You big grizzly bear."

Bo shoots Ernie a warning glance. "Don't be a fool."

"Let her go!" Ernie demands.

Bo pulls me by my hair. "So you brought your little faggot friend with you, huh?"

Ernie gasps. "Oh, no, he didn't," he says under his breath.

"Bo, let go of my hair." I grimace at the pain.

After one good pull, he pushes me away from him. I turn around to face him, and Ernie slips his hand in mine. I see that Bo hasn't bothered to put a shirt on, and the expression on his face is beyond frenzy.

"Let's just go," Ernie says.

Bo looks at me in disbelief, and his voice cracks. "You just busted out my window."

"So what? Who's that woman up there?" My eyes begin to water, as I can't repress the increasing stinging feeling in my chest.

His reply is sarcastic. "Shawni, you're the one who needed some space, right?"

"I didn't mean forever."

Ernie squeezes my hand. "I said let's go."

I ignore Ernie, snatch my hand from his, and ask Bo as I fight the tears that are forcing their way out of my eyes, "Are you sleeping with her?"

He narrows his eyes. "She's just a client."

I let the tears flow, there's no use fighting it any longer. "You asshole," I say through angry tears.

He lets out a laugh. "Oh, so, now I'm the asshole."

"Who is she, Bo?" I ask.

He smirks. "A friend."

Instantly, I lunge toward Bo's chest. Maybe I can scratch him to death. His eyes, his nose, his chest, his . . .

Ernie grabs my wrists, pulling me back. "Shawni!" He holds me. "Let's just get out of here."

Bo tilts his head. "How's Zin?"

I shout. "For the last time, Trip is nobody to me!"

"What?" Bo replies.

Or was that Ernie? Maybe it was both of them.

Bo looks, dazed, confused, and angrier. "Trip?"

"Shawni," Ernie whispers. "We need to get out of here."

"Woman!" Bo's breathing increases as he bites his bottom lip. "Ahh! Trip? Zin? What is this?" he shouts at the top of his lungs.

A light flicks on behind us, but I'm afraid to turn around. Bo stretches his arms out and moans even louder.

Neither Ernie nor I move, and I suspect it is for the exact same reason. Bo suddenly reminds me of the reason why I was always afraid of *The Wizard of Oz*. It was that scene when Dorothy first encounters the Lion, and he roars.

Bo reaches inside the shattered window of the Denali and removes the brick from the seat. I flinch, afraid he's going to throw it directly at Ernie and me. Ernie must think the same thing, because he buries his head into my back, and I hear him murmuring something about walking through a valley of a shadow of death and fearing evil.

Bo hurls the brick at the back window of the Denali, and it shatters in slow motion. The sound of glass breaking is accompanied by the jolting sound of sirens.

Ernie speaks with his lips pressed against my back. "Help is on the way, girl."

Bo is still looking at me. "Trip, the photographer? The one I saw you talkin' to at the party tonight? What? You fuckin' with him, too?"

"No," I reply.

The sirens are getting closer and closer.

"I don't believe you, Shawni. After everything I've done for you? Everything we've been through?"

"Bo . . ." I fight off more tears.

He walks over toward the approaching police car, and calls back to me, "You're full of it, Shawni."

The officer driving stops the car and gets out. "What's the problem here, Mr. Delaney?" he says, as the other officer gets out as well.

I turn to face the passenger side police officer, who bears a remarkable resemblance to the actor Scott Baio, a definite cutie pie. The other one, the pudgy one, who just happens to be the one Bo knows, is casually leaning against the side of the car.

He shakes hands with Bo. "How've you been, man?" he asks.

"Been better, that's for sure."

The officer looks around. "We received several calls from neighbors complaining about a disturbance."

Ernie lets go of my wrists and moans under his breath as he stands up straight.

The other police officer turns his flashlight on, and aims it at the Denali. "This yours?" he asks Bo.

"Yeah," Bo replies.

The officer walks over to the window and peers in. "Any idea who busted the window out?"

Bo looks at me scornfully. "Any idea, Shawni?"

The police officer looks back and forth between Bo and me, and then he eyes Ernie before looking back at Bo. "We got a report of two people wearing ski masks, looking suspicious in the area. Any of you know anything about that?" He aims the flashlight at the ski mask balled up and lonely on the ground next to the Denali. "Anyone know the owner of that there ski mask?"

"Shawni?" Bo continues to look at me.

"I . . ." is all I can manage to get out.

The officer shines the light at me. "That there ski mask belong to you, ma'am?"

I close my eyes. "Can you get the light out of my face, first?"

"Shawni," Ernie whispers, "play it cool."

Bo's officer friend nods at Bo. "Can we speak to you over by the car, sir?"

Bo glances at me, "Sure." He joins the pudgy one by the car.

Scott Baio's twin walks over to the Denali, flicks the flashlight back on, and inspects further.

Ernie nudges me. "I told you to leave. Damn! Now we're going to jail."

"No, we're not," I whisper back.

The officer inspecting the window looks back at me. "Did you break this window, ma'am?"

"What window?" I reply. I look down and notice his badge. "Officer Wolfe?"

He smiles back at me. "Ma'am, you don't see that window busted out?" He shines the light back on the Denali.

I can't say anything.

The pudgy one returns, and approaches me. "Ma'am, my name is Officer Craig. This here is my partner, Officer Wolfe. And I'm afraid, unless you have any proof against this gentleman's claim that you busted out his window—"

"What?" I cut my eyes at Bo, who scowls as he stands with his arms folded across his chest. He told on me!

The officer continues. "According to this gentleman, you and your friend here approached these premises wearing ski masks and attempted to break into his living room window. Then you allegedly proceeded to bust out Mr. Delaney's car windows. Do you wish to disagree?"

I roll my eyes. "Excuse me, but do I look like the type of woman who would throw a brick through a window? I mean, really? As if I don't have bigger and—"

"Ma'am," he interrupts, "you mind explaining how you knew it was a brick that broke the window?"

Ernie growls. "Damn . . ."

The officer glances back at the police car. "You two mind coming with us down to the station?"

"Oh, Lord!" Ernie cries. "On what grounds officer?"

The officer looks at Ernie, and shrugs calmly. "Oh, disturbing the peace. Attempted breaking and entering. Destruction of property. We'll figure something out. Either of you been drinking tonight?"

We both shake our heads no.

The other officer is standing directly behind me now. "Ma'am, you have the right to remain silent . . ." He pulls my wrists and a clicking noise locks them into place. As he continues to talk, all I see is the back of Bo's bald head walking—away.

"Asshole!" I hear myself shout at Bo, as the officer pushes my head down, forcing me to get into the backseat of the police car.

I hear Ernie smack his lips, and I look over and realize that he's sitting right next to me. "I told you," he says.

I roll my eyes at the evil guard who is threatening me with a pair of fingernail clippers. "You're kidding, right?" I ask her.

She looks back at me and blows her bangs off her face. "We gotta cut 'em off." She shrugs. "Sorry."

"Sorry?" I reply. "It's not like I'm a criminal!"

"Lady, I'm not gonna argue with you," she says. "Everyone that comes in here has to get their nails cut." She gestures with the clippers. "Now, are you gonna cooperate, or should I call a supervisor? And if I were you, I'd cooperate, because, I'm telling you, if she has to cut 'em, it'll take a lot longer for 'em to grow back than if I do."

"Fine." I slip my fingers through the bars.

One by one, she cuts off each of the tips of my delicately French manicured fingernails. I don't know if the tears are coming back because, on top of everything that has happened, my fingernails are being destroyed, or because of the reality these are steel bars that my hands are resting on.

"Phone's over there." She points with the paper cup that now contains fingernail tips that once belonged on my now repulsive-looking hands. "You do realize that you're here until Monday?"

"Excuse me?" I reply.

"No bail on Sundays, sorry," she says. "Let me know if you need another blanket." With that, she walks away.

"I don't think so," I shout. "My fiancé is an attorney—thank you very much!" I say to the back of her as she makes her way down the hallway, shaking her head.

She glances back. "Monday. Sorry."

I turn around and face the cell. A twenty-something ghetto-fabulous girl wearing a too-tight denim outfit, a ridiculously long hair weave with blond streaks, and a pissed-off expression on her face, frowns back at me.

I immediately turn around and face the bars again. I can't stay in here until Monday. Are they crazy? This is absurd! There are murderers on the street, killing people for crying out loud. And I have to stay in here and look at dingy gray walls and smell month-old funk with this drug dealer's girlfriend as a roommate because I threw a damn brick through a window? Oh, and there is no way that I am sitting on that mattress. I've got a mattress for my dog that's more acceptable.

I glance down the hallway. Where did that fingernail stealing witch go? That's a really cold thing to do, cutting off a woman's fingernails. This is so ridiculous. "Miss?" I call down the hallway. "I'd like to see a manager, please?"

I wait for moments.

I clear my throat and call again. "Miss?"

The only response I get is a laugh. From my new roommate.

How am I supposed to make a call if I don't have a quarter? It's bad enough that I have to subject myself to using a public, jail public at that, phone, but I don't even have a quarter! I dig around in my pockets as I stand at the pay phone, hoping for a miracle amid the lint that they allowed me to keep after I was forced to empty my belongings into a plastic bag.

My roommate's voice has an echo as she speaks. "You gotta call collect."

Collect?

"Thanks," I say without turning back to look at her.

I pick up the receiver, and I'm so upset that I have to force myself to remember his phone number. "Collect from Shawni Baldwin," I whisper to the operator.

My fiancé is an attorney, I said. Yeah right. What fiancé? I can't believe he had another woman over there. And he allowed them to take me away in a police car!

What's taking this operator so long?

I never should have listened to Ernie. What was I thinking? Then again, maybe Ernie was right. If I hadn't gone back up there . . .

Ernie refused to talk to me all the way to the station.

I cannot believe Bo let them arrest me!

Oh my goodness, I can't stay behind these bars until tomorrow. I'll . . . I'll . . . I would say I'll die but there is no way I'm dying before I find out who the hell that woman was sitting on my fiancé's couch.

The operator finally returns. "I'm sorry, but the party declined to accept charges."

"What?" I reply. "No, wait a second. Can you click back over and tell him that I'm—"

"Ma'am," she interrupts. "The party has already hung up."

I slam the phone down.

I pick the phone right back up and hope that Duran is staying at Mommie's tonight.

The operator returns. "Go ahead with your call."

"Shawni!" Duran's voice is groggy. "I must be buggin'. What the hell is going on? Calling from jail?"

"Duran I'm in prison. Bo and I had a fight," I whisper and try not to cry.

"What? Did he hit you? Where are you? Where is he?"

"I'm in Brooklyn. Duran, come get me. Please!"

"I'm on my way."

"They said I can't leave until Monday."

"Shit. No bail on Sundays. What the hell happened? Where's Delaney?"

"He's at home. Duran, I don't care. Just get me out of here."

There is a lot of movement on the other end of the phone and then the sound of keys jiggling before he says, "All right, sis, remember, 'Ran's the man. I'm gonna handle this. I'll be there to get you asap. I'm on my way to Brooklyn. You all right, baby girl?"

"No." I close my eyes.

"Hold yourself together. I don't know what the hell is going on, but you just keep thinkin' about the fact that I'm paying Delaney a visit to find out, all right? You just focus on that, and everything's gonna be cool as soon as I handle that, all right?"

"Duran hurry."

"Be cool," he says before hanging up.

I don't believe this is happening! I would say it feels like a dream, but it doesn't. It feels like I am dead smack in the middle of someone else's life. Then again, it feels more like a joke. Like any second now someone is going to come down the hallway, and they'll be laughing. You can go home, now, they'll say. And I'll walk out of this cell and Bo will be standing there, and he'll be laughing also. Gotcha, he'll say.

Right.

My roommate walks over to the bars, puts her hands in her back pockets, and then yells for the guard to come. Then she turns to me, "You see how stupid these bitches are? I asked for a Bible three hours ago, these hoes ain't brought it yet."

I hear the fingernail villain's voice before I see her making her way down the hallway. "What is it, Teena?" she mumbles.

"Didn't I ask for a Bible?" Teena replies. "Dang, is that asking for too much up in here?"

"We're trying to find you one." The guard replies, and then looks at me. "Did you want one, too? It's slow tonight. You want some water or something?"

"No thanks," I reply. I don't want any reason to have to even think about using that disgusting toilet.

"I'll be back," the guard says and walks away.

Teena looks at me. "These bitches make me sick up in here, you know? Asked for a Bible, I don't know how many times, then here she comes tellin' you they're slow tonight. If you're that slow tonight, can I get my Bible? I mean, I wasn't asking for a damn t-bone, you know?" She smacks her lips—black lined and with entirely too much purple lipstick on them. "You know the worst thing in life is really wanting something or needing it, and not being able to get up and get it your damn self, having to wait on somebody to get it for you. I mean, damn, I ain't never been one to beg, but shit, is that what I got to do?"

I shrug. What am I supposed to say?

She looks me up and down. "What they got you for?"

Okay, should I lie and say murder, so she'll think I'm tough and won't try to beat me up? Think fast, Shawni. "Attempted burglary," I finally reply.

She scrunches up her eyebrows. "Whaaaat? Well, ain't that some shit? I mean, you look like one of them silly rich bitches be comin' up in here for a punk d.u.i or somethin'. Never can tell."

I better figure out what type of criminal I'm dealing with here. "What'd you, um, do?" I ask.

"Man, they better be lucky they got me, 'cause I ain't playin'. Shoot. They lucky they got me before I busted *all* that fool's windows out."

Now I really feel like I'm dreaming.

I clear my throat. "You busted out someone's windows?"

"Hell yeah. Shoot, ain't no piece gonna make no fool outta me! My grandmamma told me: Don't let no man make no fool out of you. Shoot, I'm up here bein' down with this piece, lookin' out for him in a way he ain't never had no woman checkin' for him, you know? I mean, holdin' it down for him when shit was rough. Nickel didn't have a car when I met him, but he rolled mine. And now that he got his new ride, he got the nerve to have some acne havin' bitch up in the car with him? And I haven't even rode in it yet? Oh, hell no."

"So, it was your boyfriend?" I clarify.

"*Ummm hmmm.* You always know when a piece got somebody in the car with him, when you call and he's all actin' shady, talkin' about what's up—voice all deep like he's talkin' to one of his partners or some shit—and all tryin' to get off the phone all quick, tryin' some punk ass line about havin' to call you right back. I ain't stupid."

Let me call you back. I'm busy. Those were Bo's words.

"Nickel thinks he's slick, but I'm a bold bitch. I bet I'll roll up to the crib, bust the window out," she says.

I wait for her to calm down, and ask, "At his house?"

"Hell yes. Heard he had some skinny ho up in the car, rollin' around, profilin' and stuff. He lucky the police came when they did."

"So, what else were you going to do?" I ask.

She looks me up and down and squints. "What, you the police or somethin'? I'm sayin', 'cause you all interested and stuff!"

I shake my head.

"You know"—she looks me up and down—"you better not be."

"I'm not. Really."

She laughs without smiling, but she laughs. "Nah, you straight. I can tell—you one of them dizzy hos, but it's cool. You ain't gotta be all up in my business though." She sniffs and turns her head, and then turns back to look at me. "You a Christian?"

I'm too nervous to answer, but she's looking at me insistently, so I take a deep breath. "I believe in God, yes. I pray."

"Yeah, me, too. I be prayin' all the time. And it be this priest up in here some weekends that be prayin' with you and stuff, if you ask him to. That's my boy, Father Gerald. He ain't here tonight, but if you come on certain weekends, he'll be here."

Even if Eddie Murphy, Gregory Hines, Michael Jordan, Pierce Brosnan, Blair Underwood, and that cute little Ben Affleck were waiting for me in this cell, there is no way I'm coming back. No way.

"Yeah," Teena continues, "he always be readin' this scripture to me out of the Bible. Thought maybe you was a religious girl. Thought maybe you could help me remember them words. Father Gerald is a cool dude. I be tellin' him all about my problems, and he be helpin' me understand 'em. They ever bring me a Bible, I'm gonna find that scripture. Watch."

"So, what's the point of it?"

"What?"

"The scripture."

"Shoot," she replies. "I grew up in the church. I used to sing in the junior choir, man, we used to be tight. We could blow, I'm tellin' you. Sometimes I be wantin' to go back there so bad. I ain't ready, though. But I'm gonna go back one day—watch. I'm gonna go back and shock all them fools up in there. They gonna be like, Teena, you came back? Watch. I be needin' God sometimes though. I know I ain't right up in my head. God don't like me actin' ugly and stuff. That's why I love me some Father Gerald. He be tellin' me that God still love me. He said God gone forgive me if I ask him to. That's right. He tellin' the truth, too, it's right there in that scripture. I'm gone find that scripture, too—watch."

Soon, my mind drifts off to the droning sound of Teena's complaints about the jail system, her boyfriend, and on and on and on. I try not to cry as I close my eyes and fall asleep.

Sanford! Oh, my goodness, my poor dog is going to starve to death! I'm going to starve to death. There is no way I'm eating anything out of this place. I'd rather eat Sanford's Pedigree. Poor Sanford is probably dying to go outside.

The male guard standing on the other side of the bars, holding two trays of food looks at me. "Morning. You ladies want some grub?" he asks. He's young—probably twenty-five, and clean cut. His hair cut close, with a part down the center, he looks like a baseball-playing type of guy.

Teena groggily sits up. "You ain't gotta be all loud. Dang."

He shakes his head. "You back in here again, Teena?"

She puts her hand on her hip as she sits on the bed. "And?"

"Why don't you just start making reservations?" he replies.

"Forget you, Harvey. Punk." Her nose flares open a little. "What's for breakfast?"

He looks at me sympathetically. "How you doin'?"

"Fine," I reply.

"Harvey." He nods.

"Shawni," I say, expressionless.

He glances down at the food. "You want some bacon?"

She stomps her foot. "Hell, yeah! And some eggs and grits, too."

I look away. "No, thanks."

Teena yawns. "Well, bring me hers and some damn orange juice, too." She retrieves her tray, and then stands there as he walks away. She yells after him. "And where's my Bible?"

He doesn't answer.

I have to get out of here. I march over to the phone again. If he doesn't accept my call this time . . .

"Collect from Shawni," I insist into the phone. I feel weak, and numb, like at any moment I'm going to faint.

A moment passes, and then the operator returns. "Go ahead with your call."

His voice is calm. "What, Shawni?"

"You asshole."

"Don't call me with that, Shawni."

"Do you have any idea where I am Bo? Any idea?"

He yawns. "They settle you down in there yet?"

"Look, whatever. Would you just go over and feed Sanford?"

"Sanford's cool."

"You fed him?"

"Yeah."

"Well, maybe you do have a heart."

"So, you're dealin' with Mr. Photography Man, Trip, now, huh? Shawni, damn. I try to give you the world, the finest things in life, and you'd rather settle for some simple ass pimp daddy lookin' fool?"

"Look, I just called to ask you to feed Sanford."

"I saw you grinnin' all up in his face at the club, then last night, out of nowhere, you bring his name up. So give it to me, for real. What do you have to say for yourself?"

I take a deep breath. "First, who was she?" I ask.

"Who was who?" he asks.

"Bo, you know what? Don't play dumb with me."

"I told you—a client. Damn. Got 'Ran over here questionin' me this morning, and I already told you what was up with her."

"When did she leave?"

"Who said she left?"

"She's still there?"

"What time did Zin leave?"

" 'Bye, Bo."

Click.

I don't believe this!

Suddenly, Harvey's voice commands my attention. "Sure you aren't hungry?" He's back with my tray of food. "I'm gonna give 'em both to Hungry Hippo over here." He winks at Teena.

She snatches the tray. "Give me my food." And then she looks at me. "Your frail ass need to eat somethin'."

I look away from her. "I'm not hungry."

Harvey smiles. "I got some doughnuts."

"No, thanks," I say.

Teena laughs. "Well, bring them glazed hos to me then. How come you ain't offer me no doughnuts? What? Just 'cause mine is sewn not grown don't make that longhaired ho no better than me. You got some glazed ones for real?"

Harvey appears not to pay any attention to her as he leaves, but I notice a soft laugh escaping from the side of his mouth as he turns to walk away.

A moment later Teena whispers to me, "So, what was all that about? Your man creepin' on you or somethin'?"

I do not answer her. I close my eyes, and try as hard as I can to go to sleep.

I tried to cry myself to sleep, careful not to make any noises that would indicate to Teena that I was afraid, but no tears would come. Too angry to cry, I slept in a ball in the corner, on the floor, throughout most of the day. I'd wake up every now and then to the sounds of Teena cursing at someone on the phone, or at the sounds of doors slamming somewhere in the distance. I imagined Mr. Doughnuts sitting with his feet propped on a desk, watching us on the surveillance camera, which I refuse to turn toward. I must look awful. So I turned to face the wall. Now, I'm face-to-face with Teena, who's bearing a strange expression, an awkward suggestion of disgust. What could she possibly be so disgusted about just by looking at me?

She's sitting up. "Why don't you just get up on the bed? Damn. You're makin' me uncomfortable," she says to me. "Aren't you tired of sleepin'? You been asleep all day."

I ignore her. If I'm still enough, she'll think I'm still sleeping.

She smacks her lips. "Bitch, I know you hear me, but it's cool. Stay your ass down there on the floor. I was just tryin' to be nice."

Nice? She just called me a bitch!

I'm so hungry, and I have to go to the bathroom again, and I hate going to the bathroom over there. I peek down at my fingernails, ragged and pathetic.

I wonder what Ernie is doing. I hope he's okay.

Despite my anger, a tiny part of me hopes Bo will be waiting for me, that things between us will revert back to the way they were, that this will all just be a bad dream.

I don't bother to look back at Teena as I step out of the cell. I feel her eyes on me, accompanied by her murmuring *you'll be back.*

I'm free now, and I've had to look at Teena long enough, so I do not turn back. I pause for a moment as I realize that no one ever brought her Bible, and I'm shocked by the sympathy I feel for her. Yes, it truly is a bitch to desire something, and to be completely unable to get it for yourself. Simple things, such as a Bible, should not have to be begged for. In a strange way I'm sorry that Teena can't leave with me, but I wash that thought away as the door closes behind me and the guard locks it again, locking Teena inside. She'll be back next week, begging again for a Bible, for attention, for orange juice. I will not.

The hallways don't seem as long as they did coming in. I turn the final corner, and for a split second I am disappointed, but just as quickly my heart flickers with relief. Duran's eyes are tired and uncertain as I approach him.

We sign the stupid papers in silence, both of our emotions muted on purpose. I don't even care when she tells me that the charges have been dropped, I already feel as if I've been through a prison term. All I want is to get home and take a long steaming hot bath in the whirlpool, and figure out how to feel like myself again.

Once we're outside, his voice is uncharacteristically somber, "You all right, sis?" he asks as he pulls me into his arms. I bury my face into his chest, and I am reminded of how simply wonderful that feeling is, so safe, so secure—my brother's arms.

Perhaps I'm too exhausted, perhaps too embarrassed, or maybe I'm too relieved, but I'm still unable to cry.

I hug him as tight as I possibly can. "Thank you," I say into his chest.

He pulls me tighter. "You're shaking."

And it's funny, I hadn't even realized, but he's right. I am.

I sigh as I peek out from his chest and catch a glimpse of my own hand. "They cut my nails off."

He looks down at my fingers, swallows at the sight, but doesn't say anything.

As we walk toward the car, I don't look up. I keep my head buried in Duran's chest, and he holds me. He doesn't let go until we reach the car, and I finally look up to see Mommie's Benz. I glance inside, but she isn't in there.

I look at him, "Mommie . . . ?"

"She's still in Aspen. I didn't call her." He unlocks the passenger door, and waits for me to get in.

He gets in on the driver's side, adjusts the rearview mirror, and starts the car. "Where do you wanna go eat?" he asks.

"Nowhere. Home." I lean my head back onto the headrest.

"Shawni, you need to eat. You're shaking. And you know, big brother would cook you somethin', but I'm not Delaney, not all skilled in the kitchen like that." He laughs as he whips through the parking lot.

I try to sound as calm as possible. "I just want to go home, okay? Can you just take me home?"

"Shawni," Duran slows down at the end of the parking lot, and stops before turning out into traffic. He glances in the sideview mirror. "Yo, isn't this your boy?" He honks at a blue minivan pulling up to the side of us. Ernie is hanging out the passenger side window, waving.

Duran rolls his window down. "What's up, man?"

"Chile, I'm just happy to be free!" He gestures with his wrists. "You all right, Bonnie?"

I nod, and say sincerely, "I'm sorry, Ernie."

"This, too, shall pass," he says.

I try to smile. Too weak. Too close to tears. Can't.

Duran nods at Ernie. "All right then, man, later."

The driver of the minivan, who I can't see, honks and pulls off.

"Duran, really," I say. "I'm tired. I just want to go home. Just take me home."

"I will, *after we eat*." He looks at me with a serious expression. "*After* we talk. You didn't tell me you dogged out Delaney's windows, Shawni."

I'd rather listen to Teena in prison than listen to the speech I know I'm in for from Duran. I close my eyes and sigh. "Just make it somewhere in Queens or something. Somewhere where I don't know anyone, okay?"

. "Cool with me, " he replies, and turns the volume up on the radio—Hot 97.

Duran is sitting across from me in the booth. Carly's Diner. Small and unnoticed by the average passerby, but the food has always been good here. He dumps another container of cream into my cup of coffee. "Drink up."

I stir it, blow it, and drink a little. Not because I want to, but because I have to remember what happened exactly, and stirring helps me think. Everything seems hazy.

"What got into you, Shawni?"

I drink some more of my coffee.

He looks baffled for a moment. "You really dogged Delaney's window with a brick?"

"I was upset."

"You were trippin'! All up at the club, all up on 'Sef. Delaney said he peeped you flirtin' with Trip. Yo! I peeped you givin' Zin the grin. Then I get a call from you in jail, gotta come bail you out! Man, I can think of a lot of people who'd do jail time, but not you. It's crazy, yo. I'm just straight up trippin'. So, what'd you do to him?"

"Who?"

"Bo! Shawni, chill. I get this call from you in the middle of the night from jail and you said you and Delaney had a fight. I would wreck things if he or anybody else ever did something to hurt you—and you know this—but Delaney didn't do anything. You're the one who went over there doggin' out windows and acting crazy. You didn't tell me all that."

"Nice of you to take his side."

"I'm not. I always have your back, but what you did was ill. I saw the damage. And you're up in his window wearing a ski mask? Sis, come on!"

"He wouldn't call me back, and I was freaking out about it. I went over there and there's this other woman over, Duran. I just lost it."

"Had you been drinking?"

"No."

"You would do something like that in your right frame of mind?"

"A friend stopped by and we got a little high—" I don't finish because Duran is giving me the eye. "What?" I ask.

"Trip?"

"What difference does it make who it was?"

He continues to give me the eye.

I look away.

"Getting high is stupid, Shawni. You see how stupid it made you act?"

You have no idea, my brother.

He continues, "And why is it okay for you to have Trip over but Delaney should get his windows dogged for having company?"

"You are taking his side!"

The waitress arrives at the table and puts Duran's blueberry pancakes and my wheat toast on the table. I pick at a piece of toast, and nibble on the edge.

"Put some jelly on that, Shawni," he says. "And this isn't about taking sides. It's about principle."

"I don't want jelly. Would you stop telling me what to do?" I roll my eyes.

Duran snatches the toast out of my hand and starts buttering it himself. He rips the top off a container of strawberry jelly and scrapes that on as well.

I watch, annoyed. "Why are you buttering my toast, Duran? I like it dry."

"Because you need to eat. You look like shit. Man, you know what it's like to see my sister all messed up like this, comin' out of jail over some punk shit?"

"Well, I happen to like it dry," I inform him.

"Eat," he says firmly.

I take a bite of the toast, and it does taste an awful lot better with jelly on it, but that's not the point.

We eat quietly, and I do everything to avoid looking at him, even though I know that he's staring at me. When I finally do look at him, his plate is empty, and he's looking at me, waiting.

I push my now-cold cup of coffee away. "Can we just go? I'm ready to go home."

He gives me a weird, sympathetic expression, but doesn't say anything.

"What?" I ask. Something's wrong. I can sense it.

"I'm gonna take you home, Shawni, but I just want you to be prepared."

"Prepared?" My heartbeats are noticeably heavier now. "Sanford?" I say weakly.

"Naw, Sanford's cool."

Whew. "Well, what, then?"

Duran says quietly, "Sanford's in Brooklyn."

"Okay," I nod. "No big deal. We'll stop in Brooklyn and pick him up."

"Delaney's ticked, Shawni. Real ticked. I think you need to just play it cool, all right? I just want you to play your cards a certain way."

"What do you mean play it cool?"

"Just listen to me, all right?"

Is this a joke? "Take me home, now."

"Shawni, listen to me," he demands. "I'm gonna tell you like it is, all right? You need to go home and get yourself together. Take a day or two and just reevaluate some things, figure out what you want, and focus on appreciating the things you have. 'Cause, I'm givin' it to you like this: You're my sister, and you know I'd do anything for you. Anything. But when you're wrong, I gotta keep it real with you. And you're wrong. You're stupid for getting high. You're out of line, and you need to check yourself. Delaney's my friend—yes—"

"But I'm your—"

"Yes!" He interrupts. "Let me finish. You're my sister—yes. Delaney's my boy—yes, but I know for a fact that he's a good man. He loves you. You need to go on ahead and step out of his world if you're not tryin' to be down with him, all right? That's all I'm asking you to do is reevaluate what you want."

"Whatever. Take me to Brooklyn to get my dog. Take me home."

"Shawni, you said yourself that you didn't think you were ready for marriage, all that stuff about men coming a dime a dozen. You're always talkin' that jazz. Then you're up in the club—"

"What about Bo! I'm telling you, there was a woman over there! What about that?"

"Yeah, well, you need to just let that ride. She's nobody, and I know this! Just like Trip. Just like my boy Zin. Understand? All I need is for you to promise me that you'll cool yourself off for a few days, just focus on trying to figure out what you really want. Then, when you holler at Delaney, you can come right with him. That's all I'm askin' you to do for me. Can you do that?"

"I want my dog."

"Well, technically, since everything's in his name . . ." He laughs. "I mean he did pay for the dog."

I glare at him. "Don't go there. You think you're so smart, using some sort of reverse psychology."

He looks at me sincerely. "All I'm sayin' is that I love you, sis. On the real."

"Just take me home."

"Are you gonna be okay? I can put some business on hold, stay with you tonight—no problem. How's that sound?"

I put my hand on my leg to try to stop my foot from tapping uncontrollably. "I'll be fine."

"Let's roll."

My walls never looked this white. Maybe it's because Bo just painted them a month ago, or maybe it's because the ones in jail looked as if they'd been painted with smut. It's quiet. No Sanford for now, but I'll get him soon enough. No Teena. No Duran—no way was I letting him come up and lecture to me for the rest of the day. I'm home, and all I need is me.

"You have no messages."

The light wasn't blinking, but I checked anyhow.

The entire way home all I could think about was taking a bath, washing my hair, scrubbing my face, putting on clean clothes—

something fluffy and comfy. I couldn't move quickly enough. Despite feeling refreshed now, I am still tired. In fact, after my marathon in the bathroom, I can barely muster the strength to slide under the sheets, but I do, and I'm delighted by how good my bed feels.

There is no quiet breathing of a canine in the room, no sounds of paws across the hardwood floor into the kitchen to gulp down water. No whining to go outside. This silence will take some getting used to, and I lie here, trying to do just that.

I turn on my back, find a comfortable position, and my ears find enjoyment in the noise that the water in the mattress makes. After it quiets down, I move again on purpose, realizing that the room sounds much better with noise.

The stereo in the living room seems like a journey away. Maybe if I close my eyes, keep them closed, relax, and ignore the silence, sleep will come.

It doesn't.

Although my body feels tired, I'm not really sleepy. Perhaps I need exercise as opposed to rest, to revitalize myself.

It's twelve noon, why should I be lying here in bed just because I've had a misery-packed weekend? Why not get up, get out, get some fresh air, and get my rhythm back? I don't need his credit card. Whatever. I unlock my safe, grab some cash, and call for a car.

Ten blocks down Madison Avenue, and five down Fifth, and I can't decide which store to go into. Oddly, I am unable to decide what it is that I even want to buy. I can't remember what's fashionably in for this season, and then I'm disturbed by the fact that I even tried to remember. I've always been a trendsetter, so why do I even care what anyone else is wearing?

My determined march across Forty-second Street is suddenly jolted, and I lose my balance as someone shoves me from behind. A hand, however, immediately helps me regain my balance.

"My fault," a male voice says. "Are you okay?"

I look up at the tanned and smiling face of the dark-haired young man who has pulled me out of the flow of walking traffic, and has now stopped walking himself. He stuffs his basketball under his arm, and looks concerned. He's wearing New Balance gear from head to toe, like either he just stepped off the court or he's a spokesman for that line of athletic gear.

"These people are pushing," he says. "That guy almost knocked me down."

"I'm fine." I smile.

"Nice smile. You a model?" He grimaces at a passerby who brushes against him. "See what I'm saying? People keep pushin' like it's really that big of a rush. You from around here? I'm from Louisiana, not used to this."

"Oh, holiday traffic, Monday before Thanksgiving," I say. I start walking, but beach boy pulls my forearm again.

"Are you a model?" he asks again.

"No. Are you on *Baywatch*?" I try to keep walking.

"*Baywatch?*" He scrunches up his eyebrows. "Why'd you ask that?"

"What makes you think I'm a model?" I say, trying to pick up my pace.

"I was just askin'. You look like one." He keeps up with me.

I remind myself that I don't care what this charming kid from Louisiana thinks. I don't care if I live my entire life without another man's approval. I walk faster, but beach boy does, too. I look back at him and courteously say, "No, I'm not a model. Thanks."

"Why'd you ask if I play on *Baywatch*?" he asks.

"Same reason. You just look the beach-boy type."

"Oh, now, that's funny." He softly touches my arm. "Hey, can you stop a minute?"

I do. And I'm unable to be as annoyed as I'd like to be. This boy next door seems so sweet, and I wish I could just be myself because normally I'd enjoy this conversation, but I can't. I sigh. "What?"

"It's so hard to meet people here." He looks distraught. "I'm in town with my church's youth group that I coach for. All I've been around is junior high school boys every day of this entire tournament, and I'm getting ready to go bonkers. I'm eager to get out and meet some adults, you know? But no one stops to talk to anyone around here," he says.

"Welcome to New York. Sometimes you don't want to stop and talk to someone."

He tosses his ball up in the air. "Oh. That's why everyone seems so tense?"

Do I look like an official tour guide to understanding New Yorkers, or what?

He tilts his head. "You're just so gosh darn pretty. My wife loves those *Glamour* and *Vogue* magazines. She told me to get an autograph if I saw a model, and I just thought you ought to be one."

I don't feel like being so polite anymore. My face is distorting into a frown, but I consciously shake away the tension, swallowing the heaviness in my throat.

I turn to basketball boy. "I'll tell you what—stand outside the Condé Nast Building, that big gray building right up the street here. That's where a lot of fashion magazines are housed. You're bound to see one coming or going eventually. Then you can get your wife an autograph."

He looks baffled for a moment, and then he says, "Okay."

"Have a good one." I turn away.

"Hey, wait," he says.

I look back at him.

"Did I offend you? I didn't mean to."

I do the best I can to conjure up a grin. "Of course not."

He yells at me as I walk away. "You ought to head over there, too, you know? Let 'em sign you up for the cover." He laughs.

I turn around, want to yell to him, but he's gone. There are only faces now. Too many strangers looking at me. I suddenly realize that I'm standing near the middle of Times Square, directly in front of the ESPN Zone restaurant, and I've stopped walking. My heart rate is dashing and my breathing is frantic. I can't remember where I'm going.

No tears, but the verge is so much more intense.

If there were a musical score to accompany this scene in my life, it would be blaring right now. Heavy brass. Loud drums. Clashing cymbals.

I want to run, but my feet won't move.

I look around.

Businessmen.

UPS men. FedEx men.

Dreadlocked men.

Tall men.

Short men.

Black men. White men. Spanish men. Jamaican men.

Smiling men. Men smiling at me.

Men.

I want to close my eyes, to escape, but I need to see the path back to Fifth Avenue, and I need to get back to Baby Blue. I need to get in my car. To go home. And then I realize that there is no Baby Blue to get into.

I put my stilettos to motion, and quickly make my way to the nearest corner. For once I am thankful for the cabdrivers that force their way across traffic to stop for someone who may or may not need a ride. The someone is me, and I do. I climb in, blurt out my address, and pull the door closed.

I'll be okay as soon as I get home, I try to convince myself.

Only, in my heart, I know that what Duran has always said is right. I'm a terrible liar.

"Hello," he answers.

"Bo," I say, annoyed by my own confusion and desperation.

"Shawni," he says, his voice softer than I've heard lately.

I don't know what to say, can't remember why I called.

The volume from his television fades. Football.

How can he be watching football when I just got out of jail!

He clears his throat. "We need to talk."

My eyes. They won't blink. My heart? It is still. I don't like what my instincts tell me his tone of voice is saying.

"Uh," I laugh nervously, and bite my tongue to stop the tears. "I think we do."

"I'm tired," he says bluntly.

Something tells me that he doesn't necessarily mean he's in need of a nap.

He sucks his teeth. "I give all I can. You said you were tired of livin' with your mother, that you finally wanted to move out, and I tell you, baby, come live with me. You say no, you want your own pad, you've never had that, and you want to experience being on your own. I tell you to find a spot that you love, and it's yours. You said your favorite color was blue. I give you the keys to a new Lexus—*blue*. It's yours. You wanna go here, you wanna go there—wherever. Baby, what do I always do? Whatever you want. 'Cause it makes me feel so damn good seeing you happy, seeing that smile.

You wanna stop modeling, I tell you I'll take care of you. I'm not a perfect man—far from it—but what'd I ever ask of you? I'm not hard to please. Just be there. Be mine."

His voice quiets, but then I hear a loud bang, as if he threw something. He doesn't say anything for several moments. Only breathing.

My mind races. "Bo?"

"What!" he retorts.

"You're right," I say. "And that's what I've been trying to tell you. It's not you, it's me."

I cannot *believe* I just said that! It's not you, it's me? How old and trite is that?

But it's true.

He laughs a little. "Not me, huh? Yeah, well that's not hard to believe. I don't know what else I can do for you, Shawni. Damn straight it's you."

"Can you just try to be there for me?"

"Shawni."

"Yes?"

"I need some space."

"What?"

Those are *my* words! I've said those words before—to so many nice guys. But not Bo, never Bo, he's a keeper. I don't need space from you, Bo. Don't you dare use that line on me!

"Baby," he says, "you need some space, too."

"What are you saying?" I hold my chest. "Are you breaking up with me?"

"I don't think we can be together right now. I'm not up for these bullshit games."

"Games? Bo, who's playing games? Who was that bitch I saw

getting up from your couch? What about that? Who was she? You wanna talk about games?"

"She's just a friend from law school. I told you that, woman. Obviously you just don't trust me."

"That's nerve! You were acting all insecure the other night."

"Whoa! Bo Delaney is a lot of things, but I'm not insecure."

"If you say so."

He waits a moment. "Let's just play it by ear. You let me know when you've found another place, so I can get out of the lease."

"Excuse me? So, now what, you want me to move out?"

Silence.

I clear my throat. "Bo? Are you telling me to find somewhere else to live?"

"I'm not saying you have to be out today."

"Fine!"

He sucks his teeth. "Look, this doesn't have to be ugly, Shawni. We can handle this like the two adults we are. I'll be considerate of your—"

"Oh, don't patronize me!" And I hang up. Only I think I hear him beat me to it.

I position myself at my vanity table, smooth its skirt down, and fold my hands across the top of it. Shawni Baldwin, I tell myself, you are going to be okay.

Images, twenty years ago, of me in this same position—sitting at a vanity table, talking to myself, suddenly play across my mind. Mommie's table was much larger, or so it seemed, but I used to sit there and long to be where I am today. Grown up.

I pucker, glance down at the tube of lipstick, and the pink seems too dull, so I put it down. I relax my lips and dig around in my case of lipsticks for brighter shades. There are dozens to choose from, but I keep shuffling through them, and I can't decide. Reds. Oranges. Browns. Berries. Pinks. Maybe I can't pick because I'm not really thinking about selecting a color to paint my lips with, but instead I'm stressing over the fact that I'm getting ready . . . for nothing.

My doorbell is not going to ring.

Darling, peek out the window, she used to say when we'd hear a car door. See if that's Daddy.

And I could hear the sounds of Duran down below, hurrying to the door. Daddy's here, he would yell up to us.

I'd look over at Mommie sitting at her table, so beautiful.

It meant she was going to have a marvelous evening out, and she was going to come home late, and I would be lying there, determined to be awake when she came in. Sometimes I'd manage to stay up, but other times she would accidentally wake me, creeping up the stairs. Occasionally there would be other footsteps. Daddy. I would squint to see their shadows easing toward her bedroom. Heavy-eyed, I'd blink my way through a prayer for Daddy to still be there in the morning. He never was. Not once.

The family outings that the four of us shared were few. I'm remembering the time when Daddy took us to a festival, and there was a carousel. I must have been seven or eight, but I rode it anyhow and Mommie and Daddy accompanied me. Duran was a few feet away, sitting atop a fence, laughing, teasing me for riding such a kiddie ride, but I didn't care. Mommie was standing on one side of me. Daddy was on the other. Both of them protecting me from falling.

I scoot my chair up now, and try to get as close to the mirror as I possibly can. I don't look so different after all these years. My face, my hair—minus the ponytails of course—and my skin all seem the same. My eyes though . . . My eyes have changed. I hadn't noticed.

I snatch a tube of mascara, and eagerly apply some to my eyelashes.

My eyes, whether made up or not, are different now.

Where is the sparkle that used to flash back at me when I stared into the mirror?

No matter how hard you try, Shawni, those eyes aren't going to shine.

You were a little girl then, Shawni. It's gone. That's right, look away.

I fumble up from the chair. If I can just make it into the living room. There are no mirrors in there.

In the living room, I reach the bar. A bottle of vodka. Too weak to pour it, but I hold it tightly. My head aching, my body exhausted, I sit down and grip the side of the couch.

And I couldn't move, two nights ago, this very same spot, away from the singe of cruel fire. And it was my fault. I shouldn't have played with it.

I swallow it dry. It's tasteless.

The window behind the couch, behind me, is cracked open, and there's a breeze coming in. I turn around and look out, and my neck is stiffening. The wind is so pleasant—November air. No pretty view to enjoy, though. Luxurious place with every amenity you could want, but even with such lavishness it's still New York, and my view is of a fire escape.

I turn back around, eye the CD shelf. I should get up, put a CD in—stop the silence, too loud for my headache.

And this confirms it. I must be going crazy. Because I have not gotten up, I have not put a CD in the player, but I suddenly hear singing.

A voice, from somewhere. *"I sing because I'm haa-aaaa-pyyyy . . ."*

The window can't be singing.

"I sing because I'm freeee-eeeee . . ."

I blink a few times as I make my way over to the window. It's not the window singing, I realize as I look out, and down below.

"His eye . . . is on . . . the spaaarrrr-rowwww . . ."

A woman is standing on the fire escape below me. I can see the top of her head—long, skinny braids. Dressed in a flowered house-coat, she is sweeping, unaware that I am up here listening—peeking down at her as she sings in an alto voice, effortlessly soulful.

"And I know-ohhh, He watches . . . He watches meeeee . . ."

I close my eyes, gripping the bottle tighter, letting the breeze caress my face, and I listen.

"I singggg becaaause I am haaaap-pee."

Happy.

"I sing beeeecaaaaaause I'm free-eeeeee . . ."

Free.

"His eye—"

I slam the window shut; everything is too loud. Her voice, though muffled, is chasing me. The breeze is gone, and now there isn't enough air in the room. The bottle is gripped in my hand, but I do not want to drink anymore. I want to rest.

I look down at my hands, what is left of my fingernails, and I think of her words. She said I had it all, and I wasn't grabbing it. For the first time I see that my hands are her hands. My opportunities were her chances.

Who will I become?

Happy. Free.

I wish the noises would slow down. Too loud. The floor, so hard, stops my fall.

A male voice says, "Chile . . ."

My eyes hesitate, and then open.

My teeth chattering, but without sound, and in slow motion.

So chilly in here.

Faces. Several of them. Sad. A uniform. Police. All so mournful. Voices.

A hand grips mine. Mine feels puffy.

His voice, familiar, speaks again, hollow and far away. It sounds like an echo, coming closer with every word. "When it rains, it pours."

And his face, though my vision is blurred, is becoming recognizable.

And now his voice is clear, as he says, "But this here is a monsoon."

Ernie.

SIX

Severance Agreement

I remember a dullness, a muted feeling. I remember trying in vain to think, to be conscious, to come back to being, to feel again. I remember wanting to lift my arm—too heavy. I remember gritting my teeth, and holding my breath. I remember wanting so bad to let go of something, and realizing that it was someone's hand, and then not wanting to let go. I remember being too weak to cry, but still feeling tears on my face. I remember opening my mouth, and the smell of alcohol.

I'm lying here now, squinting, trying to see, and I don't remember getting in this bed, nor do I recall anyone putting what looks like a tube in my arm.

All of me hurts.

I'm moaning, wanting to open my eyes, needing someone to help me open my eyes, because I can't seem to stay conscious long enough, but every time I try to speak, to ask for help, no words come out. It's like a nightmare, and I want to wake up from it, but I can't, so I just accept it and keep sleeping. I think for a moment that someone is flickering the lights on and off, but I'm realizing now that those are my eyelids opening and closing.

Someone is kissing my face. My skin feels sweaty.

"Stop," I hear myself mumble.

"No," a voice whispers and kisses my cheek again.

I'm struggling, determined to keep my eyes open; and when I'm finally able to, he leans in for another kiss—this time on my lips, and I see an image of Bo as he pulls away, after kissing me again.

"Bo?" I hear myself whisper.

"Shhh." He kisses me again.

"Where's . . . ?" I can't remember what I was going to ask.

A different voice speaks this time, a woman. "Is she waking up?" Mommie.

I am able to keep my eyes open now as I turn my head. She's walking toward me; her salt-and-pepper hair is pulled back into a bun, and her eyes are puffy, red-stained, and anxious.

Mommie, are you crying? I try to ask, but the words do not come out.

Her face approaching. I'm startled by her expression. Fear. She leans down and rubs my arm, and her tennis bracelets make a clinking noise against the railing of the bed.

She looks down at me, her eyes concerned. "How do you feel?" she asks.

"My head hurts." I am shocked and relieved that I actually hear the words this time. I attempt to sit up. Bo gently pushes my shoulder back down.

"Lie down," he says quietly.

I'm remembering a dry feeling in my mouth. I recall asking someone what was happening to me. I remember someone wiping the tears off my face. Ernie. A cold chill in a hallway. Screaming.

"You want some water, baby?" Bo kisses me another time.

Why does he keep kissing me?

"No," I reply. "Where's Ernie?" I ask, my voice hoarse, my throat sore.

Mommie rubs my arm gently. "He went home, darling. He was here all night. I told him to go get some rest."

All night?

Bo brushes my hair, and it feels like it's hard and clumpy. "You feel okay, baby?" he asks.

Mommie taps my arms. "I'll go get the doctor," she says, before hurrying out of the room.

The doctor? This is a hospital room?

Bo's voice is soothing, but different, as if he's uneasy, but straining to not sound uneasy. "We're gonna get you home. Get you back to health." He says it as if it's a question rather than a statement, almost like he wants to add "if that's okay with you."

"What's . . . ?" I start to ask what's wrong with me, but then I remember.

Someone pounding at the door. Not being able to get up.

Bo is squeezing my hand, grasping for confidence. "You'll come to Brooklyn, baby. We're gonna make this right."

A new voice with a Jamaican accent fills the room. "Hey, trooper."

A short, petite, dark-skinned woman wearing blue scrubs walks toward me. She smiles, "They tell me you're feeling a little better, hmmm?" She retrieves a stethoscope from around her neck.

I jump at the touch of the cold metal she puts on my chest. "I'm not sick," I say.

She nods. "Are you having a hard time remembering?" She takes my hand in hers. "Squeeze my hand for me?"

I squeeze quickly. Now, leave me alone. I'm not sick.

I close my eyes and swallow hard, and it hurts.

Bo continues to brush my hair with his hand as the doctor continues to talk.

I wish he would stop touching me.

I open my eyes, and shove him in his stomach. "Would you stop?"

Everyone stares at me. Shocked.

I glare at Bo but try to soften my tone of voice. "Please?"

He looks hurt, offended, embarrassed. He sucks his teeth, gets up, and walks out of the room.

Soon after he leaves, Dr. Jamaican-Accent takes a really deep breath. "Care to tell me what you remember about yesterday? The events that took place?"

I shrug. "I wasn't feeling well."

She makes a ticking noise with her tongue as she reads my chart.

I close my eyes, begin wishing as hard as I can for this woman to go away, disappear. "I just felt really ill," I say.

She nods. "Ah, I see."

I tilt my head. "Normally, I'm fine."

She hums a little, makes that ticking noise again, and takes another deep breath. "Any new circumstances in your life lately? Major emotional changes that could cause such a psychological collapse?"

I close my eyes, begin wishing again. Go away, woman. Go home to Jamaica, find a way to get your groove back. "Nope. I got engaged recently. That's about it," I say. Now, can you leave me alone?

"Ah," she replies. "I've met Mr. Delaney." She tugs on my toe, which has a startling effect, causing my eyes to widen. She's smiling. "I do believe that just a moment ago was the first time I've seen his eyes dry since you arrived here yesterday."

Mommie, whom I'd almost forgotten was still in the room, adds, "We all love her so much."

The doctor tugs my toe again. "I can tell." She glances at the door. "I'll be back soon, to talk some more, Ms. Baldwin. I'm juggling right now."

I nod. "Juggle on."

My wish finally comes true. She leaves.

And then I remember. My fiancé also just dumped me. I'm not engaged anymore.

"Shawni," Mommie walks to the foot of the bed, puts her hands on her hips, and frowns. "You are being very impolite to Bo and to your doctor. Do you realize how happy we are that you're okay?"

I moan as I pull my arm up to see what is irritating my hand, and then remember the tube. "What is this?"

She forces my arm back down on the mattress and stares at me viciously. "You almost died. Do you realize how dehydrated you are?" She suddenly reaches up and covers her mouth, and her face distorts into a strange frown. Her voice cracks. "Shawni . . ."

I clear my throat. "My throat hurts."

She's wipes a tear and pinches her nostrils together. "I'm not surprised."

"My head hurts." It's stuffy, like there's cotton in my ears, and people keep adding more.

"The doctor said—" she begins.

"I need some Tylenol," I interrupt. "I don't care what the doctor said. My throat hurts."

Her tennis bracelets are even louder this time, clinking on the railing. She takes a deep breath before pulling me by my chin—her cologne overpowering me. And then she says softly, "Do you have any idea how happy I am to hear your voice?"

"Mommie . . ." I say through clenched teeth.

She pulls my chin again. And then she lets go. And then she leans over me, and her lips meet my forehead. A firm kiss on my forehead is followed by one of her wet tears landing on my face.

I squint, bite my tongue—do anything to hold back the tears.

She whispers in my ear. "I love you so much."

I bite my tongue again. "I just didn't feel good, that's all."

She gently rubs my arm. "I know," she says. She clears her throat. "Your brother's out in the waiting room. He'll want to know that you're awake now."

I close my eyes and listen to her heels leave the room.

I love you, too, Mommie.

It's funny how you can associate certain scents with people. I must have drifted off to sleep, but now I feel someone kiss my cheek, and I recognize the smell of his hair gel—minty—before I even open my eyes.

I look up to see his face, tearstained, with a steady stream of new tears, and I immediately close my eyes again.

"Duran." I force a smile, still refusing to cry. "I'm okay."

He tries to sound strong. "I shouldn't have left you there by yourself."

"Duran." I nod away his words. I look up at him, still forcing a smile. "Really, I'm okay."

"What's wrong, Shawni?"

I look around the room, making sure that he and I are alone.

Then I realize that I don't know for sure what's wrong. So I don't answer.

I close my eyes. Was there ever a time when Duran didn't use that brand of hair gel? I enjoy the scent.

"Did Daddy come?" I ask him.

He doesn't answer. That means no.

A soft knock on the door wakes me up. I look up and Bo peeks in. He waits a moment before stepping all the way in, and he's holding a tiny plush white teddy bear in one hand, a paper cup in the other. Mommie and Duran are sitting at the foot of my bed, and Bo hands Mommie the cup.

He smiles at her. "Cream, no sugar, right?"

She nods. "That's very sweet." She touches Duran's arm, "Shawni, your brother and I are going to step out for a moment. We'll be back," she says before they leave.

Bo walks over to my bed, sits the teddy bear on the table next to me, and waits a long time before he speaks. When he finally does, I can't even bring myself to look at him.

He sighs. "Shawni. I just . . ." And then he sighs again. His hand cupped over his eyes, he doesn't complete his sentence.

I try to pull myself up, but roll my eyes at the stupid tubes coming out of my hand, and just lie here instead.

He grips the railing. "Baby, when I got that call. Ernie was so frantic. My heart just . . . Damn, baby . . . You don't know. What would I have done if he had told me what I thought I was about to hear? I thought I was never going to talk to you again, the way Ernie was screaming."

"I'm glad you know he has a name now," I say as halfheartedly as possible.

"What?" he asks quietly, confused.

"Thank you," I say, "for not calling him out of his name for a change."

"Yeah . . ." he replies. "I got you a little teddy bear. I thought he might make you smile. Figured he'd have better luck than me." He picks up the tiny white teddy bear, and holds him out to me. A blue silk bow around his neck.

I eye the bear, not wanting to care. "Cute," I say unenthusiastically.

Bo simply nods, puts the bear back on the table, and sits down on one of the chairs.

"Shawni," he says gently, "I've never felt so disconnected from you. Help me understand what's wrong? Please."

That may be the first time I've ever heard Bo use the word *please*.

I fall asleep knowing that he's sitting there, staring at me, but I do not reply.

"Where's Mommie?" I ask him as I sit up in bed, notice the Jell-O in front of me, and decide to nibble on it.

It's Wednesday evening, and obviously Bo isn't going anywhere, so I may as well talk to him. He's sitting over there, looking up at ESPN's SportsCenter—football highlights—and he turns to look at me, visibly surprised that I've started a conversation with him for the first time since I woke up yesterday morning. He smiles a little. "Uh, 'Ran took her home to get some rest. You were asleep, and they just decided to slip out. Ernie called again, wanted to know how you were feeling."

I answer dryly. "I feel fine."

He gets up and turns the television off, walks over to my bed, readjusts the railing, and slides in beside me. Only half of his solid body will fit, so I scoot over, giving him as much room as possible. He takes the spoon from my hand, and starts feeding me the Jell-O, his body so warm next to mine, and he smells so good, a breezy scent. His brown turtleneck feels so soft as his arm touches mine.

I take a bite of the Jell-O and then push the spoon away. "I don't want anymore," I say.

He eyes my fingernails curiously.

"Yeah, you see what they did to me? That's what they do to women in prison, you know."

He chuckles. "Baby, you did not go to prison. There's a big difference."

"Whatever. I don't want any more Jell-O."

"Okay." He puts the spoon down. "Glad you ate that much."

He takes my hand and affectionately kisses each of my fingernails, taking his time on each one. "It's messing with my mind—seeing you in here like this. And I can't fix it."

I look away. "Hmmm . . ." I shrug. "And what if I weren't in here?"

"It was driving me crazy not seeing you," he replies, still kissing them.

"You're the one who said you needed space."

He takes a deep breath, gently letting my hand go. "What the hell was I supposed to do? I'd rather walk away, be one up, than stick around and get played, baby. I won't do it." He pauses. "But I'm not leaving your world until I know you're okay. I mean that." His kiss against my forehead is warm and quick. "You know you're my boo."

It's one of those moments. I don't know if it's necessarily surrendering, but it's realizing that not giving in is taking up too much of your energy. And all of a sudden you'd rather just end the battle, because it's too difficult to remember why you're fighting in the first place. And in your heart you know that you really don't want to fight anymore, even if you would never admit that.

I hold up my hand, tubes and all, spread my fingers apart, and wait for him to put his hand in mine. He does. Truce. I sigh.

He pulls my hand to his lips, and kisses it—hard. I immediately feel that twinge in my stomach, that tingly feeling that only Bo's kisses produce, and I silently hope that he doesn't let go. And he doesn't.

Dr. Jamaica said I could go home. I acted as if I were happy, because it seemed appropriate, but actually, I think I should stay here longer. I think they should ask me more questions.

Bo seems happier than even I do when the doctor leaves the room. "I'll help you get dressed." He rubs my knee. "You'll rest better at home. I want you to come with me to Brooklyn." He stands up.

Although I'd rather go home to Soho I don't bother to say anything. As long as I can sleep, a few nights in Brooklyn will be okay.

Glorious uninterrupted sleep.

Bo helps me up, and I notice a fluffy baby blue cotton jogging suit at the foot of the bed. The blue, I admit, does make me smile a little.

He grins, a pleased look of accomplishment. "Now there's my little smile."

Okay, I feel a little weak, but hardly enough for a wheelchair. I'm so irritated as I sit here waiting at the curb in front of the entrance to the hospital, a nurse standing behind me just in case I roll away in this thing. So unnecessary.

Finally, Bo pulls up in Baby Blue, and he gets out to help me into the car. "Thank you." He nods to the nurse.

She waves at me, a look of concern. "Take care of yourself."

I nod, and Bo replies, "We'll take good care of her."

I wait for him to get in on the driver's side. "Where's the Denali?" I ask.

He puts the car in drive, and shrugs a little. "The shop. Had a little scratch on the window. Nothing the car doctor can't fix." He winks.

"Oh." I nod, remembering again.

He pulls up to a stop sign, and leans over to reach into the glove compartment, pulling out a key ring that's holding three shiny silver keys. He slips his index finger into the ring, twirls it around a few times, and laughs. Just as he is about to pull away from the stop sign, he gently drops the keys into my lap.

I stare down at them, confused. "What?" I look at the keys.

"I want you to stay in Brooklyn—with me."

"What?" I ask, not sure if I heard him correctly, hoping that I didn't hear him correctly.

"Your own set of keys. We can worry about the other place later."

"Bo . . ." I sigh.

"Well, you know," he says proudly. "Your mother wanted you to stay with her. Ernie wanted you to stay with him. 'Ran was ready to move in with you in Soho. But I want you to—"

"What are you talking about? Since when do I have to live with anyone?"

He drives in silence for a moment, his mood changing to serious. "Baby, you know we can't let you be alone right now."

"What?" I snap my eyes at him.

"This is serious business here, Shawni. The doctor doesn't think you should be alone."

"You know what? Let me tell you something. I don't care what you or the doctors or Ernie or anyone else thinks. Okay? None of you!"

"Okay." He nods. "But you're still coming to Brooklyn."

"Sorry about your door," Ernie's voice says after I answer the phone.

"What door?" I sit up in the bed, Bo's black satin sheets causing me to slide a little bit.

Ernie smacks his lips. "Oh, well then, you must not remember when we had to pry it open? Chile, you were out of it! Eyes rollin' all up in your head like that damn *Exorcist* movie. Mess comin' all out your mouth. Shoot, if Ricci Malone had seen what I saw he would have said hell naw I didn't want her to model for me—shoot, that chile is tore up from the floor up."

I laugh. "Ernie . . ."

"It's good to hear you laugh," he says, and then he whispers. "Answer me—yes or no. Is Baldy-man still standing right there?"

I hear Bo in the bathroom, and answer, "No."

"Good. Now, I just want you to tell me right now. Do you want to stay there with him? Because, chile, my place is yours. I'll come get you. You want to leave, get out of there, call me. Just call me and say Clyde, it's me Bonnie—that'll be the code, and I'll be on my way, okay?"

I smile. "I'll be okay, Ernie. He's actually being really sweet."

"Yeah," he replies. "A guilty conscience will work the hell out of you. Well, you know who to call if you want to leave," he says.

I'm lying in bed, and I look up to see Bo standing in the doorway. He yells for Sanford to get off the satin bedspread. Each time Bo yells, Sanford jumps down, waits a moment, and then jumps right back up to lie down next to me.

"Bo, let him stay," I whine, and playfully pat Sanford's head. "He missed me."

"Damn." Bo frowns at Sanford.

"Be nice to my dog!" I playfully warn him.

He gives Sanford another disgusted look, and then looks at me. "What do you want to eat?"

"I'm sleepy. Nothing." I push my head further into the pillow and continue rubbing Sanford.

"You have to eat," he says to me, and then looks back at San-ford. "All right, dog, get on down."

Sanford jumps down, but stands next to the bed and begins licking my face.

Bo groans. "Lettin' that dog lick all on your face! Go on, now," he commands Sanford.

Sanford whines, but after a moment he resentfully trots out of the room.

"He just misses me," I say.

A chuckle escapes from Bo's mouth, and he tries to fight off a smile as he walks over to the bed and lies down next to me. "You couldn't get a cute little terrier or something?" He lays his head on my shoulder.

"You know I like my men big." I laugh and kiss the top of his head.

"So that's the only reason you love us, me and Sanford, because we're big?"

"Yup," I say jokingly as he rubs my leg.

He leans his head back and looks up at me. His mustache so perfectly thin, his skin so rich and dark. "That's it, huh?" He smiles.

"Well, Sanford's cute. *You*, on the other hand, I don't know." I laugh.

"Yeah, all right." He lays his head back on my shoulder and continues rubbing my leg.

"I'm sorry about the Denali," I whisper and enjoy his soft caresses.

"I'm sorry, too, baby. We've both been acting so childish." He stops rubbing for a moment. "Everything is going to be okay."

"Shawni, it's your mother," Bo's voice wakes me up as he forces the phone into my hand.

I roll over and mumble, "I'll call her back."

"Shawni, come on, she's been calling all day." He puts the phone up to my ear anyhow.

All day? What time is it?

"You're still sleeping?" Mommie's voice says.

"What time is it?" I moan as I notice the night seeping in through the curtains.

Bo pauses before leaving the room. "Almost eleven o'clock."

Man I have been asleep for a long time. "Hi, Mommie," I sigh.

"Go back to sleep, darling. I have Daddy on the three-way. He just wanted to say hello."

"Daddy?" My heart leaps as I open my eyes.

His voice is gentle and sympathetic. "Hi, kitten. How do you feel?"

"Hi," I yawn as I sit up. "I'm okay. Just tired."

"I called you in the hospital, but you were resting. It's probably a virus."

A virus?

"Yeah, I'm okay," I say.

Mommie interrupts. "Shawni hasn't been taking very good care of herself. Bo said she's barely eating."

"I eat plenty. Daddy, are you still coming for Christmas?"

"I'll be there," he replies. "I wanted to be there tomorrow for Thanksgiving, but . . ."

But what, Daddy? Say it. Come on. Go ahead.

Mommie's voice cuts in again. "Darling, Shawni needs her rest."

"I'm sure." Daddy sighs. "Listen, Shawni, Mommie tells me you're finalizing plans for the wedding?"

"Yeah . . ." I look over at Bo, who's changing into his pajamas.

His purple silk pajamas . . .

Daddy sounds pleased. "Good. Well, listen, keep me posted. Your mother can just forward me the bills. July will be here before you know it."

"I know, Daddy."

"Well, kitten," he says, "get your rest. I'll see you soon, okay?"

"Okay."

And Mommie adds, "Shawni, I'll be checking on you."

"Okay."

And I hang up the phone and sigh.

Bo pulls the covers back on the other side of the bed, and crawls in beside me. "I wanted to let you sleep, but she's been calling all day. Why don't you get out of your clothes, get cozy?"

I smell something cooking, and ask, "What's that?"

"The turkey—gonna let it cook overnight."

He's wearing the same purple pajamas he had on that night.

He notices me staring at his legs. "What's wrong, baby?"

"Nothing."

He yawns. "You want some soup or something?"

"No." I turn away from him and allow my head to sink back into the pillow.

"You need to eat something, you haven't all day." His slips his arm around my waist and pulls my body in toward his.

"I said I'm not hungry." I push his arm off of me.

He could at least have the decency to wear a different pair of pajamas.

He raises his voice. "Why'd you push me away like that?"

I squeeze my eyes closed. "I'm sleepy."

"So, what. Now I can't hold you because you're sleepy?"

"Just drop it."

He doesn't say anything for a moment, but his breathing gets heavier.

He finally speaks. "Drop what?"

I don't answer. I just want to go back to sleep.

He sucks his teeth. "So, I get ignored now, huh?"

"I'm sleepy," I say again.

He laughs a quick, fake laugh, and then I feel him get up from the bed and walk toward the door. He kicks the garbage can. "I'll be basting the damn turkey if you need me," he says before he leaves the room.

I pull the blanket over my head. "Turn the light off," I yell.

A moment later the room slams into darkness.

Magnificent darkness.

Sleep. Glorious . . .

"I dreamt about Duran last night," I break the morning silence between us.

Bo doesn't look away from the stove. "Yeah, he called last night. I told him you were, you know, sleepy."

"Well, I was. What do you want me to say? I was exhausted. I still am."

He retrieves the pitcher of orange juice from the refrigerator, grabs a glass, puts it on the table in front of me, and pours it full. "Vitamin C should help—I can't seem to."

I roll my eyes at the glass. "Thanks."

He goes back to the omelets. "So, what'd you dream?"

"I don't know. I just know he was in it." I pick up the glass and clear my throat

He turns back to look at me. "What?"

"Bo, you know I don't drink orange juice. The acid."

He comes over and snatches the glass from me, which causes a few drops of juice to splash onto my face.

I sigh. "You didn't have to snatch."

"What do you want to drink then?"

"Nothing."

He pulls open the refrigerator door and takes out a plastic jug of water, and pours some of it into a clean glass. "Here," he says, slamming the glass down in front of me.

I just stare at it. I never drink water without lemon. He knows that.

I get up, retrieve a slice of lemon from the refrigerator, and squeeze it into my water.

And I know that this is so not about the lemon, but I don't know what to say.

A few moments later he sits a warm plate in front of me, and a picture perfect omelet stares up at me.

He sits down across from me and begins eating his omelet. In a tone of voice suggesting an effort to be polite, he asks, "So, how'd you sleep?"

"Fine," I try to match his tone of voice. "And you?"

"Well, besides the fact that every time I get an inch too close to you, you're tellin' me to scoot over, I think I slept okay."

I barely even remember him getting back into bed.

"Bo, I was tired, why can't you understand that?"

He continues to eat his omelet, but in silence.

I look down at mine, and I haven't taken a single bite.

I glance over at the stove and notice that sitting on top of it is a pan holding a golden brown turkey, stalks of celery sticking out of it.

I nod at it. "The turkey looks great."

"My parents invited us over, but I told them we were gonna chill out over here this year. I didn't tell them why."

"Why not?"

"Because they'd ask too many questions."

"Nothing to ask."

"Oh?"

"Nope. I'm fine."

He sucks his teeth. "Well, I'd rather us spend some time alone anyhow."

I shrug. "Okay."

He looks down at my untouched omelet. "Woman, why aren't you eating?"

"I'm really not hungry."

"Baby, you have to eat."

I push my chair back and get up from the table. "I'll eat it later," I say, as I start up the stairs. "I'm going to take a shower."

I usually prefer my water to be as hot as I can endure, so hot that it's an intense pleasure, but I adjust it to cool instead. Pleasure is not the goal, escape is. I decide to let it run for a few minutes while I undress.

I stare at myself in the mirror, the sound of water trickling a musical score to the sad and pitiful reflection that listlessly gazes back at me.

My hair looks horribly greasy. My eyes are horrid—dark and sunken—and my lips are chapped, stained white. I need a facial. I need my hair set. I need Ernie. I need to get away. To sleep.

I've never looked this thin. But then again, it's how a paper doll looks with clothes on that matters, right?

I ease into the shower, needing the water to soothe me, to comfort me. It does. I just stand there, letting the water drum my body into a dream, and I imagine the rhythms of Jamaica or some Caribbean place. Joyous. And I imagine that I am dancing freely to the music of the water.

I don't know if it's possible to fall asleep standing up or not, but I think I must have, because I don't hear him come into the bathroom, but now I suddenly feel Bo's muscular arms from behind, wrapping themselves around me, holding me, waking me up. I'm annoyed at first, at the interruption of my serenity, but then I realize that his arms feel as comforting as the water—maybe even better.

He kisses the back of my shoulder, slowing down the tempo, but a slow groove is just as nice sometimes. "Why's the water so cold?" he asks.

I gasp as I realize how cold the water has gotten. I don't remember turning the temperature down. Did I really have it that cool?

He reaches up, turns the hot water up, and kisses my shoulder again. "Hey, baby." He holds me tighter, pulling me closer to his chest, so solid.

I close my eyes, wrap my arms around his neck. "Tighter," I plead.

He pulls me even closer as the now warm water produces a new pulsating rhythm, with a hypnotizing effect. It cascades over our bodies as we hold each other in silence. Somewhere amid the water is another falling ocean—my teardrops—but because they are washed away, I doubt Bo even notices.

When I turn around to face him, I am uncomfortable with looking at him, so I let my head fall back, completely submerging my hair into the stream of water. He kisses me, hard and then gentle and then hard again, all the way down to my navel, and then back up.

As we wash each other in calculated strokes, I finally open my eyes and watch his hands. So unhurried. I am, too, but only because I'm so weak.

He leans down a little, kisses me—his kisses passionate, so honest, so good.

I put my hand under his chin, pull him back down to me, and kiss him back. "Turn around," I whisper.

And when he turns his back to me, like so many other days before, I begin cleansing it, kneading it, taking pride in watching him feel good. He hangs his head in satisfaction, giving in to the pleasure of my nurturing caresses. And I think to myself "He truly is easily pleased."

"That was Sherm." He tosses the cordless onto the couch.

I nod as I continue to rub Sanford with one hand, and bite off a piece of the carrot that is in my other one.

He taps my leg. "There's a showcase tonight at the Brooklyn Moon. I told him I'd try to swing by. I want you to come with me."

"A showcase on Thanksgiving night?"

"No doubt. This is a prime night. Everybody's gonna be out tonight. And I want you to come with me—it might put you in the holiday spirit."

"I don't feel like it."

"Come on, now. Be nice. We don't have to stay long, just for maybe two sets. How's that? Go on, go get dressed."

"I don't feel up to it. Besides, Sherm didn't know what he was talking about with the last showcase, right? I'm not wasting my Thanksgiving night."

He laughs, squeezes my thigh. "So time spent with me is wasted now, huh? Come on, baby, go get dressed. We'll go up there, give it fifteen minutes. If you're still not with it, if the vibe is whack, we'll come back home. Deal?"

I grudgingly take a final bite of my carrot, and put the remainder of it in Bo's mouth. He immediately starts crunching on it as I get up.

"Fifteen minutes—that's it," I say, and Sanford follows me as I head upstairs.

Bo must be changing channels on the television, because as I'm going upstairs I hear the sounds of a football game fill the room. Then he yells to me. "Put on something sexy."

I decided on a cream-colored Calvin Klein pantsuit. It's as "sexy" as he's going to get from me tonight. I pull my hair back into a tidy ponytail, notice that my ends are frizzy and in need of conditioning, and decide to pull it back into a bun instead. I add a pair of gold hoop earrings, bronze lipstick, and a spray of Giorgio. I have a long talk with myself in the mirror, telling myself that fifteen minutes won't kill me. Argue with myself that it only takes a second to die. Convince myself that I might actually feel better if I go out. Remind myself that I was already dressed, and I may as well get it over with.

His eyes brighten as I enter the den. "Baby . . ." He smiles.

"Hmmm?" I giggle.

He gets up and pulls me into a hug. "You look so good." He kisses my forehead.

"Thank you." I bat my eyes and follow him over to the couch, where he pulls me onto his lap. Just as I do, the phone rings.

"Hell-ooooh," I answer it playfully.

"Shawni?"

"Hi, Mommie," I reply, and realize how happy I sound.

"Well," she laughs a little, "you certainly sound better."

I get up from Bo's lap and head into the kitchen. "Happy Thanksgiving."

"Well, thank you darling," she says.

And then she takes a breath. And then she doesn't say anything.

"Mommie?"

Her glass clinks as I hear her set it on the table. "Happy Thanksgiving to you, too, darling. Did Bo cook?"

"Yeah," I say. "Did you?"

"No, I really don't have an appetite today. I offered to cook for your brother, but I haven't seen him all day."

"Really? He's still in town?"

She sighs. "He's off handling some business, he says."

And she does it again—takes a breath and then doesn't say anything.

"Mommie, is everything okay?"

"Oh," she laughs again. "Of course. I just thought I'd call and check on you. I'm glad you're having a happy Thanksgiving."

"So," I say, purposefully nonchalant, "heard from Daddy today?"

She hums. "He'll probably call later."

I watch the cupboard above the refrigerator where Bo keeps all his liquor, and think "Just a little holiday cocktail—a taste."

I pull myself up and sit on top of the counter next to the refrigerator. "Are you okay?" I ask her.

She laughs. "Peachy. He'll call later. He always does."

I'm reaching up, almost able to touch the door of the cupboard, when I lose my balance. Whoops. I hear Bo coming, and decide to jump down from the counter. "Well, I'm sure he will. I'll call you back in a little bit, okay?"

"Okay, darling," she replies.

I think about her sitting there, probably in a gorgeous house gown, her glass in one hand, her cigarette in the other, and only the sounds of Nat King Cole to keep her company.

"Mommie, if you want, I can come over," I add.

"Of course not. Enjoy your evening. Give my love to Bo, okay?"

"Okay."

I hang up the phone just as Bo walks into the kitchen. I remind myself that I am an adult and that no one has any jurisdiction over what I do, so why should I alter my actions simply because he entered the room? So I sit back down on the counter and reach for the shelf.

He watches me, and calmly asks, "What are you doing?"

"Nothing," I reply. Finally able to reach the vodka, I pull it down from the shelf.

He walks over and snatches the bottle from me. "You haven't even eaten. Eat a piece of turkey. Drink some ice water."

"I ate a whole bag of carrots." I snatch it back.

"No." He raises his eyebrows, and takes the bottle from me again.

I go to grab it back from him, but he raises it above his head. I shrug. "Fine. I can drink my iced tea plain. It's not that serious, Bo."

"I guess I'm supposed to eat the whole damn turkey by myself?"

I shrug and turn away from him to grab a few pieces of the sliced turkey, and drop them into Sanford's dish.

He doesn't respond, just looks at me blankly for a few moments. And then he sucks his teeth, "We'll leave as soon as the game's over." He goes back out into the living room, taking the only bottle of vodka with him.

Rum will just have to suffice. I grudgingly retrieve the bottle from the shelf and mix it with my iced tea. I go back into the living room.

Bo is wearing Eternity, I realize as I cuddle next to him. He smells so good—that stuff should be permitted by license only.

It's not exactly Mommie's Brew, but it actually isn't too bad with rum. Already, I'm less tense. I take a sip of my iced tea mix, and then lean in and give a little nibble to Bo's ear.

Maybe I can make him forget about going out to the showcase, I think as I blow down his neck.

An odd look crosses his face, and he glances at me out of the corner of his eye. He frowns. He looks down at my glass, and then turns to look at me. He takes my glass, and I'm hoping that he's going to put it on the table so that we can go upstairs, but he doesn't. He puts the glass to his mouth, and drinks a little of it.

Oh boy . . .

I'm a grown woman. I can drink whatever I want.

He looks at me with disgust, sucks his teeth, and then finishes off my half-full glass in what looks like one single gulp. He hands the now ice cube–filled glass back to me and then turns his attention back to the never-ending football game.

Whatever.

Bored and in need of something to keep me awake for the remainder of the game, I reach over to the coffee table and grab the *Vibe* magazine—thick yellow letters at the bottom of the cover— Cris, Mo, Al, and Zin; Vibe gets personal with The Gentlemen.

I want to put it down, forget I ever saw it, but Bo is absorbed in the game. What can it hurt?

Bo clears his throat. "Page ninety-six, baby."

I do a double-take. Did he really just say that? "Excuse me?"

He laughs. "Go on and check 'em out—ninety-six."

I toss the magazine back onto the coffee table.

He's staring at the screen, smiling because of whatever is making the crowd go crazy at the game, smiling because he thinks he read my thoughts.

"Hello?" I pick up the cordless, relieved that it rang, giving me a reason to excuse myself from the football game of the year.

"What's up, sis?" Duran's voice sounds uneasy. "How ya feelin'?"

"I'm okay." I sigh.

"Yeah?"

"I am," I say.

"I'm glad."

"Where are you?" I ask.

"Check it. I'm outside. I need to holler at you for a minute." His voice sounds even stranger now. "Yo, just tell Bo I need to give you somethin', all right?"

"Is everything okay?"

"Yeah, it's cool. I just need to holler at you."

"I'll be right out," I say before hanging up the phone.

"Tell him to come in and get some of this turkey," Bo says as I slip on my leather jacket and head out the door.

Duran hands me a Smoothie drink after I close the door to Mommie's Benz.

"Strawberry and kiwi." He winks at the Smoothie. "Still your favorite?"

"Duran, you're so sweet." I sip on it to be polite, to show my appreciation for his thoughtfulness, but I'm much more interested in his seriousness.

"What's up?" I ask as I watch Duran put the car in drive and pull away from the curb.

"I just need to holler at you," he says. And he turns the corner at the next block, pulls over, and turns the headlights off after he puts it in park. He leaves the car running, rap music quietly playing from the speakers.

"About what?" I ask.

"About a few things." He looks over at me and winks. His diamond-hoop earring is glistening as usual.

"Few things, like what?" I wish he would just say what it is.

"First things first. Man, I'm buggin'. You have me on a real unbelievable buggin' trip." He looks at me. "I've never seen you look so out of it."

I turn and look out the window. An elderly lady walking up her steps. I concentrate on counting each one.

"Things are that bad, Shawni?" he asks.

"No, Duran." I turn to him.

He swallows, hard. "Man, 'cause no amount of bullshit is worth that." He looks away this time. He talks to the driver's side window. "I guess some things will have you trippin' to the point of stressin', but yo . . ."

"Is this what you brought me out here for?"

He puts his hand to his forehead, scratches his eyebrows. "I felt like, in there, in that waiting room, I kept thinkin' that if you weren't going to be okay . . . shit, I was gonna have to die or something. I couldn't take it. I promise you, I better check outta here before you or Mommie, because either one of you messed up is just some shit I don't think I'm equipped to handle." He sighs. "But no, that's not all I wanted to holler at you about."

"Go ahead. What is it? You have me out here."

He looks away again, puts his hand on the steering wheel, taps his knuckles on the steering wheel, and grips the steering wheel.

"Duran! What?" I shout, and punch him in his arm.

"Ah!" He rubs his arm and laughs. "You didn't have to hit me, man." A moment passes, another song begins playing, a new beat for him to tap his knuckles to on the steering wheel as he nods his head. Finally, he says, "Naw, I just wanted to see you, just for a minute, just me and you."

"You could've come inside. Bo would have given us some privacy."

He reaches to the inside pocket of his coat, and hands me an envelope.

"What's this?"

"A little pocket change for you." He winks. "Good job on the gear for the fellas."

"Thanks," I say.

He smiles a little. "You're out of your league with Zin, understand?"

"What?" I roll my eyes. "Whatever. Who said anything about Zin?"

"Yeah, big brother's just sayin' . . ."

"Where in the world is this coming from?"

"And don't ever let me catch you grindin' up on one of my boys—"

"Take me back. Take me back *now*," I say.

He nods. "I can do that." He turns the lights on, and pulls out into traffic heading back toward Elliot Street, and we ride back in silence. He's still tapping the steering wheel. I'm so ready to get out of this car!

As we pull up in front of the brownstone, he says, "I'm not uptight. But you know it's some things that I just have to voice my opinion about. It's all love."

"I know, but Duran, some things you don't have to say—especially more than once!"

He looks away, and I feel bad because he seems sad for a moment.

I lean in and kiss him on the cheek. "I love you for it though." I pat him on his leg.

He examines my horrid-looking hands. "This shit right here is bugged."

"It's nothing." I sigh and ease my hand away.

He eyes my fingernails for a while. "None of that should have happened. And I'm trippin' that I even have to say this, but I need to say this, and I don't want no questions asked, cool?"

"What is it now?"

"I'm gonna let you get on back in there to the man. I need to get on back over here and help Mommie get some Christmas stuff down from the closet, but first I wanna say this. You know I was thinking about what you asked me the other day about when you know if you're ready for marriage and all that. Shawni, man, I just wish you would've listened to me when I told you to just play it cool for a few days, be up off of Delaney. I needed to check some things out, then you go and end up in the hospital."

"What do you mean, check some things out?" I'm really annoyed now.

"I would never do anything or say anything that could hurt you, sis. I would never tell you to do anything that would bring you down, you know this, right? I'm not gonna steer you wrong."

I nod.

"Just, you gotta trust me more. I know I make you mad sometimes, but I gotta look out for you 'cause I don't know who else will, right?"

I nod again. "Where is this going, Duran? The point? Just tell me right now. I can take it. Does this have something to do with Bo? Is he cheating on me?"

He taps the steering wheel some more. "I don't know. All I'm sayin' is that I'm asking you to be cool until I check some things out. Just you gotta trust me, okay?"

I want to grab him by the back of his ponytail, slam his head against the steering wheel until he spits out whatever it is he's trying to tell me, but I don't. Whatever it is, he won't say it—either because he isn't sure, or because he can't. Instead of taking hold of him, I decide that maybe I don't really want to hear whatever it is anyhow.

"Fine, Duran," I say.

He nods, too, a solid nod, confirming our agreement. "I'll holler at you later then."

He waits until I'm in the doorway of the brownstone. Two honks and he pulls off. Just as he does I realize that I left my smoothie and my paycheck in the car.

"What's up with 'Ran?" Bo asks.

"Nothing." I notice that the television is turned off. "Game over?"

"Yeah," he says. "He didn't want to come in for a minute?"

"No." I sigh. "Bo, I'm tired. Go to the showcase without me, 'kay?" I give him a brief kiss. "Have a good time."

He stands there frozen. "I thought you were coming with me?"

I begin heading upstairs. "Changed my mind."

"What the fuck?" he says. "What's wrong now?" He's right behind me on the stairs.

"Nothing." I quicken my pace, hurry into the bedroom, and yank off my earrings.

He stands in the doorway, sucking his teeth. "What just happened? What did you and 'Ran talk about?"

"What difference does it make? Nothing. Brother-sister stuff." I kick off my boots, unzip my pantsuit down the side and slide out of it. I toss it on the bed.

He snatches the pantsuit from off the bed. "This is the way you treat a two-hundred-and-fifty-dollar pantsuit?"

I look at it, roll my eyes, and go to the closet to retrieve my robe.

"Shawni, I'm talking. Don't walk away from me."

"Bo, if you don't like it, hang it up then."

A cream blur hurls past me and lands on the floor of the closet.

"Fuck some clothes," he shouts. "I asked you to go to this showcase with me. You said you would. Now you're trippin'?"

"I'm tired."

"Woman, there ain't that much sleep in the world."

I turn back to him, pull my robe on, and tie it tight. "I'm not in the mood for this, Bo."

"For what? Shit." He knocks a bottle of lotion off the dresser. "Fuckin' mood changes every two seconds is drivin' me insane."

I take a breath, walk over to him, place my hand on his chest, lean in, and give him a delicate kiss on the lips.

"Keep it," he says.

"Good night," I say as I make my way over to the bed and crawl under the covers.

A moment later a burst of cool air whisks across my body as Bo yanks the covers off me.

"Who was in the car, Shawni?"

I sit up. "What?"

He stares at me, his temples pulsating. "Who did you just go around the corner with?"

"What are you talking about? Duran. I told you already. What, so now you don't think I was outside with my brother? You're crazy."

His eyes bulk. He looks around. Laughs. "I'm crazy?" He laughs again. He knocks the remote to the television off the dresser as he leaves the room. He mutters the word *crazy* again as he makes his way down the hallway.

I hear the closet downstairs opening, and then the front door slams shut.

I pull the covers back over me and concentrate on sleeping as hard as I can.

Sleep. Glorious.

I'm startled out of comalike sleep by a thud on the bed.

"Sanford?" I don't open my eyes. I don't want to open my eyes. I want to hear Sanford's breathing, to reassure me that it's him, and then just go back to sleep.

I listen. I don't hear him panting.

I peel my eyelids open. The bright red letters of the clock tell me it's 4:35. I look at the blinds. No light peeking in—that means it's 4:35—A.M.

"Sanford?" I say again.

Still, no panting.

I sit up, and look at the other side of the bed. A pile of something. I can hardly see what it is. The room is so dark.

"Who's there?" I ask as I fumble for the lamp. I squint as I adjust my eyes to the light.

Bo. Standing there. His leather jacket on. His face tense. He stares at me.

"What?" I ask. "I can't believe you woke me up like this!"

He looks down at the bed. A pile of clothes. My clothes. A pair of my jeans. A sweatshirt. My cropped leather jacket. My leather boots.

"What?" I ask again.

He answers in a playfully authoritative voice. "Get up. Get your clothes on."

I pound my fist on the bed. "It's almost five o'clock in the morning, Bo!"

He smiles, shrugs, walks over to me. He sits down on the edge of the bed. "Baby, I'm asking you nicely. Would you please get up and put your clothes on?"

I look at him.

"Come on, now," he says. "Hurry up, I wanna take you somewhere." And he taps me on my thigh, and gets up. "I'll be outside," he adds before he leaves the room.

I look at the clock again. I can't believe him. This better be important.

The late night/early morning November air is warm and still. I close the front door behind me. The street is quiet. He's sitting on the stoop, waiting, biting his bottom lip.

"Okay, Bo, here I am. What?"

He looks away from me, down toward the bottom of the steps.

My eyes follow his gaze.

The Harley.

I cut my eyes back at him. "Bo, please." I roll my eyes.

He takes my hand and pulls me over to him.

I look down at him. "You're serious?"

He bites his bottom lip again, and stands up. "Come on. Spur of the moment, adventurous type of stuff, like we used to do," he says. "Let's go."

The starting up of a motorcycle in the middle of the night is enough to make all the neighbors open the windows and spit curses at us, and that's the last thing we need. So after Bo starts it—the noise boisterous—he gestures for me to get on. I hurry up and do so.

He looks back at me. "Ready?"

I pull my body against his, and hold tight to his waist, and nod.

My body is pressed against his as hard as I can, I say a quick prayer as we head out into the sporadic flow of middle-of-the-night traffic. I have no idea where I'm going, or why it has to be in the middle of the night, but as I hold him tightly, his leather jacket soft and welcoming, I remind myself to breathe out. Bo's been riding for years. He's careful. There's less traffic at night. We'll be okay. I need to just relax. And I do. I lay my head against his back, and give in to the ride.

Slow and monotonous at first, we ride through Brooklyn for a while. Things look different at night. I've never noticed. The markets that are so alive during the day with rows of colorful fruits and vege-tables, men with cardboard tables out in front of the stores playing dominoes or checkers, children zipping past on scooters, and various people stopping to shake, sniff, or squeeze for freshness, are now quiet. A steel gate is pulled down in front of the store, making every-thing seem deserted.

Crossing the Brooklyn Bridge, Bo picks up speed. I hold on tighter as he leans forward a little more, the pull of the bike making me feel a little uncertain, but the rock-hard feel of Bo's body re-minds me of who I'm with.

There is nothing like the feeling that the person you're with can protect you from whatever may come. I smile at the feeling of being shielded.

We ride for a long time, up the highway where there is a clear view of the Hudson, I watch the water—black at night and never-ending. I find myself in a trance as we zip alongside it.

He peeks back at me, and shouts. "You okay, baby?"

I squeeze him. Yes.

He veers to the right, pulls off the highway, and exits onto Riverside Drive. We cross 125th over to Broadway. He turns right and heads back downtown.

Manhattan is different. Closed buildings also appear vacant, but there are more people out. Walking. Laughing. Happy. Having en-joyed a night of partying and finally accepting that it's over. Dawn is approaching. I almost wish we'd stayed on the highway, now that the view of the water is gone, the stop and go of the traffic lights is frustrating. I decide to enjoy what images Broadway has to offer.

Cabs weaving in and out, rushing downtown, rushing uptown. I catch a glimpse inside of a yellow one. A red-haired girl passed out, asleep against the window. I laugh out loud as I think about how much fun she probably had tonight, imagining how her evening culminated in her being so exhausted. Probably so worn out from dancing, or maybe too drunk. Stoned perhaps.

We approach Times Square. Lights make it seem like daytime. And I think about New Year's Eve last year, when Bo and I were right here watching the ball drop. And the memories flow. And this is what I do for the rest of the ride, all the way back to Brooklyn. Focus on Bo.

I've grown so attached to the constant hum of the motorcycle that when he finally turns it off, the silence of early morning seems deafening.

He pulls his helmet off, rests his forearm on the handlebars, and sits there for a few moments. It takes him awhile to catch his breath, and I take my helmet off while I wait.

My hair is sweaty, and my legs feel as if they're humming.

He sits up and looks at the sky, shaking his head.

I wipe the sweat off the back of his head before I get off the bike. And when I stand up I realize that my entire body still feels the vibration of the motor.

He lets out a long breath. "Damn, that felt good."

I nod in agreement.

He's looking at me. That look. He grins. "Baby, you look so good right now. All sweaty."

I wait while he puts the bike away. I wait, knowing, anticipating.

"You look so good right now, too," I say, my heart pounding as he opens the front door.

Sanford's breath warm against my palm as I pat his head in passing through the living room. Bo's body pressing mine up the stairs, he bites the side of my neck. "No," he says to Sanford. "Stay." Tripping up the stairs, both of us are so ready, so impatient.

I laugh, pull Bo's leather jacket off, love the sound of it falling back down the stairs, can't wait to get the rest of our things off.

Sanford is whining as Bo slams the bedroom door, and then there are a few scratches as Sanford pleads to come in here with us, and then Bo yells for him to hush, and he does.

Explorative kissing like when we first met. Curious.

A faint cry slips out of my mouth. I can't take this intensity. I'm too eager to actually do any of the work. "Hurry," I whisper as he unwraps the clothes, moist from sweat, from both of our willing bodies.

"Baby . . ." he groans, trying to move as quickly as he can. His breathing hurried, his movement forceful, he grabs the comforter and pulls a bunch of it into a ball—unable to contain himself, he has to get a grip for a moment. He bites his bottom lip—hard. His eyes needing me.

I lie back onto the bed, so ready I could yell. I look up at him, my eyes pleading, needing him, too.

That vein on the side of his head. His chest, so ridiculously alluring, coming closer.

His heart beating against mine, he lies there for a brief moment.

He bites my earlobe. I stroke his back. What's left of my nails skid their way up and down, and up and down.

No way. I'm never living without this man.

"Good morn-ninggg." A high-pitched accent sings loudly into the phone. "Ms. Baldwin. Is that you?"

"Yes." I push Bo's heavy arm off my stomach and sit up. He moans a little and turns over on his back. "Who's this?" I ask.

"This is Dr. Whitney. From the hospital? How do you feel?"

"I'm okay."

"Well, I just wanted to call and check on you—see how you are coming along. That is not something I always do, but I wanted to be sure to call you. May I ask you a few questions? Would that be okay?"

I slide my legs from under the sheets, and when I do, Bo wakes a little.

"Where you goin', baby?" He moans.

I hold a finger up, point to the phone, and mouth the word *doctor*. I look around for my robe. "A few questions?"

"Yes, just a few questions that I want to ask you since you've been home. Is that okay?"

I tie my robe and go into the bathroom. "Okay . . ."

"I spoke with your fiancé the other day, and he tells me that you are sleeping quite a bit."

"A little. I've just been tired."

"Has this just started—the heavy sleeping—or was this before the incident?"

I sit on the edge of the bathtub, one leg over the other. "I've always been a heavy sleeper."

"I understand." She pauses. "How is your appetite? Still not eating?"

Why is Bo telling this woman all of my business? "I eat when I'm hungry," I say.

"You see, Ms. Baldwin, this is something of my concern. I don't want to see you back in the hospital again. You are sleeping a lot lately, you are having appetite loss . . . These are things that concern us, that make us think you might suffer from depression right now, that you are likely candidate. Have you been taking the medication we prescribed for you?"

"Yes," I say.

No. And I'm not going to. And I'm not one of those people who sit around feeling sorry for themselves, drawing sad faces and rose petals with daggers through them in my diary. I saw a girl in high school do that once. I don't need any medication. I'm fine.

"You see, sometimes we have depression and it is not a thing where we are necessarily crying all the time," she says.

I despise those moments where it feels as if someone has just read your mind, making me wonder if there is something I don't know, that maybe some people can read minds.

"There are other symptoms of depression besides crying. Have you had some life-changing event take place? Not doing or enjoying the things you did at one time? I don't want you to think that you have to continue to feel this way."

"Dr. Whitney, I can't thank you enough for calling, but I feel fine. I'm not depressed, and I don't need any medication."

She waits a moment. "I do hope you take care of yourself. Let us know if there is anything we can do to help you."

"Thank you." I roll my eyes. "Thanks again for calling."

The mirror is so honest, it's almost rude. I catch a glimpse of myself on my way out of the bathroom and have to stop. Forget feeling depressed, I look depressed. I look like I've had a hard life, and I should not look like this after such an intense night of love-making. I should be glowing. The ends of my hair are frizzy. If I had a pair of scissors in my hand right now I'd whack it all off.

Somewhere—I feel around underneath the bathroom sink—I have a bag of hair rollers. Tired, wanting to go back to sleep, I am relieved when I find them, and determined to find the energy to stand here and roll my hair up.

I don't know how Ernie can possibly do this every single day the way he does, all day long. My arms are tired after putting in only seven rollers. Too tired to continue, too frustrated to undo what I've already done, I decide that I'll just call Ernie in a little while and beg him to squeeze me in today, and I take my half-rolled head back to bed.

Bo doesn't open his eyes as I crawl back under the covers. "What'd the doctor say?" he asks.

"What'd you say to the doctor, is more like it!" I punch my pillow and try to get comfortable again.

"Say what?"

"You told her I was depressed?" I turn my back to him.

"No." He yawns. "I told her you wouldn't get out of bed and that all you want to do is fill up on damn ice water here and there. She's the one who mentioned depression."

I stare at the ceiling for a while.

"What time is it?" he asks.

I look at the clock. "Almost ten o'clock," I answer dryly.

He yawns. "See, you keepin' me up all night," he teases. "I wanted to be out of here by nine."

"You're working on the day after Thanksgiving? What's there to do?"

He sits up. "What isn't there to do? You gonna be okay if I leave for a few hours?"

"Stop treating me like I'm suicidal or something."

"You know I didn't mean it like that, baby." He gets out of bed, and Sanford jumps up and barks. "What you lookin' at Sanford? You need to go outside?" he asks, and Sanford whines in response.

Doors open and close. The front door opens awhile later. Bo taking Sanford out. Bo and Sanford coming in awhile later. The bathroom door opening. Closing. The shower door. Water running. Can I please get some quiet in here?

Just as I am about to fall back asleep to the comforting sound of Niagara Falls coming from the bathroom, the phone rings.

Go away, Dr. Whitney. No, I don't think I'm depressed. Please stop calling.

I fumble for the phone. "Hello?" I wait, cringing, hoping it's not her again.

No response.

"Hello?" I say again.

Click.

Whatever.

A moment later it rings again.

This time I'm really annoyed. "Hello!" I wait.

"Uh . . ." A female voice. No accent. A soft, high pitch. "Hi."

"Hi . . ." I wait.

In a nervous, but sweet-sounding voice, she asks politely. "Is Bo home?"

I listen. Niagara Falls is still flowing. "Yes," I say, "who's calling?"

She doesn't say anything.

"Hello?" I sit up. "Who is this?"

"Uh, I asked to speak to Bo," she says.

"Okay," I bat my eyes, "and I asked who this is."

"Look, is he there or not?" she says, her voice no longer sweet.

I glance at the Caller-ID box. Private. "Are you gonna tell me who this is or not?"

She clears her throat. "Look, if you're not going to put him on the phone, since you're all up in his business, being his personal secretary, can you just ask him if he still plans on meeting me for breakfast? He's late."

A huge—no, a massive—boulder falls from the ceiling, hits me in the chest, and for a moment I can't breathe. I look up. There is no boulder. My chest, however, feels as if there was.

"Meeting you for breakfast?" I ask.

Shawni, don't you dare let this woman hear you get upset.

"He was supposed to be here at nine." She has the audacity to sound annoyed.

For breakfast, huh? What about you wanting to be at the office by nine, Bo?

She sighs. "Just tell him to hit me on my hip, leave me a voice mail if we're still on for breakfast or not. Tell him Cherry called."

Didn't I ask her earlier what her name was?

"Sure," I say as pleasantly as I'm able. "I'll give him the message."

Click.

Boom. I kick the bathroom door. A moment later Niagara Falls trickles to a hush.

"Shawni?" he calls.

"You better hurry up," I shout at the door as loud as I can. "It's getting late."

It's probably that same bitch that was over here the other night. I hurry down the stairs. I look at the couch. Sitting on the couch with her robe on, like this is her man's house or something, like she can just come in here—to my man's house—and sit on his couch, and fix her robe, while I'm standing outside the window with a damn ski mask on, trying to get in, ending up locked behind bars because of it!

I plop down on the couch.

Play it cool, Shawni. Don't you dare let him know you're on to him.

I feel around under the coffee table for the phone book, and call the first car service I notice in the yellow pages. I tell them to be here in ten minutes.

How can he do this to me? Liar! To the office on the morning after Thanksgiving? I should have known something was up. Instincts never lie. You wanna go out here and sneak around with Miss Cherry, huh? Well, Shawni Baldwin will not fill the shoes of the little housewife at home who's stupid enough to believe that her man is at the office on the day after Thanksgiving.

When Bo descends the stairs, dressed in a sexy maroon suit, freshly shaved, smelling good, he's in an interestingly good mood.

Dressed to impress, huh?

I tilt my head. "You look nice."

He looks down at his suit. "Thank you. Come gimme a kiss. I'm rollin' out."

Oh, sure Bo, I'll give you a kiss. This'll be the last damn kiss you'll ever experience from these lovely lips. You better enjoy this moment.

He heads toward the door. "You got me feelin' all nice after last night." He laughs. "Makin' a brotha feel like he can conquer the world!"

Oh, really? You asshole.

I fake a giggle. "Well, you worked up an appetite didn't you? Don't you want to eat a little breakfast before you go?"

He pauses. "Nah, I'm cool. I'll eat in a little bit."

I already know.

I wait for the door to close behind him. Wait to hear the car start up, and then I say to my dog, "Be back in a bit, Sanford." I pat his head, grab my purse, and head out the door.

Coast clear, so I slide out the front door. The tail end of Baby Blue is a blur at the end of the block, but it's definitely still visible.

"Follow that Lexus," I say to the driver.

"What Lexus?" he asks.

"Hurry up." I point ahead. "And don't get too close. Just follow it."

"Lady." He turns around, a slightly surprised look across his face. "If this is some kind of a high-speed chase scene you're looking for, I can't help you. Where are you headed?"

I grunt. "Listen, I will pay you well, okay? All I'm asking is for you to follow the Lexus and you're *not* doing a very good job of it. Can you put this thing in drive already? Please?"

He turns around, mumbles what sounds like a few curse words in his native tongue, and begins driving.

All the way to Manhattan, my driver does a good job of keeping a reasonable distance as instructed. Around Twenty-second Street, he asks with a smirk, "Can I at least know who we're following?"

I decide to humor him. "F.B.I. I'm undercover. Special assignment. The man we're chasing is a spy."

He waits a moment, unsure of whether or not he should laugh, but suspecting that he should believe me. "Espionage?"

"Yes."

He turns down the volume of National Public Radio. "What country?"

I laugh. "The H.S."

"H.S.?"

"Yeah. *Ho*nited States."

He turns back, sees me smiling, and a smile sneaks across his face as well. "Funny."

The office? It's on Fifty-ninth. But we follow Bo all the way up to Ninetieth! The City Diner.

"Now what?" my new partner in crime asks.

I tell him to park. I don't know. Ernie isn't here to tell me what to do. What not to do.

Bo gets out and, unbeknownst to him, I observe him paying the meter, crossing the street, and going inside the restaurant.

"Can you wait here?" I ask.

He looks uncomfortable. "Lady, it's a busy day, lotsa traffic."

"I said I'll pay you nicely," I remind him.

He doesn't answer for a moment, looks annoyed, and shrugs. "Five minutes."

I spot the back of his bald head as soon as I step inside. All the way in the back of the diner, at a table, not alone. Didn't anyone ever tell you that you should never sit with your back to the door, Mr. Delaney?

A petite little thing sitting across from him. Light-skinned. Hair dyed red. Leaned in, looking down at something on the table. Both of them looking down at something on the table.

"Ma'am?" The host approaches me. "Is there something we can help you with?"

I glance at him. "My party has already arrived." I head down the aisle.

Odd looks from several people. What are they looking at? There is even an outright gasp from one lady who immediately looks away from me. She whispers something to the lady dining next to her. She gasps as well.

"Ma'am?" I hear the host calling from behind.

I quicken my speed. Marching toward him. Can't get down here fast enough.

Still looking down, neither of them hear me coming. Good. It always hurts more when you don't know it's coming.

Whap! I slap the back of his bald head as hard as I can. Whap! I slap it again.

He snaps around. "What the . . . ?" He holds his head. His eyes? Wider than a deer's facing headlights.

I look at her. You're next.

But Bo takes hold of my arm first. "Shawni?" He hurries to grab my other arm. "Shawni!"

Both of my arms pulled behind me, my body is yanked into the booth, next to him, my eyes glaring at the cute lil' thing sitting in front of me. Twenty-four, twenty-five years old, big gold hoop earrings, a Fendi purse sitting on the table, wearing a black Christian Dior business suit, a scared shitless expression on her face. I look her cold into her dark brown eyes, "Cherry?" I ask.

She looks at Bo.

He looks at me. "Shawni, what are you doing?"

I wiggle with all my might. It's a workout comparable to Tae Bo, trying to free myself from his impossible grasp. A weak, "Because . . ." finally escapes from my exasperated body.

He clenches my forearms even tighter, forcing my chest to push out. I glance down. My robe falling open, and now I'm the one who gasps. My robe.

"Bo," her tiny voice speaks up. "Do you want me to leave?"

I kick underneath the table, hoping to crush her shin. I miss. "No." I glare at her.

Bo mutters under his breath. "I don't believe this."

I shoulder him as hard as I can, my only weapon.

"Woman!" He jerks me even harder.

The host arrives at the table. "Is there something I can help you with?" He looks at me.

Bo tugs my arms once again. "No, we're leaving."

The host nods. He looks at me. Nods again. "Please, if you will." He says quietly, and walks away.

"Cherry," Bo says to her in a professional tone of voice. "We'll set something up for next week." He looks down at the papers scattered about the table. The papers scattered about the table. Papers. Business papers. Contracts. Oh, boy.

He clears his throat and says to her, "Why don't you fax everything to the office, and I'll look it over? We can go from there."

She begins gathering the papers, stacking them up in a neat pile. "Okay," she says.

"Shawni," he says through his teeth, "go." And he nudges me out of the booth.

As if he is the officer, and I am the arrestee, he keeps my wrists behind my back, sucks his teeth, and forces me out of the diner.

That definitely was not the same woman from the couch the other night.

"Bo," I say when we get outside and he finally lets go of me, thrusting my arms away from him, a disgusted groan as he does. He crosses the street. I follow. "Bo?" I call after him.

He doesn't answer me.

"Bo!" I try to keep up. "Well, when she called the house this morning—"

He looks at me out of the corner of his eye, is about to say something, but doesn't. He gives me a really appalled look instead.

"I forgot to tell you she called," I say, trying to keep up with him. "She was so rude. I thought . . ."

As he nears the car, he pulls out the keys. "I don't believe you, Shawni." He unlocks the doors.

I hurry to the other side and jump in before he has a chance to lock me out. "Bo, just listen," I beg. "I'm sorry."

He very calmly starts the car. He very calmly pulls out into traffic. He very calmly says, "This is more than I can deal with. Too much."

"Can you just hear me out?"

His jawbone is pumping faster than my heart is beating as he runs a red light. He glances in the rearview mirror. "Get off my tail," he says.

I turn around. Shoot. "Oh, pull over. It's the cabdriver. I need to pay him."

"Woman," he says, "I promise you, you get out this car and you will not have a chance to get back in."

And he turns the radio up as loud as it's ever been, gives me an "I dare you to" look when I try to turn the volume back down, and looks straight ahead as he drives.

The cabdriver pulls up alongside us. Our music is too loud for me to make out what he's saying, but his window is rolled down, his face is now maroon in color from shouting so loud, and then there is a gesture in the universal language—the one where sound is not needed for comprehension. The finger.

"Bo!" I shout. "I have to pay the cab. He'll call the police!"

His cheeks puff with air. He'll huff, and he'll puff, and he'll blow me the hell out of this car if I don't sit over here and keep my mouth shut. He slows down for the next red light, jumps out of the car, and storms over to the cab. Shouting back and forth. I can't make out what they're saying, but they're both shouting. Bo tosses a few bills into the car and the cab speeds off—running the red light, his hand hanging out the window, still giving me the finger.

Bo slams the door shut, turns the radio down, and then turns it completely off. "Forty dollars for some bullshit, woman. Forty dollars for you to catch a cab all the way uptown to interrupt a meeting with me and a potential client. Now I have to drive you all the way back downtown over some bullshit!" He cuts a look at me. "This is too much for me. Lookin' like Florence Jefferson, you decide to come out in public in your damn house robe and rollers—"

I don't hear a single word after this. Rollers. I reach up. Rollers. I look down. Robe. Oh, my goodness, what am I doing? Did I really just do this? Is this really happening?

He drives faster. "This is some fatal attraction type of bullshit, Shawni. I can't handle this. Naw, hell naw, I can't. No. I *cannot* handle this. I won't."

I swallow. "Bo, I'm sorry. She called this morning, and— Why don't you say something about the fact that she was rude to me when she called?" I raise my voice.

"Woman," he says calmly. "Do I or do I not give you your phone messages? You decided to wait and humiliate me before you bothered to tell me that the woman even called, before you give me a chance to tell you that she's young and immature, but can sing her ass off? How was I supposed to know how she talked to you if I didn't even know she called? Huh? You don't mention a word about her calling until now. What—she's rude when she calls means I'm on some shady stuff? Shawni, damn! I don't need this." He sucks his teeth again.

"I already feel bad enough as it is, can you just hear what I'm saying? You said you were going to the office. You didn't mention anything about breakfast with some woman named Cherry! And then she calls saying you're late for breakfast, and she was rude to me. She wouldn't tell me her name—"

"So, how'd you know her name then, Shawni?"

"Well, after I kept asking her! Then she says it with an attitude. 'Tell Bo Cherry called. Tell him to page me.' What was I supposed to think?"

He clenches his jaws tighter. "You could have asked me. I would have told you."

"But you said you were going to the office. You didn't say anything about breakfast—"

"Woman! I have breakfast all the time with clients. Since when do I need your approval?" He groans. "I can't deal with this. All the clothes, the jewelry, all of it—you can take. This is it. I'm through. You have to go. You have to! Go stay with your mama, your bullshit ass brother—"

"Whoa! My *bullshit* ass brother? What does Duran have to do with anything?"

"Yeah! You haven't been right since Duran filled your head with whatever he told you. Comin' in the house, actin' all sour. You think I want to live all paranoid like this, wondering if you're gonna be sneakin' up behind me to come slap me in the back of my head. Yeah, your bullshit ass brother!"

"Duran," I say through my teeth, "doesn't have anything to do with this. Your name didn't even come up when Duran and I talked. Why are you so worried about what Duran and I talked about?"

"I swear I should've listened to my mother. I swear!"

I sit up, turn to face him directly, and ask, "What's that supposed to mean?"

"She always said you were nothing but a gold diggin'—"

I shriek. "She said *what*?"

"Just, don't say anything else to me, Shawni. Drop it. When we get back to Brooklyn, I'm tellin' you now, call somebody to come get you, go to Soho, get your stuff, and get the hell—"

"Excuse me!" I pound the dashboard a few times. "I beg your mother's pardon, and I beg *your* pardon for not putting her in her place, but I am *hardly* a gold digger! I have never needed a man for anything!"

He laughs heartily. "Yeah, right! You need a man like you need your next breath. You can't do a damn thing for yourself. I'd like to see you sit there with a straight face and tell me you've never needed a man for anything. You couldn't last a day. You'd have a nervous breakdown before you even live a day without a man."

That stings.

I want to hit him. I want to slap him. Really. I want to do a lot of things, but it's as if I'm in a time warp, some type of twilight zone. I'm sitting here, a crazed woman in my robe and with rollers in my hair, in broad daylight, and I'm wondering how I got here, and how I can get back.

"What's happening to you?" He sighs. "You used to be the most confident woman I'd ever met in my entire life! That was the most extraordinary thing about you, Shawni. You were like no other woman I had ever— Now, what? It's back to the same type of bullshit drama these other females like to bring? I can't deal with this. Take it all. I don't care!"

"No! How about you and your mother give it all to some gold-diggin' hoochie when you find one—she's such an expert at spotting them! Just give me my dog, that's all I want! I can buy my own damn clothes. Sanford. That's it. That's all I want."

"Deal."

SEVEN

Ready or Not

"You know, at night, if you stare out a window, it eventually becomes like a mirror," Ernie tells me.

"Really?" I reply uncaringly as I continue to gaze out the window at nothing in particular. But eventually what he has just said resonates, as with each passing moment my reflection is more apparent. He's right. The sun has set, and Shawni stares back at me now. Lifeless. Pouting. My arms folded across my chest. I cringe at the sight of me.

"Over there lookin' like Anna," he says.

"Anna?" I get up, close the blinds and join him on his couch. "Who's that?"

"Chile, Anna Rexia." He laughs. "Let's order a pizza or something—you need to eat."

"Not hungry."

"Well, if you plan on staying here with me I am not about to watch you waste away. I almost lost you once, and I'm not gonna let you starve yourself to death. That bald-headed lawyer-man is not the bomb, and you can find another. You're supposed to be Miss America, chile. Five dollars, remember?"

I look around at Ernie's bachelor pad, its decor animal-print inspired—everything from leopard to zebra to snakeskin is everywhere. A small one bedroom, but it's comfy, definitely tight for two people, but he insisted that I take his bedroom.

"Ernie," I sulk, "I have nothing."

"No"—he holds up his finger—"you have a brother, a mother, and a best friend who love you. Even when we can't remember why we love you, we still do." He winks, and then nods at Sanford, asleep by the front door. "And that dog over there loves you. You need to pull yourself together."

"That's not what I mean." I grab a pillow and ball it up with all my might before burying my head into it.

What am I going to do without him?

His voice is as tired as it is stern. "Look, Shawni, my father always told me that happiness and inner peace depends on how you measure yourself as a man—or in your case a woman. If you want to measure yourself, your entire existence, on whether or not you have a so-called good man in your life, and whether or not he's giving you the keys to a Lex and a condo, then hell. Right now, yes, you are a failure. But, if you . . . Shawni, look up here! Look at me."

I lift my head and wait, focusing on his eyebrows. I don't want him to look into my eyes directly, just in case what they say is true, about looking into someone's eyes.

"But," he continues, "if you measure your worth based on your heart, your intentions, and what type of person you are, you might find different results. Hell, I wanted to be a damn ophthalmologist, but I never had the patience for studying. Dropped out my freshman year of undergrad, started doing hair, and eventually went on and got my license. You think I wasn't depressed the year my brother graduated from Princeton? You think I wasn't feeling sorry for myself the year that my would-have-been graduation date passed? But Daddy looked me in my eye and told me that I'm a good person, I have heart, and I care about people."

I nod halfheartedly.

"Chile, talk to me, please. You're starting to look like a zombie. Go put some makeup on or something, looking tore up from the hardwood up." He snaps his fingers in front of my eyes. "Can you hear me, chile?"

I almost laugh, but sigh instead. "What I mean is that I had what seemed like everything, and lost it, but there was always Bo if nothing else. And now look."

"So, in other words, you took him for granted?"

"No."

"Why is it so hard for you to admit that you need someone?"

"Because I don't."

"That's what I mean right there. You did, too, need Bo."

Sanford comes over and licks my face and whimpers a little. Even he gets stirred at the sound of Bo's name.

Ernie raises an eyebrow at Sanford. "I know that dog isn't hungry again. Look, I'm gonna have to go to the store and get some Pedigree or something if he thinks I'm gonna fix him another plate of sausage."

"No." I'm amused at why Sanford is really whining. "He's not hungry, just giving me a kiss, that's all."

"You need to do some Copperfield magic on that Doberman, turn him into a man, see. Because that, right there, is the kind of love, loyalty, and attention I'm talking about. You need a man like that, chile," Ernie says.

"I felt so stupid when I saw all of that paperwork on the table. When did I become so paranoid?"

"Paranoid, my ass! What about the woman on the couch? That's not paranoia, now is it? Stop beating yourself up, girlfriend. You're human."

"Do you think he slept with her?" I say weakly, fully knowing what Ernie's going to say.

"Who, Bo? He's a man, chile. The question is how many times. You said yourself she was sitting there in her robe. I mean, I hate to be blunt, but . . ."

"How do I get back to my old self again, Ernie?" I sit up.

"Shawni," Ernie sits down beside me and exhales, his voice forcefully calm. "First of all, you should have asked him if he's messin' with couch woman. But then again, if he is, let her have him. Who wants to be going around man-sharing anyhow? You know? Who wants to be all up in a relationship knowing that he's got another woman on the—" He catches himself, gasps, and cups his hand over his mouth.

"It's okay." I shrug. "Go on and say it. Another woman on the side. Go ahead and finish saying what you were going to say, Ernie. It's the truth."

His hand falls away from his mouth, a sympathetic expression. "I'm so sorry, girl."

"I just need to get away for a while."

"No. What you need to do is go pay Miss Mother a visit. Now *that's* what you need to do. I'm sorry, for what I almost said, girl, but have you ever thought that maybe she's the reason you deal with men the way you do?" He holds his breath for a moment, and then, "Chile, it was just a thought. Don't be mad at me, okay?"

I shrug.

How can I be mad at you, Ernie? You're right.

Dressed in an ivory chiffon robe, her hair hanging loose, and her glass in her hand, she pulls the door open. "Hello, my love," she says. "Come on in."

Nancy Wilson is quietly singing from the stereo when we get to the back den. A game of solitaire is spread out across the coffee table. An Agatha Christie novel on the arm of the couch. Mommie gestures with her glass. "Drink?"

"No thanks." I take a seat on the rocking chair.

She turns the radio off before sitting down on the couch. "Didn't Ernie want to come up?"

"Just me."

She looks at me with a sad smile. "You look so gloomy."

I gaze at her, a woman who has aged so gracefully, still stunningly gorgeous, so sophisticated, such a remarkable presence, with such a graceful way of being, and I realize that if I could go back twenty years the image would be precisely the same. Me, sitting with my mother, admiring her beauty as she sits there so effortlessly elegant. With that damn glass in her hand.

"I'm not gloomy," I say.

An easy nod. "Okay." She leans back a little.

I look down at the cards on the coffee table. "Solitaire, huh?"

She glances at the cards, and then back at me. "What's wrong?"

If I could just open my mouth, talk to her, express my feelings. If only things were that simple. If only she could read my mind like when I was a little girl and I'd walk in the room and she'd just know. Her thin hand across my cheek felt like a whisper from the sky sometimes, telling me everything is going to be okay. This is the woman who has always been my icon of existence, how can I say anything now that may hurt her feelings? How can we talk and not have the discussion erupt into an argument?

"I tried to call you earlier today," she says.

"I'm at Ernie's."

She looks uncomfortable, a curious look, and she waits.

"Did Bo answer?" I ask.

She raises her chin and studies my face. "I left a message for you to call me. I thought that was why you called and said you were going to stop by."

"No. I just wanted to see you."

"Well, good." With a nonchalant sweep, she gathers the playing cards and begins stacking them into a neat pile. "Sweetheart, you are eating, aren't you? You look terribly thin."

"Ernie made chicken earlier."

"Oh?" She smiles. "Good?"

"Ernie's a great cook."

"Here." She hands me a pink envelope from the desk. "This came in the mail for you."

I don't bother to look down at it before stuffing it in the pocket of the jacket Ernie let me borrow. Then I toy with the string from the hood as I say, "Bo and I aren't doing too well."

Mommie gives her stack of cards a quick shuffle before putting them on the table. "Did you have an argument?" She picks up her glass.

I nod. "Pretty bad."

"What about?"

"I don't know. I guess I embarrassed him."

"In public?"

I nod. "It just makes me think that I'm not ready for marriage."

She takes another drink. "Possibly not, but darling, couples have arguments all the time."

"It's more than that." I shake my head. "I think I'm afraid of commitment."

She starts to respond, but instead waits for me to continue.

I take a breath. "The other night there was this woman, Mommie. Sitting there, on his couch. And he wouldn't let me in. How am I supposed to just swallow that?"

She widens her eyes, and blinks. "Oh, really?"

"Yes."

"And did you ask him who this woman was?"

"His friend from law school."

"Okay. And you don't believe him?"

"No."

"Why not?" She pauses. "Duran tells me you've had company recently."

She shakes her glass, now only filled with ice, and heads toward the kitchen—more than likely for a refill.

I follow her down the hallway, and I say quietly, "So now there are a million things running through my mind."

"I'm listening," she says.

First she gets the vodka from the cupboard.

"Mommie, I was talking to Ernie earlier, and he said something that made sense to me, and I just need to share it with you, okay?"

"Sure." She takes the iced tea from the refrigerator. "Go ahead."

"Ernie thinks that I measure my existence based upon whether or not I have a man in my presence, and that when I don't, I can't handle it. And in all honesty I can't really say that he's completely wrong."

"Interesting," she says.

"I mean, I've never wanted to be one of those women who can't cope because they didn't have their father around. I suppose in a way Daddy was, but maybe because of not having him, and things being so great when he *was* around, and Ernie thinks—"

"This Ernie," she interrupts, "sure has a lot of opinions. Ever tell Ernie what people think about him?"

I sigh. "Just hear me, okay?"

She mixes her brew.

I close my eyes, listen to the familiar rhythm that the spoon and glass make as she mixes. Always mixing her brew. "I used to think that nothing else really mattered to me besides someday becoming a fashion model, and having a prince to call my own. And being like you." I sigh.

Her eyes watch me with nervous anticipation. "Where's this going?" She drinks a little.

"Well, you know, I used to see you with Daddy, and how happy you were to be with him, and it made Duran and me so happy to see you happy. But when you weren't with Daddy, when Daddy didn't come—*couldn't* come, you changed."

Her face stone silent, she stares back at me as she drinks.

"I don't mean to hurt your feelings, Mommie, but when Daddy couldn't come you were different, you did just what you're doing now. You drank too much. You became irritable. You didn't . . ." I look away as I try to continue.

She softly clears her throat. "I didn't what?" she says curtly.

Get it off of your chest, Shawni. Don't back down now. Be brave. Say it. She's already mad, how much worse can it get?

I grimace as I force myself to continue. "I really do feel pretty messed up when I don't feel validated. And lately I've been feeling really vulnerable, and I don't know what I would do if Bo cheated on me."

"Don't kid yourself, darling, there is not a woman on earth who can single-handedly be everything for a man. Don't fall into that 'I'm getting married and now we should be everything for each other' way of thinking. The man said she's a friend, so be it. Don't you have friends of the opposite sex?"

"But he wouldn't let me in!"

"Would *you* have let you in? Duran tells me you were hanging out on Bo's window ledge like a wild woman."

"Mommie! I'm sitting here telling you that Bo has another woman, and you're going to turn around and make this about me? You know what had to be going on if she was over and he wouldn't let me in. It's obvious."

"Perhaps." She hums as she thinks. "But the man says that wasn't the case. Duran even cosigns for him. Sweetheart, you know your brother wouldn't do that if it weren't legitimate. When a man gives you his word on something, you just shouldn't question it for a second unless you have hard evidence. You have so much to learn, darling. When a man is handling his business, you step aside and let him handle it. You don't pop in, sneaking up behind him to see what he's doing."

"You talked to Bo, didn't you? He told you what happened!"

She sighs. "I sensed that he was upset. And I did have to pry it out of him."

"I bet he didn't tell you how rude the woman was when she called this morning, did he?"

"He said something about it, yes. But sweetheart, listen to me, okay? When I tell you you have a lot to learn about men, I'm not kidding."

"I wouldn't have gone down there if she hadn't called this morning saying he was late to meet her for breakfast. I wouldn't be so paranoid if I hadn't gone down to Brooklyn the other night and seen another woman, half dressed, on his couch!"

"Okay, let's be blunt," she says, her eyes ready to talk business.

"All men cheat at some point, okay? That's what you need to know right here and now. I'm just gonna go ahead and tell you right now. All men cheat. It's unfortunate but that's the way things are."

She shrugs. "Call it what you will. It's what I've learned for fact, Shawni. It took me years to accept it, too. I see so much of myself in you, darling. I was the same way, scared to death of commitment. Allow me to save you the turmoil. You go on thinking that Bo is never going to have a little something on the side throughout your entire marriage, and you're going to have high tides to row, okay? Accept it now and your marriage will be a lot easier."

"We broke up, Mommie," I spit out. "There isn't going to be a wedding." I face her and wait for her reaction.

"Darling, with everything that you're going through, I'm sure you just need some away time to clear your mind. Everything will be fine."

"I hope so. But there isn't going to be a wedding. It's over."

A scorned look in her eyes, she holds her glass up as if to say cheers, and an eerie smile crosses her face. "Congratulations." She drinks a little. "What you wanted, right? To not get married and then blame it on me?" She downs the rest of her drink, looks at the glass, shakes the ice around some more, and then very casually and effortlessly she just drops it. Pieces of glass and ice shatter about.

I look down at the glass. More shattered pieces. "Mommie, I'm sorry, why'd you drop your glass?" I go to get the broom.

I'm stopped by the sound of glass clinking and I look back to see the heels of her house slippers cracking across the glass as she leaves the kitchen. I hurry to follow her.

She heads back into the den and sits down.

"Mommie?"

She just sits there, looking right through me, going to that place that is beyond me, a place I cannot see, a place where she ignores me calling her name, a place I've seen her visit before. Duran urging me to just leave her alone for a while.

"Mommie?" I plead in front of her as I wait for her to say something.

She puts her hands together, her nails perfectly manicured as usual, a double coat of red polish, and she says quietly. "We'll discuss this later, darling."

My mind rushes desperately, "I thought that if I told you how I felt, maybe it'd help . . ."

What did I think I was going to accomplish?

I start rambling, saying a lot of things, anything to relieve the tension that my remarks have created, to ease my increasing guilt about continuously hurting her.

But she's already said it. *We'll talk about it later*. It's a proven fact that no matter how long I try to persuade her, the verdict is not going to change.

A brochure, pale pink, matching the envelope, falls out after I rip open the envelope. There is a beautiful silhouette of a woman with an abstract setting in the background. The woman's head is slightly bowed, it reminds me of that Picasso painting *The Blue Nude*, only happier.

"What's that?" Ernie asks as he drives away from Mommie's building.

"Just some mail for me that was sent to Mommie's."

"How'd it go?"

"The usual."

You Are Not Alone! The brochure reads across the top in bold letters. An odd sensation comes over me as I continue to read. Who sent this?

Dear *Shawni Baldwin*,

**Troubled? Unhappy? Overwhelmed by crossroads?
Not yourself lately? Feel like you're at the end of your rope?
Tie a knot, and hold on! *Help is on the way.***

You are not alone, and someone who cares about you wants you to know. This is an invitation to freedom! Freedom from the fears that you are afraid to face. Freedom from the things that are prohibiting you from being the person you ought to be.

You are *not* alone!

A space has been reserved and paid for by someone who cares about you for our next retreat. Please call the toll-free number below to verify that you will attend. You will *not* be alone!

ETERNAL HOPE WOMEN'S RETREAT CENTER

Further instructions will be given when you call!
Please don't pass this by!

"Thanks Ernie," I say sarcastically.

"For what?"

"This invitation. I know it's from you."

"If I sent you an invitation, you're gonna have to tell me where the party is and what time it starts. Invitation to what?"

"Very funny, Ernie. Did he call while I was gone?"

"Who?"

"*Ernie!* Who do you think?"

"Nope. Bo the ho didn't call."

"I don't need to hear that!" I snap. "Did you or did you not send this?" I hand him the paper.

He reads it, shakes his head, and hands it back to me. "Somebody sent my brother and his wife on one of those couple's retreats like that a few years ago."

"Some sort of a hoax, huh?"

He smacks his lips. "Hell naw. Shoot. My brother said they came back and made whoopee like jack rabbits every day for like two months."

I laugh a little. Whatever. Probably some sweepstakes gimmick.

Two o'clock. A.M.

I tiptoe out into the living room. I can't tell who's snoring louder—Ernie or Sanford.

I feel around in the dark for the couch. "Ernie?" I whisper.

He jerks up. "Hmm? What's wrong?"

I kneel and slide down on the floor in front of the couch. "I can't sleep."

He lets out a long breath. "Guess that means I won't be able to either, huh?"

"I just keep thinking about him." A pang in my chest. "What if he's with someone?"

"Shawni, it doesn't mean anything. Filler hos. That's all. You know, can't be with the one you love, get a filler ho. You've done that yourself, remember? Trip. Zin the Gentleman."

"I can't do this." I feel around and grab the leg of Ernie's cotton pajamas and tug. "Ernie, help me. I don't want to be by myself."

He sits up. "Now that we've reduced my presence to phantom status . . . But my feelings aren't hurt, chile. Come here." He pats the couch.

I crawl up onto the couch next to him, and he puts his arm around me. I nestle my head onto his chest. "I can't take it," I say.

He rubs my arm. "It's just something you have to get through, that's all."

"Just look at my life. It's in ruins!"

"Oh, shut the hell up, Shawni! Tell that to the folks living on the streets and the folks on their deathbeds. Your life isn't ruined, chile. We just gotta get through this. It'll be okay."

I close my eyes. "I just wish I could stop thinking about him."

"So stop trying to. Why? Maybe thinking long and hard is what you need to do."

"I refuse to sit here drowning myself in regret. If he wants it to be over, I'll just have to deal with it."

"Why is it so hard for you to admit that you need him? You're human."

I think for a moment, and then say, "Because I don't."

"If you say so."

Without intending to I slept most of the day on Sunday. I'd wake up every now and then to run to the bathroom, and then crawl right back into bed. I heard Ernie take Sanford outside once, and I tried to say thank you, but I was too sleepy. I also remember waking up to see Ernie's eyes, wide open, staring down at me. I wanted to say something, but I fell back asleep instead.

I don't even have the strength to look down at Sanford, who is begging for my attention. The energy that I finally have to get out of bed is minimal as I make my way into the kitchen.

"Oh, my goodness!" Ernie shouts. "Shawni, would you please at least eat a piece of toast or something? Please don't make me see you in the hospital again."

The sun is yelling wake up as it coats every corner of his olive-colored kitchenette.

"I'm just sleepy. Is it Monday?" I rub my eyes.

"Umm hmm." He hands me a mug.

"What's this?" I make my way over to the small round table and sit down.

"Coffee. French Vanilla," he says.

"Thanks for taking Sanford out," I say.

"Dog's bigger than me—big old thing took *me* out. You're welcome chile. I got him some dog food."

"When did you go to the store?"

"As if you would know—you've been so out of it."

I pat my leg for Sanford to come, and he does. "What's all this sticky stuff on his mouth?" I try to scrape off the cream-colored mess around his mouth as he whimpers and tries to avoid my pulling at it.

"Oh." Ernie leans over and eyes Sanford's mouth. "Hell, that dog wanted some of my butter pecan. What I look like telling a big Doberman no?"

"You gave him ice cream!" I shout.

"What? Will it hurt him? Oh, Lord the dog's gone die!"

"No," I laugh. "I guess a little bit won't hurt him, but Ernie, he's a dog."

He gets up and wets a paper towel for me to wipe Sanford's mouth. "Ernie didn't know, shoot. Ernie was just trying to satisfy the dog's begging."

"I know. Thanks, Ernie."

"Girl, you have to eat. You want some cereal at least? Fruity Pebbles or something?"

"Do you have Frosted Flakes?"

He smiles. "Lord, yes."

"Okay. I'm gonna lie down for a few more minutes, and when I get up I'll have some, okay?"

"Chile . . ." He moans as I leave the kitchen.

On Tuesday morning Ernie tried to wake me up. He was leaving for work and said I could drive him and keep the car if I wanted, said that I could come get my hair done if I wanted—his treat. I sat up in bed, smiled at the thought, and then went right back to sleep. It was noon before I woke up.

Sanford was begging me to go outside. I remember contemplating calling Otto and paying him to take Sanford out, but reality shot through my chest when I realized that I wasn't at home and that the condo would never be home again.

I groggily made my way to the front door to take Sanford out, and I realized that all I had on was a T-shirt. I rummaged through Ernie's clothes and found a pair of green sweatpants and put them on. They were too short—way too short. I broke down crying right on the bathroom floor. Sanford licked my tears as I wept.

With my only changes of clothes over at Bo's, I finally put my dirty ones back on and took Sanford outside.

I came back in and went right back to sleep, with Sanford stretched out snoring beside me.

I heard the phone ringing all day, but it seemed too far away to reach.

The place was dark when I heard Ernie come in.

"Chile . . ." I heard him say softly as he washed my face. Whatever he said after that, I don't remember. All I know is that I begged him through my tears to just let me sleep. I would get up in a minute. I remember how my face felt pleasantly refreshed, and then I just fell asleep again.

The weird thing is, I don't remember dreaming anything.

It was as if I were dead.

That was Wednesday.

On Thursday I wanted to get out of bed, so I did.

"God, you probably are dying to go out," I mumbled. "Sanford?" I squinted as I looked around the room.

"I took him out earlier." Sanford's voice came from the corner of the bedroom. He was sitting on the floor doing a crossword puzzle. He looked peculiar with reading glasses on. Then I realized that it wasn't Sanford. Of course it wasn't Sanford. I did a double-take. Sanford can't talk.

"Ernie." I looked at the clock. "What are you doing home? It's only two o'clock."

"Can I take a lunch break?" He rolled his eyes. "I'm not like you, Anna Rexia. I *like* to eat."

"I'm just not hungry," I grumbled as I made my way into the bathroom. "That's a long way to come for just lunch."

"Shawni, maybe you should go ahead and take the medication."

"I'm not sick. You take them."

"Your brother called," he said before I closed the bathroom door. "He says he'll be back in town tomorrow. Wants to see you."

If I didn't know it was definitely me, I would have thought it was a stranger staring back at me in the mirror.

She was feeble. Sickly.

Her eyes were puffy and barely opened, dim.

I thought you only get bags under your eyes from a lack of sleep?

Her hair was dry, looked matted even.

She was too tired to do anything about it.

She was even too tired to cry again.

"Has he called?" I asked Ernie as I crawled back into bed.

"If you're talking about Duran, no. Your father, no. Bo, I wouldn't tell you if he had. Chile, I gotta go back to work. I fed Sanford. Please be finished with all this resting when I get home. I'm really worried about you." He kissed me on my forehead.

I tried to go back to sleep, but it wasn't as easy.

I rolled over and picked up the phone.

I wanted to call Bo, so I dialed, but I didn't push the right numbers.

"Hello?" I said as I tried to keep my eyes open.

"Hello?" an unfamiliar voice replied.

"Sorry, wrong number," I heard myself say before hanging up.

That evening when Ernie got home I asked him if Bo was on the answering machine.

"No," he replied.

"Has he called at all this week?"

"No," he said again. "I brought us some Chinese."

I ate as little as I could.

Ernie left late Thursday evening to go to the grocery store. He made me promise not to kill myself while he was gone. I literally had to say, "I promise not to die while you're gone," before he would leave the apartment.

And I tried to go back to sleep, but I couldn't. I reached over and grabbed my purse, dumped the contents of it out on the bed, and felt around for my phone book. Yusef answered on the first ring. He couldn't believe I was calling, wanted to know why I was calling—

hadn't I gotten him into enough trouble that night at the club? He said Duran's always tripping. I told him that that was something he didn't have to tell me about. He asked if I was okay. From his tone of voice I could tell that he knew what had happened. I asked him for Zin's number in Atlanta, told him I needed to talk to Zin about some clothes for a gig next month. He said he didn't have his home number, but he had his pager. I told him that that would do. I didn't tell Yusef this, but I needed a fix. Real bad. I needed to get away. I was going to call Zin and suggest me coming to Atlanta for a visit. Yusef's so gullible. He believed me.

Zin's voice startled me at first. What was I going to say? I hung up.

I dialed his pager again.

"This is Zin." His voice was rushed, music playing in the background. "Yo, I can't call you back if you don't leave a message, so you know what to do. Holler."

Beep.

I froze for a moment, looked around the room to make sure no one was watching, which was silly, there was no one here besides Sanford and me.

"Hey," I said. "This is Shawni. I just called . . ." I laughed. "Why don't you give me a buzz? I've moved." And I messed up a couple of times as I tried to recite Ernie's phone number. I finally got it right, pushed the pound sign, and hung up.

Maybe I just needed to get out, go see a play, get my mind off of everything—on something else, someone else.

I skimmed through my phone book for a while. I hadn't done that in a long time. I had to literally think hard and try to remember faces of guys I hadn't talked to in awhile. For one of my ex-boyfriends, I only had his mother's phone number, and he was the only one I thought I would actually enjoy talking to. I was getting ready to call her and ask her for the phone number to where he's stationed in Germany, when the phone rang.

I answered in a hurry. (This is how I know that things were getting pretty bad. I would never have answered the phone in a hurry.) "Hello?"

"Hey, girl." It was Ernie. "I was just checking on you. I was going to make fish for dinner tomorrow. What kind should I buy?"

I thought it was going to be Zin calling back. Instead Ernie was bugging me about food! "Tuna's fine," I said.

"Tuna?" he repeated. "How's that for a fine dining experience?"

"Tuna, Ernie!" I shouted, and hung up the phone.

Then I sat up and again felt around amid all the stuff from my purse for my phone book. I felt a piece of paper and wondered what it was. I picked it up. Looked at it. Pale pink. You Are Not Alone, it reminded me.

I figured it couldn't hurt to call the number and see what they say. I could always just hang up. If they asked me for my social security number, I'd know it was a gimmick.

An operator answered. Her voice was friendly. "Eternal Hope," she said.

"Is this some type of a cult?" I asked.

"Who's this?" she pleasantly replied.

"I got this thing in the mail last week."

"Let's start with your name."

"Shawni," I say.

"Great!" she exclaimed. "We're so glad you called."

Was I supposed to answer her? Was this a joke?

"Who is this?" I asked.

"My name is Kaitlyn. I'm a woman of Eternal Hope."

I wanted to hang up, but didn't.

"Shawni, I'd be happy to confirm a reservation for you?"

"Wait. I don't even know what this is yet."

"Well, it's an all women's retreat, and most of the details are kept confidential until you actually go through the program. I can tell you that we were founded in 1987, and we've been helping hundreds of women across the country who are experiencing new challenges ever since. Someone thought this might be a rewarding experience for you, and has paid for your space. I can also tell you that I am a woman of Eternal Hope, and that I have been happier ever since."

She does sound quite chipper.

"Can you at least tell me who sent me this?" I ask.

She hesitated. "I can tell you that it is someone who cares about you very much, and that they're very concerned about you. They want you to know that you are not alone. Would you like me to confirm your reservation?"

"You said someone who cares about me?"

"That's right. And they're very concerned about you."

If it wasn't Ernie, could it be Mommie? Duran? Bo?

"Well, can you tell me if it's a man or a woman at least?"

She laughed. "No, but I can tell you that I'd be happy to confirm the reservation. Should we anticipate seeing you tomorrow?"

"So soon? I don't know."

"Well, there are other dates, but why wait?"

"I don't know . . ."

"Just get a pen and a pad and take down the information." She sounded as if she was smiling.

I snatched a pen and piece of scratch paper from the pile of junk, and prepared my hand to write. "Okay," I said. "I'm ready."

"We know you are," she replied.

EIGHT

Detox

*t*oday is Friday.

I'm supposed to be there by six o'clock.

It's almost four.

Should I go? What if it's a scam?

But then, what if turns out to be what I truly need?

Kaitlyn told me to pack only underwear, so I wash the extra pairs that I have with me, borrow Ernie's backpack, and prepare to leave. My hand is tense as I dial the number to the car service as Kaitlyn had instructed.

If they take me into the woods and kill me, will anyone find me?

If they drive me off of the face of the earth, will I even desire to come back?

I don't know.

I don't care.

The only thing that is keeping me standing is the wish of what this could be.

Maybe someone really does care about me.

Maybe this retreat will really help.

A voice is screaming from the pit of my stomach, begging me to be me again.

Months ago I knew who I was. I was happy being in my own skin. I had everything I wanted. Today I have no idea who I am, or what to do in order to feel like myself again.

I don't even recognize my own handwriting as I write the note.

Ernie—Thank you for everything. Please take care of Sanford. I owe you so much. I'm very sad. Gone away until Monday—to find freedom.   Love, Shawni

I give Sanford a piece of sausage as I leave, and I'm down the hallway and out the door before I realize that I forgot to cook it.

Looks like I just murdered my dog, I sigh.

The car is waiting with a pink flag on the antenna—just like Kaitlyn said it would.

There is a moment where I do not want to go inside the building. I want to look back, to go back, but at the same time, if I can just make it to the door. I'm afraid that if I don't keep walking, I will break down again.

But this flash of ambiguity passes, and I compose myself. I will not cry. I move toward the white ranch-style building. I have to go inside. Inside this retreat center, I am told I will find freedom. Freedom from what, I don't know. But I do know that it sounds nice.

"Your name?" the petite woman asks as I walk in. She's holding a clipboard and is ready to write something as she waits for my reply.

I look around, and the purposefully cozy atmosphere surprises me. The den has yellow carpet, floral wallpaper, and a very large fireplace. I expected a hospital setting, but this just looks like some-one's country-styled living room, or at least a hospital trying to emu-late one.

"Shawni Baldwin," I say.

"Welcome, I'm Kaitlyn." She extends her hand, and I can't imagine any other face matching her voice anymore. She is just as pleasant in person as she was over the phone. She nods up. "The others are all in chapel, so you should hurry and join them. I'll take your bag." She slips the backpack off my shoulder, and I suddenly feel naked without it.

She tells me to take the stairs at the end of the hallway, and to go into the first door on my left. "You should be able to hear every-one from the hallway," she concludes. "Good luck to you," she adds.

I count the sixteen stairs on the way up because I am willing to do anything to keep my mind off crying. Kaitlyn was right, I hear voices coming from behind the paint-chipped white door.

What is strange, however, is that the voices are laughing. She did say the first door on the left. This has to be it.

Maybe this is all a joke.

A dream, perhaps?

A surprise party?

I quietly open the door, and I'm surprised at how close everyone is. I imagined "chapel" to be a huge room with maybe fifty or sixty pews and a balcony, and with a pulpit in the front. Instead, this "chapel" has only eight oak pews, with green cushions that are age-stained. There is no balcony, and the "pulpit" is only a podium with a microphone. There is a small organ in the front, and a poster that says You Are Not Alone! propped in front of it. I suddenly notice how quiet it has gotten as the seven or so faces stare back at me. Well, they aren't actually staring—just looking, and smiling.

"Well, thank goodness," a shapely bleached blond woman, wearing a blue sweatshirt and faded jeans, says with a grin. Her teeth are nicotine-stained and her perm has grown out, and something about her makes her seem nice. Her voice is rough, yet welcoming. "You must be the Princess?" She smiles.

"Princess?" I ask nervously, and notice that all the faces are smiling curiously back at me, so I try to smile, too, but I'm so nervous.

"Sure. We all said we'd call you Princess, since you arrived so fashionably late, you know? Like royalty." She smiles and her eyes squint as she waits for me to respond.

"Oh." I try to laugh. Then the others laugh, and that helps ease my uneasiness.

"I'm Linda." She extends her hand. "I'm going to be your retreat leader. It's good to have you with us. Shawni, right?"

I shake her hand and want to say "Nice to meet you also" but I'm still so nervous. Maybe I'm just hungry? I should have had a little vodka at least. Something to help me relax. Too late now.

"Well"—she rocks back and forth on her white Reebok tennis shoes—"we were waiting for you, so I guess we can get started." She tells everyone to have a seat in the first three rows of pews and then takes her place behind the podium. She puts her hands in her back pockets and waits for us to settle.

I sit on the end closest to the aisle, and a woman with chestnut brown hair and too many freckles sits down next to me. She smiles, gently, and says hello. Her voice is quiet.

"Hi," I say, and I'm surprised that I was able to manage that much.

Linda leans into the podium and begins talking. "I think everyone knows my name by now, but for any of you who didn't catch it, I'm Linda." She clasps her hands together. "I'm going to be your retreat leader, which means I'll be with you from now until you leave here Monday morning."

Monday morning?

I eye the door in the back of the chapel, the same one I just willingly walked through.

What am I doing here?

"I think it's best if we just be as open with each other as possible from here on," Linda continues. "If my breath stinks, don't smile and pretend like it doesn't, tell me. Because you better believe I'm gonna tell you."

Everyone laughs except me.

The woman sitting next to me lets out a soft humming laugh.

I'm starting to panic.

"Really," Linda continues, "I know there is a thing called tact, but I'm really a straight-forward type of gal, and that's the way I hope you'll be with me during your stay here at Eternal Hope." She clears her throat and stands up straight. "Of course, there will be other leaders that will be with us throughout the weekend, but I am the only one who will be here from beginning to end."

"We need to, unfortunately, set down ground rules. You know, like they used to do at camp and we never paid any attention? Well, not much different here. Rules are rules, and they have to be followed. But before we get to the rules, I'm supposed to tell you about myself, so that's what I'll do."

Linda smiles, and leans down on the podium again. The room is silent as she rubs her index finger along the edge of the podium and stares down. Finally she looks up and gazes out at us. "I've always hated this part. I like just getting to know people naturally, but, well, they make me give you my bio, so here goes. My name is Linda. Well, I've said that. I'm uh, thirty-seven years young. I'm a third-year woman of Eternal Hope. I have a seventeen-year-old son."

She pauses and smiles, a forced smile this time, which seems out of character for her. Up until this point, her smiles seemed to flow easily.

"My son," she continues, "is somewhere in this country. God knows where—I don't. I haven't seen him since he was thirteen years old. He uh, ran out on me, ran away from home one night. That night his daddy had beat me so bad that I couldn't hear out of either ear. I didn't even know it was him saying ' 'Bye Mommy' to me 'cause my ears were throbbing so bad. I kept thinking it was my husband saying 'stop sobbing, stop sobbing' but nope, it was Scotty, my boy, saying ' 'Bye Mommy.' "

We all seem to be breathing with a common rhythm now, cautious about how loud.

"Wasn't so bad getting beat up like that, you know? Compare that with having your only son say ' 'Bye Mommy,' and not being able to see what he looks like one last time, nor have the strength in your jaws to ask him where he's going. I just know that I was lying on the kitchen floor, and I heard the back screen door close. And I sighed to myself because I thought that was just like Scotty to be careful about not letting the door slam, you know? Real sweet kid, always was.

"So anyhow, I slept on the kitchen floor that night, too weak to get up. Cat woke me up next morning wanting to eat, licking my swollen eyes. I tried to open 'em but I couldn't really see when I did—swollen so bad. Could see enough just to feel around and feed the cat. Figured it out later that my man had run out on me, too. House was empty, except for the cat."

Linda laughs and shakes her head, "I used to think if it weren't for that damn cat I'd a died on that floor, went into a coma or something. For a long time I wished I had." She pauses. "But I know now that I had to get up—in more ways than one."

She exhales. "So, a few months later, I got a letter from Scotty, saying something like 'Hey Mom, hope you're feelin' better. I'm okay here at Grandma's.' Grandma was my husband's mother—never liked me much. A couple of weeks later, I got the invitation to Eternal Hope. I had no idea what it was, but I knew I hadn't eaten in days, and that without my husband I had no idea where my next meal was coming from. I didn't have a job—no skills, no money, no son, no nothing. I thought I'd at least get a meal out of it. Turns out I got my life back. Came here, and my life changed. Did you hear me ladies? My life *changed*." She adds, suddenly upbeat again, "And it's *still* changing."

As I look into Linda's face, not even three feet from my own, it's really hard to accept that this is a true story. How could anyone have done that to her? I glance at the woman sitting next to me, and she has unfolded a Kleenex in her hand and is dabbing a tear out of the corner of her eye. I immediately turn my attention back to Linda, who isn't crying, and focus on her. I don't want the woman next to me to inspire me to start crying.

Linda continues, "When I first left the program, I left all cleaned up with a new outlook on life. Got out, and the first thing I wanted to do was get my son home. It was a week before his fourteenth birthday, and I called. He had run away again. He left a note, they said, saying 'Tell Mom I hope she gets better.' That was the last time anyone heard from him.

"So six months later and another abusive relationship later, I ended up right back in here. I wanted to change my life again—desperately—and I did. Harder the second time, though, because I wasn't doing it for my son, so I could take care of him. I was doing it for me, so I could take care of me. And that's what I'm doing now. Taking care of Linda.

"So." She smiles. "If you're sitting there wondering what on earth you're doing here, just look around and know that you're all thinking the same thing. You're not alone. Ladies, please trust that the retreat does work if you let it. But you have to be willing to let it."

She waits a moment, and then, "And that's enough about me." She smiles.

Everyone begins clapping, and it is startling, because the applause is so loud and sudden. I'm jolted into thinking that I should probably leave, slip out, and go home now. I'm looking around at these women, and I'm thinking that they all probably have stories like Linda's. Stories about men leaving them, abusing them, and getting beaten and raped. I don't have that story.

I'm a twenty-nine-year-old ex-model. I leave men; men don't use and abuse me. I've never been left by a . . . Okay, so no man has ever hit me. I have an overprotective brother who with one phone call could have the guy who hit me spitting out his own teeth in an alley somewhere in the Bronx. No, I do not fit the profile of a battered woman. Thank you very much.

Then again, why am I here? My life is . . . I don't even know my life anymore.

Linda's soliloquy, and her words about her life changing, keep echoing in my mind, and I can't leave. I want change, too. What'll I miss if I leave?

Unexpectedly, I feel something in my hand and look down. It is a soft Kleenex, and the dark-haired woman with too many freckles who is sitting next to me is slipping it to me. I look up at her tear-stained face, and she nods for me to take it. I do, and hold it to my own face and realize that I want to bury myself inside this Kleenex. I notice the color of the tissue. No biting of my tongue or twitching of my nose stops the tears from streaming down my face now. I never thought I'd see the day when not even the color baby blue brings me joy.

How can I leave? I have nowhere else to go.

The door in the back of the chapel opens and Kaitlyn enters, her hair bouncing as she makes her way to the podium, grinning. As I look around, I notice that she and Linda are the only two in the entire room who are smiling. Everyone else is wiping her tears.

"Gosh, Linda!" Kaitlyn says. "What'd you say to everyone?" She and Linda laugh.

"This always happens on the first night," Linda assures us.

Kaitlyn takes a deep breath. "The next thing we need to accomplish is getting your room assignments, your complimentary Eternal Hope jogging suits, so you can be nice and comfy all weekend, and introductions. You've met Linda, I know. And I've met all of you. I know a lot about you all, but I know you have a thousand questions for me. First, I'll tell you that I'm Kaitlyn, as you all know, and I'm a woman of Eternal Hope. You'll understand what that's all about soon enough. And I promise you that by the time you go back on Monday morning you will know who submitted your name. That is the least of our concern right now. Let's briefly introduce ourselves first. Just tell us your first name, and something special about yourself, okay?" She scrunches up her nose and nods at Linda.

"Okay," Linda agrees. "Let's just go around the room. How's that?"

And so we do. I have no idea what the first three women say, because I am fretfully anticipating my own statement. I hear nervous laughter as the ladies talk, as the voices get closer to me.

"My name is Debi," I hear someone say on the other side of the woman sitting next to me. Her voice is clear and strong, and commands attention. "I'm thirty-two and I'm from Jersey," she says.

"I'm . . . uh . . ." the woman next to me wipes her nose. Her freckled face is flushed now as she speaks. "I'm Janet, and I really don't know what to say about myself. I'm, uh . . . I'm from Brooklyn. Is that enough?"

Linda and Kaitlyn both nod and smile before simultaneously nodding at me.

Everyone is looking at me.

"Shawni?" Someone's voice snaps my attention. Linda says with a smile, "Isn't it?"

"Yes," I clear my throat and say, "My name is Shawni, and I guess I can't really say where I live because I don't really have a . . . I'm originally from Milan, but I moved from there when I was a little girl. I, uh . . . I grew up in Manhattan." I wipe my eyes.

"Okay." Linda nods. "That was everyone, right?"

Then again, that wasn't so bad.

Kaitlyn responds to Linda. "I think so. Now, Linda, did you notice anything peculiar about the introductions?"

"As a matter of fact," Linda laughs, "I did."

I eye both of them suspiciously, and as I glance around I see that the other women are doing the same.

"Ladies," Kaitlyn says cheerfully. "It's okay. Notice the sign over here." She points to the poster board in front of the organ. "Remember our slogan, 'you are not alone.' But did any of you notice that not one of you mentioned anything regarding men."

I gasp without meaning to.

So does the woman sitting next to me, Janet.

Debi does, too. Hers is the most audible of all.

Linda and Kaitlyn are both laughing.

"That tells us," Linda says, "that there is always hope. Perhaps some of you have programmed yourselves to believe that your existence is dependent on a man. Perhaps some of you feel like you are less of a woman because you don't have a man. We already know that one of you has just gone through a third divorce. But rejoice, ladies! The first step is realizing that you are someone regardless, and I think each of your introductions demonstrated that."

I never went to college, by choice. I was making more money modeling in high school than most people were making with master's degrees. I figured I could learn without chasing a degree. But I did use to imagine what it would have been like to live in a dorm. Now, it looks like this weekend will give me a taste of that.

The sheets are clean, I hope, but I can't believe that I am actually not in the least bit appalled by the idea of having to sleep in the bottom bunk of a bed that other people have slept in. My roommate turned out to be my heavily freckled brunette pew-mate from earlier, Janet. She smiles gracefully as she climbs to the top bunk.

We were told that we would have until ten o'clock to rest, shower, put on our pink cotton jogging suits, and meet in the den.

Kaitlyn said that we would find something on our beds, and sure enough there is a large pink envelope waiting on the bottom bunk with my name typed on the front. Inside is a pale pink sheet of paper—a brief, typed note—addressed to me, and there is also a sealed white envelope, which I place on the bed while I read the pink note.

> Welcome, Shawni! We are so delighted that you have decided to join us! You will not regret your experience this weekend.
>
> As you know, someone who cares about you has submitted your name as an ideal candidate for this retreat. Enclosed, please find an unsigned letter from that individual. Please note, however, that you will not know your sponsor's identity until the conclusion of the weekend, at which point you will certainly be aware.

Get your rest. Tonight will not be easy.
Detox begins at ten o'clock!

The letter is on pearl white stationery with unfamiliar cursive handwriting in black fountain ink.

Dearest Shawni,

Please do not take this letter as a retroactive retort, but instead know that what I'm going to say to you is what I have enveloped inside my heart for the many years that I have known you. It is only now, at this point, that I feel the urge to reach out to you, that it will behoove you to hear this and to truly experience Eternal Hope.

Shawni, you have become the most selfish bitch that I have ever encountered in my life! We have always spoken of a "friendship" that you and I have; yet I must point out to you that a friendship, in my definition of the word, is something that two people share. It is not a boastful attempt on one person's part to suck the loving life out of the other as long as breath exists. Friendship is loyalty.

I don't mean to hurt your feelings, but I love you enough to tell you how I really feel. Sure, despite your flaws you offer a lot to the world, but it's been difficult for me to remember that about you lately. I hope I can again someday soon. I hope that you will get the help you need.

Please be open to your experience at Eternal Hope. That's the only way it will be successful. This is the time to ask yourself *why* you do the things you do. Okay? I'll see you soon.

My Best

I hug my pillow, crawl into bed—not caring about anyone having slept here before, and wait for sleep to come. I highly doubt if I will be able to get up at ten. How will I lift my heavy heart from this bed? Is any of what this person wrote about me true? I've heard the saying all my life, but not until now do I know how accurate it is. The truth really can hurt.

"Shawni?" Someone's hand is cool on my wrist as they gently shake it. "I hate to wake you, but it's almost ten."

I'm surprised that I was actually able to fall asleep. The last thing I remember is a letter, a really mean letter. It takes me a moment to realize exactly where I am and that it is Janet who is shaking my arm.

"Oh." I try to sit up. "Thanks. I think I'm just gonna lay here."

The door to our room suddenly opens and Linda's rough voice accompanies her smiling face, "Detox begins in fifteen minutes, ladies. You better get a move on." And she closes the door.

"I'm tired, too," Janet says. "Hopefully, they'll let us rest when we get back." She bends down to tie up her shoelaces.

I didn't bring any tennis shoes.

All I have are my boots—stilettos.

They didn't tell me to bring comfortable shoes, and I wasn't thinking.

"I can't go," I say as I stare down at her K-Swiss. Her hands move cautiously, as if the shoe will be hurt if she tugs too tight. "I don't have any tennis shoes," I tell her.

"Oh." She finishes tying them and stands up. I hadn't noticed that the front of the jogging suits have "Eternal Hope" embroidered in a barely visible, darker shade of pink across the front. "What size are you?" she asks, her voice a natural whisper.

"They said to only bring—"

"About a nine?"

"Eight and a half." I sigh.

"Here," she reaches into her flower printed duffel bag and re-trieves a pair of beige satin slippers. "Might be a little big, but they should be more comfortable than those." She eyes my boots, which I hadn't bothered to take off as I slept.

"Thanks," I sigh easily.

I don't know what's wrong with me, but for some reason I don't care that I don't know anything about this woman and her personal foot hygiene. On the sink in our small bathroom I discover a pink shopping bag with "EH" on the front. "Shawni" is written in pink on the white ribbon tied on the handle. Inside are all sorts of toi-letries, a towel set, and a small pink notepad and pen.

"Got your paper and pen?" Janet says after I emerge from the bathroom.

"Yes," I say, "and thanks again for the slippers."

"Sure," she says quietly as we leave the room and head for detox, whatever that is.

This is crazy. No, ridiculous. It is the stupidest thing I have ever heard of in my life. Obviously everyone in the room, besides Linda of course, is feeling the same thing.

"What?" Debi sits up straight.

"What'd she say?" Janet whispers to me.

"Excuse me?" I look at Linda, who is leaning against the wall in the den as we sit scattered around the room on the couches and vari-ous chairs listening to her instructions. "What was that again?" I ask.

"That's right, ladies." She laughs, but I don't see a damn thing funny. "For the next four hours you will begin the process of detox, where you must talk to one another, nonstop, about yourselves, for as long as you can. Not a single word, however, should reflect anything regarding men. You can talk about anything under the sun, anything that is on your mind—except men. And the deal is that the first one of you who says anything about men—*anything*—has to confess something, and confession can be about anything. Got it? Rule is everyone has to talk. You are not allowed to be quiet. Someone stops talking, someone else better pick it up. Everyone talks. Got it? Okay. So, I'll start the timer—"

"For four hours?" I hear someone ask.

"That's what I said!" Linda smiles as she turns the hand on her timer. "Four hours. Starting . . . now." She puts the timer on the shelf above the fireplace.

Janet nudges me—and I nudge her right back.

Maybe we should both make a run for it.

These people are mental cases.

Is it humanly possible to have a four-hour conversation without talking about men? I could build a pyramid with my bare hands easier.

"Look," Debi's voice is articulate and strangely familiar. I suddenly realize that I know that voice. I look at her intensely for the first time—and I know that face. She's very pretty, a gorgeous mahogany complexion, conservative hair. She looks around. "I don't know about any of you, but there is no way that I am going to sit here for four hours and talk about nothing."

Linda nods with an amused smile. "Try," she insists.

Just as Debi begins talking again I realize why I know her voice. I didn't recognize her without her signature pearl necklace and blazer, suit, sweater, whatever, but she is definitely Debi Graham from that daytime talk show. "It's no secret that I like to talk, I love to talk," she laughs. "But I would much rather talk about—"

"Watch it," Linda warns. "Be ready to tell us a secret if you mention anything regarding them."

"This is impossible," a petite woman with long braids suggests.

"Preposterous."

"Outlandish."

Linda is nodding repeatedly and gesturing for us to keep talking.

"What?" Debi looks around at all of us. "What are we supposed to talk about?"

"Flowers?" An older woman with glasses hanging from around her neck suggests sarcastically.

Linda claps and continues to gesture for us to keep going.

"I . . ." I don't know why I start talking, but I do. "I like sunflowers."

Everyone laughs, including me.

Debi smiles and gives me a high five. "Honey, roses for me."

Janet whispers. "Azaleas anyone?"

Linda's face is turning red with excitement as we continue to talk about flowers.

The first time I mess up, I accidentally say something about Eddie Murphy. Well, it was Debi's fault because she's talking about Rodeo Drive being a great place to shop and it makes me think about how Rodeo Drive is in Beverly Hills, and then I think about *Beverly Hills Cop*, and then . . . I messed up, so I had to tell a secret.

"I don't have a home anymore," I say, and surprise myself when I don't shed a tear. It feels good admitting it out loud to someone else.

Linda's smile fades as she hands me a Kleenex. "Just *in case*," she says.

The second time I mess up, the subject is breakfast, and I instinctively think about omelets, and mention the fact that my fiancé makes the best turkey and cheese.

"He has another woman" is my confession.

The timer goes off several hours later, but we keep talking, because we all seem to want to, and Linda assures us that it's "okay" and that it happens every time. Our detox ends up lasting until almost five o'clock in the morning. Each "secret" gets longer in detail, more intense, and more personal.

"I miss Milan. I miss my father" is my last secret. Funny, I never said it out loud before. I need the Kleenex now.

Linda urges us to find a corner in the room and to write whatever we feel like writing in our journals. It's five-thirty in the morning, and I'm the last one to leave when I finally finish writing.

"You better get some sleep," Linda says. "Our first speaker is at ten."

"Okay," I close my notepad and head back to the room.

The lights are off, and so I tiptoe in so as not to wake Janet.

"I can't sleep." She surprises me by whispering from the top bunk. Because the sun is beginning to rise outside, I don't need to turn the light on to see that her face is troubled, stressed, and tense. "Guess that was our first experience at good old Eternal Hope, huh?" She pulls her hair back and begins braiding it.

"Yeah," I say as I crawl onto the bottom bunk. "I wrote a lot in my journal."

"I didn't know what to write about. I don't know what I'm doing here." She sighs and I hear her fall back onto the bed.

I don't know what I'm doing here either, but a part of me is glad that I am.

"Before you came in," she says, "I was just thinking, wondering what I'd be doing if I were at home tonight."

I snuggle close to my pillow and yawn. "And what would you be doing?"

She hums an I don't know sound. "Probably listening to Alanis or Indigo Girls, trying to go to sleep, trying not to think about Sonny."

"Who's Sonny?" I ask.

She doesn't answer.

"Janet?" I whisper. "Are you sleeping?"

"No," she says. "Just thinking. When's your birthday?"

"September thirtieth."

She hums. "Libra."

"Yeah . . ." I reply.

"Libras. Unable to function without balance in their lives. My mother once told me that life is about balance. She's a Libra, too— said we should think of life as walking. Said if you lose your balance while you're walking, you'll fall. It's like that in life, too, you know? I'm a Cancer."

"Oh . . ." I feel myself drifting off to sleep.

She yawns. "I wonder if there's some correlation between zodiac signs and women who have a dependency on men." She laughs. "Maybe some of us are predisposed by our birthdays."

I laugh, too. "Funny." I yawn. "Detox was kind of fun, huh?"

She waits a moment. "Yeah, in a way, it was."

NINE

Ode to Hettie Jones

"**I** knew I was a man junkie," she begins. Our first guest speaker is a very pretty Asian woman. Her jet-black hair is pulled back into a loose ponytail. Her round cheeks appearing even more swollen when she smiles, she's bubbly, and from the moment she stepped in front of the podium, her happiness was evident. She's wearing a loose-fitting floral dress, and she looks totally at ease.

"I guess I knew, I mean really knew the night of my fifth anniversary of being manless, so to speak. My husband and I had been divorced a long time by then. I was home alone, and I was sitting there feeling sorry for myself, thinking about how alone I really was—and had been for such a long time—when the phone rang. It was a prank caller, but I wasn't annoyed. I felt a strange twinge of delight in the fact that my prankster was a man." She laughs, as do all of us who are seated on the pews.

"So I kept trying to get him to keep talking to me." She laughs some more. "And eventually he grew very silent, and then hung up. I freaked out. Went to C-Town, tossed a box of doughnuts, a bag of Doritos, and some Oreo cookies in a basket. Waited in the longest of all the lines because that was the line where the cashier was a man.

I used to always pick the male cashiers, try to spark up conversation—all to no avail. I was desperate as all get out, and no man is attracted to a desperate woman. I ate every crumb of the goodies. Cried myself to sleep that night. I'm a six-month woman of Eternal Hope, and I've been losing weight ever since I came. I never knew that my addiction to food was because I wasn't dealing with my real pain until I came here. And it wasn't until I came here that I really reached inside myself and accepted why I felt so worthless without him. It's never about the substance, it's always deeper."

I laugh occasionally, as she continues, but only because I hear other people laughing. Although she is quite funny, the truth is that I am completely awestruck by what she said, and I find it very difficult to concentrate on the rest of her speech. Words echo relentlessly in my mind.

I never knew that my addiction . . . was because I wasn't dealing with my real pain . . .

It's never about the substance.

When she finishes her speech, everyone responds with applause.

Linda puts on a slow tempo new age CD and tells us all to feel free to journal, and that in twenty minutes we'll have open discussion. I am also surprised when I see Linda and our speaker both writing in their journals.

I thought they were cured? Why are they journaling?

As I begin to write, I think about how peculiar it is that I awoke so easily this morning. I only got three hours of sleep, yet I was the first one down to chapel. My energy is escalating as I write, as if I could write for hours. Then I think that there is a chance that all the excessive sleeping was a good thing. It's strange, but I feel completely rested now. I can't explain it. All I know is that twenty minutes seems highly insufficient for trying to transcribe all that I am feeling right now, so many thoughts.

Our next speaker isn't until one-thirty, so Linda informs us that lunch is ready for us in the dining room.

Spaghetti. A big old plate of carbohydrates. I look down at the steaming plate of noodles, thick red sauce with onions and green peppers, huge meatballs.

I think about eating around the noodles, as I pinch off a piece of one of my meatballs. The taste is rich, like wine. This sauce is incredible. I take another pinch.

"Is it just me," I whisper to Janet, "or is this sauce really good?"

She smiles as she finishes her mouthful. "It tastes okay."

Maybe I'm just hungry. What am I talking about? I'm starving.

These noodles taste like heaven—well, if heaven has a taste.

"You ladies doing okay?" Linda asks as she walks past.

Debi, Janet, and I are sitting in the den, our stomachs stuffed, and chatting as we wait on our next speaker.

"Fine." Debi speaks on behalf of all three of us.

"Next speaker in twenty minutes; see you upstairs," she says as she walks away.

"So, what do you do?" Debi looks at Janet. Debi's mahogany skin is flawless. She must use Clinique—or maybe she just has naturally beautiful skin. She crosses her legs and waits for Janet to answer.

"Teach music—elementary school," Janet says as she pulls her hair back into a bun, finalizing it by sticking her pencil in the middle to hold it in place. "What about you?" She looks back at Debi.

"Finally," Debi laughs, "someone doesn't know who I am."

"Are you famous or something?" Janet whispers.

I finally get the nerve to ask. "Aren't you a talk-show host?"

Her eyes widen, "You watch my show?"

Her topics are boring to me. The guests always appear to be acting with their she stole my baby's daddy from me stories. Seen one, you've seen 'em all. She really could use a stylist. Her choices of clothes are a shameful drag. I've definitely seen her show, but I hardly watch it.

"A few times," I say.

"Well, listen!" She leans in and looks me in the eye. "It better not end up in the tabloids that I was here. If it does, I'm coming to see you." She sits back and laughs.

At first I thought that she was serious, but the more we talk, the more I realize that Debi has her very own sense of humor. There is a little bit of sarcasm in everything she says. She has a unique opinion about everything, and I am captivated by her confidence.

She sighs. "I know my sister is the one who sent me the brochure. Yesterday when I saw everyone crying and carrying on I thought I would want to kill her come Monday morning. But actually I kind of like this. I mean, well, I could do without all the crying."

"I have no idea who submitted my name," Janet says.

"Me neither, come to think of it," I add.

"It took me a long time to acknowledge my dependence, huh Linda?" A salt-and-pepper haired woman standing at the podium winks at Linda. Looking to be in her late fifties, she's wearing a pink silk blouse and pink lipstick. Her brown skin appears soft, and a few wrinkles frame her dark mascara and heavily eye-shadowed eyes. She leans onto the podium. "Women, four times I endured this program. It would work, I'm not kidding, each time, and then I would consistently go into this denial thing. Thinking, I'm sixty-five years old . . ."

Did she just say sixty-five?

Wow, I would never have guessed.

She pauses to retrieve a Kleenex from the box on the podium. "I knew this was going to happen," she sniffs and then blows her nose. "I thought, I'm sixty-five years old, who on earth am I kidding! I should be knitting, being a grandmother or something. There I was sitting in a room with a bunch of women going through detox again. Before my first time coming here, my husband had passed away, and believe me when I tell you that I loved that man, but it didn't take long. After he died, I was dating all different ages, different races, different everything. I couldn't get enough of my new-found freedom, but I never took the time to really experience being alone. I never had been, and the thought frightened me. I was loyal to that man for forty years. I knew him more than I knew myself. I never took the time to have a love affair with me.

"My kids turned on me, because I was dishonoring their father," she continues. "In a way, maybe I was. But men were my refuge. I didn't know anything else.

"Let me tell you, when there's someone in your life who you can't live without, when you lose yourself in the midst of losing them, ladies, you're putting your faith in someone else, and your faith belongs to your creator, and to yourself. Women of Eternal Hope, I am here to tell you that it need not be crack cocaine or even rum. If you can't stand without it, it's a dependency. If you'll do anything to get it, compromising your integrity, it's a dependency." She looks down, takes a moment, and her voice cracks as she continues.

"So I came here, got out, felt good, and then when I went home I fell into this ridiculous boastful denial about how I didn't need Eternal Hope, or anyone to help me, because I was not like those women. I found myself right back here each time. The third time I committed myself like you wouldn't believe. I had to find peace.

The more disappointing relationships I went through, the more I was losing my family, my friends, my peace of mind. I was losing myself."

She lowers her head again, and this time it is a few moments before she continues.

"I've always had too much pride, you know? Just too much." She looks up at us, her face flooding with tears. "Believe me when I tell you, pride can be a mighty hindrance to freedom. And through experiences like this and by the grace of God, you can be free." She lowers her head again before gaining her composure enough to continue. "I'm a two-year woman of Eternal Hope, but I'm also an almost seventy-year victim of self-impediment. I exist now. Don't be afraid to admit that you are flawed. Even with every imperfection, you do exist." She walks away from the podium.

The applause is soft as Linda embraces her.

I begin writing before we're even instructed to start.

"I looked up one day, while I was driving my route," our four o'clock speaker begins. She's solid, the type of body that screams *I work out!*—and I'm not just talking about aerobics. I'm talking like Angela Bassett in the movie *What's Love Got to Do With It*—working out. She's wearing a turtleneck dress and leather boots. Her blond hair is a pageboy cut, and her movements aren't stiff. She just looks very disciplined, to put it best. She reminds me of a jockey. "And there were about four people left on the bus. I was almost finished for the night.

"And I was incredibly amazed at the sudden shudder in my chest when I realized that all of my remaining passengers were men. The bus was quiet. It was late on a Thursday. I was starting to slow down without realizing. This guy in a suit, cute guy, says, 'Are you okay,' and I just kept thinking of the fact that I was the sole female on the bus."

She looks up at the ceiling as she continues, remembering. "And at the next stop there was a woman standing there, waiting with a stroller. I sped past her. I didn't want any other woman on my bus. Just me. I wanted all of those men for myself. I was crazed. I didn't want to let any of them off at their stops. I was just driving, missing stops, crazed. One of them finally talked me into giving him the wheel, and my heart was beating so fast when he did because he lifted me out of the driver's seat, and he smelled so good. I couldn't say anything. He pulled the bus over, and let them all off. I got fired. I started getting stoned again, tried to smoke away the shame of being a sex addict. I threw away the brochure four times, and the fifth time it came I called the number.

"It took coming here for me to learn why I craved men so insatiably. Why every man I encountered was a potential screw. Compulsive. And I was resentful that I even had to deal with this . . . this bizarre addiction. I was so bitter that I couldn't just get it together. Then I came here. But I left Eternal Hope, and I was petrified of men for a year. I wouldn't even talk to my postman, I was so afraid of that obsessive behavior coming back. Years before that, I had screwed my cable man—didn't even know his name, just screwed him. And it was never the sex that I was addicted to, but that's what I once believed.

"So for a year after Eternal Hope I was celibate, and my best friends got weird on me because, well, everyone thought I had become a dyke or something because I just refused to date. I was scared that dating again would knock me completely off balance. I slowly became a hermit. I missed my brother's hockey tournament because I had screwed his coach once, and I no longer trusted myself.

"I came back to Eternal Hope. There had to have been something I missed to help me cope, right? I didn't even stay for the whole retreat the second time. It hit me during my second detox that what I was craving, what I needed was to feel desired by a man. I was an army brat. My father was a sergeant. You think he had time to play hide and seek with me? Yeah, right. Oh, and the base was a fantasssstic place to grow up, even had myself a real close companion—Private Perverted Dick, the forty-something-year-old man who I gave my virginity to at the age of twelve. I would have told my father, but quite honestly I liked that attention. I left the day I turned eighteen. Had nowhere to go. Then I met a man in an airport. He took me in. He was the most charming motherfucker you could ever imagine."

She continues as her face is burning red, but in a manner that seems fitting for her military upbringing, only one tear falls, "He had me so dazed that I didn't even admit that I was a prostitute, that he was my pimp. I was just helping him make money for the business we were going to own someday, and it felt so damn good—until afterward, when the johns would leave me alone on a musty mattress with nothing but an achy heart and the disgusting desire to do it again. I was so lost—spiritually, emotionally. I was so stupid. I had nowhere to go . . . refused to go back to the base. Sick of feeling appalled by the smell of my own skin, I finally grew a backbone and left him. Gave him a kiss one morning, told him I was going out for a smoke, and just never went back. I got a job driving a bus. Saved up every dime I could, and got my own place. But my heart was still with me, and nothing changed. Then I got the invitation to Eternal Hope. And here I discovered that there is hope, Eternal Hope for me, for anyone. I felt like such a freak, admitting what I'd been through. And then someone told me that I was giving my demons permission to punish me over and over again for my mistakes, and that they would keep on until I denied them access.

"Many of the women at my second retreat were just like oh I'm a housewife but I can't stop flirting with the meter reader, and I thought if I told them what I was guilty of they'd think I was a slut. But I still opened up. And it didn't matter what people thought of me. I was getting it off my chest. And it helped."

She stands erect as she concludes. "I have a steady boyfriend now. And he's enough. And I'm still celibate." She sighs.

After dinner we're told to meet in the basement for Recreation.

I ate two plates of macaroni and cheese.

It was the best macaroni and cheese I had ever had in my life.

The basement is fairly empty and reminds me of a ballet studio with the mirrors and the bars. Pink plastic balls are scattered throughout the room.

"Grab a partner," Linda chimes as she pulls Janet next to her.

I look up, and Debi is standing in front of me with a questioning expression.

I smile. "Sure."

"Here we go," Linda says, pulling a whistle from her pocket and giving it a long blow. "Two square. One ball per pair, okay?" She picks up a ball and she and Janet sit down facing each other, and we all do the same.

The rule is that you toss the ball to your partner, and then they have to name a woman that they admire and a reason why they do. This seems simple enough. Linda warned that the trick is to remember whom we named.

"Jenny Jones," Debi says first, "because she's such a compassionate host, genuine."

I catch the ball and hold it. "Uhh . . ."

"Keep the ball moving, Shawni," Linda shouts from across the room.

"Marilyn Monroe?" I giggle. "Because she was so stylish and sexy."

"All right, all right . . ." Debi nods as she catches the ball. "I'll say . . . Umm . . . Okay, Star Jones, because she always has something profound to say."

"Okay," I catch the ball. "What about . . . oh . . . Diva Diana Ross, because she is the definition of glamorous."

"Rosa Parks. Because she stood for something."

"Beverly Johnson. She is one of the prettiest women, most supreme models, ever to be captured on film."

"Tina Turner. Because she had the guts to leave Ike."

She and I both burst out laughing.

"Ah . . ." I try to stop laughing. "My mother. Because she's so sophisticated and has so much natural elegance."

"Okay," she calms her laughing, "my sister because I know she's the one who sent my name to these folks, and she's so sweet."

Linda blows her whistle. "Now, ladies, keep the ball going back and forth, but this round you have to name the same woman and then tell what you don't admire about them, okay?" She blows the whistle again.

The other women are beginning, but Debi has a blank look on her face.

"What's wrong?" I ask.

"Who'd I say first?" She laughs.

"Jenny."

"Right." She catches the ball. "Okay, Jenny Jones. And, I wish she could get more recognition. She's underrated, and I think she settles for it."

"Okay." I pause after catching the ball.

"Marilyn," she reminds me.

"Right," I giggle. "I don't admire the way she was a mistress to the president. Not cool."

"Rosa Parks," she changes her voice to a whisper. "Girl, I am not gonna sit here and try to think of something I don't admire about Ms. Parks, okay? That's just a no-no."

"Okay." I catch the ball and I laugh. She skipped Star Jones, but I don't bother to remind her, because it just means this game will be over sooner anyhow, and I'm tired of this. What's the point? "Beverly to me is like Rosa to you, okay? She's the greatest. That's a no-no, too."

"So." She catches the ball. "Tina. I don't admire the fact that she stayed with Ike as long as she did, you know? I guess that's the only thing."

"My mother." I catch the ball. "I . . ."

What is the point of this brainless game?

I can't tell this stranger what I don't admire about my mother.

I toss the ball back to her.

"Your mother, what?" She waits.

"I don't know. Your turn." I sigh.

"Well"—she clears her throat—"you won't say anything about your mother, my lips are sealed on my kinfolk." She huffs.

"Fine." I roll my eyes.

Soon the balls quiet and conversation halts.

"In your journals, ladies," Linda stands up. "Please write whatever you feel, but try to stick to the qualities you suggested about the women you admire. How are you like them? What qualities do they have that you have and admire about yourself? What qualities do they have that you wish you could change?"

As I begin to journal, I can't even begin to think about Ms. Ross or Beverly Johnson. All I can think about is Mommie, and the qualities that I don't like about her.

I keep hearing Linda tell me to be honest in my journal, because, after all, no one is going to read it except me. I keep thinking about the anonymous letter I received and how the person suggested that I be open.

Dare I write that Mommie is like Marilyn, only Daddy isn't the president?

I hear my pen drop as I make my way out of the room.

It's no one's business. The last thing I need is for someone to ask me why I'm crying. I feel way too comfortable with these women to run the risk of actually telling someone.

It's no one's business.

Shaking from my tears, afraid of my fears, I burst into a bathroom stall, lock the door behind me, curl up in the corner, and try to make it all go away.

"Shawni?" Someone whispers as the bathroom door creaks open.

I don't answer. I hold my breath. If they can't hear me, they'll leave.

"Shawni, it's Janet. Are you okay?" My roommate taps on the stall.

How'd she know I was in here?

"Please come out?" she whispers.

"In a minute," I tell her.

"I need someone to talk to. Will you listen?" She sniffs.

I'd much rather listen than talk.

"I didn't like that game." She's sitting in front of the sink, her face flushed as she blows her nose. "And I'm tired of crying."

I finish splashing my face with water and join her on the floor. "Me too."

"I don't think I belong here." She sighs as she hugs her legs and rests her chin on her knees. "Everyone seems to know so much about themselves. You know when we journal? I don't write anything—just song lyrics."

"Really?" I think about the pages and pages that I've filled in mine. "I've written a lot."

"Probably because you know what you're feeling. I don't, Shawni. I'm crying all the time, and it's not because of what these women are talking about. I just feel so sad, and I don't know why."

"Not at all?"

"No," she says abruptly.

"Maybe you're not being honest with yourself. Linda said that you have to be totally honest with your journal. I think it helps when you are. I sometimes feel like I could write forever, and I know it's because no one else is going to read it."

"That's awesome. I just . . ."—she closes her eyes—"I just don't know what to write."

"So, what lyrics do you write? Your own?"

She laughs a little, and she has a tiny dimple hidden in her freckles. Her smile fades quietly as she sighs. "No. I wish I were that talented. I write down lyrics that I remember. That I sing. That I teach."

"Like what?" I ask.

"Depends. Sometimes Gospel. Sometimes Tracy Chapman—she really moves me. Or Indigo Girls. Or whatever I'm feeling. Sarah Vaughn. I love music so much."

"Really?"

"Ummm hmmm . . ." She hums and opens her eyes. "Do you realize how close it is to Christmas? A couple of weeks away, and it doesn't even feel like it. When I was teaching we'd always have our rooms decorated to remind us, put us in the mood."

"I thought you said you are a teacher?"

"Well, I am." She sits up straight. "Just not right now. I'm sort of suspended for a while, but it's okay."

I want to ask her what she could possibly have done to get suspended from teaching, but I don't. I don't because part of me doesn't really want to know, and also because her soprano humming takes all of my attention.

It's a lovely melody.

She smiles, and her eyes begin to water as she sings, *"Oh . . . heaaaar the angels' voices . . . ohhhh . . . night . . . oh . . . night diiiiivine . . ."*

"What's that song?" I interject.

She leans back and continues to sing, *"Faaaaaaallllll on your kneeeeees . . . oooohhh heaaaar . . . the angels' voices . . ."*

"What's that song?" I ask urgently.

It is the loveliest song I have ever heard in my entire life.

She ignores me as she keeps on singing, *"Oh . . . falllll on your kneeeeessss . . . hear the angels' voices . . ."* She stops singing, buries her head in her lap, and succumbs to quiet weeping.

"Janet?" I crawl over to her and put my arm around her. "Are you okay?"

I think that maybe ten minutes pass as she quietly cries, and I sit here in wonderment.

Those words were so lovely.

"Janet, you have such a beautiful voice." I try to brush the hair away from her face, but she keeps her head buried in her knees.

Eventually, when she does look up, her tears have stopped but her voice is still shaky. "Thanks." She wipes her eyes and blows her nose.

"If I had your voice," I tell her, "I'd sing all of the time."

She sniffs. "Yeah, you think so. No talent in the world is worth sharing if you're not happy inside. I hope you get something out of this retreat. I see you writing in your journal, and I just think there's so much hope for you, you know?"

"No." I shake my head. "There's hope for you, too. Linda said—"

"No," she interrupts. "I'm just not ready. I'm leaving."

I barely pay attention to our nine o'clock speaker. The only thing I can think about is Janet's quiet good-bye as she flipped her floral duffel bag over her shoulder and waved. I felt defeated as I sat on my bottom bunk, unable to reason with her, to get her to stay. I felt like a part of me was leaving with her. We had come together. I wanted us to make it through this together. I couldn't even say good-bye to her. I couldn't believe that she was actually leaving. I watched my feet instead of her.

She sighed when I reminded her that I was still wearing her beige slippers. "Keep them," she said in her signature whisper.

And she left.

Just like Darlene, my best friend when I was young.

We made a pinky swear one day in Central Park. Sitting with delicate lace napkins (because paper ones were far too ordinary for us), with our legs crossed, nibbling on tomato sandwiches, she grinned at me. Darlene said, "Shawni Baldwin, from Milan, swear we're best friends."

A few months later her family moved away. She said she would write. She never did. My letter was returned. Addressee unknown. I never heard from her again.

Alone. Afraid to be alone. Afraid to look afraid, I stood on the curb as they drove away. Our pinkies held high in the air until we were out of each other's sight.

Alone on the stage, my last show.

Alone, without my man.

Desperately needing to feel sheltered all of my life.

Without Daddy, I have always felt abandoned. Alone.

And Janet. I hadn't known her long, but she was leaving, and there was nothing I could say to change that.

I think I might need another notepad after tonight.

We have to play that stupid game again after breakfast on Sunday morning, only we have to use five men as opposed to women—and they have to be men we know personally.

I'd rather be in detox.

"My brother, Duran." I toss the ball. "Because he protects me."

"My friend, Ernie." I toss the ball. "Because he protects me, too."

"My father." I toss the ball. "Because. He protects . . ."

"My ex-fiancé, Bo." I toss the ball. "Because he protected me."

"My dog Sanford." I toss the ball. "Because . . ."

I really don't see the reason for this. Now I have to think of things that I don't admire about them? Can this just be over already?

"My brother, Duran." I toss the ball. "He gets overprotective sometimes."

"My friend, Ernie." I toss the ball. "He can be so blatant."

"My ex-fiancé, Bo." I toss the ball. "Because he's so good to me, but so bad for me."

"Sanford." I toss the ball. "His love is so unconditional, and it seems unfair to him."

Debi waits with a frown.

"What?" I sigh.

"You forgot your father."

"Oh." I catch the ball. Maybe if I just say it I'll feel better. "My father. Because he's not here. He's in Milan, with them, like he always is." I toss the ball back. "Happy?"

"With who?" she whispers.

"His fucking family!" I shout. "His wife and his kids. Okay?"

The balls continue to bounce, all of the ladies are shouting, and no one notices what I've said. I'm glad.

Debi thrusts the ball back at me. "My ex-husband, Darnell. Because he used to beat the shit out of me."

Debi and I stare at each other as our pink ball bounces away from us, lonely.

She stares at me.

I stare at her.

And slowly, we both begin to smile.

And then we both laugh. And it feels good.

And the conversations around us are still continuing.

And what we've said doesn't matter to anyone in the room. Only to us.

"Well," Kaitlyn takes the podium. "How's everyone feeling?" She smiles.

I am drained, and inspired, and nervous, and I'm feeling so much right now that it is utterly overwhelming.

"Probably tired," Kaitlyn suggests. "I know. Remember, I've sat in the pews. I've been through this program. I know how exhausting it can be. We've lost two of you, but that's okay. For those of you who are still here, only twenty-four more hours, okay? Hang in there. If you're not feeling something yet, you will."

I look around the room. I hadn't noticed anyone besides Janet leaving. I'm trying to remember all of the ladies who were here yesterday, and I sigh when I don't see the older woman with the glasses hanging from around her neck.

I think her name was Audrey.

I wonder why she left.

"Sunday afternoon is always fun," Kaitlyn says. "I highly doubt that any of you will need any Kleenex for this one, okay?" She claps her hands three times and the back door of the chapel opens.

Four women wearing surgical scrubs and carrying pink picnic baskets emerge and march down the aisles.

I knew this was too good to be true.

Now I guess they're going to try to do some kind of surgery on us.

I should have escaped when I had the chance.

"These women," Kaitlyn gestures to them as they stand in front of the podium. "Kim, Gala, Bonnie, and Argia—are here to give you an Eternal Hope makeover. Kim will be giving each of you a back massage, Gala will be doing facials and eyebrows, Sally will be doing your nails, and Argia your hair, okay? It'll be fun. Trust me."

Argia is a tall, solid, dark-skinned woman. Her hands are heavy and warm, and her voice is very deep, yet somehow gentle.

"How are you?" she asks as she puts the heavy gray cape around my neck.

"Okay?" I say, nervously.

Please don't let her ruin my hair.

"Cap treatment?" she says, her voice deep and slow.

"That's a deep conditioner, right?" I ask.

She parts my hair. "Scalp is a little dry."

I feel so nervous, and tense—and then I look across the room and see Debi. She's getting her eyebrows waxed, sitting comfortably in a chair, her hands casually folded across her chest, and she's laughing about something. She doesn't seem to be in the least inhibited by this situation. These are complete strangers making us over, and no one else seems to be concerned about it.

Why am I being so uptight?

I smile. "I'd like a cap treatment, yes."

I take a deep breath and consciously try to slow my breathing.

"Tell me about yourself," she says as she twists a jar open. "Got any kids?"

"No, but I have a dog."

"Oh?"

"His name is Sanford."

"Sanford, huh?"

"Yes, he's a Doberman. He's a sweet dog."

"I see." She begins applying the contents of the jar onto my hair. "Married?"

"I was," I say, and then catch myself. "I mean I was engaged. I've never been married. We broke up. Well, he dumped me."

I can't believe I just told this complete stranger that.

But she's so angelic as she nods, encouraging me to continue, as if this happens all of the time. She's used to it. She doesn't mind listening if I want to continue.

So, I take another deep breath, smile, and keep talking.

My hair turned out ravishing. Almost as nice as when Ernie does it.

As I'm laying here getting my massage, Kim's elbows piercing my back with pleasurable pressure, I think about my life, and how I ended up here.

If someone had told me a year ago that I would someday end up at a retreat, I would have rolled my eyes and laughed. Whatever. If someone had told me that I would one day feel as if I couldn't live without a man, that my 'men come a dime a dozen and I have five dollars' philosophy would have to be labeled hypocrisy, I would have laughed. Whatever. There really is a comfort in knowing you're not alone.

I realize I'm humming out loud as she massages me, and my eyes pop open.

"Go on," my masseuse assures me. "Let it out. Moan. Groan. Everyone does that."

If someone had told me a year ago that Bo and I wouldn't be together, I wouldn't have believed him or her. I would have never thought that someday I would have to learn to live without him. But I may have to do just that, and that's going to be okay.

"As you know," Linda sits in the rocking chair after all of us gather—feeling fantastic after our makeovers. "Tonight is your last night here. If you're anything like I was, like most women who come through here, you're a little nervous. You bet your ass I was shaking, wondering how in the hell I'm going to go out into this world, full of men, and not find some low-life to cling to!

"I have bad news for you, ladies. You're not cured. It doesn't happen in a weekend. This is just the beginning; this retreat is just the foundation for you to build your strength upon. All I can tell you is to just keep going! If you find yourself picking up the phone to call him, and you know damn well he's not good for you, ask yourself why! And then answer yourself honestly.

"Maybe you're sitting there thinking that you've beat it, or that you don't even have a problem. Maybe some of you don't believe you even belong here. Well, only you can decide that. You're the only person who can label yourself. And you're the only person who can help you. You have to do the work. And it's tough. You don't get cured. You cope.

"Maybe you'll find yourself back there again. I can't get my life together, buy a house, travel, be happy unless I have a man in my life. Heck, we're sexual beings. You don't have to try to live without, but if you do have to live without, you have to be able to survive. Eternal Hope is not here to teach you how to live without a man, we're here to help you live with yourself.

"And I just want to remind you," she concludes, "that this weekend is ending, but Eternal Hope is always here—every single weekend. When you leave in the morning, you'll get a card with a phone number to a twenty-four-hour-a-day support hot line. Call anytime. Talk to whichever counselor is on line. You'll also be getting instructions on how to invite someone you might be concerned about to this retreat. Remember, it is an ongoing process. It doesn't end tomorrow morning. When you leave here, it begins. And every day, to thine own self, be true."

Our final speaker is surprisingly a man.

"Evening ladies," he smiles. He's a conservatively dressed brown-skinned man, very unassuming. He straightens his tie and laughs. "I bet by now some of you are ready to throw eggs at my entire gender, huh?"

"Stone him," someone yells and we all burst out laughing.

"Right." He laughs. "Stone me. Well, I don't fault you for that. There are some men I would love to see stoned. There are three times more, however, who are decent. I'm a man, as you are already aware, and I'm proud of my respect for women. And no, I am not here to tell you that I was strung out on a man."

We all laugh.

"But," he pauses and waits for the laughter to quiet down. "My mother was. She was the sweetest, most giving, most generous woman to ever live, and her name was Hope. I started running this retreat center in her memory. She lived her entire life devoted to a man who was not devoted to her. I used to make excuses, like 'Mama it's all right. Dad's just out with the fellas,' when he'd stay gone all night. And Mama just accepted it. I wish to God I would have said, 'Mama, you deserve a better man!' But I never did. Now I've dedicated my life to saying it on her behalf.

"When my father left, I saw my mother age real quickly," he continues. "Sadly, my mother chose not to cope. I miss her terribly, every day, and every single day I think about how dark that place must have been for her, to think that she couldn't live alone, without him. Ladies, you are the hope. You are the chance that my mother did not give herself, and you are not alone. You are never alone. You have yourself."

Someone calls out, "Are you married?"

He laughs. Such a pleasant smile. "Yes. Very happily so. Fourteen years."

"Lucky bitch," she responds.

We all laugh heartily, even our speaker.

It's midnight, and I'm sleepy. I have just finished writing in my journal, and there is only one empty page left. I hope I have the strength to go back and read all of this stuff, as Linda said I should when I get home. I know that it feels good when I write it, but I don't know how it will feel to read it.

I wish Janet were here.

It's so quiet being alone in this room.

I'm not even sleepy, come to think of it.

Suddenly the door bursts open and a flashlight is aimed at the ceiling. A whistle blows and someone screams, "In the den! Hurry, hurry!" And they slam the door.

As soon as I enter the den, bright pink confetti falling blinds my vision. Pink and white balloons are hanging everywhere. And the room is full of people, new faces.

"Congratulations!" Everyone is shouting.

"What the hell?" I hear Debi's voice behind me.

"Shawni!" I hear someone shriek.

I turn around to follow the voice that is so familiar, but just as I do I hear Debi scream, and I look to see who Debi is running toward.

"Tonya!" she says and grabs a woman who looks like she could be her twin. "I knew you had something to do with this. I told everybody. I said, my sister . . ." she closes her eyes and her face scrunches as she fights back the tears.

"Shawni, over here!" I hear someone say.

I turn around and my first instinct, for some reason, is to run away. She's holding a bouquet of sunflowers, wearing a black leather dress, and her jet-black Asian-styled bangs are the first thing I recognize.

My eyes widen. My jaw drops. "Abigail?"

"Shawni!" She runs over to me and grins. "You did it!"

"I did? Did, what?" I ask, completely confused.

What is Abigail doing here?

"You're a woman of Eternal Hope!" She laughs and proudly holds the sunflowers out toward me. "Here."

Abigail.

We used to call her Abi.

We used to have so much fun together, doing shows . . .

"I'm so confused." I look around. All of the women from the re-treat are in the den now, people are snapping pictures, and laughing, and crying, and hugging. "Abi? You're the one?"

"Uh-huh." She bites her frosty pink-colored lip and nods.

"How'd you know I came?" I ask.

"It's part of the experience, your sponsor being here to con-gratulate you. Kaitlyn told me."

"Abigail . . ."

"Come on." She pulls me in for a hug. "I'm so proud of you, Shawni. So glad you came."

I think mostly I'm crying because seeing Abigail reminds me of that night.

Let my boyfriend buy you a drink, she had said.

He was so handsome. A Sicilian God.

I got high with him. He was her boyfriend.

How can I face her now?

She releases me from the hug. "Let's go talk."

I reluctantly follow her down the hallway, and join her on the stairway by the front door.

She pulls a pack of cigarettes from her Prada purse and lights one up.

"Abi! I can't believe you're the one who sent me here. How'd you know?"

She takes a smoke from her cigarette, waits a moment, and then lets out a graceful puff. "Everybody knows, okay? We've all known it for years. You're a hopeless flirt, and you crave men like a drug. It's no secret—if that's what you thought. And then I heard about you being in the hospital."

"Who told you?" I ask, half embarrassed and partially angry that anyone knew.

"You know the industry. People talk. I overheard it somewhere."

"Great!" I say. "The entire world knows. So that's why you sent me the invitation? Because you thought I'd gone crazy?"

"Shawni"—she tilts her head and looks at me sympathetically—"I knew there was more to it than just you guys breaking up, like everyone was saying. But you know, when you turned down Ricci I did think you were losing it. We all did. Even then, something inside of me knew that there was more to it, that there was something wrong, that you were really going through something."

I sigh. "I was worn-out by the like-me, like-me game."

"No, shit. I could tell. I've been there." She looks uncomfortable for a moment. "But then, that night at the Millennium Rush party. Here I was so happy to see you, and then, when I saw the way you looked at Trip . . ."

She knows! Oh no!

She's going to burn me with that cigarette.

She makes an appalled face, but then relaxes. "I couldn't do anything except laugh to myself when I saw the way you were looking at my boyfriend. I was trying to be nice for old times sake, having him buy you a drink, and what kind of thanks do I get? You brought out your old bag of flirting tricks."

"Abi, I'm so sorry." The words flee from my mouth just as I realize how sincere they are.

"I knew you left with him. He ditched me, got the keys. I watched him. I saw you get in the car with him. Did you fuck him?"

"Abi, no. I swear. And I had no intentions."

"Actually . . ." she taps on her cigarette, "I believe you. I really do. He's such a sleaze. Dick head."

There's a long silence, and all I can think about is that time we did that show, and we were so excited about those Fendi makeup cases.

"Abi, do you remember the time—"

"Fendi?" She smiles a little.

"How'd you know?"

"Every time I think about you, I think about that. We were so excited, so young, so naive. Everything was so much more fun in those days."

"I agree," I say.

"Now look at us. I'm having to fight depression every time I don't get the attention that I used to, and every time I lose another guy—unsure if it's because of me or him, but feeling like shit regardless. I'm being told at twenty-eight years of age that I'm too old for the business. Thirteen- and fourteen-year-old girls showing up at shows, getting more and more attention. We were so naive. I'm so much smarter now, and so, of course, now they tell me that I'm a bitch."

"Abi, you're international! You are still working aren't you?"

"Actually," she bites her bottom lip, "I got a call from Ricci."

Whoa.

I nod. "Are you going to take it?"

"I already did. I'm sorry, kid. You're the only person I know who'd—"

"Abi," I interrupt, "you deserve it, okay? I'm happy for you. Ricci's huge."

Karma. She does deserve it. No such thing as luck.

I look at the door that leads outside. "I hope I'll be okay when I leave here. I don't want to be sad anymore."

She puts her cigarette out on the side of a garbage can and throws it away. "No. No way. Not after this weekend." She walks up a couple of steps.

"Thank you," I say. "For the invitation."

"You're welcome." She looks back at me. "But all I did was suggest it. You did the work, and that's what's important. Doesn't matter how you ended up here. Now, come on, there's cake and stuff in there." She walks up a couple more steps.

"Abi, wait." I say, and wait for her to stop and turn around again. "Why'd you care so much? Even after you saw me leave with Trip?"

She gives me the vibrant smile that has gotten her so much attention from top designers all over the world. "Ever read poetry, my dear?" she asks.

"No, not really," I reply.

"There's a poet. I don't know the poem, but the last line," her smile fades slightly as she tries to recall it. "Hettie Jones is the poet, and the last line says: 'Having been her, befriend her.'"

TEN

The Burden of Eve

I can hardly wait to see Sanford, but I'm a little unsure of whether I should tell Ernie about my weekend. He'll probably have something cynical to say, and I want to savor the inspiration.

Something feels strange as I walk into the building. Maybe it's because I haven't been here in three days. And then I notice that the door to Ernie's apartment is cracked open.

I push it all the way open, close it gently, and then ease into the hallway. "Ernie?"

The couch is pulled out into the middle of the floor, and so are both of the end tables. Shoes are scattered everywhere, and there is a huge hole in the center of the living room wall with several dark scuffmarks around it. Something is very eerie about this.

"Ernie!" I shout frantically.

Suddenly an image whizzes through the living room and into the kitchen.

Was that him?

"Ernie?" I shout again as I run after it into the kitchen.

Sure enough, it's him. He's wearing a white surgical mask, huge yellow plastic gloves, like the ones you use when you wash dishes, and he has a tool belt around his waist—only there aren't any tools, just several spray cans. He's holding a hammer as he wraps both arms around the refrigerator. He strains to pull it out of the corner.

His voice is muffled behind the surgical mask. "I'm glad you're here. Put that bag down and help me move this thing."

I put the backpack down on the kitchen counter and help him pull the refrigerator out into the middle of the kitchen floor. "What are you trying to do?"

"Shhhhh!" He holds up his index finger and holds his breath.

I follow his eyes as he looks around the kitchen floor suspiciously. He is acting really weird.

I feel as if I am in the twilight zone.

"What's wrong with you?" I demand. "And what are you looking for?"

Suddenly he gasps and runs past me, out the kitchen, back through the living room, and into his bedroom. I immediately run behind him, and I shriek when we get to his bedroom. It's a disaster. Shoes are everywhere. Rolled up pages of newspaper are everywhere. His bed and dresser are pushed out into the middle of the floor. On the bottom of the wall, right where the phone jack is, is another hole in the wall, with dark smudges like the one in the living room.

"What happened in here?" I shriek.

"Shush!" He looks around the room guardedly.

"Ernie, no. I want to know—"

"Chile, shut up and grab a shoe." He pulls out one of the spray cans from his tool belt and tosses it to me.

"Raid?" I read the label.

"Use it. Grab a shoe, too." He tiptoes over to the closet and bangs on the door with his hammer. "Come on out here, Jerry," he says.

Jerry? I lean toward the closet and eye it suspiciously. "Who's Jerry?" I whisper.

His eyes widen. "He's about the size of a lightbulb if you see him."

"See who?" I whisper.

"Chile, you moved out for a weekend and a mouse moved in. You hear me?"

I immediately toss the bottle of Raid onto the bed.

He smacks his lips and picks it right back up. "What're you doing? You better grab a weapon and help."

"Help you do what, Ernie?" I roll my eyes. "Kill a mouse with a bottle of Raid?"

"The Raid is for the eyes, chile. All you have to do is blind him. I'll get 'em with the hammer." He peeks behind the chair in the corner, and then pulls it away from the wall.

"Ernie, I can't believe you're tripping out over a tiny little mouse."

He puts his hand on his hip and widens his eyes. "Excuse me, but when I'm sitting down at my kitchen table, getting ready to enjoy my bologna and cheese, and I got a horsedog begging me for a bite, and then a wanna-be Disneyland spokesperson runs his little scrawny tail across my kitchen table and looks at me like he wants a bite, too, oh it's a big deal. Oh, he's got to die."

"They're more afraid of you than you are of them." I can't believe he's busting holes in the walls over a little mouse.

"I don't know who told you that lie, but ain't no way in this galaxy that that rodent is more afraid of me than I am of him. You hear me?"

I look around the room. "Just tell Sanford to get him. He's trained."

His eyes widen even more, and he very methodically walks out of the room.

"Ernie?" I follow him. "Where are you going?" I pat my leg. "Sanford?"

Ernie goes back into the kitchen. "Come on, Jerry! Tom is ready to clobber your little ass."

"Where's my dog?" I look around.

"He wasn't in the kitchen?" Ernie begins easing out of the room.

"No," I say, my heartbeats quickening. "Where is he? Did he get out? The front door was cracked."

He stops walking, and turns back around to face me. He slowly pulls the mask off as he sighs, "I left the door open for Jerry to leave."

"So, where's Sanford?"

Just then I notice Ernie's mouth. His bottom lip is dark and swollen. "Shawni . . ."

I take a step toward him. "Have you been in a fight? What's happened to you?"

"Chile, I don't know where you've been, but people have been looking for you. I told 'em I don't know! All I know is she left me a note talking about going to find freedom. I said, 'Hell check the Underground Railroad. I don't know.' What was I supposed to say?"

"To who, Ernie? Who was looking for me? And where the hell is my dog?"

"Well, it's like this." He sighs. "It was a cool and windy Friday evening when I got off work—"

"Ernie!" I walk over, stand directly in front of him, and as I stare down at him I desperately try not to murder him with my eyes. "Talk!"

"You ain't gotta be all rude, all up in my face and stuff."

"Damnit!"

"Okay, okay! I got your note, saw that invitation on the dresser, and thought you had gone a little, you know." He does a crazy gesture with his finger pointed at his temple, "And so, when he called—"

"When who called?"

"Mr. Clean."

"What happened?" My heart races as I clench my teeth.

"See, what happened was I was really nervous about you, and I didn't know if I should be calling your mother and them. Then Bo called, and he just caught me at a moment when I was really concerned about where you were."

"And?"

"So, he asked if I knew when you'd be back, and I told him no, that I thought you might have gone to a retreat. So, he said yeah right, and laughed, you know. He found that really hard to believe. Then he said he had to take the dog to the vet."

"The vet?" I yell. "Ernie, Sanford didn't need to go to the vet! Did you let him take my dog?"

"Chile, I believed him. I see why you be gettin' all messed up over him. He's smooth as butter. He said he was just gonna come by here to get the dog and take the dog to get his rabies shot. Chile, you know me, I'm thinkin' if the dog need a vaccine for rabies, I'm not trying to stop nobody from taking him to get it, you know what I'm sayin'?"

"So you let him take my dog? Ernie, how could you?" I stomp my foot and fight back the tears. "Sanford didn't have a vet appointment! He already had all his vaccinations."

"Well, I know that now. Because, chile, when lawyer man got here, it got ugly. It was somethin' uuuugggggleeee. I'm tryin' to tell you. He was all where the fuck is she? Who did she go out of town with? I know your little faggot ass knows where she is, and you know I didn't appreciate that business. So, I showed him the note. Told him, I didn't know any more than him. He told the dog to come, and the dog went. I said, oh no, I don't know if I should let you take the dog, 'cause by now I had figured that he wasn't even thinkin' about gettin' the dog a shot."

"What'd he say?"

"Chile, somethin' about tellin' you that your dog was gonna be a stuffed trophy or roadkill or—"

"He said what?" I don't bother to fight back the tears.

"Your hair looks nice. What you do, get it done?"

"Where are your car keys?" My lip trembles.

"I tried to stop him, Shawni. I did, I did. The dog wouldn't listen to me. Baldy said come and he went, like he was a servant or something."

"He's trained to obey commands, Ernie."

"Well, he wouldn't obey me. I said stay and he went."

"So how'd your lip get all messed up?"

"That's what I'm tryin' to tell you, chile. I tried to stop him."

"He hit you?" I don't wait for his answer, and head into the living room. "Where are the keys?"

"Chile, don't go to Brooklyn. I don't have time to be buying no black suit for your funeral. You better be like Farrah and just burn his bed."

"I gotta go." I head toward the door with his car keys.

Just as I'm slamming the door shut I hear Ernie shout "Come on out here, you cheddar cheese eatin' little shit."

He's laying on the floor in front of the black leather couch, holding a bag of Cheetos, no shirt on, his herringbone glistening, and he's wearing a pair of black sweatpants. His eyes snap away from the television when I burst through the unlocked door.

"Woman!" he shouts. "What the fuck is wrong with you? Comin' up in here like that!"

Sanford gallops toward me and immediately begins licking my hand.

"Hi, baby poo-poo!" I lean down and kiss him on his nose. "Sit, for Mommie, okay?" I ask, and he obeys.

"Damn, Shawni, you can't just be bustin' up in here like that."

"The door was unlocked."

He stands up and tosses the bag onto the couch. "Unlocked doesn't mean feel free to fuckin' enter!"

"You know what? I don't really care. You asshole. How dare you take my dog?"

"Who paid for the son-of-a-bitch? I think that makes him mine." His nose flares up as he steps toward me and sucks his teeth.

"What are you trying to prove?"

"Where've you been?"

"You told me to leave, remember?"

He takes a deep breath, and although his vein is protruding on the side of his head, he calmly sits down on the couch. "You're not gonna tell me where you've been, huh? So why are you here?"

"Did you hit Ernie?" I ask, and I think for a second that I'm seeing things as I notice that Bo's bottom lip is a little swollen. "Did Ernie hit you?" I squint to verify the puffiness.

"You think I'm gonna let some little fool faggot swing on me, and not punch him back? You smokin' crack or somethin'?"

"You mean," I laugh out of disbelief. "Ernie swung on you first?"

"Damn faggot."

"Unbelievable."

"Oh, what? It's funny that a faggot swung on me, huh? Yeah, that's some Saturday Night Live comedy, huh?"

I try to stop laughing. "I'm sorry. I just . . . Ernie didn't mention that he hit you, too."

"Yeah, well, he's lucky I let him keep his teeth. Damn queer."

"Bo, he's my friend and he was just looking out for me, okay?"

"You know what? I'm not tryin' to hear that. Go on back over there with him, that's where you want to be. Or go back to whoever you were with all weekend."

"Actually, I was at a retreat."

"Save it."

"It was the best thing that could have ever happened to me. It helped me to put some things in perspective."

"I'm not trying to hear this, woman."

I walk over to the couch and sit down next to him. "Can I just tell you about it?"

"I said I am not trying to hear this."

I snatch the remote control off the table and turn the television off. "Please?"

He sucks his teeth, clears his throat, and then, "What?"

So I get up and stand directly in front of him. "Last week I was so down and out, so depressed. All I did was sleep and cry and sleep and cry, and all I could think about was you."

"Should've thought about all that before."

"What, before I came over here and saw some woman on the couch?"

"Yeah, after you spent the day with that Marvin Gaye wanna be fool, then you decide to come to Brooklyn lookin' for me. Comin' over here high and carryin' on."

"So how on earth can you possibly justify that woman sitting on your couch half naked?"

He does a double-take. "Half . . . ? Woman, please!"

"In her robe. Yes. I saw it!"

"Here we go again. Why are you so paranoid? Who's here with me now, huh? Who do I work hard to take care of? Why are you pressed over somebody who means nothing to me? Nothing! And why do I have to work so damn hard to show you how much I love you?"

Urgh. The *l* word. I love you, too, Bo, but now is not the time for that.

"Who said anything about being pressed?"

"Where's all this coming from, Shawni? Damn."

"I don't even know why I'm talking to you. I just came to get my dog."

"Listen." His voice is soft as he walks over toward me. "Baby, I'm not messin' around with anyone, if that's all you need to hear. All weekend I've been shooting pool, doing paperwork, and mad as hell because the only woman I want to be with is off with some fool. I said some things the other day strictly out of frustration. You just had me so upset . . . But I'm tired of all this foolishness. I want you to stop trippin' and let this stuff ride. There's only one woman that I want, and I'm trying to love her the way she deserves to be loved, but she won't let me. There's no other woman for me except you, baby." He takes my hands.

I slide my hands out of his. "But who was she?"

"I told you, a friend. We went to law school together. She came over and she was upset about some things. I dealt with it and I haven't talked to her since."

"But you wouldn't let me in."

"Can we please just forget that that ever even happened? I don't give a damn about her."

I don't know what to say. I'm even at a loss for thoughts.

He puts his hands on my waist and pulls me in a little. "So, when are you coming home?"

"Yeah, right," I say on impulse, as I pull back from him.

"Let's make this work, baby. Forget all the dumb stuff."

"Look, I know I'm not the easiest person to love, but I—"

"But I do. Forget all the rest. There's no stopping me if you'll just let me, baby. My love is bond. I mean that. You think I would put up with so much if I didn't want this?" His voice cracks. "Baby, come on. I'm tired of this."

He kisses me on my neck as he continues. "Now, are you gonna act right and let me love you?" He's showering my neck with soft kisses, and holding my hands as he does.

And this time I can't pull away.

How does he always do this to me?

"Don't you know," he says as he begins unzipping my jacket. "I could have so many other women. But I don't want any of them. I want you. I want you." He pulls my jacket off and throws it across the room onto the couch. "I'm so sprung on you, baby. Come on . . ." He casually pulls my sweatshirt over my face, and tosses it across the room as well.

It lands on the couch and the pink "EH" lettering stares back at me.

He's unsnapping my white-lace bra . . .

"Bo—" I stop him by grabbing his hand. "I want to tell you about this weekend."

He leans in and kisses me gently at first, and then I am slowly escorted into the land of complete passion. His kissing me evolves into us kissing. The kisses are fiery, and seemingly eternal.

I can't stop myself.

I don't want to stop.

I hear the soft hush of my bra as it lands on the couch.

I whimper between kisses.

He continues by carrying me up the stairs, and easing me onto the bed.

"I'll be right back," he whispers and leaves the room.

My heart is racing as I attempt to hold on to the memories of those EH letters. Think, Shawni. What happened this weekend. What happened . . . ?

Congratulations, Shawni! Those were Abi's words.

Suddenly I hear the stereo come on downstairs. Otis Redding's voice fills the air, raspy and sincere.

"I've been loving you too long," he sings, "to stop now."

I feel like screaming for help, because I know that I won't be able to control myself when Bo gets back up here.

And I'm right.

"Baby"—he kisses each of my fingers—"let me show you how much I love you?"

"I love you so much, Bo," I think I say out loud, but maybe I don't. Maybe I just think it.

His fingertips . . . on the small of my back . . . pulling me closer . . . and closer . . .

Ecstasy.

I'm taking a shower, alone, because Bo is sleeping. I'm shaking as I pour the liquid soap onto my body. Bo is the best man I've ever known, the best lover I've ever had, and the handsomest man. Why do I feel so guilty about having made love to him? What's wrong with me? Was I wrong to make love to him? I mean, his touch, it just feels so good, so right.

To thine own self, I hear someone say, and I honestly jerk because it sounds as if they are actually in the shower with me. I sigh when I realize that my thoughts are screaming so loud that it sounds as if they are in fact talking to me.

To thine own self be true.

Well, I am being true to myself, aren't I? Bo loves me, and I honestly love him, too. I've never felt so protected in a man's arms, so desired.

This is crazy. I'm turning myself into a nut case, for goodness sake. There is absolutely no reason why I should feel guilty.

"You smell so good." Bo kisses my back as I climb into bed next to him.

I turn over and kiss him on his head. "You're so incredible." I sigh before turning back over.

He nibbles on my shoulder.

"But . . . " I begin.

Bo's nibbling stops, and we're both still. "But?"

I sit up. "I just think I need some time alone, Bo."

"Say what, now?"

I push the covers back. "I don't know if I'm ready." I turn to face him. He's lying there with a surprisingly eased expression on his face as I continue. "I think maybe I just need some time to find myself."

"Find yourself, huh?"

"See, the thing is . . . " I get up and go look out the window.

There's a little girl walking down the sidewalk, probably seven years old.

"The thing is *what*, Shawni?" Bo says.

I'm watching the little girl, and thinking about my journal, and Eternal Hope, and my life.

"Bo, I had to grow up so fast. I was this little sophisticated child, and I was so confused about leaving Milan, and my father, and the only life I had known. You know I used to ask God and myself all the time, I used to wonder, how come we're not good enough to be Daddy's family, you know? Like, why couldn't Mommie be his wife instead of her? How come he had to go home to them every night, and not us? Why did we have to be the ones to leave Milan? No little girl should have to contemplate such things.

"And," I sigh, "sometimes I think, on the other hand, that I've lived my entire life too sheltered."

"Oh, is that right?"

"I love you so much, Bo, and I don't want to hurt you, and I don't want to lose you, but this weekend I tapped into a part of me that is wondering if I really can survive with just Shawni. And I need to find that out. And I need you to let me walk away to do so."

"This weekend, huh?" He sucks his teeth, and I turn around.

I hate when he makes that noise.

"That's what I've been trying to tell you," I say, and roll my eyes as he sucks his teeth again. "This weekend, I went on a retreat. It was incredible."

"I'm supposed to believe that, right?" He sits up.

"Believe what?"

"That you were at a retreat." He gets out of bed.

"I'm serious. Didn't you see my shirt? The *EH* stands for Eternal Hope. It's an incredible place where women come together and just figure out why they're dependent on men."

"You know, I have tried, for the last time, to make this shit work." He puts his hands behind his head. "You'd rather run around tryin' to find yourself, shit—go! I'm through. Save your speech woman; I'm gonna go ahead and make this easy for you. You got your mutt! Go." He gets up, walks out, and slams the bathroom door.

I've gone downstairs, retrieved my EH sweatshirt and bra, and now I'm sitting on the edge of the bed in silence as I listen to him showering. I feel like crying, and I consider crying, even try to cry, but I can't. Maybe I'm tired of crying. And in a way I feel good about what I've said. No need to cry. To thine own self be true. But I can't leave just yet. There's one more thing I must say.

He comes out of the bathroom, zipping up his pants, the ones that always hit his thighs in all the right places.

"Still here?" he asks without even looking at me.

"Bo?"

He laughs a quick, fake laugh. "Save it, Shawni."

"Not only have you been generous and good to me, but actually the day you proposed to me is the day I think I started needing to free myself. So much pain that I may not have otherwise realized. Thank you, for everything."

"Yeah, you get through finding yourself, and yourself needs a car to get around in, don't come calling me talking about you're sorry."

"I can buy my own car, Bo. I'll be okay."

"Good luck."

"Fine." I pat my leg for Sanford to come, and he does. "I guess we'll get going then."

"'Bye," he snaps.

And so Sanford and I leave.

"Champagne?" Ernie holds up a bottle of bubbly as Sanford and I walk into the living room.

"No, thanks." I say as I unhook the belt from Sanford's collar and take my jacket off. "For what?" I ask dryly.

"Jerry's dead." He turns up the bottle.

"Oh? How'd you get him?"

"Went down to the hardware store. Bought a bunch of traps. Got a bunch of those chunks of cheese from the market. *Bam!* Had 'em within an hour. Watch your toes around here though."

Ernie calmly takes a careful look and says, "Oh, no, you're in the zombie mode again. What happened?"

"I can't believe you hit Bo, Ernie. You shouldn't have done that."

"Tell me about it. It was like hitting a brick wall. I still can't feel two of my knuckles."

"See, that wasn't very smart."

"So what happened? I see horsedog is back."

"It's definitely over this time. Bo and me."

He nods, unsure of what to say for a change.

"But I'm okay with it."

"Champagne?" He holds the bottle up again.

"No, thanks." I smile. "It's so crazy. This weekend was like the best thing that could have ever happened to me. I'm so glad I went."

"I'm just glad you're safe. I was worried sick." He sits on the couch. "Sin called."

"What?" A smile accidentally eases across my face. "Zin, you mean?"

"Same thing. Left his home number. You want it?"

"What'd he say?"

He shrugs. "There was a message on the machine. Just said for you to call him at home in Atlanta. Said he was leaving for L.A. on Monday. Left that number, too. You gonna call him?"

"I don't know. I'm really curious about him, but a part of me thinks that the only reason our paths crossed was because I needed to be challenged to look deeper into things. He's like that." I take a breath, try to slow the tempo of my heartbeats. He called. "Then again, who knows? Anyhow, I'm really sorry I had you worried. I was so gone. Gave Sanford uncooked sausage even."

"I was wondering how he got that raw piece of meat. He ain't stupid, he didn't eat it. Gave it to me when I got home—guess he wanted me to cook it." He laughs.

"Ernie, I really need to tell you something." I sigh.

"Is it serious?"

I smile. "Nope." And I look him right in his tiny little brown eyes. "You are a great friend, Ernie. And I love you."

He looks away. "Don't do that. Don't be getting all sentimental on me like that."

I laugh. "I don't think I ever told you that. And it's been on my mind a lot the last few days. I am fortunate to know you."

"Yeah, yeah." He brushes his hand in the air a few times, and then he looks at me. "So, what happened this weekend?"

I look at him. So loving in his own way, yet so much pain underneath that tough exterior.

"What?" He groans. "Okay! Okay! I love you, too! Damn."

And we both laugh.

"So what's going on?" I ask Duran as he drives me over to Mommie's. "There's something you're not telling me. Don't play dumb." I playfully sock him one in his arm. "Talk!"

"Oh, that really really hurt." He laughs, rubbing his arm.

"I can make it hurt if I want."

"What happened with Delaney?"

"Nothing new. We broke up."

"Broke up, huh?" He looks annoyed.

"Yes."

"Man, you're so hardheaded! Didn't I tell you to be cool until I found some shit out?"

I look at him blankly. "What's wrong with you?"

He looks at me, totally ticked off. He taps his ear. "You don't listen, Shawni!"

"How can I listen"—I bang my ear, sarcastically imitating him—"if you don't tell me anything?"

He laughs out of frustration. "All you had to do was play it cool

until I found some things out, but no, you go and jump to all kind
of conclusions."

"What are you talking about?"

"Yo, Delaney's not fuckin' around with Adonna."

"Who the hell is Adonna?"

"Adonna Dawkins. Damn. The woman you saw on the couch.
His classmate from law school. She was sweatin' him up at Justin's
that night. He saw her, spoke, said hello, and kept rollin'. But she
was sweatin' him mad crazy all night. I was sittin' right there when
he told her he was engaged. That bitch didn't give a fuck. She was on
it. Then when you told me you saw some woman on the couch that
night, I knew that's who it had to be."

"And you didn't tell me!"

"What was there to tell? That's why I told your little hardheaded
and hot-tempered spoiled ass that I wanted you to be cool until I
found out if something was going down or not. No, you go on and
high tail it anyway."

"So? That doesn't mean he's not messing around with her."

"He's not. I did what I had to do, and I know this. She told me
herself how she'd do anything to get him back. They used to have
some shit goin' on back in law school, I guess. It's been some years
and she'd do anything to have Delaney again. But he wasn't havin' it!
She tried every trick in the book, but he wasn't having it!"

"Yeah, right. How do you know she wasn't lying?"

"I don't. But I know a players game. I'm a player. I know the
game, and I've talked to Delaney. I told you from jump he's good
people. If anything did go down that night, Delaney's on some
Hollywood actin' stuff, and so is she, because they're both playin' the
hush-hush role like you wouldn't believe, like some thespians. He's
not peepin' Adonna, I'm tellin' you. Here I've been workin' my ass
off tryin' to find this out, and you don't listen for shit!"

I don't know what to say. Maybe it's possible that what Duran is saying is true.

"Shawni," he says, "I've never steered you wrong, have I? And I never would. You messed up. Big time! And don't think I don't know about you calling 'Sef for Zin's pager number.

"Yeah," he nods, "you keep on being hardheaded when big brother tries to warn you. Don't come cryin' to me. You go ahead and mess around with Zin. Wait until he drops some old guru spiritual bullshit on you to talk you out of your panties like he does all these women out here lookin' for some deep-ass intellectual bullshit from a man. Go ahead, let him make you all dizzy and shit with his funny-colored eyes. Don't call me when you fall into the pile of hos that he's lured into his den with some old philosophical game, all right? Don't call me, 'cause I've already warned you! I'm his manager, Shawni. I know his game. I've seen it too many times."

What if he's right? What if he's right about everything?

Duran's really upset now. "Don't—"

"Okay!" I shout and bang my fist on the window. "Enough. I heard you. I heard everything you said. And, by the way, I didn't break up with Bo because of her. It's much more complicated."

He huffs, and he sulks, and he drives in silence.

My brother. The father I've always had.

I was a grown-up little girl, during my childhood in Milan, balancing playing hopscotch and jacks with the game of keeping secret the intricacies of my family's complex situation. And even now, after all these years, I am afraid of the bravery that healing is going to require.

She's just come in from shopping, taking boxes wrapped in

lovely silver and blue wrapping paper and big silver bows, and placing them under the tree.

I offer to help.

She says she's got it.

I glance at the nametags. To Duran, love Mommie. To Shawni, with love from Mommie. To Duran. To Shawni.

Doing the best she can, still, after all these years, to make the holidays so special.

I'm thinking about Debi. A strong, beautiful woman, a successful talk-show host, but at the same time a woman addicted to a man who shows his love by pounding her precious face, for so many years attempting to destroy her faith in herself. Janet, afraid to look her demons in the eyes, to tell them to step back and allow her to be happy again. I'm thinking of all of them. Women searching for the strength to stop giving pain permission to wear the mask of love, to finally face the agony of leaving as opposed to enduring the heartache of staying.

There's solace, even when you feel the weight of the entire earth on your heart, in knowing that there are people whose stories are more complicated than yours. But it seems unnecessary now to compare my hurt with theirs and rejoice in not having it quite that bad. It doesn't really matter how scorned you are, there is commonality in all heartache. Pain is pain.

"Ernie said you had gone away for the weekend," she finally tries to begin a conversation. "I called on Friday evening. Were you out of town?"

"Kind of," I say.

"Duran was looking for you, too."

"I talked to him. He's the one who dropped me off here."

"I see," she says. "Hungry? I made tuna salad earlier."

My heart smiles. Mommie makes the best tuna salad. "I'll get some in a little bit," I say.

A long silence. An unrecognizable distance between us. So much to say, so little to say.

She exhales. "So, where do we begin?"

And, courageously, I propose, "At the places we've left off."

She nods. "Okay, that's pretty broad, but okay."

"Mommie, I never want to hurt you," I tell her.

"Ah." She stops me, raising her pointer finger. "No hurt. Say it. Okay?"

I take a long breath, and only because she has said that I am brave enough to begin. "When I was growing up I used to wonder how come we weren't good enough to be ordinary. I always thought that you deserved more."

"Okay"—she twiddles her thumbs a little—"that's fair. You're being honest, I know. But, sweetheart, it's never been a question of whether or not I've ever been good enough. I was in my prime. I was living the high life, the fast and thrilling life. Why would I have wanted to get married, and be settled down when every night there was late-night champagne with impeccably dressed and romantically inclined millionaire business tycoons with private jets and adventurous plans? Your father, darling, was only one of the most incredible men I encountered. It's what I chose, darling, not what I was worthy of."

"I just wish we could have had regular lives. No hidden elements. No illusions from a distance," I finally admit to her.

"You know, I think maybe that sounds nice. Maybe if I had realized before that your father wasn't going to be one of the ones I would be able to turn loose . . . But, you know, I've never been really skilled at reasoning. It's about what I want at the moment. And,

Shawni Kaye, you have a very similar trait. A good thing, but it can also be dangerous."

"And I always wanted Daddy to be there in the morning," I confess.

She takes a breath. She starts to say something, but stops. A sigh. A smile. "Me too."

"I could never have admitted that before."

"But you want to know something else?" She continues, "I've known a lot of people, and believe me every family has more there than what's captured on the family portrait. No one is truly ordinary. And in all fairness, you can't blame everything entirely on me, darling. I didn't lie down and make two babies by myself. Your father made a choice, too. Maybe not the best choice for you and Duran, or even for him and me, but it's the choice that we made. You see? You can't put all of the blame on me."

She crosses her leg, her red slacks narrow and crisp. "Sure, sometimes I've wished to the point of near obsession that he could be there with you and Duran, but he wasn't, and he wasn't going to be. So, I moved you and your brother back to the States to try and lessen the pain that, yes, I played a role in inflicting upon you. You think it didn't hurt me, too? Seeing how my choices had affected my children?"

"Mommie, it's okay." I force myself to sound cheerful, and then I sit down next to her. I can't bear to see her troubled. Her wounds are my wounds.

A tear wells up in her eye, and her voice is strange. "I would love to be able to say I'm sorry, but I just love him—so much. If only I could have known how you'd be affected."

"I'm not asking for an apology, Mommie."

What do you do when you thought you had so much to say,

and suddenly it all seems different? You thought you had to get it all out, but you don't. You realize that it's not that she didn't know what you were feeling. She, like you, just wasn't ready to deal with it.

"Shawni, you're so strong," she says.

"And you are, too," I remind her.

She smiles, but that tear in her eye taints it. "Really, you are. And you're so beautiful."

I nod. "And so are you. So beautiful."

"Sometimes I look at you," she says, "and it's all I have, you and Duran. And I'm able to admire what I did that is good. I'm thankful for that." The tear finally falls.

"I've missed you," I tell her.

A reassuring nod, and then she says, "I'm here, darling."

And I realize now that it must have been hard, to say the least, all these years, standing where she's stood, trying to justify her choices, having to forever carry the burden of other people's pain, constantly reminded that her children are eternally incomplete. If she could do it all again, would she? Or would she make different choices? Is it even worth contemplating? We're here. What's done is done. My life is up to me from here on. The choices are now mine.

Walk, Shawni. Walk and balance.